Taylor Crest

Circa 1420-1602

Smithsonian Institution, Catalogue No. E-1749.

abbycat group

&

PUBLISHING

BRANDS

STORIES BUILT
TO **LAST**

abbycat group

&

P U B L I S H I N G
B R A N D S

S I N C E   2 0 2 5

www.abbycatgroup.com

THE

BASTARD

OF

TAYLOR'S END

AGP

THE

BASTARD

OF

TAYLOR'S END

JACK CHASE

Published by Abbycat Group
An imprint of Abbycat Group LLC, operating as AGP | Abbycat Group & Publishing Brands
Palm Desert, California
www.abbycatgroup.com

ISBN 979-8-9998644-1-3 (Hardcover)
Library of Congress Preassigned Control Number: 2025927632

Cover design by FRAMEWORKS
Book design by FRAMEWORKS
Text set in EB Garamond

"The Dragon and the Prince" (original play by) © 2025 Jack Chase

First edition, December 2025

Printed in the United States of America

10 9 8 7 6 5 4 3 2 1

For my Tata, the first artist I ever knew.

*And for William Goldman, master of the story that
knows it's a story.*

"The absence of alternatives clears the mind marvelously."

Henry Kissinger

ACT GUIDE

The realm festers beneath crowns of gold and robes of ermine.

In the shadow of the Taylor dynasty, where majesty masks tyranny and courtly grace conceals the executioner's blade, the kingdom's sinews strain toward rupture. Upon the mud-soaked margins of a village whose name history shall not remember, a bastard child of no lineage prepares to topple an empire.

Jamie possesses naught save the breath in his lungs and the fire in his breast; no patrimony, no remembrance of gentle birth, no promise of tomorrow's dawn. Yet when the headsman's axe cleaves asunder his sole sanctuary, sending him into the wild margins where civilization surrenders to chaos, fortune grants him congress with a figure of darkest legend: a warrior shrouded in obsidian mail, whose very name whispers across the realm like wind through gallows timber.

What commences as covenant born of desperation transforms into odyssey through carnage and cinder, through the arithmetic of vengeance and the cruel algebra of survival. As sedition stirs in the kingdom's marrow, Jamie conceives a stratagem most audacious: to breach the very heart of the Taylor court through that singular art the crown yet holds sacred—the ancient craft of players and painted stages.
'

Beneath the mask of wandering mummers, Jamie and his spectral confederate shall perform the ultimate masque, one scripted not in ink but in blood, destined to conclude not with applause but with the death-rattle of dynasties and the birth-cry of revolution.

The Bastard of Taylor's End, *wherein kingdoms fall and bastards rise.*

PROLOGVE

THE MAN THAT RODE VNTO FYRË, AND THE
BEGETTING OF THE RED PRINCE

The Northbury Massacre

23 November 1578

At first, it was the drums.

Low, deep, rolling thunder that rattled your bones before your ears could catch it, that tightened the chest, made your breath hitch in the back of your throat. The rhythm was ancient. It had been heard before, in another time, another life, when men fought like animals and their wars were carved in blood.

Then came the horses.

Whining, restless, pounding the earth with hooves that churned the soil like thunderclaps. The screeching sound of leather against leather as the raiders braced for impact. Then the hiss of steel unsheathing, one after another—sharp, clean, a sound like breath sucked through clenched teeth. Torches snapped to life in the dark. Their light sliced through the shadows, making the night shudder with their glow.

When the first rooftops caught fire, Northbury did not look

like a town anymore. It looked like hell had arrived on Earth.

The Beverley raiders hit the western gate at full gallop, swords gleaming orange under torchlight. The first guard didn't scream—his head simply rotated into the dirt, and by the time it landed, five more had fallen. Arrows flew through the sky like locusts. Then the horses came through the courtyard. Old men were pulled from their beds and slaughtered in their kitchens. Women were dragged by their hair into alleys, screaming until their throats collapsed. Children were tossed against walls or trampled underfoot.

Sir Felix Ryder sat astride his horse at the ridge, staring down at the ruin below. The fire was a living thing, devouring everything in its path, curling around the bodies, twisting them in its dance. Smoke billowed in jagged columns, dark and thick, blotting out the stars. There was no fight, only a purge. And in the center of it all, the black-and-crimson banner of the Beverleys flapped like the wing of the Devil himself.

Rowan Campbell sat beside him on a dapple-gray gelding, peering through a battered spyglass. His beard was streaked with ash.

"Bloody Scots," he said, low and sour.

Felix didn't answer. His face was set like stone, not a twitch, not a flicker in his cold blue eyes. He didn't need to speak. The world below him was speaking enough.

"I'm meant to return," Felix said, his voice breaking the silence between them, low and steady.

Rowan lowered the spyglass, his eyes narrowing as he scanned the chaos ahead. "Then go," he said, voice gruff, but with a touch of something that lingered beneath the surface. "I'll hold them."

Felix didn't look back. His jaw tightened.

"Reinforcements from the castle will come?"

"They better." Rowan's words were clipped, the bitterness sharp.

Felix turned his horse, spurring it into motion.

"Take watch," he called back over his shoulder. "Keep what's left."

Rowan's mouth opened, but Felix was already gone, riding down the hill at full gallop, the hooves pounding, kicking up mud as he cut through the firestorm below. Rowan watched him go, his back to the inferno and the future.

In the nursery of Taylor's Castle, a different battle raged.

Queen Anya Taylor was dying.

She didn't know it yet. Not in the way you know you're dying. But she could feel something dark unraveling in her womb, something tearing, something failing.

She had been screaming for hours. Blood soaked the sheets. The midwife looked like she'd bathed in it. Her hands were shaking. Her voice stayed calm, but her eyes screamed panic.

"You're doing beautifully, Your Grace," she lied.

King Tobias Taylor II knelt beside her, young and terrified, caught in a world that demanded more from him than he could give. His face was pale, his eyes wide with helplessness. Of course, Tobias had taken the crown not from birthright but by force and charisma, for there was no royal blood in his veins. With Anya's womb dying beneath him, he knew the Taylor line, by blood, as he knew it, ended with her. He felt as he looked now, like a boy playing at the role of monarch; unfit for a crown, unready for the weight of a kingdom.

"You're almost there," he whispered again, though he had no idea what that meant. "Almost there, darling."

Anya screamed again, a long, sharp sound so primal it seemed as if it might split the air itself. Something in her snapped. Her body convulsed, the world spinning out of—

A sound filled the room.

Tiny.

Wet.

Furious.

The child was out.

The midwife held him aloft, red and glistening. He was howling, an unearthly cry, raw and desperate, like something torn from the very fabric of life. A beast, an angel, something caught between worlds.

"A boy," the midwife announced, her voice carrying the

shock of something she hadn't expected. "A healthy one, Your Grace."

Tobias stared at the child, his expression frozen. He didn't know whether to weep or to vomit. His mouth moved, but the words caught in his throat.

Anya, fading, turned her head to look at him. Her lips quivered.

"Toby…"

"I'm here," he whispered. "I'm right here, my love."

"Promise me."

"Anything."

"Keep our boy safe. Promise me you'll keep our Little Prince safe."

Tobias nodded, his throat raw and ears ringing. "I promise."

Back in Northbury, Rowan Campbell led the charge into hell.

Heat blazed against his armor, smoke clawing at his lungs, ripping at his throat with every breath. Around him, Northbury screamed. A crushed child lay beneath a wagon axle to his left, body twisted unnaturally, hand outstretched as if it had been reaching for something, or someone.

Rowan didn't stop.

A woman shrieked ahead, dragged into an alley by her hair, her legs kicking, a flash of steel rising above her.

He didn't slow.

Couldn't. The only thing left to do was ring the bell or die trying.

In the blur ahead, a ghostly figure stepped into view; no armor, just leather and black warpaint smeared like a permanent scream across his face.

A longbow was already drawn.

Rowan leaned into the gallop, eyes ever fixed on the church spire barely visible through the haze. If he could get there, if he could hold the steps, maybe he could give the last dozen souls something to cling to. Maybe he could carve out thirty more seconds of—

Thwack.

Rowan's mind went blank.

The arrow sunk into his right knee like a stake through rotten wood. The pain was so sudden, so excruciating, it didn't even register as such at first. It simply felt like gravity had betrayed him. One moment he was in the saddle, charging into legend. The next, his body was weightless, hurtling through the air like a rag doll.

He hit the ground shoulder-first, his arm folding under him with a sick crunch as the rest of him skidded across the cobblestone. His sword flew from his grip, clattering into the dark. The back of his helmet cracked against a stone wall. He rolled once, then again, and again, before settling in the ash face-down, everything around him muted except the ringing in his skull.

He tasted copper. Dirt. The world tilted.

His horse vanished into the fire.

He tried to rise. Just a hand at first. But even that motion tore something inside him and sent a howl out of his mouth that barely sounded human. He collapsed again, the arrow still jutting from his knee, blood pulsing around the shaft in hurried, throbbing bursts.

And all he could see now were boots—enemy boots—trampling past. None bothered to finish him.

The fire would take care of that.

Felix's horse nearly collapsed from exhaustion when he reached the gates of Taylor's Castle. He threw the reins to a guard.

"What's the word, Sir Felix?"

"Northbury's gone, that's the bloody word. Lock the gates."

The guard paled. "Right away, Sir Felix. Your Queen is in the birthing ward."

Felix didn't stop moving. His armor clanked like a dirge.

He reached the ward just as the Queen slipped into stillness.

Tobias was sitting beside the bed, one hand clutching hers, the other clutching nothing. His face was blank, red-eyed. Broken. Felix tried to lend a comforting hand. Tobias batted it. Felix moved to the cradle instead.

The boy stared up at him with wide green eyes, unafraid.

Felix stared back, and something ancient stirred inside him, deep in his chest.

Outside, the bells began to toll.

Rowan lay in the blood-drenched mud, half-conscious. Fire licked the edges of the thatched roofs. The air was hot, thick with soot and death. His leg was fire. His sword was gone. His ears were full of smoke. All around him, Northbury howled.

A figure knelt beside him. A girl—barely seventeen. Hands red with his blood, wrapping his knee with torn cloth.

"Stop it," he growled.

"Shut up," she muttered, knotting the bandage tighter.

"Rescuing a soldier. That makes you stupider than me."

"Don't die. I'm not wasting a good dress on a corpse." She met his eyes. "I'm Ruth."

He coughed blood. "Rowan."

Northbury burned into dawn, settling into a carcass of its former self.

Felix stood in the highest tower of Taylor's Castle, watching the ash fall like snow. In his arms, the boy slept. Oblivious. He would never know the smell of the burning streets. He'd keep him hidden. He'd keep him safe.

Because somewhere in the woods, past the tree line, past the rivers and moors, past all that was noble and rotten, something had ended, and something else was just beginning.

And soon, it would wear a crown.

ACT I

THE BOYE RAISED IN SHADEWES

The Dragon and the Prince

A Tragedie.

Written by B. Oddfellow, Gent.

Printed in London by Thomas Creede, dwelling in Thames Street, at the signe of the Eagle and Childe.

1 6 0 2

P R O L V G U E

Enter CHORUS, cloaked in smoke and ashes, bearing a single taper.

CHORUS. When stone begets a crowne, and bloodline turnes to boast, The pyre of pride shall flame the mountaines ghost. From shadowed hearth to throne of hammered gold, This tale of two sonnes shall now be told. One taught that strength is steele, and feare the law, The other bent ore bookes, who seekes to knowe, not draw. Yet wisedome oft is buried in the bones of youth, And kinges who cannot heare shall never knowe the truth. What is a monster but the shape of what we feare? What is a crowne but pride made stone to weare? The wheele of fate turnes slow, but turneth sure, What seemes most safe is seldome most secure. Attend: the village sleeps beneath the yoke, And none dare name the beast the kingdome woke.

Exit CHORUS.

ACTUS PRIMUS, SCAENA PRIMA

A humble chamber, high in the castle. Bookes and parchment scattered. A single windowe frames the mountaine farre off. Rushlight.

Enter PRINCE LEO, reading alone.

PRINCE LEO. Here in this quiet cell of dust and page, I trace the wordes of every ancient sage. Beyond these walles, the kingdome spreads its weight Ore simple folke who labour, watch, and wait. The village sleeps; the shepherd tends his fold; None speake, for speaking hath not made men bold, Not in a realme where kinges define what's true, And monsters are whatever kinges pursue. They whisper of a beast in Harthfells snowe, A dragon vast, whom none alive doe knowe. My father calls it scourge, and blight, and bane, But what if feare itself hath forged the name? I reade of creatures older than the throne, Whose silence speakes a tongue this court hath never knowne.

Thunder heard, farre off. LEO riseth, looking toward the mountaine.

What thunder calles from yonder craggy height? Perhaps the beast is not what wakes the night? Perhaps the monster dwells not there, but here, Where pride hath made its home and nursed its feare.

Exit LEO.

SCENE 1

JAMIE

1602

They tore through the brush, a boy and girl with the sun at their backs, breathless, reckless, the forest ringing with their laughter. Branches whipped at their faces; roots caught at their ankles; the earth itself seemed to conspire against their flight. But they ran anyway, because running was what they had, and joy was brief enough that you seized it when it came.

Lillian Spires had learned many lessons in the span between girl and woman, but keeping quiet was not among them. She cut through Whiteheart Creek and sent water flying in silver arcs. Her skirts hung heavy with it, dragging at her legs, but her laughter was louder for the defiance, louder for the years that had tried to teach her silence.

Jamie Campbell chased her downhill, lungs burning with the effort. His boots, cracked leather held together by stubbornness and wire, slipped on the wet stones, sending him stumbling like a drunk. Everything about him spoke of barely held together: his patched breeches, his shirt gone gray with too many washings, the way he carried himself as if apologizing for taking up space in the world.

The ground opened before them, rolling down toward Taylor's End in waves of green that had once been wild but now bore the scars of cultivation. Fields carved into neat squares, hedgerows planted to mark boundaries, the slow conquest of order over chaos that marked the advance of civilization. But it was the castle that commanded the eye, drew it up from the humble geometry of village life to something that belonged to legend.

Taylor's Castle rose from the valley floor like a mountain of worked stone, its towers piercing the evening sky with deliberate arrogance. Shadow pooled at its base, stretching across the village like a blanket thrown over a corpse. The place had stood for nearly two centuries, weathering sieges and storms with equal indifference. Kings had been born within those walls, and kings had died there. The very stones seemed to whisper of power, the kind that bent nations to its will and crushed rebellion beneath iron heels.

The village huddled at the castle's feet like a beggar at a nobleman's gate. Taylor's End: a collection of timber and thatch, smoke-stained and weather-beaten, where common folk pursued their small concerns beneath the gaze of their betters. Merchants called out from their stalls, hawking goods that would never grace a lord's table. Children chased dogs through the muddy streets, their laughter bright and brief. Guards lounged at corners with hands on sword hilts, watching everything with the lazy attention of predators between meals.

Commerce and fear moved through the streets in equal measure, as natural as breathing. Men bowed when knights passed, kept their eyes down when tax collectors made their rounds, spoke in whispers when matters touched on those who lived behind the castle's walls. This was the order of things, had always been the order of things, and would always be the order of things until the stones themselves crumbled to dust. At twenty-four, Jamie was already older than the King and the King's elder brother both, but the burden he carried belonged to no bloodline, for Jamie was a bastard, though perhaps his greatest sin, according to the monarchy, was that of being a commoner, and when combined, age was of little query.

From a low door stepped Rowan Campbell, rag in his weathered hands, limp in his gait, face carved by years that had taken more than they gave. His right knee dragged behind him like dead weight, legacy of some old wound that had never healed proper. Even his voice carried the scar, a slur on every second word that marked him as broken in ways both seen and hidden.

Twenty-four years of raising another man's bastard had aged him beyond his span. His shoulders, once broad enough to bear a knight's armor, now curved inward as if the weight of disappointment had finally bent them past repair. The cottage behind him was no better, a converted shed with walls that leaked rain and let in winter, where two men lived on what barely fed one.

"Jamie! Supper!"

The call carried the weight of routine, the same words spoken at the same hour for more years than either cared to count. Jamie turned toward the sound, still breathless from the chase, grinning with the unconscious joy of youth that had not yet learned to apologize for itself.

"Lillian and I saw a dragon!"

Rowan's hands worked the rag with deliberate patience, drying fingers that had once wielded sword and lance but now knew only the honest calluses of a smith's trade.

"How big?" he asked, playing his part in this familiar dance.

"Bigger than Taylor's Castle."

The old soldier's mouth twitched; not quite a smile, but close enough to pass for one. His eyes flicked toward the mountain of stone that dominated their world.

"You and your legends," he muttered. "Perhaps it could do us all a favor and sit on it one of these days."

There was venom in those words, carefully hidden but present all the same. Twenty-four years of servitude hadn't dulled the edge of old resentments. He gestured toward their humble door with hands that trembled slightly—age or anger, impossible to say which. "Get inside."

Jamie's grin faltered. "Can Lillian stay?"

The hope in his voice was painful to hear. Here was a young man who had learned to expect disappointment but could not quite stop reaching for more. Rowan's expression softened, though kindness and cruelty often wore the same face when poverty made the choices.

"I've only enough for you. Her father'll want her home anyway, I imagine."

Jamie's shoulders sagged. He lingered only long enough to smile back at Lillian, memorizing the way the dying light caught in her dark hair, the stubborn set of her jaw that promised she would never quite submit to what the world demanded of women.

"Later."

"Later," she smiled.

Then she was gone, melting back into the gathering dusk like something half-remembered from a dream.

Inside, the hut smelled of smoke and goat hair, of meals stretched too thin and hopes worn threadbare. The single room held everything they owned: a rough table, two stools, a pallet for sleeping, hooks for their few possessions. It was a poor man's palace, and they were its kings. The stove ticked with heat, the only sound in a silence that had grown comfortable over the years. Rowan lowered himself to his chair with the careful movements of a man whose body had declared war on his ambitions. They ate their thin soup without speaking, spoons scraping against wooden bowls in rhythm with the eternal music of survival.

"Feed the goats after, will you?" Rowan said.

"I know."

"So," Rowan said at length, "the carpenter's girl?"

Jamie felt heat rise in his cheeks. "She's a friend."

"Aye. And I'm the King of England."

Rowan's laugh was a cough, bitter and warm all at once.

Then came the sound that killed all pretense of peace.

Horses. Iron shoes striking mud. The creak of leather and the rattle of steel, the martial symphony that announced the approach of those who held power and were not shy about using it. Rowan's smile died like a candle snuffed by wind.

They stepped outside together, boots sinking into mud that never quite dried in this low place where the castle's shadow pooled like stagnant water. The evening air brought cookfires and fear, two aromas that were now linked in Taylor's End.

The King's Watch had arrived. Six riders cutting through the village without slowing, their horses' hooves churning the road to soup. Merchants scrambled to clear the way; children pressed themselves against doorframes; dogs slunk into alleys with tails between their legs. At their head rode Sir Arthur Richardson, tall as a tree and twice as unbending. His shoulders were broad as a castle wall; his face carved from granite that had never learned to smile. When he dismounted, it was with the weight of a man who carried authority like it was welded to his bones. Every movement spoke of violence barely contained, of strength that had never met its match.

"Rowan."

"Arthur."

"You owe the castle another five crowns," Richardson said. "That's a hundred bits now."

Rowan's jaw worked like he was chewing gristle. "I can count."

"Can you?" Richardson's smile was carved from the same stone as his face. "Time has a way of clouding a man's mind. Especially when that man chooses to forget his obligations."

"I need more time."

"Time's all you've had, old man. It's grown expensive."

The words hung between them like drawn blades. Around them, the village held its breath.

"I was a soldier," Rowan said, and the words carried all the dignity he had left.

Richardson's laugh was winter wind through bare branches. "Mate, the king is dead. Three years in the ground and longer in spirit. You're entitled to nothing. You barely were then. Now, if I forgave ev'ry man his taxes, what work would I have left?"

"My goats, Arthur, they—"

The slap cracked the air like lightning.

Rowan's head snapped sideways, blood welling from his split lip. Villagers gasped and stared at the mud. Jamie's hands balled into fists at his sides.

"Your goats?" Richardson jabbed a gloved hand toward the warped sign above their weathered shack, letters faded but still legible: Campbell Metals. "You're a blacksmith, ain't you?"

"Yes." The word came out thick through Rowan's swollen lip.

"Then sell some bloody swords."

Richardson swung into his saddle with fluid grace. Iron hooves tore the road as they rode out of Taylor's End.

Rowan wiped blood from his mouth with the back of his hand. He looked at Jamie, and in that look passed all the knowledge that mattered: debt and power were the true lords of this land, and mercy was a luxury reserved for those who had no need of it.

The goats still needed feeding. The forge still needed tending. Life still needed living, even when living felt like slow drowning.

Some men were born to command kingdoms.

Others were born to survive them.

SCENE 2

THE BLACK PRINCE

The study at Taylor's Castle was a monument to dead things preserved. Dark timber rose in panels of ancient oak, each board carved with heraldic beasts locked in eternal combat, their scaled bodies writhing in relief as though the wood itself remembered being forest. The grain ran vertical, drawing the eye upward to a ceiling lost in shadow, vaulted and distant, where centuries of smoke from tallow candles had stained the stone the color of old blood.

No tapestries softened the austerity. No warmth lived here. This was calculation made architecture, a room designed to remind lesser men that beauty required discipline, and discipline required the excision of sentiment.

Prince Damien stood at the narrow window slit, a vertical gash in stone three feet thick, and watched the courtyard below with the attention a naturalist gives insects. Carpenters moved within entrenched scaffolding in their crude choreography, hammer strikes punctuating jokes shouted loud enough to carry up the castle wall. They were building the moat Lionel had ordered, because kings, when frightened, preferred remedies that were visible, expensive, and entirely beside the point.

The sound of their laughter reached him. Coarse. Unrestrained. The kind of joy that came from stupidity, from never having looked deeply enough into the world to see what it actually was.

Damien's hand rested against the stone. Cold. Solid. Honest in a way flesh never was. Stone didn't pretend. Didn't perform virtue or loyalty or love. It simply endured or it crumbled, and there was purity in that binary.

He had been born close enough to power that men called him prince, and far enough from it that no one ever forgot the smell of where that title came from. Tobias had recognized them because it was useful. Nothing more. Two boys born to a woman who sold herself in rooms like the ones Lionel favored, elevated by paperwork and silence, royal only in ink. Damien had learned young that blood was a story men told themselves when they wanted theft to sound like inheritance. Tobias had known that story better than anyone and married it when conquest alone wouldn't suffice.

In his other hand, something trembled.

He brought his palm up slowly, opening his fingers with the care of a man unwrapping something precious and fragile. The dove sat in the cup of his hand, white feathers catching the weak afternoon light that filtered through the window slit. Its head moved in quick jerks, eyes black and glassy, feet gripping his skin with tiny claws that pressed but didn't pierce.

Beautiful. Objectively so. The curve of its breast. The symmetry of its wings folded against its body. The unblemished white of its plumage, unmarked by the filth that defined everything else in this kingdom.

He studied it the way a theologian studies scripture, searching for meaning in form, for truth in design. The bird was pure because it was simple. It knew hunger and fear and the imperative to fly. Nothing else complicated its existence. No ambition disguised as service, no cowardice dressed as wisdom, no weakness pretending to be strength.

"Rare is the unity of beauty and purity."

His voice emerged soft, barely above a whisper, the tone a priest might use to deliver benediction or curse. The two were indistinguishable if you understood that both were judgments pronounced on the inadequate.

The door behind him groaned on hinges that had needed oil for a decade and would never receive it. Someone had decided long ago that the squeal served as announcement, that it gave the room's occupant warning of approach, and so the maintenance had been neglected with purpose.

Damien didn't turn. He knew the pattern of that particular entrance, the apologetic shuffle that always preceded it.

"My Lord."

Falstaff's voice carried the reedy quality of wind through a cracked window. Thin. Uncertain. The sound of a man who'd spent his life calculating exactly how much deference was required to survive and had decided the answer was always more.

"First Councilman Falstaff." Damien kept his eyes on the dove. "To what do I owe this pleasure?"

The word pleasure was delivered with the faintest emphasis, just enough to let Falstaff know that his presence was tolerated but not desired, that he existed in this room on sufferance and should conduct his business with appropriate brevity.

The dove's head turned. Its beak opened slightly, a pink tongue visible for a moment before it closed again. Such a small thing. Such perfect economy of design. Nothing wasted. Nothing excessive. Just wings and bone and the ability to rise above the filth below.

Damien released his fingers.

The bird pushed off from his palm with a flutter of white, a brief chaos of feathers and air, then found the window slit and arrowed through it. Gone in seconds. A white smudge against the gray of the castle's outer wall, shrinking as it climbed, becoming indistinguishable from cloud as it reached altitude.

Free. Unburdened. Pure.

"I've received word Lord Henry is nearing the gates. He's prepared to make an offer."

Falstaff's words came quickly now, emboldened by Damien's silence, by the illusion that silence meant permission to continue speaking. The councilman had never understood that silence was judgment withheld, that the absence of correction was not approval but patience stretched thin.

Damien turned.

"An offer?"

Falstaff stood near the door. Thin as parchment and twice as fragile, the old councilman was. He had mastered the art of occupying space without claiming it, of being present without being noticed. His robes hung loose on a frame that age had winnowed down to essential elements, his face mapped with lines that spoke to decades of worry, of nights spent calculating how to survive another day in a court where survival required sacrificing dignity in increments so small you barely noticed it disappearing.

"He'd like his daughter—er, Margaret, I believe—to take your brother's hand."

Damien's mouth twitched. Not quite a smile. More an acknowledgment that the universe had delivered exactly the kind of tragicomic development he'd predicted.

"Hmph."

His palm closed on empty air, fingers curling into a loose fist where the dove had been. The warmth from its body was already fading. Everything warm faded eventually, returned to the temperature of stone.

He walked toward Falstaff. The councilman's eyes tracked the approach, pupils dilating slightly, a mammalian response to the proximity of something predatory.

"And the other matter?"

Falstaff's throat bobbed. His hands twitched toward each other, fingers knotting briefly before he forced them still. "Nothing yet, my Lord."

The response was expected. Disappointing but unsurprising. Men in chains rarely cooperated on timelines that suited their captors' convenience. Henry Beverley was proving as stubborn in defeat as he'd been foolish in war.

"I'll be down in a moment."

Damien stopped three feet from Falstaff. Close enough to smell the fear-sweat that had begun to bead along the old man's hairline. Close enough to watch his breathing accelerate. Close enough to see the exact moment when the councilman understood he'd been dismissed and began calculating his exit.

"Councilman?"

Falstaff froze. "Yes, my Lord?"

"Where is my brother?"

The question hung between them. Simple. Direct. Requiring an answer that both men already knew but that needed to be spoken aloud because the speaking of it would force the councilman to choose between honesty and loyalty, and watching men make that choice was how you measured their worth.

Falstaff's mouth opened. Closed. His eyes cut sideways toward the door as though escape might still be possible if he moved quickly enough.

But he was old. And Damien was patient. And they both knew how this ended.

"The brothel, my Lord."

The words came out strangled, as though Falstaff himself were responsible for Lionel's appetites, as though proximity to failure made him complicit in it.

Damien nodded once.

Falstaff fled.

The door groaned shut behind him. The study returned to silence. Damien stood in the center of the room, alone again, surrounded by carved beasts frozen in perpetual violence, and felt the familiar contempt settle back into his chest where it lived permanently.

His brother was in a brothel. At noon. With court convening within the hour. With Henry Beverley approaching the gates in chains, daughter in tow, ready to kneel and offer his bloodline in exchange for mercy he didn't deserve and wouldn't receive.

And Lionel was drunk. Or getting there. Probably both.

Damien crossed to a side table where a basin of water sat beside a cloth. He dipped his hands. The water was cold. He washed his palms methodically, removing any trace of the dove, any residue of warmth or feathers or the brief contact with something that had been beautiful.

When his hands were clean, he dried them. Folded the cloth precisely. Set it beside the basin at a right angle.

The brothel was a quarter mile away, through corridors that descended from nobility to necessity, from stone that bore the weight of centuries to timber that creaked under the weight of vice. Damien walked through them all with the same measured pace, his boots striking stone then wood then stone again.

The brothel announced itself before he reached it. Sound leaked through the walls. Laughter. The kind that came from wine and nakedness and the temporary amnesia that both provided. Music played somewhere deeper in, a fiddle badly tuned, notes stumbling over each other in a rhythm that suggested the player was as drunk as the audience.

The door was open. Of course it was. Lionel probably hadn't bothered closing it. Probably wanted anyone passing by to know exactly where he was and what he was doing, wanted his presence to be witnessed and therefore validated. *Look at me. Look at how I don't care about your judgment. Look at how free I am.*

Except none of it was freedom. Just another cage built from appetite and weakness, bars made of flesh and wine, a cell you could walk into and out of but somehow never truly left.

Damien stopped at the threshold.

The room stank. Sweat and sweet wine and something beneath both, something organic and sour, the smell of bodies used hard and put away unwashed. The air was thick with it, humid, clinging to skin and clothes, invading nostrils with aggressive insistence.

Lionel sat tangled in silk sheets that had started the day white but now bore the stains of their defilement. Wine. Lipstick. Other fluids best left unidentified. Three women sprawled around him in various states of undress, all young, all pretty in the way that poverty made women pretty, sharp-featured and hard-eyed beneath the performance of pleasure.

Wine moved between mouths. Lionel tilted a bottle toward one girl's lips, poured too fast, let it run down her chin in red rivulets that painted her throat and chest. She laughed. Threw her head back. Performed joy with the skill of someone whose livelihood depended on convincing drunk men they were having the time of their lives.

Another girl leaned against Lionel's shoulder, her hand tracing patterns on his chest, fingers moving through the sparse hair there with practiced laziness. Her eyes were vacant. Watching something on the far wall that wasn't there.

The third had fallen asleep. Or passed out. Her head lolled against the pillows, mouth open, one breast exposed where the sheet had fallen away.

And Lionel. Twenty-two years old, King of England for three, crowned in a ceremony that had taken six hours and cost more than most villages earned in a decade, sitting in a brothel at noon, half-drunk, fully pathetic, grinning with the desperate enthusiasm of a child who'd found a puddle to play in, baffled that the adults refused to join him.

"Brother!"

The word came out too loud, slurred at the edges. Lionel's face split into a grin that showed wine-stained teeth, his eyes bright with something that might have been joy if you didn't look closely enough to see the fear beneath it.

The fear was always there. Always visible to anyone who bothered to look. Lionel was terrified. Permanently. Of his crown, of his court, of his brother, of the world that demanded more from him than he had to give.

So he drank. And fucked. And pretended the fear would drown if he poured enough wine on top of it.

It never did. Fear floated.

Damien stepped into the room. The door closed behind him with a soft click that somehow carried more weight than a slam would have.

"Lord Henry's just arrived."

"Fantastic!" Lionel reached for another bottle, found it, brandished it toward Damien. "Pour yourself some wine, yeah?"

The offer was genuine. Enthusiastic. Lionel actually believed that Damien might want to join him, that partaking in this degradation might somehow be appealing, that the stink and the sweat and the performance of pleasure-for-crowns was something brothers shared.

"I'd like you to tell the girls to leave."

Damien's hands hung loose at his sides. His posture was relaxed. Everything about his body language suggested this was a request, a preference gently expressed, something Lionel could choose to honor or ignore as his brotherly affection dictated.

Everything about his eyes said otherwise.

"But we're having so much fun, brother! Aren't we, ladies?"

The women laughed. Too quickly, too loud. The sound of people who'd learned to read danger in silence and were now trying desperately to fill that silence with noise loud enough to drown out what was coming.

Damien waited. Didn't move. Didn't blink. Just stood there, a statue of controlled violence, letting the laughter die on its own, letting the silence return and settle and become uncomfortable.

"Tell them to leave."

His voice dropped. Quieter. But the quiet carried weight, pulled air from the room, made breathing difficult for everyone except him.

Lionel's grin faltered. Cracked. The fear beneath it leaked through.

He waved a hand. Dismissive. Trying to reclaim authority even as he surrendered it. "Go on."

The women moved. Fast. Professional. They'd been in rooms that turned dangerous before. Knew when to perform and when to flee. They snatched their clothes from wherever they'd been discarded, didn't bother dressing, just clutched fabric to their chests and ran for the door.

Their giggling continued in the corridor. Fading. Becoming

distance and then silence.

Lionel stood. Unsteady. The robe he'd been wearing hung open, tied loosely at the waist, exposing his chest and stomach, pale skin gone soft from inactivity and indulgence. He swayed. Caught himself. Tried to arrange his face into something regal.

Failed.

"Here already?"

The question was plaintive. Childish. As though Henry Beverley's arrival was some kind of betrayal, some breach of etiquette, as though prisoners had the luxury of choosing their own schedule.

"It's past noon. You'd do well to clean yourself up."

Damien assessed his brother's body with clinical eyes. Cataloging the damage. Wine stains on his robe. Lipstick on his neck. His hair matted with sweat. His eyes bloodshot and unfocused.

This was England's king. This was the man who sat on their father's throne, who wore their father's crown, who spoke law with their father's authority.

This was what happened when weakness inherited power.

"Do you enjoy patronizing me?"

Lionel's voice tried for anger. Landed somewhere closer to petulance.

Damien smirked. "You're an easy target."

"And you're a bully."

The accusation hung between them. True. Obvious. Completely irrelevant. Damien was a bully in the way stone was hard, in the way winter was cold, in the way gravity pulled objects downward. These were simply facts about how the world worked.

It was a familiar dance, a tired one, really, the routine they performed where Lionel pretended to have dignity and Damien pretended to respect it.

"Half-drunk and robed may be your idea of serviceable, but I assure you it's not the court's. You wouldn't want your pecker to slip out during proceedings, would you?"

Lionel's face went scarlet, humiliation blooming across his

cheeks in mottled patches, rage and shame bleeding together until they were indistinguishable.

"Serviceable is what I say it is," he huffed. "I am the King."

There it was. The phrase Lionel deployed whenever backed into corners, whenever forced to confront his own inadequacy. I am the King. As though saying it enough times would make it true. Would transform the crown from burden into authority. Would grant him the power that should have accompanied the title but somehow never had.

"You'd also do well to strike that phrase from your vocabulary."

Damien started for the door. His work here was finished. The message had been delivered. Lionel would clean himself. Would present himself in court. Would perform his role adequately because the alternative was standing before nobility while stinking of wine and whores, and even Lionel wasn't drunk enough to believe that was acceptable.

"Any man who must repeat his authority has none."

He glanced back. One last look. One final judgment delivered with the weight of years of disappointment.

"Now. Sometime today?"

Then he was gone. Out the door. Into the corridor. Leaving his brother alone with the wine and the stains and the shame.

Behind him, silence. Then the sound of something breaking. Glass shattering. Lionel throwing a bottle perhaps, or hurling furniture, or just collapsing under the weight of being exactly who he was and knowing it wasn't enough and never would be.

Damien walked back toward the castle proper, toward the throne room where Henry Beverley would soon kneel and offer his daughter and pretend this was negotiation rather than surrender.

The world was full of chaos. Full of Lionels and Henrys and Falstaffs, men who believed their wants mattered, who thought weakness deserved sympathy, who confused survival with virtue.

And above them all, watching, was Damien. The only one who understood what they refused to see. That cruelty wasn't passion. It was principle. That violence wasn't chaos. It was the purest form of reason. That beauty and purity were rare not because the world lacked them but because the world didn't deserve them.

The dove was gone. Flown away into sky and distance.

Everything else remained.

SCENE 3

THE COURT

The throne room had witnessed one hundred and eighty-two years of cruelty dressed as justice, and the stones remembered every drop of blood spilled in the name of order. Thirty feet of carved granite rose to a vaulted ceiling where shadows pooled like standing water, undisturbed by the pale afternoon light that struggled through arrow-slit windows. The air tasted of old smoke, the kind that gets into the walls and never leaves. No tapestries softened the austerity. No warmth lived here. This was a room built to remind men that power didn't need to justify itself.

Above the dais, carved into the gray rock with the obsessive detail of men who understood symbolism as weapon, the Taylor crest dominated the wall: two dragons, serpentine and ancient, locked in eternal combat, their tails braided together in a knot that suggested neither would ever win and neither would ever surrender. Some said it represented the dual nature of kingship—mercy and wrath, justice and vengeance. Others, after enough ale, whispered it just meant the Taylors had always been at war with themselves.

Lionel arrived late, which surprised no one who knew him.

He climbed the steps with the careful precision of a man trying not to reveal how recently he'd been horizontal, his black robes—silk, imported, worth more than a village blacksmith earned in five years—hanging slightly crooked across his shoulders. Wine still perfumed the air around him, mixing with whatever soap the brothel girls used, he moved through the world with the permanent anxiety of an actor who'd forgotten his lines but couldn't leave the stage.

The throne swallowed him. Too big for his frame, too heavy with history, it made him look like a child playing dress-up in his father's study. His fingers found the armrest and began their familiar percussion, a nervous habit he'd never managed to break. His other leg bounced. A vein pulsed in his temple.

Damien stood to his right, half a step back, close enough to whisper advice but far enough to make clear he had no interest in doing so.

Where Lionel drowned in fabric, Damien wore practicality like a second skin. Steel breastplate over leather; bracers on his forearms, one reinforced beyond necessity; boots made for walking, not ceremony. No crown. No ornament. Just the tools of violence, well-maintained and ready. He stood six and a half feet tall, which meant most men had to look up to meet his eyes. Most men chose not to. His hair—black as pitch, long enough to tie back but currently loose—framed a face that might have been handsome if it ever bothered to express anything resembling warmth.

The height disparity between the brothers was real but required no theatre. Lionel sat elevated by throne and title. Damien stood elevated by the simple fact of his presence, the way certain men occupy space as if they'd purchased it with blood and planned to collect interest.

The doors opened.

The sound rolled through the room like distant thunder,

iron hinges groaning under the weight of oak thick enough to stop a battering ram. Every head turned. Conversations died. The court held its breath.

Henry Beverley entered in chains.

He'd been a king once. You could still see it in the way he walked, even with iron on his wrists—the muscle memory of authority, the spine that refused to bend despite everything time and war had done to the flesh around it. Fifty-four, maybe older. His beard had gone thin and gray, threaded with white along the jaw. His coat, once fine and fitted, hung loose on a frame that had shed thirty pounds since the last time he'd worn it for anything other than surrender.

His hands were bound in front of him, the manacles connected by a short length of chain that clinked with each step. The iron had rubbed his wrists raw. Dried blood crusted the edges where the metal bit deepest. He didn't try to hide it. Didn't look down. His eyes stayed level, locked on the middle distance, refusing to meet anyone's gaze but refusing to show shame.

Behind him, keeping pace but separate, came his daughter.

Margaret Beverley. Nineteen years old and moving through the room as if it were a dream from which she might wake if she could just remember how. Her hair—black as her father's had been before age bleached it—fell past her shoulders in waves that caught what little light the windows offered. Her eyes were a deep, piercing blue, and they stayed fixed on the floor three feet ahead of her as if she had memorized that exact distance and found safety there.

Her gown was indigo, expensive once, now showing wear at the hems where the fabric dragged across every floor she'd crossed in the past week. She held herself carefully, arms at her sides, hands loose, breathing shallow and controlled. Everything about her posture suggested a girl who'd learned that invisibility was the best defense available to women in rooms where men decided their futures.

Four guards flanked them, swords sheathed but hands resting on hilts in the universal posture of men prepared to draw steel if anyone breathed wrong. At the front walked Richard-son, tall and grim, his expression carved from the same granite as the walls. He'd ridden back from Taylor's End less than two hours ago. Rowan Campbell's blood still stained his glove, a rust-brown smear across the knuckles that he hadn't bothered to clean.

The procession reached the base of the stairs and stopped. Henry knelt.

It took him longer than it should have. His right knee buck-led first, then his left, and for a moment it seemed he might topple forward and crack his skull on the bottom step. But he caught himself. Found his balance. Settled into the position with as much dignity as a man in his position could manage.

Margaret remained standing, head bowed, hands now knot-ted together in front of her stomach as if she were trying to hold herself in one piece through force of will.

The room waited.

Lionel leaned forward, elbows on his knees, studying Hen-ry with the expression of a man examining a horse he might purchase if the price came down. He let the silence stretch. Let it pull tight. Let every second remind everyone present who controlled time itself in this room.

Then he spoke.

"Hello, Henry."

"Your Grace," Henry said, voice steady despite everything.

Lionel smiled. "How was your trip?"

"Fine, Your Grace."

Lionel's gaze drifted past Henry to Margaret, lingering there with the appraisal of a man considering a purchase. "Your daughter." He paused, letting the moment breathe. "I find her lovely."

Margaret's shoulders tightened. She didn't look up.

Henry's jaw worked. "Thank you, Your Grace."

"I understand she will take my hand as Queen."

"What of our land, Your Grace?"

And there it was. The question that mattered. The reason Henry knelt in chains instead of hanging from a gibbet. His daughter's hand in exchange for his family's ancestral holdings, two hundred years of Beverley blood poured into Scottish soil now to be signed over to the Taylors in a marriage contract dressed up as alliance.

Lionel's smile sharpened. "You've surrendered it, have you not?"

"I was assured an understanding might be reached."

"While your demented seed and his army lurk?" The warmth drained from Lionel's voice like water from a cracked cup. "D'you think me stupid?"

"Your Grace—"

Lionel stood. The movement was sudden, graceless. He descended two steps, then three, closing the distance until Henry had to crane his neck backward to maintain eye contact.

Damien watched his brother descend and felt something familiar stir in his chest. Not quite contempt, not quite pity. Closer to the weary awareness of a man watching a drunk stumble toward a cliff and knowing there was no point in shouting a warning. Lionel performed his authority the way children performed adulthood, with exaggerated gestures and borrowed phrases, never quite understanding that real power didn't need to announce itself.

Their father, for all his faults, would have handled this differently. Tobias had possessed the gift of silence, the ability to make men confess their sins simply by looking at them long enough. He'd understood that kingship was nine parts theatre and one part murder, and he'd been talented at both.

"Here's something I would like to understand," Lionel said, voice rising now, playing to the gallery of courtiers and guards who lined the walls. "When does it end, Henry? The Beverleys have been vying for the throne for hundreds of years. And what exactly is it you've conquered? Peasant farmers? Sheep?"

He paused, letting the rhetorical blade twist.

"Small children and their mothers in Northbury?"

Margaret flinched. Barely. Just a twitch at the corner of her mouth. But Damien saw it.

Northbury. Twenty-four years past and still a wound that

wouldn't close. Three hundred dead, most of them civilians, burned alive or cut down in the streets by Beverley raiders who'd mistaken brutality for strategy.

"The land does not forget your crimes," Lionel continued, warming to his subject now, riding the momentum of his own rhetoric. "Of course, it seems you've been more successful in producing incompetent dullards and cocky fairies like your son than actual victories, and I suppose now..."

He gestured toward Margaret without looking at her.

"Wives? So, again, I ask you. When does it end?"

Henry's jaw tightened. Muscles bunched along his neck. His bound hands clenched into fists. But his voice, when it came, stayed level. Stayed diplomatic. Stayed locked in the role of penitent supplicant that survival demanded.

"Your Grace, I humbly—"

"Is that how you thought you'd obtain my sympathies?" Lionel's voice cracked like a whip. "By calling it humility when you're here in chains, trading your crown and your daughter for the privilege of breathing?"

The air in the room changed. Went thin. Brittle. Courtiers who'd been pretending not to listen stopped pretending. Guards straightened. Even the shadows seemed to lean forward, interested now in how this would end.

Margaret's hands were shaking. She knotted them tighter in her skirt, knuckles white with the effort of keeping still.

Henry's eyes stayed down. "War is... complicated, Your Grace."

It was the wrong answer. Everyone in the room knew it. Perhaps Henry knew it too and said it anyway, because some part of him—the part that remembered being king, remembered giving orders instead of taking them—couldn't quite bend far enough to beg.

"Are you suggesting I don't understand the concept?"

Lionel's voice had gone quiet now, which was somehow worse than the shouted. Quiet meant he'd stopped performing and started feeling, and feelings in men with absolute power tended to end with someone bleeding.

And that's when Henry made his choice.

Something shifted behind his eyes. Some calculation completed. Some final tally of costs and benefits that concluded he had nothing left to lose except his pride, and pride at least died clean. His head tilted up. His lips pressed into a thin line, then pulled wide into a smile, sharp and cold and vindictive, the smile of a man who'd decided that if he was going to hang, he'd at least get to speak his mind first.

When he spoke again, the submission was gone. What came out was pure venom.

"I was picking my brother's corpses up off the battlefield while you were still sucking on your whore mother's tit."

The court inhaled as one.

"Call yourself a King, eh? Claim you understand what war is? That crown must be digging into your juvenile brain sooner than I figured it might. So, *yes*, I am saying you do not understand the concept."

Lionel's face went blank. For three seconds he simply stood there, frozen, his expression caught between shock and rage, unable to process that a person had addressed him in the manner he addressed servants. Then his hand moved to his sword hilt.

"It seems you've taken me for some kind of cunt, old man."

Henry's smile widened. "And if I have?"

"I would be forced to correct you."

The old king laughed. It was a terrible sound—dry, bitter, carrying twenty years of defeat and disappointment, the laugh of a man who'd lost everything and discovered it wasn't as bad as he'd feared. Fear required hope. Hope required believing your choices mattered. Henry Beverley had run out of both.

"I simply see you for what you are. A spoiled little boy, playing dress-up in the robes of a consort *throne-leecher* who borrowed his crown and left it to bastards."

He raised his voice now, projecting it past Lionel to the guards, the courtiers, anyone with ears.

"A spoiled little bastard boy!"

Lionel's hand tightened on the sword. He descended another

step, close enough now that Henry could smell the wine on his breath.

"You accost me under my foundations. Belittle me, curse me. I only wonder, what sort of memento would your brothers in the mainland prefer? Your shriveled cock and balls, or that bald head of yours that's led them to so much success?"

The threat hung in the air like smoke, visible and choking. Every person in the room understood what they were witnessing: a king learning, in real time, that authority without respect was just permission to be hated.

Lionel held the moment, milking it, trying to reclaim some scrap of dignity through dramatic pause. Then he spoke, voice low and flat.

"Guards."

They moved fast. Two grabbed Henry by the arms, hauling him upright with enough force to dislocate something. The old man grunted but didn't scream. Richardson stepped forward from his position by the wall, one hand resting on his sword hilt, watching Henry with the dead-eyed patience of a man who'd learned to love his work. The same hand that had split Rowan Campbell's lip two hours ago now flexed with anticipation, already deciding where the first blow would land.

Henry thrashed once, testing his captors' grip, finding it solid. Then he stopped struggling and poured everything he had left into words.

"I will not give my life to a faux monarchy! Much less to a pompous, illegitimate swine! The spawn of a brothel rat!"

Damien's voice cut through the madness like a blade through silk.

"All monarchy is illegitimate, old man."

Everyone stopped. Guards froze mid-drag. Courtiers turned. Even Henry went still, his head swiveling to find the source of the voice.

Damien stepped forward. One step. Just enough to draw every eye in the room, to shift the center of gravity from his brother's theatrical rage to his own terrifying calm.

Their eyes locked.

And Henry saw him. Really saw him. Not the armor or the height or the theatrical cruelty that Lionel wore like costume jewelry. He saw the real thing, the cold, patient brutality of a man who didn't need to shout because he'd learned that violence spoke louder than words and fear lasted longer than pain. Henry had watched Damien grow from a quiet boy who stood in his father's shadow into something darker, something that made even hardened soldiers nervous.

"One might even say that's the beauty of it."

Damien's smile was a terrible thing. It reached his eyes and somehow made them colder.

Henry's face drained of color. All the defiance, all the bitter humor, all the performance—it slid off him like water, leaving behind only the exhausted resignation of a man who'd finally met someone he couldn't bluff.

His voice dropped. Went sober.

"Your father should've drowned you when you were born."

Damien's smile widened.

Henry was dragged from the court, his voice still echoing down the corridor. Curses and prophecies and prayers all tangled together until the doors slammed shut and cut him off mid-sentence.

The room breathed again. Slowly. Carefully. The way you breathe after nearly drowning.

Margaret stood alone in the center of the floor.

She hadn't moved during the entire exchange. Hadn't looked up. Hadn't made a sound. Her head stayed bowed. Her hands stayed knotted in her skirt. Her breathing stayed shallow and controlled. But something had broken inside her. You could see it in the way her shoulders curved inward, the way her spine bent just slightly, as if her body had finally accepted what her mind had been denying: she was property now, to be bartered and traded and used however these men decided.

Lionel climbed back to the throne. Sat. Tried to arrange his face into something resembling authority. Failed. He looked shaken, young, aware that he'd lost control of the room and entirely uncertain how to get it back.

He cleared his throat.

"Escort the lady to her temporary chamber."

Damien nodded once. He crossed the floor, his boots echoing throughout the throne room, and finally stopped in front of Margaret. He didn't speak. Didn't touch her. Just stood there, waiting with a bottomless, quiet patience, until curiosity or fear or simple exhaustion forced her to lift her head.

Their eyes met.

Up close, she was younger than he'd expected. Not in years—nineteen was nineteen—but in the way she held herself, like someone who'd been protected from the world's teeth and was only now learning they were sharp. Her eyes were red but dry. She'd cried herself out somewhere between here and her father's cell, and now there was nothing left except the hollow resignation of someone too tired to be afraid anymore.

Damien held her gaze for exactly three seconds. Then he turned and walked toward the door.

She followed.

SCENE 4

YOU'RE A GOOD MAN, ELI

Jamie lay on his back staring at the ceiling beams, counting knots in the wood because counting anything was better than thinking. Rowan's snores rattled the walls, a rhythmic sawing that had become as familiar as his own heartbeat over the years. The old man slept like the dead—hard and immediate, the sleep of exhausted bodies that had given up arguing with their circumstances.

Jamie waited. Counted to a hundred. Then two hundred. Listening for any change in Rowan's breathing, any shift in the pattern that might suggest consciousness returning. When he was satisfied, he peeled back the threadbare blanket and swung his legs over the edge of the pallet, moving with the care of someone who'd spent years sneaking out and knew exactly which floorboards groaned.

His boots waited where he'd left them, worn leather shaped to his feet by countless miles of walking. He slipped them on without lacing them, just tucked the tongues in and stood slowly, distributing his weight across the balls of his feet. The door was three steps away. He made it in two and a half, skipping the middle board that always creaked, and eased the latch open with both hands to muffle the sound.

Outside, the night air hit him cold and clean, washing away the close staleness of the hut. He breathed deep, tasting woodsmoke and horse dung and something green underneath it all—the forest reasserting itself now that the sun had gone down and men had retreated indoors.

Taylor's End at night was a different creature than Taylor's End by day. The industrious bustle of commerce gave way to something looser, messier, more honest. Voices carried from open windows, arguments and laughter and the rhythmic creak of beds working overtime. A drunk sang somewhere in the distance, off-key and enthusiastic, some ballad about a sailor's wife that got progressively more explicit with each verse. Dogs barked at shadows. Somewhere a baby cried, thin and reedy, the sound cutting through everything else like a knife.

Jamie walked with his head down, hands in his pockets, just another young man with nowhere particular to be and no reason to hurry getting there. The streets were mud and horseshit, never quite drying even in summer, perpetually churned by cartwheels and hooves and boots. Lanterns hung from hooks outside taverns and brothels, casting pools of yellow light that did more to deepen the shadows than dispel them.

He found Micah leaning against a porch rail outside the tanner's shop, picking at his teeth with a splinter of wood. Twenty-two years old and already going soft around the middle, Micah had the look of someone who'd given up on ambition and found contentment at the bottom of a bottle. His clothes hung loose on his frame, patched and re-patched, held together more by habit than thread.

"Rowan know you're here?" Micah asked, not looking up from his dental work.

"He'd never have it. Where are we going?"

Micah grinned, finally meeting Jamie's eyes. "Taylor's Ale.

Lillian and Ava said they'd meet us there."

They walked side by side through streets that grew louder as they approached the commercial heart of the village. The sounds of drinking and whoring mixed into a kind of music—crude but honest, the soundtrack of people trying to forget their circumstances for a few hours before morning came and demanded payment for the night's pleasures.

Taylor's Ale & Comfort squatted at the intersection of two muddy roads, a rambling structure that had started as a modest taproom and metastasized over the years into something that served every vice the Crown hadn't explicitly outlawed and several it had. Light spilled from the windows. Music leaked through the walls; fiddle and drum and voices raised in songs that would have gotten you thrown out of church.

Micah pushed through the door and Jamie followed, stepping from relative quiet into a wall of noise that hit like a physical thing. The main room was packed shoulder to shoulder with drunks in various stages of decay: farmers spending their week's wages, merchants celebrating successful swindles, soldiers on leave looking for fights or women or preferably both. Prostitutes worked the room.

The air was thick with smoke and sweat and spilled beer, so dense you could almost chew it. Someone had vomited in a corner and made a halfhearted attempt to cover it with sawdust. Nobody seemed to mind.

Micah navigated through the chaos with the confidence of someone who knew the territory, leading Jamie past tables where men shouted over dice and cards, past alcoves where transactions of a more intimate nature were being negotiated, down a corridor that grew progressively darker and quieter until they reached a door at the end.

Beyond it, four men sat around a battered table playing cards with the grim concentration of people wagering more than they could afford to lose. None of them looked up as Micah and Jamie passed. Whatever they were doing, they wanted no witnesses.

The barrel room smelled of fermentation and wood rot and

was filled with large casks. Micah went straight for the nearest tap, pulling a dented canteen from inside his coat, and began filling it with the offhand ease of someone who'd done this a hundred times and gotten caught maybe twice.

He was screwing the cap back on when a voice cut through the quiet.

"Sneaky fucker."

The man in the doorway was tall and rail-thin, built like he'd been stretched on a rack and forgotten there. Eli Richardson. Forty-something, though the years had been unkind and added a few decades to his face. His left eye was glass, the socket around it webbed with scars that suggested someone had tried to remove his head and only partially succeeded. The rest of his face bore similar geography—white lines cutting across tanned skin, the permanent record of a life lived violently.

"You gonna pay for that, young man?"

Micah didn't look particularly concerned. "What are you so hung up for? We've won the war, haven't we?"

"Were you there?"

Micah's grin widened. "Obviously. Tell him, Jamie."

"Fuck off," Jamie smirked.

Eli's good eye found Jamie. Not the quick appraisal of a stranger, but something slower. Something that lingered a half-second too long, the way you look at a thing you've been watching grow for years and still can't quite believe. The scars on his face shifted as something moved beneath them.

"How are you, young man?"

The words came out warmer than anything else Eli had said. Softer. The voice of a man asking about more than he was saying. Jamie shrugged. The gesture was automatic, the universal armor of young men who didn't know how to answer questions that mattered.

"Eli's a man of many vocations," Micah announced with the grin of someone about to say something stupid. "Whoring, mostly—"

The smack came fast—open palm to the back of Micah's head, hard enough to rattle teeth but not hard enough to do real damage. Eli's hand was already returning to his side before Micah finished wincing.

"If you ever want to put some extra bits in your pocket," Eli said, his attention still on Jamie with an intensity that felt like being measured for something Jamie couldn't name, "you just come down here. I know Rowan's been having trouble with the castle. It's the least I could do for a legend."

Jamie nodded, unsure what else to do with that. The idea of Rowan Campbell being anyone's legend seemed laughable until you remembered he'd survived Northbury, and most men who'd been there hadn't.

"But for now, you lot need to scram," Eli gestured toward the door. "It's a full house, can't have you mucking about."

Micah was already moving, pulling Jamie back through the card room—the four men still hadn't looked up—and into the main hall where the noise hit them again like surf.

They stopped by the bar. Micah leaned against the scarred wood with the satisfaction of a job well done, patting the canteen hidden under his coat.

"This... *This* is what it's all about, mate! Music, girls, ale—what more could you need?"

Jamie looked around at the sweating, shouted mass of humanity and felt his head start to throb. "It's a little loud, mate."

"The village it is." Micah hoisted the canteen slightly, producing a slosh. "We got what we came for, didn't we?"

Then Lillian appeared through the crowd with Ava in tow, and Jamie forgot about the noise.

"Now we really got what we come for, eh?" Micah grabbed Ava around the waist and kissed her with the enthusiasm of youth and alcohol, all technique and no subtlety.

Jamie and Lillian hugged. It was careful, almost formal, the embrace of two people who wanted more but hadn't quite figured out how to ask for it.

"Is your father alright?" Her voice was soft, pitched low enough that only he could hear it beneath the din.

"He'll manage."

"Those knights," she said, barely above a whisper. "They're

so awful."

"Let's leave before Eli kicks my ass, right?" Micah had come up for air and was already pushing toward the door. "That includes you lot!"

Outside, the night felt quieter by comparison, though the sounds of the village hadn't actually dimmed, they'd just been drowned out by the concentrated chaos of the tavern. The four of them walked without destination, letting their feet carry them where they would, passing the bottle Micah had stolen with the democratic generosity of drunk people who'd forgotten tomorrow existed.

They ended up on a hill overlooking Taylor's End, a gentle rise on the eastern edge of the village where shepherds brought their flocks during the day and young people brought their secrets at night. From here you could see the whole sprawl of the village laid out like a map, tiny points of light marking where people gathered to hold back the dark.

Micah flopped down in the grass and stared at the stars. "It all looks so small from here."

"The buildings?" Jamie asked, settling beside him. "Or the people?"

"Both. Makes you think."

"About what?"

Micah took a long pull from the bottle before answering. "Down there, everything looks so big and real. But from up here, the buildings are just little boxes, the people... they're just these little specks. I've lived here my whole life and, until now, I never realized how small it all really is."

Jamie studied his friend's face in the starlight, noting the unfocused eyes, the slack mouth. "Are you alright, mate?"

"Splendid." Micah thrust the bottle at him. "You'd do well to catch up. Call yourself a man..."

He stood suddenly, teetering at the edge of the slope with his arms windmilling for balance. For one terrible moment it looked like gravity would claim him, send him tumbling down into the dark. Then he caught himself, laughing with the relief of someone who'd just remembered they were immortal.

"So I can fall down this hill with you?" Jamie asked.

Micah grabbed Ava's hand, pulling her upright with more force than grace. "Let's go, Ava—Jamie and I aren't on the same page, you see—"

"Where are you going?"

"A brush, Jamie. A brush!"

They disappeared into the darkness, giggled like children, leaving Jamie and Lillian alone on the hilltop with the stars and the stolen ale and all the words neither of them knew how to say.

Jamie shook his head, smiling despite himself. When he turned back, Lillian was watching him with an expression he couldn't quite read.

"So," she said, "what are you going to do?"

"Hmm?"

"Do you want to stay here?"

He frowned, genuinely confused. "Stay where?"

"Taylor's End."

The question landed heavier than it should have. He'd never really thought about it in those terms. You stayed where you were born because that's what people did. You learned your father's trade and married a local girl and had children who would learn your trade and marry local girls and the wheel kept turning until you died and got buried in the same earth that had fed you.

"S'pose I could work for my father," Jamie shrugged. "Make swords, all that."

Lillian nodded, but her eyes had gone distant.

"I hate it here, Jamie."

"Well, what will you do?"

"Travel. Maybe see the world."

He couldn't help but smile. "What do you know about the world?"

"That's why I want to go, you buffoon."

"Fair enough."

He took a drink, letting the cheap ale burn down his throat, giving him something to do with his hands. "Well, where would you go?"

She shrugged, but there was calculation behind it. She'd been thinking about this, planning it in whatever private spaces her life allowed.

"Maybe London. I want to be an actor."

Jamie's brow furrowed. "An actor?"

"Proper. On the stage."

"Like the Shakespeare bloke?"

"Once, before my mother left Taylor's End, she took me to see a play at The Globe in London." She shifted, pulling her knees up to her chest, wrapping her arms around them. "At first, I thought the idea was... silly, you know? Grown-ups playing dress-up and shouting at each other in front of thousands of people. It all seemed... embarrassing."

She paused, and Jamie waited, sensing this mattered more than she was letting on.

"But by the moment the intermission came, it occurred to me that, during the show, I hadn't thought of anything else. Everything I thought I knew about my world just... went away. Like I was on the stage me self. And when it was over, everyone stood up and cheered and clapped and cried. And I wondered: what must it be like to be on that stage? To be clapped for like that? To be admired?"

Jamie thought about that for a moment; the idea of becoming someone else, of stepping into a different life like you'd step into different clothes. The appeal was obvious when your real life consisted of goats and poverty and watching your father get slapped in the street.

He placed his hand over Lillian's. Her skin was warm despite the cool night air.

"I'll come with you."

"Jamie..."

"The old bloke will manage. You'll need someone to protect you, won't you?"

She laughed. "Like you'd be much help."

"The play. What was it about?"

Lillian looked at him, and it was then that something passed between them that had nothing to do with words.

"It was about love."

Jamie's hand tightened around hers. The moment stretched, pulling taut like a rope taking weight. Then, finally, they were kissing, falling back into the grass together, the bottle tipping over and spilling forgotten into the dirt.

"Thank the Gods!"

They jumped apart like they'd been burned. Micah stumbled toward them out of the darkness, waving the nearly empty bottle above his head like a trophy. Behind him, Ava was rebuttoning her shirt with the efficient embarrassment of someone who'd just been caught doing exactly what everyone assumed they were doing.

"It's about time you two lovebirds admitted to it."

Jamie scrambled to his feet, face hot. "I should stab you with that fucking bottle."

"You talking dirty to me now?" Micah swayed, grinning like an idiot. "Because, you know, I'd save that for later, eh?"

Jamie tackled Micah into the grass and they rolled, laughing and cursing, all elbows and knees and the kind of brutality that passes for affection between young men who haven't learned better ways to express themselves.

Later, walking through the emptier streets on the village's edge, Jamie and Micah passed what remained of the bottle back and forth. The girls had gone home. The night had gone quiet. Even the drunks had mostly stumbled back to whatever holes they'd crawled out of.

"Are you going to marry that girl?" Micah asked, his words starting to slur together at the edges.

"Hmm?"

"Her father hits her, you know."

The words landed cold and hard in Jamie's stomach. "I didn't know that."

"He's a proper prick, always has been. But she's a good girl."

"I don't know much else."

"You don't know much of anything."

"Says you, you thick-headed cunt."

Micah laughed and opened his mouth to respond, then stopped. His hand shot out, gripping Jamie's arm with sudden intensity.

"Is that the King's Watch?"

Jamie followed his gaze. Twenty feet ahead, maybe less, a group of mounted knights was moving through the street at a walk, their horses' hooves striking the packed earth with rhythmic thuds. Six riders, maybe seven, hard to tell in the dark.

"It better be or we're fucked."

"You recognize any of them?"

Jamie squinted, trying to make out features in the dim light of the few remaining lanterns. Then the lead rider passed under one and his face became clear.

"Yeah, actually. The one in the front... Arthur Richardson."

"Is he the one who came to your house?"

Jamie nodded, already sensing where this was going and powerless to stop it.

"That *cunt...*"

Micah started walking toward the knights, and Jamie had no choice but to follow because leaving him alone seemed worse than whatever was about to happen.

"Micah!" he hissed, but it was too late.

They caught up to the mounted men, and Micah planted himself directly in Richardson's path, forcing the knight to rein in his horse.

"Sir Arthur?"

Richardson looked down at him with the expression of a man discovering dog shit on his boot. "What do you want, lad?"

"I'm just wondering. What does it take to be a knight? Apart from having a small pecker."

The street went quiet. The other knights shifted in their saddles, hands drifting toward sword hilts. Jamie felt his mouth go dry.

"You'd do best to keep walking, mate." Richardson's voice was flat, carrying no heat but all the more dangerous for it.

"I only ask because my pecker's quite small, and I think I'd be perfect."

Richardson glanced at his men—some silent communication passing between them—then swung down from his saddle with fluid grace. He was huge up close, shoulders like a bull, height that made even a full-grown man feel like a child.

"Say that again."

Micah opened his mouth, probably to make things exponentially worse, but his body had other ideas. His face went pale. His throat worked. Then he lurched forward and vomited directly onto Richardson's breastplate; a thick, reeking stream of ale and dinner that splattered across polished steel.

Time seemed to stop. Micah looked up, saw what he'd done, saw Richardson's expression shift from annoyed to murderous, and tried to run.

He made it three steps.

Richardson's hand shot out, catching him by the collar, and slammed him face-first into the mud. Then the beating began.

Richardson didn't hurry it. Each punch was measured, deliberate, delivered with the practiced efficiency of someone who knew exactly how much damage he was doing and enjoyed every second. Face, ribs, kidneys—he worked methodically, painting Micah's body with bruises that would last weeks.

When he was satisfied, Richardson grabbed a handful of Micah's hair and shoved his face into the mud, grinding it there like he was stubbing out a cigarette. Then he spat on him.

"Ought to sober you up." He straightened, brushing mud from his gloves. "Not bad for a man with a small pecker, eh? Now, act like a little cunt one more time and I'll have yours cut off and worn around my neck, you understand? Eli won't be able to help you then, y'hear me?"

Richardson's eyes found Jamie in the shadows. They stared at each other across twenty feet of darkness, and something ancient and indiscernible passed between them.

Then Richardson mounted his horse, signaled his men, and rode off into the night.

Jamie rushed to Micah's side, helping him up from the mud. His friend's face was a mess: split lip, nose streaming blood, one eye already swelling shut. He leaned heavily on Jamie, barely able to stand.

"Micah, I—"

"Just... help me home, will you?"

Jamie got an arm around him, taking most of his weight. "It's okay. It's okay."

But it wasn't okay. Nothing about this was okay.

They made it back to Taylor's Ale & Comfort, and Eli took one look at Micah's face and went white.

They laid him on a cot in the barrel room. Eli knelt beside him with a wet rag, cleaning blood with shaking hands.

"He was drunk," Jamie said, the words tumbling out too fast. "Started in on some knight in the street. Beat him bloody."

"Which knight?"

"Arthur Richardson. Same one that's been harassing my old man."

Eli froze. Dropped the rag into the bucket. The sound of water sloshing was very loud in the sudden silence.

"Did... I'm sorry, do you know him?"

"Arthur's my brother."

The words spread through the room like ink in clear water. Jamie opened his mouth, closed it, opened it again. "But he's—"

"He's a cocksucker is what he is."

Eli sat on the edge of the cot and reached down for a bottle between his feet, took a long pull that suggested he was trying to drown something. When he set it down, his finger went to his left cheek, tracing the white scar that ran from eye socket to jaw.

"His doing. Nearly cut my bloody head off for a laugh." His good eye found Jamie's. "No man's this fuck-ugly without a reason."

"How old were you?"

"Barely six."

He drank again, and in the silence Jamie heard everything Eli wasn't said, the decades of brotherless brotherhood, of learning to live with a face that made children cry and women look away, of knowing the man responsible wore royal colors and slept sound at night.

"Micah might not be my son. Not by blood, no, but he is my boy. I've only ever wanted the best for him, ever since he was dropped on my steps." Eli's voice had gone soft, almost gentle. "Of course, Taylor's End can't be safe for much longer. Not like it was."

He looked at Jamie then, and his one good eye was wet.

"You should get back to your corners, Jamie."

"I can stay with him."

"*Jamie.* Go home."

Jamie understood. This was private. This was family business, whatever that meant in a world where brothers cut each other's faces and fathers beat their daughters and love was something you stole in moments on hilltops because tomorrow it might be gone.

"Good night." He paused at the door. "You're a good man, Eli."

Outside, the night had gone cold. Jamie walked home through empty streets, tasting blood in his mouth though he hadn't been hit, feeling his knuckles ache though he hadn't thrown a punch.

Tomorrow, Richardson would come for Rowan's taxes.

Tomorrow, everything would change.

But tonight, he'd kissed Lillian Spires under the stars, and for a few stolen moments, the world had been exactly what he'd wanted it to be.

SCENE 5

Four women circled Margaret in the chamber that would never be hers, their hands moving with the trained competence of servants who understood that beauty was constructed, that nobility required architecture. Pin here. Tuck there. Pull the waist until breathing became negotiation. The dress was cream silk, imported from somewhere she'd never see, cut to reveal the architecture of her body in ways that made her skin want to crawl off her bones and hide in corners.

It fit because they'd measured her three times the night before. Had run their hands over her flesh with the detachment of cartographers mapping territory they'd never own.

The mirror showed what they'd made: a girl in white, face painted the color of bone, hair braided with pearls that clicked together when she moved her head. Her eyes focused on nothing. Had learned overnight that focusing meant seeing, and seeing meant understanding, and understanding would break what little remained of her that could still be broken.

They complimented her. Called her *radiant*. Said the king would be pleased. Their voices were bright and false.

She counted stones in the wall. Forty-three visible from where she stood. Forty-four if you counted the chipped one half-hidden by the curtain's edge. Numbers were clean.

Dawn broke over Taylor's End like judgment, gray and cold and indifferent to what it revealed.

Richardson and his knights rode in through mud that sucked at hooves with obscene sounds, six horses moving in formation, iron and leather and the promise of violence incarnate. The sound of their approach was a drumbeat, steady and inevitable.

Merchants saw them coming and discovered urgent business elsewhere. Children vanished into doorways before their mothers could call them. Dogs stopped barking.

Rowan saw them through a crack in the wall, his good eye pressed to the gap where timber had warped away from timber, and counted riders. Six. Recognized Richardson at the front by the way he sat his horse, by the particular arrogance of his posture. His stomach dropped.

He'd known this was coming. Had known since yesterday, since the slap that split his lip, since Richardson's promise that debt collected itself with or without permission. But knowing and experiencing were different countries.

The door opened.

Margaret's heart kicked once. Hard. Then went quiet in a way that felt like surrender.

Lionel entered and stopped. Stood framed in the doorway like a painting of a king, black robes edged in gold thread that caught morning light and threw it back in expensive patterns.

"Leave us."

His voice carried the casual authority of men who'd never been refused, who'd learned young that the world rearranged itself around their preferences if they spoke loudly enough.

The women curtsied. Scattered. The door closed behind them with a sound like a coffin lid, soft and final.

The room shrank. Air became scarce. Margaret stood in her white dress and felt the walls press closer, felt the ceiling drop, felt the floor tilt beneath her feet though nothing moved except her perception.

Lionel crossed toward her. Slowly. His eyes moved over her body with the attention livestock inspectors gave cattle at market.

"How'd you sleep?"

The question was performance. He didn't care about her sleep.

"Just fine, Your Grace."

Her voice came out steady. She was proud of that. Proud that fear could be swallowed, that training held even when everything inside her was screaming.

"No need for formalities." He stopped three feet away. Close enough to smell him. Wine and something beneath it, something organic. "You're far too beautiful to be this meek."

"My apologies."

"Nothing to be sorry for."

His hand moved. She tracked it peripherally, didn't let her eyes follow directly because that would be acknowledging, and acknowledgment felt like permission. His fingers found her exposed back. The dress was cut low, skin bare from neck to waist, and his hand settled on her spine like a brand.

She made a sound. Couldn't stop it. A small noise that might have been surprise or revulsion or just her body's involuntary response to being touched by something cold and unwanted.

"Is something wrong?"

Yes. Everything. Your hand. This dress. This room. This castle. This marriage. This life that was being written onto her body in touches she couldn't refuse.

"Your hand is cold."

He smiled. Found that amusing. "Apologies."

His fingers stayed where they were. Began to move. Traced down her spine slowly, vertebra by vertebra, each small bone a station on a journey he was taking without permission.

"You're thinking of your father, are you?"

The question landed sharp. She'd been careful. Had kept her face neutral. But he'd seen something, some flicker, some tell she hadn't controlled fast enough.

"I was."

"You worry for him?"

"I'm not sure."

The truth. She *wasn't* sure. Her father had brought this on them. His wars. His pride. His refusal to bend when bending might have saved them. But he was still her father.

"I have no intention of taking your father's life."

The lie sat between them like a third presence. Obvious. Ignored.

Rowan turned from the wall crack and crossed the hut in three limping steps, his bad knee screaming with each movement, a symphony of old damage conducting itself through bone and sinew.

He shook Jamie awake. Hard. No gentleness. No time.

"Jamie...*Jamie!*"

The boy stirred. Made sounds that suggested consciousness was approaching but hadn't arrived. His eyes opened halfway, unfocused.

"What?"

"Wake up, lad."

Jamie sat up. Confused. Then he saw Rowan's face and understood that the world had changed while he slept, that whatever was coming had already started, that this was the moment his life divided into before and after.

"You needn't be afraid."

Lionel's voice carried reassurance the way rotting meat carried flies.

He reached into his robe. Produced a small wooden box. Opened it with the flourish of a man presenting treasure, revealing a pearl necklace inside, each bead perfectly matched, strung on silk thread thin as spider web, expensive and beautiful in the way that objects become beautiful when their cost exceeds their function.

"This is your home now."

He lifted the necklace with both hands. Approached. His fingers brushed her neck, settling the pearls into place, working the clasp with practiced ease.

He stepped back. Admired his work. His hand came up and smoothed her hair.

"Treat it as such."

Margaret's hand rose involuntarily. Touched the pearls. They were cold against her throat. Heavy. Each bead a small weight contributing to a larger burden.

"They're beautiful."

"They are."

Rowan threw everything within reach into a canvas bag that had been empty yesterday and now had to hold a life. Bread. Hard and old but still edible. Dried meat wrapped in cloth. The dagger he'd kept hidden beneath the floorboards for twelve years, oiled and wrapped and waiting.

"You *must* go."

Jamie looked through the wall crack. Saw the horses. Saw Richardson dismounting. Understanding hit him cold and complete, knowledge arriving all at once like water through a broken dam.

He started shaking his head. *No.* The universal refusal. The child's first defense against reality.

"Jamie..."

"I can't leave you."

The words came out strangled. Desperate. True. He couldn't leave. Couldn't abandon the man who'd raised him, who'd fed him, who'd taught him what little he knew about surviving.

Rowan grabbed his shoulders. Held tight. His hands were shaking, but his grip was solid.

"Yes, you can. Jamie, you *must* listen—"

"Where am I to go?"

"Get to Northbury. There's good people there."

The instructions were simple. Insufficient. A map with one landmark. But it was all Rowan had to give and giving it cost him everything except the last thing, which would cost more.

"Now, please, go."

Jamie nodded. Not because he agreed. Because arguing would waste seconds they didn't have, because words were luxury and time was currency and they'd just run out of both.

Rowan pulled him close. They held each other. Father and son in everything except blood. The old soldier's chest hitched once. Twice. His breathing went ragged. Then he pushed Jamie away with force, with violence, because gentleness would make leaving harder and leaving was already impossible.

"*Go.*"

Lionel's hand found Margaret's shoulders. Pushed them back with the pressure of a man rearranging furniture, adjusting an object to achieve a desired aesthetic.

"Don't slouch. You have a woman's body. Show it."

He circled her. Once. A complete orbit. His eyes cataloging, his judgment pronounced silently but visible in his expression. Satisfaction. She'd passed inspection.

He started for the door. The audience was over. She'd been prepared, adorned, instructed. Now came the waiting, the hours between preparation and execution, the interlude where brides were meant to contemplate their good fortune.

"I'll send the slaves in to give you a proper bath. Ceremony will be at noon."

He was halfway through the doorway when she spoke. Surprised herself by speaking. Some part of her that hadn't been beaten down yet, hadn't learned to be silent, hadn't accepted that questions were rebellion.

"Is that necessary?"

Lionel stopped. His back to her. Shoulders tensing. The posture of a man who'd heard something unexpected and was now processing whether it constituted disrespect.

He turned. Slowly. Their eyes met, and she saw him register the question, saw his mind work through the implications, saw him arrive at the conclusion that she'd just made a mistake and that mistakes required correction.

But she'd already said it. Already committed. And some stubborn part of her that remembered being a king's daughter rather than a war trophy didn't care that this was foolish, didn't care that defiance had consequences, didn't care that she was about to learn what those consequences felt like.

"I'm sorry?"

His voice was soft. Dangerous.

Margaret knew the risk. Knew she should apologize, should bow her head, should demonstrate the proper deference. Pressed anyway.

"I can bathe myself if that's alright."

The air went thin. Oxygen evacuated. Breathing became work.

"You question me?"

"I didn't—"

He crossed the room. When he reached her his hand went to her throat and closed, fingers wrapping around her neck, thumb pressing into the hollow where her pulse lived, hard enough to make breathing an effort.

"Despite what you may have concocted in that delicate little head of yours while being escorted from your pathetic little homeland by my army, this isn't a partnership. Some may think it means peace, but it's less than that."

His grip tightened. Her vision began to tunnel. Black crept in from the edges.

"It means I *won*."

Jamie grabbed the bag and slipped out the back door, moving

low and fast, his body remembering every game of chase he'd played as a child, every time he'd snuck out to meet Lillian, muscle memory taking over where conscious thought had fled.

The morning air hit his lungs sharp and clean. Cold. The last cold clean thing he'd taste for days. Behind him, Richardson's voice carried through the dawn like a bell tolling, loud and inexorable.

"Come on out, Rowan. Haven't got all bloody day, mate."

The words were casual. Jovial even. The tone of a man conducting business he found neither pleasant nor unpleasant, just necessary, just part of the day's work.

Jamie ran. Fifty yards to the tree line. The field was open. Exposed. If they looked his direction, he'd be visible, a figure moving against grass that didn't move, a rabbit fleeing across open ground while hawks circled overhead.

He didn't look back. Looking back would slow him. Slow was death. Fast might not save him but slow would definitely kill him. His boots tore through grass. His breath came ragged. The bag bounced against his hip, heavy with supplies that had seemed insufficient in the hut and now felt like ballast, like anchors trying to drag him back to where Richardson waited with steel and judgment.

Rowan walked out into the street. Into the morning. Into the attention of six mounted men who'd come to collect what he owed and had brought more than enough force to guarantee collection.

Richardson stood twenty feet away. Snake-eyed and grinning.

Behind him, five knights sat their horses with the patience of men who'd done this before, who understood that theatre required audience and they were playing their part by watching, by bearing witness, by transforming murder into spectacle.

"Arthur..."

Rowan's voice was steady. Remarkably so. He was proud of that. Proud that fear could be contained, that courage wasn't absence of terror but continuation despite it.

Richardson closed the distance in three strides. His fist drove into Rowan's stomach like a battering ram hitting a gate, all his weight behind it, nothing held back.

Air exploded from Rowan's lungs. His diaphragm spasmed. His knees buckled. Gravity took him but Richardson's hand was there first, catching him by the collar, gripping fabric and pulling, dragging him toward the center of the street where everyone could see.

Margaret's hand moved to her throat.

Touched the pearls.

They were still there. Still cold. Still heavy.

Lionel had left. The door had closed. She was alone except for the bruises forming beneath expensive jewelry.

Her legs gave out. Just stopped holding her. Stopped doing the work of keeping her upright. Let gravity reclaim her.

She collapsed to her knees. The silk dress pooled around her, beautiful even in her breaking.

The sobs came. Hard. Violent. Loud enough that the servants in the hall would hear. Loud enough that they'd know exactly what their king had done.

She didn't care. Let them hear. Let them know.

What could they do about it?

Nothing.

What could she do about it?

Nothing.

"Get on your knees, old man."

Richardson's voice carried across the street with the casual authority of a man issuing instructions to a servant, a request that was really command, a suggestion that was really threat.

Rowan obeyed. What choice did he have? Refusal meant they'd force him down anyway, meant he'd arrive at his knees through violence rather than cooperation, meant the end result was identical but the journey was more painful.

His bad leg screamed. Twenty-four years of chronic pain compressed into a single point of extraordinary agony as his knee bent and his weight settled onto earth that was cold and wet and would shortly be red.

Still, he knelt. Back straight. Head up. Refusing to give Richardson the satisfaction of seeing him beg, seeing him break, seeing him demonstrate that fear had won even if death would.

Richardson drew his sword. The blade sang coming free of its scabbard, that pure metallic note that musicians tried to replicate on instruments but could never quite match, the sound of steel sliding against steel, promise and threat combined in single sustained pitch.

He placed the flat of the blade on Rowan's shoulder. The steel was cold through his shirt, cold in a way that had nothing to do with temperature and everything to do with finality. This was the cold of endings. The cold of last things.

"For the record, I had great respect for you as a young man."

The words were probably meant as eulogy. As acknowledgment that Rowan had been something once, before age and poverty and a shot knee reduced him to this: a man kneeling in mud waiting for steel to end what time hadn't been kind enough to.

Rowan looked up at him. Their eyes met. He gathered saliva in his mouth. Spat. The bloody phlegm hit mud between them, a final communication, a last message that said everything words couldn't.

"Eat a cock."

Richardson's smile died. The pretense of respect evaporated.

"Very well."

He lifted the sword. The crowd held its breath. Time stretched. Somewhere a baby cried, high and thin and ignorant of what was happening. Somewhere a door slammed. Somewhere life continued because life always continued, indifferent to individual endings.

The world kept turning. Merchants would sell their goods. Children would grow. Dogs would bark. The sun would set and rise and set again.

And Rowan Campbell would be dead.

Jamie crouched in brush fifty yards away, watching through a gap in branches that framed the scene perfectly, that gave him clear sight line to his father kneeling in mud while Richardson raised his sword overhead.

He saw everything. The posture. The angle. The moment when the blade reached apex and paused there as though giving the universe one last chance to intervene.

The universe declined.

The sword came down.

Jamie's vision went white. His breath stopped. Sound left the world. A scream tried to form in his throat but couldn't find purchase.

He ducked behind cover. Pressed both hands over his mouth. Hyperventilated. The sobs came in short violent bursts that he couldn't control, that shook his entire frame, that felt like they might tear him apart from the inside if he didn't find a way to stop them.

His father's blood was soaking into Taylor's End.

The earth drank it down and asked for more.

In her chamber, Margaret stood. Eventually. After the sobs subsided. After her throat went raw and her eyes went dry and crying stopped achieving anything except making her face swell.

She stood. Straightened her dress. Touched her neck where Lionel's fingers had left marks that powder wouldn't cover. The pearls clicked together. Small sounds. Delicate. The music of her imprisonment.

The door opened. Servants returned. Different ones. They

didn't meet her eyes. Began preparations for the bath she'd said she didn't need, that Lionel had decided she needed anyway.

They filled a copper tub with water carried from kitchens three floors below. Hot at first. Then warm. Then tepid as time passed and they made multiple trips because the tub was large and three women could only carry so much.

Margaret stood motionless while they worked. A statue of a bride. A monument to surrender. The dress would come off. The bath would happen. The ceremony would follow. Her life would proceed along rails that had been laid without her input, toward a destination she hadn't chosen.

She counted the trips they made. Fourteen. *Fourteen* journeys up and down stairs to fill a tub for a bath she'd said she didn't want, to prepare a body for a marriage she hadn't agreed to, to make beautiful a prison she'd never escape.

The water steamed. Rose in small clouds. Dissipated. Like everything. Like her father's kingdom. Like her own future. Like the girl she'd been yesterday morning, before chains were disguised as pearls, before surrender was called wedding.

Richardson sheathed his sword. The blade slid home with a soft click that somehow carried across the silent street, audible despite distance because everyone was listening, because the crowd had gone quiet in the way crowds go quiet after witnessing something that would haunt them.

He looked down at what remained of Rowan Campbell. At the body that had been man and was now object, that had been father and was now lesson, that had been someone and was now warning.

He spat on it.

"Leave the body."

He mounted his horse. Took his time. Let the crowd watch. Let them see the ease with which he moved from murder to mounted.

"Look for that bastard of his. Rest of you, assist me in finding that twat Jeffrey Spires."

His men split. Three headed for the woods where Jamie had run, two accompanying Richardson deeper into the village, toward the carpenter's shop where Jeffrey Spires lived with his daughter, Lillian.

Jamie lifted his head. Saw them moving. Saw Richardson's group heading south. Toward Spires Carpentry.

Toward Lillian.

His grief crystallized into adrenaline. He wiped his face with the back of his hand. Came away bloody. His nose had been bleeding again. When had that started? Didn't matter. Nothing mattered except moving.

He started through the brush. Low. Fast. Using trees for cover. Following Richardson's group at distance sufficient to remain unnoticed but close enough to maintain visual contact.

The knights moved at a walk. Unhurried. Confident. Men who knew the village couldn't resist them, who understood that force was on their side and force answered all questions eventually.

He closed distance. Thirty yards. Twenty. Close enough to hear their voices now, to catch fragments of conversation that suggested they were joking about something, that murder had put them in good spirits.

They stopped at a small shack that sat alone on the village's edge. Tools hung on the outside wall with the obsessive neatness of a man who believed order was virtue, who thought that if he kept his workshop clean the world would leave him alone.

The world had other ideas.

At Taylor's Castle, the bells began to ring.

Margaret stood in her wedding gown. The bath was finished. Her hair was dry. The pearls were back around her throat.

The bruises on her neck were hidden beneath powder. Thick. Pale. The kind of coverage that looked wrong up close but acceptable from a distance, and distance was what she'd have during the ceremony. She'd be far enough away that details would blur, that the crowd would see bride rather than victim, beauty rather than damage, princess rather than prisoner.

The fear in her eyes was hidden beneath nothing. No powder for that. No makeup that could disguise what lived behind her gaze, what had taken up permanent residence when Lionel's hand closed around her throat and taught her exactly what kind of marriage this would be.

Outside, guests gathered. Nobles from across England, coming to witness the union that would end decades of war between Taylor and Beverley. They wore silk. Smiled. Pretended this was romance instead of ransom. In the throne room, Lionel waited. He'd changed into his black robes. Gold-threaded, heavy. The kind that made you sweat standing still. Beside him stood Damien, stone-faced, saying nothing, thinking everything.

"Jeffrey!"

Richardson's voice carried across the carpenter's yard with the faux friendliness of a wolf addressing sheep.

The door creaked open.

Jeffrey Spires stepped out. Squinted in morning light. He was forty. Broad-shouldered. Going soft in the middle. Carried the permanent stoop of a man who worked bent over, whose spine had curved to match his labor.

Behind him, Lillian appeared in the doorway. Her eyes found Richardson and went wide.

"Is it here?"

Jeffrey's jaw worked. "What do you think, mate?"

"Perhaps an alternative payment, then." Richardson gestured toward Lillian. "Your daughter. She's quite lovely. I know my men thought as much. She'd be a nice fit with the others, aye?"

Silence.

"Or it's on your knees, you cunt."

Jeffrey looked at Lillian. Looked at his feet. Looked back at

Richardson. His throat bobbed. Swallowing. Trying to push down whatever objection lived in him, whatever vestige of fatherhood remained.

Lillian's brow furrowed. "Father?"

Lillian's voice broke on the word. She understood. Saw her future written in his face. Saw him making the choice in real time, watched him decide that her body was acceptable currency.

He nodded.

Jamie watched from brush fifteen yards away. Close enough to see Lillian's face. Close enough to hear her scream.

"Grab her before she runs," Richardson said.

Three knights dismounted. Moved fast.

Lillian tried. Made it three steps. Her feet tangled in her skirt. She went down. They were on her immediately. Grabbed her arms. Her hair. Anything they could reach. Dragged her down the porch steps.

She fought. Kicked. Screamed. Bit one of them hard enough to draw blood. The man swore. Hit her. It didn't matter. They were trained soldiers. She was twenty-one. Weighed maybe a hundred pounds.

They wrestled her hands behind her back, tied them with hemp rope that bit into her wrists, raised red marks, would leave scars if she wore it long enough, and hauled her toward the horses. Her feet dragged in mud. Left tracks. Evidence of her resistance that would be erased by the rain.

"Father, stop them!"

Jeffrey stood in his doorway. Silent. A statue of cowardice.

They lifted her onto a horse. She thrashed. The knight holding her grunted. His grip tightened. She screamed. Another secured her with rope around her waist. Bound her to the saddle. Made escape impossible.

Richardson mounted his horse. "For the love of God, don't let her jump. Wouldn't want to waste that pretty neck."

"Father, please!" Lillian sobbed. "Please, father! Why aren't you stopping them! They're hurting me!"

Jeffrey said nothing. Did nothing.

Richardson gathered his reins. Looked at Jeffrey. A pitiful once-over. "It's best for everyone, mate."

They rode off. Lillian still screaming. Her voice carrying across the village until distance swallowed it, until she became just another sound that people heard and ignored.

Jamie's hand went to the bag.

Found the dagger Rowan had packed.

Drew it.

The blade was old but sharp. Kept oiled and wrapped for years. Waiting.

He stood. Started forward. Took three steps toward the road before logic caught up with rage and reminded him that running after six mounted knights with a single dagger was suicide by absurdism.

A twig snapped behind him.

He froze. Every muscle locked. His breath stopped.

Voices. Male. Close. Coming through brush from the north. "*Where is that fucking bastard?*"

Richardson's other men. The ones sent to find him. He could hear them crashing through undergrowth. Close. Getting closer.

Jamie's survival instinct took over. Overrode grief. Overrode rage. Reduced him to animal essentials.

Prey. Predator approaching. *Run.*

He turned and ran. Away from Taylor's End. Away from Lillian. Away from Rowan's body cooling in the street. Away from everything he'd known and everyone he'd loved. Into wilderness. Into nothing. Into whatever waited beyond the edge of civilization.

He ran for what felt like hours. Was probably twenty seconds. Time stretched. Distorted. His lungs burned. Branches whipped his face. Drew blood. His boot caught a root.

He went down. *Hard.*

The fall sent him tumbling down a steep ravine he hadn't seen coming. His body slammed into rocks. Into roots. Each impact drove air from his lungs. He couldn't stop. Couldn't control it. Just rolled. Until the ground leveled. Until momentum died. Until gravity was finished with him.

He lay there. Gasping. Bleeding. Staring at sky that was too blue to be real, too perfect to belong to a world where fathers died and friends were stolen and everything good was taken without warning.

When he could breathe again, he pushed himself up. Everything hurt.

The field stretched before him. Green. Endless. Harthfell sat in the distance, its peaks dusted with snow that looked clean and cold and impossibly far away.

He was alone now. Rowan was dead. Lillian was gone. Taylor's End was behind him, and he could never go back.

He stood. Brushed dirt from his clothes. The motion was automatic. Pointless. He was covered in mud and blood and there was no brushing that away.

He started walking. South. Or maybe it was west. The bag hung heavy on his shoulder. Inside: bread. Meat. A dagger that hadn't saved anyone.

The sun climbed. His shadow shortened. By noon he'd covered two miles. Maybe three. Moving through grassland that rolled away in every direction. Empty except for sheep in the distance.

His feet hurt. His head throbbed. Blood from the cuts on his face had dried into crust that pulled at his skin when he moved.

He kept walking. Because walking was all that was left.

At Taylor's Castle, the ceremony began.

The doors opened. Music swelled. Margaret appeared at the far end of the hall. Flanked by guards. They'd decided she was a flight risk. Taken no chances. Made sure she understood that escape wasn't option.

She walked slowly. Each step measured. Her eyes focused on

the floor three feet ahead. The same way she'd walked into the throne room yesterday. The same way she'd walk for the rest of her life.

The crowd watched. Nobles in silk. Merchants in their finest clothes. Peasants allowed in to witness royal ceremony. All of them staring.

When she reached the dais, she stopped. Lifted her head. Met Lionel's gaze.

He smiled. Warm. Genuine. The smile of a man who thought he'd won something.

She didn't smile back.

The ceremony began. Words were spoken. Vows were exchanged. Rings were placed. Pronouncements were made.

Margaret felt the pearls at her throat. Cold and heavy.

Outside, somewhere south of Taylor's End, a boy walked alone through endless fields. His father dead. His friend stolen. His life reduced to bag and blade and the long road ahead.

The sun climbed higher.

The world turned.

ACT II

THE BLACKE RIDER

Enter KING ALFRED, QUEENE EVELYN, and PRINCE CORWIN, clad in blacke armour.

KING ALFRED. A dragon stretcheth high upon the spine Of Harthfells browe, where snow and thunder dine. It seares our skies and mockes the realmes decree. Too long this wyrme hath breathed contempt on me. What is a king who suffers such a slight? Goe, Corwin; ride in blacke; restore our might. Let steele and destinie together prove That power answeres power, and crownes doe not remove.

PRINCE CORWIN. Thy will is law, good Father, and my blade is keene. The beast shall feele the edge of Wildenze unseene. Thou taught me well: that strength is borne of steele, That monsters are for slaying, not for making deale. I am the rider sent to ende this dreade; By morning light, the dragon shall be dead.

Enter PRINCE LEO, hastily, with a booke.

PRINCE LEO. Good Father, bid me journey with my kin, To learne what truthes in dragons denne doe spin. What if the beast is not the fiend we feare? What if our swordes have made the meaning cleare?

QUEENE EVELYN. Those artes are parchment yet, my gentle dove. Warre is no tutor fit for thee, my love.

KING ALFRED. Stay thou within these walles of cedard grace; The world is not for questioners to face. Let Corwin ride. Let steele decide what's right. There is no roome for doubt in kingly might.

Exeunt KING, QUEENE, and CORWIN. LEO alone.

PRINCE LEO. Though barred by love and royall-minded care, The starres doe call me to the dragons laire. My father thinkes that force alone is true, But blades can only finde what blades pursue. Bookes are my sword, and curiositie my steede; By silent foote, I goe where thoughts doe leade.

Exit LEO.

SCENE 6

The girl was not supposed to be here.

The stairs descended before her into darkness, each step worn smooth by centuries, and she followed them down because no one had told her not to, not directly, not in words she had been made to promise to obey.

The torch in her hand was too heavy for her. She carried it with both arms, the flame wavering with each careful step. It smelled of water and earth and something else beneath those things, something animal and immense.

The stairs ended. The darkness deepened. The torch pushed it back a little, enough to show her an uneven floor and walls that curved away into nothing, but not enough to show her how far the nothing went.

She stepped forward into the dark.

The air moved differently here. In and out. In and out. Warm currents that stirred the hair at her temples and carried with them the smell of smoke and something older than smoke.

She stopped walking. Held very still. Listened.

The breathing continued. Vast and slow and patient.

Her throat tightened. Her hands shook on the torch. The flame guttered and steadied and guttered again, and in its inconstant light she saw nothing, nothing at all.

She began to sing.

The song was a nursery tune, simple and repetitive, and her voice emerged thin and wavering and barely louder than a whisper.

Lavender blue, dilly dilly, lavender green...

The breathing changed. It tightened, quickened. The air in the cavern shifted, and her voice faltered.

When I am king, dilly dilly...

The breathing grew faster still. Shorter. The girl's song died in her throat.

She didn't run.

She stood in the trembling torchlight with her heart pounding against her ribs, and she waited. The breathing filled the cavern, fast and harsh, and the darkness pressed close around her.

Then, slowly, the breathing began to ease.

It lengthened. Deepened. Settled back toward the rhythm she had first heard. The pressure lifted from her, and the girl backed toward the stairs without making any sound at all. One careful step at a time. The torch held before her. The breathing steady behind her.

She climbed the worn stone steps. Reached the door.

And pulled it closed.

By the third day, Jamie had stopped counting hours and started counting breaths.

His tongue had gone thick in his mouth. His lips had cracked. The sun was a hammer. Relentless. It beat down on his head until his skull felt like it was cooking from the inside. Sweat had stopped coming.

He stumbled. Caught himself. Stumbled again.

The forest moved around him in waves. Trees bent toward him, then away, then back again.

A fly landed on his face. He tried to swat it away. Missed. His hand moved through empty air six inches from where the fly actually was. The fly crawled across his cheek. Then it was in his ear. Buzzing. The sound filled his head. Became the only sound.

He stopped walking. Stood swaying. The forest tilted. Righted itself. Tilted again.

Rowan's voice came from somewhere behind him. "Get up, lad."

Jamie turned. No one there. Just trees. Shadows.

"I said get up."

"I am up."

Jamie's voice came out cracked. Barely audible.

"You're kneeling."

Was he?

Jamie looked down. Couldn't see his legs.

"Stand up, Jamie. Keep walking."

"Where?"

"South. Toward Northbury. Good people there."

"You're dead."

"And you'll be joining me if you don't stand up."

He tried. His legs wouldn't cooperate. They'd stopped taking orders.

The fly left his ear. Crawled across his forehead. He watched it cross his field of vision. Huge. Close. Its compound eyes reflecting his face back at him in a thousand tiny, warped fragments.

And somewhere, distantly, beneath the hammer-sun and the fly-buzz and Rowan's ghost giving instructions, Jamie heard it.

Running water.

At first, he thought he was hallucinating. Wouldn't be the first time today. But the sound persisted. Grew louder as he stumbled through brush that grabbed at his clothes with fingers that weren't fingers.

Then he saw it.

A thin ribbon of water cutting through the forest floor.

He dropped. His knees hit ground. His hands followed. Then his face was in the water.

He drank. Gulped it down without stopping to taste or think. His stomach cramped. Rejected the sudden influx. Tried to expel it. He kept drinking anyway.

His whole face was submerged. Water filled his ears. Blocked out sound. The world became just pressure and cold and the overwhelming need to get more of this inside him.

When he finally came up for air, gasping, he felt halfway human again.

He was Jamie Campbell, and he was still royally cocked. His father was dead and his friend was taken and he was walking south toward a place he'd never been to find people he didn't know.

He stood. His legs held. Small victory. He wiped his mouth with the back of his hand. His lips were still cracked but the bleeding had stopped.

He started walking along the creek's edge. His head down. His bag hanging heavy on his shoulder. The bread inside had gone hard. The meat had started to smell. But he couldn't bring himself to throw either away.

The sun was dropping. Evening coming on. Another night alone approaching. He'd need somewhere to sleep. Somewhere dry. Somewhere the animals wouldn't find him.

He'd seen wolf tracks yesterday. Or thought he had. Hard to know what was real when your brain was melting.

The campsite appeared through the trees just as dusk settled in.

Jamie stopped. His body went still before his mind caught up.

He studied the clearing. A fire pit in the center, stomped out but still smoking faintly. Gray wisps rising into darkening air. Bags scattered around the perimeter.

No people visible.

His stomach growled. Loud. Insistent. The kind of growl that suggested his body was considering eating itself if he didn't find food soon.

He approached slowly. Scanning the brush. Listening. Nothing moved. Nothing made sound except the creek behind him and his own footsteps crushing leaves.

The bags were arranged around the fire pit in a rough circle, like whoever had been here had been sitting, had been sharing the space, had been civilized enough to organize their camp before they left.

One bag was open. The flap folded back.

Jamie crouched beside it. His knees popped.

He reached inside the bag. His fingers found fabric. Cloth wrapped around something. He pulled it out. Unwrapped it.

Dried meat. Dark. Tough. But real. Food.

The blow came from behind.

Thwack.

Then everything caught up at once.

White noise flooded his ears. Ringing. High-pitched. Sustained. The world tilted sideways. His balance betrayed him. He was on his knees. *How did he get on his knees?* He'd been crouching. Now he was kneeling.

His hand went to his head. Came away red.

His vision blurred. Then tripled. Three of everything. Three groups of shapes materializing from the brush.

Men. Filthy men. Surrounding him.

The shapes resolved slowly. His vision corrected itself. But there were three of them. Three men stepping from shadow into the dying light.

Their voices were muffled at first. Then clarity returned.

"Caught a live one, haven't we?"

The first man was tall. Rail-thin. His face was half-hidden under a matted beard. His teeth were brown. Several were missing.

"Pretty-looking chap. Think he'll taste better?"

The second man was shorter. Rounder. Soft in the middle in a way that suggested he'd been well-fed recently. A scar ran from his ear to his mouth, pulling his lips into a permanent sneer.

"Only one way to find out, innit?"

The third laughed. He was the youngest. Maybe thirty. Wild eyes that didn't focus on anything for more than a second. His hands wouldn't stop moving.

Jamie's head throbbed. The pain was enormous. Radiating. Blood ran warm down his scalp, over his ear, dripping from his jaw. "I mean no harm. I didn't know someone was staying here. I'm traveling."

"Not very good at it, are you?"

The tall one grinned. His brown teeth caught dying light.

"Please, just let me go. You'll never see me again. I promise."

"Thought you'd just take our food, yeah?"

"I didn't know. I'm sorry. Please, just let me go."

The three of them looked at each other. Some silent communication passed between them.

Then they burst into laughter. High and sharp and wrong.

"Right, tie his legs."

They came at him fast. Jamie scrambled backward. His hands dug through his bag. Shaking. Clumsy. His fingers found the dagger's handle. He pulled it free. Swung it side to side in wide arcs.

They laughed harder.

"Do you even know how to use that?"

"Just let me go."

Jamie's voice cracked. He hated that. Hated the fear that leaked through despite his efforts to contain it.

The tall man leaned in. Still laughing. Getting closer.

Jamie swung. Connected. The blade bit. Drew blood.

The man stopped laughing.

Time suspended. The laughter died. The forest went quiet.

"*Please*. I'll go."

He looked down at his arm. Touched the cut. His fingers came away red. He studied them.

"Got me kind of good, didn't he?"

Then he kicked Jamie in the face.

Jamie's head snapped back. The dagger flew from his hand. He heard it clang against stone somewhere. Skitter into dirt.

He landed hard on his back. Before he could move, before he

could think, rough hands grabbed him. Flipped him onto his stomach. His face pressed into dirt that smelled like rot and old blood and things that had died here before him.

Rope bit into his ankles. His feet started to tingle. Then go numb.

"I'm gonna cut you up good, pretty boy."

The voice came from somewhere above him.

"You don't have to do this."

Jamie's face was still in the dirt. His words came out muffled. Desperate. True.

His eyes found the dagger. It lay in the dirt three feet away.

The rope moved to his wrists. Cinched tight. His hands went numb immediately.

"No, we don't. But we will enjoy it."

They flipped him onto his back. The tall one stood over him. Holding an axe.

Jamie's vision blurred. Cleared. Blurred again.

He closed his eyes. Started praying. *Our Father who art in heaven. Hallowed be thy name.*

"Is he praying now?"

"Looks like it, mate."

"Fucking hell."

"I'd let you finish, mate, but I'm rather hungry."

The axe lifted. Jamie kept his eyes closed. Kept praying. *Thy kingdom come. Thy will be done—*

Blood splattered across Jamie's face. It hit his closed eyelids. Ran into his mouth. He flinched. Involuntary. Body responding before mind understood.

Silence.

He opened his eyes.

The tall man was choking. Standing over him but not looking at him anymore. Looking at something far off.

The axe fell into the dirt. Clean.

Then Jamie saw it.

An arrow.

Jutting from the tall one's neck, the fletching still quivering. Blood poured down his chest, black in the dying light. His mouth opened. Worked. No sound came out except gurgling.

He fell sideways. His eyes stayed open. Staring at nothing.

A figure moved through the clearing. Fast. Massive. Draped in black armor.

He held a sword. Long. Heavy.

The second man raised his knife. Desperate. Reflexive. The blade looked like a toy compared to what was coming at him. The sword cut through him diagonally. Shoulder to hip.

He dropped in two pieces. Blood sprayed. Hit the ground. Hit Jamie. Hit everything within six feet.

The third man turned to run.

The swordsman crouched, unhurried, and picked up the fallen axe.

He stood. Planted his feet. Then hurled it.

It crossed the ten feet between them and struck the back of the man's head.

His body ran two more steps without him. Then collapsed.

Jamie lay in the dirt. Bound. Bleeding. Covered in other men's blood and his own. Staring up at his savior.

The man was tall. Built heavy through the shoulders and chest. His armor was black plate over black leather. His helmet covered everything except his eyes.

He walked over. He looked down at Jamie for a moment.

Then he crouched. Drew a knife. Cut Jamie's ropes. Wrists first. Then ankles. The hemp fell away. Blood rushed back into Jamie's extremities. Pain.

The man stood. Turned away. Started looting the campsite.

Jamie wiped blood from his face with his sleeve. Sat up. He was going to vomit. Managed not to. Another small victory.

"You're not gonna leave some for me?"

A canteen flew at him from across the clearing. Jamie caught it with his chest. A drop sloshed inside. Maybe less.

"Cunt," Jamie breathed.

The man slung a bag over his shoulder. Turned. Started walking back into the forest.

Jamie stared after him. Blinked. Realized what had just happened.

He scrambled to his feet. Ran after the man.

"Hey! That was wicked! Where'd you learn to do all that?"

The man kept walking. Didn't turn. Didn't slow. Didn't acknowledge that Jamie existed.

"They were gonna eat me, you know. Cannibals. I thought those were only in stories."

No response.

"Can't taste that good… Anyway, where are you headed?"

Nothing.

"You don't talk, do you?"

The man stopped. Turned.

"What do you want, child?"

"Do you have a camp?"

"You're a bit touched, aren't you?"

"I have nothing. My father, he told me to get to Northbury, but…" Jamie threw his palms up. "I don't know where I am."

Silence. The man studied him.

"Northbury?"

"I think."

"You think or you know?"

"I know."

"Where are you from, boy?"

"Taylor's End."

The man froze.

"You said Taylor's End?"

Jamie nodded.

They looked at each other. Something passed between them. The man's eyes, barely visible through the helmet's slits, seemed to lighten.

He turned. Started walking again.

Jamie grinned. He followed.

"So, where are we?"

"Near Wolfpine. But I have business in Rivermouth."

"Rivermouth? It's a dump."

"We won't be there long."

"You didn't tell me your name."

"Did your father ever tell you not to push your luck?"

Jamie stopped. A thought crystallized. Obvious. Should have occurred to him sooner but his brain was still recovering from being hit with an axe handle.

"Wait... I *know* you. You're the Black Rider, aren't you? You've got the armor and everything. I'm a bloody idiot. I've heard stories about you, you know. You're the famous bounty hunter. Wanted by the crown."

"What kind of stories?"

"So it *is* you."

"What kind of stories?"

"Well, not stories. Legends, really. Like, a mother tells her children: 'Don't misbehave or the Black Rider will take you away!'"

"Children? Really?"

"Yeah. Death personified. Whole villages convinced themselves you were waiting in the dark. Women swore you hovered near cribs, listening for a child to stir, certain you'd snatch them from their beds the moment they slept too easily."

"Lovely. Any others?"

"Some say you're originally from Taylor's End. Most people, though, they just assume you're dead." Jamie paused. "Is it true?"

"That I'm dead? Or that I'm snatching babies from their beds?"

"That you're from Taylor's End."

"No."

They walked in silence for a while. The forest darkened around them. Night coming on fast. Jamie's legs burned. His head throbbed. But he kept walking because stopping meant being alone and alone meant dying and he'd had enough of almost dying for one day.

"You speak well for a mountain person."

The Black Rider's shoulders moved. Might have been a laugh.

"I'm a bounty hunter, not a fucking mong."

SCENE 7

Jamie had been right about one thing.

Rivermouth was a dump.

The village materialized out of fog so thick it felt solid. The air tasted like wet rot. Like things that had died and been left to decompose in standing water.

Shacks leaned against each other for support. Their timber was warped. Blackened. Tents sagged between them. Canvas torn and patched with scraps.

Everything looked temporary. Everything looked like it had been temporary for twenty years.

A weathered sign hung crooked at the village entrance. The letters were barely legible.

The Black Rider walked straight through without slowing. Didn't look left or right. Didn't acknowledge the eyes that watched from doorways and windows.

Jamie followed. Tried to match that confidence. Failed. He

looked around. Couldn't help it.

A woman stood in a doorway. Young. Maybe twenty. Her dress was torn. Her face was bruised.

A child sat in mud.

A dog barked.

They reached a cabin on the village's far edge. It looked worse than the rest, which was an achievement.

A horse pen was attached to one side. Empty except for two animals that looked half-starved.

"Why are we here?"

"Got to see about an old friend."

Jamie looked at him. "You have friends?"

The Black Rider didn't answer. Just gestured toward a spot ten feet from the cabin door. "Stay here."

A young drunk leaned against the door. Working his way through a bottle of whiskey. He looked up as the Black Rider approached. Squinted through alcohol haze.

"Oi! Where d'you think you're going, mate? Is it Halloween already?"

The Black Rider drew his sword. He swung the pommel hard into the drunk's face.

The drunk's nose exploded. He dropped to his knees. The whiskey bottle shattered on the ground beside him.

"*What the bloody fuck, mate*?! Broke me fucking nose, you cunt! Agh!"

The drunk's hands went to his face. Blood poured between his fingers. Ran down his wrists. Dripped from his elbows.

The Black Rider pressed the sword's hilt against the drunk's throat.

"Two horses. And don't even think about bloody moving."

The drunk's eyes went wide. Tears mixed with blood on his face. Created pink rivulets that ran down his neck and disappeared into his collar. "Then how in bloody Hell am I supposed to get the bloody horses?!"

The Black Rider ignored him and disappeared inside the cabin.

The drunk stayed on his knees. Whimpering. Both hands

pressed to his face.

Jamie stood fifteen feet away. Frozen. Watching. Not sure what his role was here. Helper? Witness? Accomplice?

Sounds erupted from inside the cabin. Shouting. Male voices. Angry. Then a crash. Something heavy hitting something else heavy. More shouting. Words that Jamie couldn't make out but that carried the universal tone of men who'd discovered violence was happening and were not pleased about it.

Then a wet sound.

Then silence.

Jamie's hand went to the dagger in his bag. His fingers closed around the handle. He didn't draw it.

The door kicked open.

The Black Rider emerged. Dragging two bodies behind him. One in each hand. Gripping their collars. Pulling them across the threshold.

He let them drop in the mud. They landed with splashes. Their eyes were still open. Staring at sky they couldn't see anymore.

The Black Rider looked at the drunk. "Horses, then?"

The drunk scrambled to his feet. Still crying. Still bleeding. But motivated now.

He ran for the pen.

The Black Rider bent. Started going through the dead men's pockets.

He pulled out a wool pouch of bits. A knife. A piece of paper that he glanced at and then discarded. It fluttered to the ground. Landed in mud.

When he was satisfied, he straightened and looked at Jamie. "Grab one."

"What?"

"The bodies. We're taking them."

Jamie stared at the corpses. They were both men in their thirties.

Blood pooled beneath them. Dark. Thick.

"Why?"

"Bounty."

"I don't—"

"Now, lad."

The tone allowed no argument. Jamie grabbed the nearest corpse by the arms. Tried to lift. The body was heavy. Heavier than it should have been.

He managed to drag it three feet before his arms gave out. His muscles screamed. His bad leg threatened to buckle. He stopped. Gasped. Looked at the Black Rider.

The man watched without helping.

The drunk returned with the horses.

The Black Rider took the reins. Secured his body to one animal in under a minute. Then he turned to Jamie.

"Need help?"

Jamie's face burned. "I've got it."

He didn't have it. But he kept trying anyway. Wrestling the corpse across the mud.

Eventually, between Jamie's stubborn pulling and the Black Rider's efficient maneuvering, they got both bodies secured.

They rode out heading south. Each mounted. Each horse with a dead man slung behind the saddle.

The fog thinned as they climbed into hills. The air cleared. By the time the sun broke through, Rivermouth was invisible behind them.

Jamie rode in silence for a while.

Finally, he couldn't hold it anymore.

"What did they do?"

"Hmm?"

"These men."

"Thieves."

"Thieves?"

"Yes."

Jamie looked at the Black Rider. At the bags hanging from his saddle. Bags that had belonged to the cannibals. Bags that had belonged to the men in Rivermouth. Bags taken from corpses. "Well, aren't you a thief?"

"Sorry, lad?"

"We're carrying the bags of dead men, aren't we?"

The Black Rider turned his head. Even through the helmet, Jamie could feel the weight of his gaze. The assessment happening behind those pale eyes.

"You mean the cannibals?"

"I just... Surely you were there for a purpose. You left their bodies—"

"I was there for supplies. Do you think anyone will miss them?"

"I—"

"They were going to eat you, right?"

"Right."

"Right. So, let's move on, yeah?"

Jamie watched the landscape roll past. Green hills dotted with sheep. Stone walls marking boundaries between properties.

"Do I really have to carry one?"

"You want your share?"

Jamie thought about that.

"How much?"

"Fifty crowns."

Jamie's eyes went wide.

"Christ."

Jamie glanced at the corpse on his horse's rear.

"Doesn't it bother you?"

"Does what bother me?"

"Killing them."

The Black Rider rode for a while without answering. The silence stretched. Became uncomfortable.

When he finally spoke, he didn't turn. "No."

Jamie waited for more.

Nothing came.

Rowan had told him to get to Northbury. To find good people.

He'd found the Black Rider instead.

He should have been terrified.

Instead, he felt something else.

The horse beneath him kept walking. The body behind him

kept swaying. And Jamie kept riding. One hand on the reins. The other resting near the dagger in his bag.

SCENE 8

Wolfpine was better than Rivermouth the way a broken leg was better than a severed one.

The buildings stood straight, at least. A smithy where hammer strikes rang out in steady rhythm. Something that might have been an inn or might have been a brothel or might have been both.

The sun was high. Hot. Jamie could feel it pressing down on his shoulders, his neck, his head.

The Black Rider dismounted in front of the general store. His boots hit dirt without sound. He tied his horse to the post with quick movements.

The animal carrying the first corpse stood beside it. Patient. Unbothered. They'd been riding with the Rivermouth thieves for two days now.

Jamie stayed mounted. Uncertain. His horse shifted beneath him.

While he waited, his eyes wandered the street. A posting board stood near the shop entrance—weathered wood covered in layers of torn notices and faded handbills. One caught his eye. A crude drawing of what might have been a dragon or possibly just a very unfortunate lizard. Hand-lettered across the top: *Barnaby Oddfellow's Traveling Stage Company*. Below it, a list of towns. Dates. The last line read:

TAYLOR'S END

PERFORMANCE AT THE CASTLE

BY ROYAL INVITATION

He looked at the Black Rider. At the bodies. At the store. "What do I... Should I..."

"Sit there."

"Right."

The store's door opened. A man stepped onto the porch.

He was forty-something. Fat. His stomach pressed against his apron. His jowls hung. His bald head gleamed with sweat despite the temperature being mild.

His apron was stained. Dark patches.

He squinted at the Black Rider. Then at the bodies. Then back at the Black Rider.

His face split into a grin. "They say to be weary of strange men bearing gifts. O'course, they didn't mention bodies."

"Oi, Ed," Black Rider greeted, flat.

The Black Rider pulled a wool pouch from his belt. He placed it in Ed's palm without ceremony, without explanation, the transaction speaking for itself.

"Rivermouth, just like you said."

Ed weighed the pouch in his hand. He nodded. Satisfied. Pocketed it. His expression shifted from jovial to aggrieved.

"Bloody maggots." He shook his head. Theatrical. "Y'know I had to have my entire door replaced because of those two cunts?

Cost me half a crown, on top of the six they snatched."

He paused. Let that sit. The injustice of it.

"Carpenter's a real bugger, too. Charged me thirty bits just for the hinges. Thirty bits! For hinges! I said to him, I said, 'Harold, these are just hunks of iron bent into shape, they're not the bloody crown jewels,' and he says to me, 'Ed, you want hinges, or you want your door to fall off?' Well, what am I supposed to say to 'at? Man's got me by the bollocks and he knows it."

Ed's hands moved while he talked. Gesturing. Illustrating.

"And that's not even accounting for the labor. Another five bits for labor. To attach hinges. Which, I'll grant you, requires some skill, but is it five bits worth of skill? That's the question. That's what I'm asking. Meanwhile, these two"—he gestured toward the corpses—"they bust in 'ere, middle of the night, smash m'door, take m'bits, break me lantern, knock over my display of imported soaps—*imported*, mind you, all the way from London—and then have the audacity, the bloody nerve, to eat half a wheel of cheese on their way out. Just stood there in me shop, eating a wheel of cheese, like they'd paid for it! Like they were customers!"

The Black Rider's voice was dry. "My pleasure."

"Nonetheless," Ed continued, "as luck would have it, Harold's the only carpenter in a bloody ten-mile radius. Maybe fifteen. Used to be Thomas, but Thomas got kicked by a horse last spring and now he can't work wood on account of his hands don't grip right anymore. Shakes too much. Sad business, that. Good man, Thomas. Terrible luck with 'orses."

He paused. Reflected. "Anyway. Thank you for catching up with them. Poor blokes. Your reward's inside." Ed's eyes shifted to Jamie, still mounted, still holding the reins of the horse carrying the second corpse. "Who's the blonde cunt?"

Jamie blinked. Second time someone had called him that. *Was this just how people talked out here?*

"Sorry?"

"Needs help getting to Northbury."

"Well, you're not far now. Two days if you don't cock about.

One if you push." He gestured toward the store. "Had a birth-day yesterday. Got some cake inside if you fancy a bite. Wife made it. Also got a bit of elk sitting on ice if you'd like to take that with you as well. Took it down three days ago. Still good."

"Sure."

Jamie looked at the Black Rider. "What about the bodies?"

Ed laughed. "They're not going anywhere, mate!"

Jamie supposed that was true. Dead men were notoriously stationary. He dismounted. His legs were stiff from riding.

He followed the Black Rider inside. Behind them, the corpses remained slumped over their horses. The sun beat down. Flies had begun to gather. Their buzzing was a low drone. Persistent. The sound of decay announcing itself.

The store was dim. Cool. A refuge from the hammer-sun outside. Jamie's eyes took a moment to adjust, the transition from brightness to shadow creating temporary blindness, shapes resolving slowly from darkness into definition.

Shelves lined the walls. Packed. Crammed. A stuffed badger on the top shelf, its glass eyes reflecting what little light came through the windows, giving it the appearance of being alive and deeply disappointed. Every available surface supporting goods that ranged from essential to baffling. Rope coiled beside rope coiled beside more rope, suggesting Ed had either found a supplier he liked or had trust issues regarding rope scarcity.

Three different kinds of soap. A rusted beartrap. A painting of a woman whose face suggested the artist had heard about faces but never actually seen one. Hammers. Saws. A fiddle missing strings. Books with water-damaged covers. A jar of something pickled that might have been vegetables or might have been something else entirely, the contents too degraded to identify with certainty. The air smelled like dust and old tobacco and something sweet that suggested the elk wasn't the only meat being kept on ice.

Ed moved behind the counter. His bulk navigated the nar-row space with practiced ease. He produced a wooden box from beneath. Opened it. Inside, crowns glinted. Real money. The kind that had weight and history and purchasing power.

"Fifty crowns, as posted."

The Black Rider approached. Counted them. Slowly. Deliberately. Each crown lifted. Examined. Tested with thumbnail for softness that would suggest counterfeiting. When he was satisfied, he pocketed the box and looked at Ed.

"The other one?"

"Right, right." Ed bent. Rummaged beneath the counter. The sound of things being moved. Shuffled. Reorganized. He emerged with a cake that had seen better days.

Half of it was gone. Consumed by Ed and presumably his wife over the course of yesterday's birthday celebration. The remaining half sagged in the middle. Structural integrity had been compromised. The frosting had melted at some point, probably during baking, then re-hardened into something that resembled wax more than food. The whole thing had the appearance of an archaeological artifact. Something unearthed from ruins. Ancient. Possibly cursed.

"My wife made it." Ed's voice carried pride. Defensive pride. The kind that acknowledged flaws but insisted on love anyway. "She's shit at baking but I love her anyway. Been married sixteen years. She still can't figure out how much sugar is too much sugar. This one's got about three times what it should. But it's sweet. I'll give her that. It's definitely sweet."

He cut two generous slices. The knife struggled. The cake resisted. He slid the slices across the counter on tin plates. Metal scraped wood.

"Eat up."

Jamie stared at his slice. It might have been chocolate. Or dirt. Or chocolate-flavored dirt. The dim light made identification difficult. The frosting caught what illumination existed and reflected it back wrong, creating the illusion of wetness that touching would probably prove false.

The Black Rider reached up. Lifted his helmet. Just enough to expose his mouth. Not the whole face. Just the necessary components for eating. His jaw. His lips. His teeth, which were surprisingly intact for a man who lived violently.

He picked up the fork. Took a bite. Chewed. Methodically.

His jaw worked with the same economy he applied to everything else. Violence. Riding. Eating terrible cake. All of it approached with identical professionalism.

He swallowed. His expression revealed nothing. No judgment. No displeasure. Just the neutral acceptance of a man who understood that complaining about free food was foolish when food cost money and money cost lives.

"Moist enough," he said.

Ed beamed. "She'll be thrilled to hear it. Tried a new recipe. Well, not new. Old. Her grandmother's. Or maybe her mother's grandmother. Family recipe, anyway. Been passed down. Probably should have stayed down, if I'm being honest, but tradition is tradition."

Jamie picked up his fork. Tested the cake with the tines. They didn't penetrate so much as chip. He managed to break off a small piece. Lifted it to his mouth. Committed.

It was sweet. Overwhelmingly so. The sugar hit his tongue like an assault. Dense. Dry. The kind of dry that pulled moisture from your mouth, that made swallowing an effort, that suggested you'd need water immediately after or risk choking.

He swallowed. His throat protested. "It's nice."

The lie was automatic. Polite.

Ed's grin widened. "She'll be thrilled to hear it. Absolutely thrilled. Forty-two yesterday. Getting old, I am. Time's a bastard, isn't it? Sneaks up on you. One day you're twenty and strong and full of piss and vinegar, the next you're forty-two and your knees sound like grinding stones when you walk. Grind and pop. Pop and grind. Every morning I wake up and it takes me five minutes just to stand. Five minutes! Just to achieve vertical! And the pissing, as I mentioned. Like passing glass. Sharp glass. Though I suppose all glass is sharp, technically. That's what makes it glass."

He laughed. Wheezed. Coughed. "But I'm alive, aren't I? That's something. Breathing. Walking. Pissing glass, but pissing, nonetheless. You could do worse."

The Black Rider ate his cake in silence. Methodical bites. Finishing it before Jamie was halfway through. When his plate was empty, he set it down carefully. Pushed it slightly away. The gesture of completion.

Then, unexpectedly, he spoke. "Your wife is kind to share."

The words landed strange. Formal. The kind of courtesy that belonged in parlors and drawing rooms, not in general stores where corpses waited outside and conversation centered on urinary dysfunction. But they were sincere. Or seemed to be. Hard to tell with the helmet concealing most of his face.

Ed looked genuinely touched. "That's very kind of you to say. I'll tell her. She'll appreciate that. She really will."

He paused. Then rallied. "The elk?"

"Right, right." Ed disappeared into a back room. The sound of his footsteps. Heavy. Deliberate. Then scraping. Dragging. Huffing. He emerged pulling a burlap sack. Large. Unwieldy.

"Took it down three days ago. Big bastard. Eight-point buck. Well, technically elk, not buck. Different species. But you know what I mean. Had to gut it on site. Too heavy to bring back whole. Been keeping it cold. Got ice in the back. Bring it down from the mountains twice a year. Pack it in sawdust. Keeps for months if you do it right."

He hoisted the sack onto the counter with a grunt that suggested his forty-two-year-old back was joining his knees in the betrayal. The sack landed with a thud. Heavy. Dense. Meat.

"Should last you another week if you wrap it proper. Maybe two if the weather stays cool. No charge. Consider it a thank you for the door situation. And the cheese. Mostly the cheese. That was good cheese."

"Appreciated."

Ed leaned on the counter. His weight settled. His breathing was elevated. The effort of moving meat had cost him. He studied the Black Rider with the familiarity of old acquaintance, with the ease of men who'd conducted transactions before and would again.

"You heading back north?"

"Eventually."

"Heard there's trouble up that way." Ed's voice shifted. Took on the tone of gossip being delivered with the weight of news.

"Taylor's lot been collecting taxes hard. Some villages got hit pretty rough."

Jamie's hand stopped halfway to his mouth. The fork frozen. The cake forgotten. His chest tightened. His ribs felt suddenly too small for his lungs.

The Black Rider's voice stayed neutral. Flat. Empty. "That so?"

"Aye," Ed nodded, warming to his topic. "Heard they killed some blacksmith in Taylor's End. Old fellow. One of their own! Didn't have the crown so they took his head instead. Just like that. Middle of the street. Everyone watching. Made an example of him, apparently. Send a message about paying your debts."

Outside, flies droned. Their buzzing carried through the open door. A constant note. The sound of decay conducting itself.

Inside, a crown clinked. Ed's hand adjusting change in his pocket. The small sound enormous in Jamie's ears.

Somewhere distant, an anvil rang. The smith working. Hammer on steel. The rhythm of creation punctuating conversation about death.

Ed shook his head. "Brutal business. Taylors don't fuck about when it comes to their crowns, do they? And this particular fellow, Richardson's his name, he's apparently quite the bastard. Big Irish cunt. Mean as they come. Works for the king directly, so he's got authority. You know the type. Thinks wearing the silk gives him license to do whatever he wants."

He paused. Spat into a bucket beside the counter. "Probably does, come to think of it. License, I mean. King's Watch generally does as they please."

He continued. His voice a drone now. Comfortable. The rhythm of a man who enjoyed talking, who stored up observations through long days alone in his store and released them when audience appeared.

"They say the blacksmith's son ran off. Smart lad. Nothing for him there now. Father dead. Home torched. They're looking for him, apparently. Richardson wants him. For what, I don't know. Probably just to complete the set. You kill the father, you kill the son. That's how these things go. Loose ends and all that."

Jamie set his fork down. Carefully. His hands were shaking. He pressed them flat against his thighs. Under the counter. Out of sight. His stomach had gone cold. The cake sat in it like a stone. Like glass. Sharp.

The Black Rider said nothing. Just stood there. Still as a monument. His helmet in place now. His face hidden. But his hands, visible, resting on the counter, were still. Absolutely still. Not tense. Not relaxed. Just still.

Inside his right glove, his finger twitched once. Barely. The leather creaked. Soft. Almost inaudible. But Jamie heard it.

Ed rambled on. Oblivious. "Of course, it's all tax business. Always is. Crown needs money, crown takes money. Simple as that. And if you don't have money, crown takes whatever else you've got. Blood, usually. They're efficient about it, I'll give them that. No wasted effort. Very practical."

He laughed. Wheezed. "Not that I'm complaining, mind. I pay my taxes. On time. Every time. Harold the carpenter, he tries to dodge them, you know. Hides bits. Claims poverty. But I pay. Because I like my head attached to my neck. Call me traditional."

The Black Rider's voice, when it came, was quiet. "The elk."

"Right, right." Ed patted the burlap sack. "All yours. Like I said, no charge. Door's replaced, cheese is eaten, we're square."

The Black Rider picked up the sack. Lifted it with one hand. He turned toward the door.

Ed called after him. "Come back any time! My wife's already planning next year's cake. Might be worse. Might be better. No way to know until you taste it."

"Looking forward to it."

They stepped back outside. Into the sun. Into the heat. Into the smell.

The bodies were still there. Exactly where they'd been left. Slumped over their horses. The sun had done its work. Accelerated decay. The smell had intensified. Sweet. Rotten. The particular odor of meat going bad, of flesh breaking down, of death announcing itself to everything with a nose.

Flies covered them. Black. Dense. Moving in patterns across skin and clothes. Their buzzing had increased in volume. No longer background noise. Now a presence. An entity. The sound of consumption.

The horses stamped. Twitched. Annoyed. But patient. Long-suffering. The way horses were when burdened with things they didn't choose but couldn't escape.

People moved through the street. Villagers going about their business. They didn't look at the bodies. Didn't acknowledge them. Just moved around them the way you move around any obstacle, any inconvenience, any piece of reality you'd prefer not to address directly.

Ed walked them toward the street's edge. His hands in his pockets. His face squinting in the sunlight. Friendly. Jovial. A man satisfied with transactions completed, relationships maintained, stories shared.

"Northbury's two days south on a good horse. Follow the river. Can't miss it."

Jamie managed a nod. His throat was too tight to speak. The words sat in his chest unspoken. Rowan's name. The truth of what Ed had described as gossip. The fact that the blacksmith had a face and a voice and hands that had built things and a son standing right here covered in his blood.

Ed clapped the Black Rider on the shoulder. "Good hunting, friend. Watch yourself on the roads. Heard there's bandits about."

The Black Rider raised a hand in acknowledgment.

They mounted. Jamie's hands found the reins. His horse shifted beneath him. Eager to move. To leave. To put distance between itself and the smell.

Jamie looked at the Black Rider. "Is there... a protocol for this?"

The Black Rider turned his head. "Yes."

Jamie waited. "And?"

"You ride."

"Right."

They rode. The Black Rider took the lead. Jamie followed. Each trailing a horse with its dead passenger swaying with every step.

Ed stood in the street watching them leave. His hand raised in farewell. When they were twenty yards away, he turned and headed back inside.

The landscape opened around them. Hills rolling away in waves of green. Trees clustered in valleys where water collected. The river to their left, visible occasionally through gaps in the vegetation, sunlight catching its surface and throwing it back in flashes.

The sun climbed higher. The heat intensified. The smell from the corpses became constant. Unavoidable. Jamie breathed through his mouth. That helped. A little.

They rode in silence.

Jamie looked at the body swaying behind his horse. At the money it represented. Fifty crowns. Half a fortune. Payment for violence. The economics of death.

Somewhere ahead lay Northbury.

Jamie didn't believe in safety anymore.

He believed in Richardson's name. In the weight of the dagger in his bag. In the certainty that someday, somehow, those two things would meet. And when they did, one of them would stop breathing.

Richardson had taken everything.

Richardson owed a debt.

Jamie would collect.

For now, he rode.

The sun climbed toward noon. The shadows shortened.

Jamie's throat was still tight. The cake sat heavy in his stomach. His head still throbbed where he'd been hit.

But he was alive. And Richardson was alive. And that meant there was work left to do.

The Black Rider's voice broke the silence. Unexpected. "I've had worse."

Jamie blinked. "*What?*"

"Cake. I've had worse." A pause. "Once it was soup."

Jamie stared at the back of the Black Rider's helmet.

He didn't laugh. Couldn't. But something in his chest loosened slightly.

"Soup," he repeated.

"Terrible soup."

"Worse than the cake?"

"Much worse. The cake was merely dense. The soup was actively hostile."

They rode.

The bodies swayed. The flies droned. The sun beat down. And two men rode south toward something that might not be safety but was at least different than here.

Richardson's name burned in Jamie's mind.

But for now, there was just the road.

SCENE 9

SCARS

The elk was tough, but Jamie didn't care. He tore into it with his teeth, grease running down his chin, fat slicking his fingers. His stomach cramped with each bite. The meat had been cooked over open flame, blackened outside and still pink at the center. He chewed slowly, letting the taste linger.

The fire crackled between them. Orange light slid across the clearing they'd chosen. Night was coming fast. The sky had gone purple, then indigo. Stars were beginning to show.

Sap popped in the burning wood. Smoke rose in a thin gray column.

The Black Rider moved around the campsite gathering what he needed. Water pot. Canteen. Bedroll. He worked without speaking.

When he reached the fire with the pot, he set it down harder than necessary. Water sloshed over the rim and struck the flames, hissing.

Jamie glanced up from his food and watched as the man found a log and lowered himself onto it. His right knee bent a beat later than the left.

He pulled a canteen from his belt and twisted the cap loose.

Then he reached up with both hands and lifted his helmet free.

Jamie stopped chewing.

The man beneath the armor was forty, maybe older. Dark hair threaded with gray. A strong jaw. Sharp cheekbones. A nose broken at least twice and never set properly.

But it was the scarring that held Jamie's attention.

A thick, raised line ran down the left side of his face from hairline to jaw, pale and roped, drawing the skin tight. Below it, burn scars mottled his neck and disappeared beneath his collar, the flesh twisted and puckered.

Jamie couldn't look away.

The Black Rider lifted the canteen and drank. Long pulls. Liquid spilled from the corners of his mouth and ran into his beard. When he lowered it, he wiped his face with the back of his hand.

His eyes were pale blue, nearly colorless in the firelight. They stayed on Jamie.

Jamie shifted under the attention. His shoulders drew in. He dropped his gaze back to the elk.

The Black Rider looked away first, turning back to the fire, but the moment had lasted too long to pass as nothing.

"Why Northbury?"

Jamie swallowed. "My father said there's good people there."

"Where is he?"

"My father? He's dead."

The man's grip on the canteen tightened until the leather creaked. For three seconds, nothing else in him moved.

When he lifted it again, he drank without pause. Jamie wondered if he meant to empty it.

"I'm sorry, child."

The words scraped on the way out.

Jamie stared at the elk in his hands. "His business, it was

suffering. He was behind on tax payments. Crown ordered his execution. Collection day."

"Hanging?"

"They took his head."

The Black Rider drew a breath through his nose. His mouth set. A faint sound escaped him, teeth pressing together. Cold air slid through the clearing.

"And you saw this."

"Along with the rest of the village."

"Do you know who did it?"

"Arthur Richardson. One of the knights."

The man's hands stayed where they were. His chest stopped rising.

"You know him?"

The Black Rider nodded once. Reached for the canteen. Drank again.

"Knew."

"How?"

The quiet stretched. The fire popped. Sap flared and burned.

"I was a knight, years back. Served the crown. Richardson was one of my underlings." A pause. "Like I said, it was a long time ago."

Jamie blinked and set down the elk. Hunger had left him. "I had no idea."

The man looked at him again. That same lingering attention. His eyes traced Jamie's face, as if mapping it. Eye color. Jawline. The way his hair fell.

"Why would you?"

Jamie picked the elk back up. Tore off another piece. Chewed. Let the silence stand.

The man leaned forward, elbows on his knees. His hands folded together, separated, folded again. Joints cracked softly. He watched the fire as though it might speak first.

It went on too long.

"Well, what happened?"

The quiet deepened.

"The Queen died."

His gaze never left the flames. Wind stirred the pines. Something called far off.

"So, I left."

"How did she die?"

The man forgot to breathe. When air finally came, it caught.

"She took ill. Happened fast."

The fire shifted. A log settled inward, throwing a brief scatter of sparks into the dark.

"Twenty-four years now," he said. "Twenty-four years running."

"What's your real name?"

He looked at Jamie.

"Felix Ryder."

"Cool." Jamie glanced down. "I'm Jamie."

Felix's attention sharpened. His eyes widened just enough to notice.

His hand began to tremble on his knee. He pressed it flat against his thigh until it stopped. Turned his face back to the fire.

"Well, Young Jamie, it seems we have more in common than I figured we might."

He leaned back against the log and tipped his head toward the sky.

"Spit out and left far behind, with no salvation in sight."

The words barely carried.

Jamie studied his face in the firelight. The scars.

Moisture gathered at the corners of Felix's eyes. The flames caught it and turned it bright.

"What happened to your face?"

Felix smiled without opening his eyes. The expression pulled uneven. "Fuck-ugly, aren't I?"

"No, I just—"

"Wrong place, wrong time, wrong side of someone's blade." He gestured toward his neck. "Flaming arrow lodged between my shoulder plate and my helmet. Saved my life. For a price."

"Do you think you could teach me?"

Felix's eyes opened and found Jamie's. Stayed there. "'Teach' you?"

"How to fight."

"How to fight? Or how to kill?"

Jamie looked down and dragged a stick through the dirt.

Felix was right.

He said nothing.

Felix watched him.

Something crossed his face and vanished.

"Morning, then."

Jamie kept tracing lines in the soil.

"Why are you helping me?"

He looked up.

Felix opened his mouth. Closed it. His hands curled on his knees, tendons standing clear.

He tried again. Failed.

Then his head tipped back against the log. His eyes drifted shut. His mouth slackened.

The snoring started.

Jamie stared. "Fuck's sake..."

He sighed and flicked the stick into the fire.

He dragged his knapsack over, wedged it beneath his head, and lay back on the cold ground.

Across the fire, Felix snored.

His hands, even in sleep, stayed curled tight.

Jamie closed his eyes.

Sleep came slowly.

SCENE 10

OVER THE HILLTOP

The hilltop broke from the forest where the trees stopped and the land opened to sky. England rolled out below in green valleys and distant villages marked by cookfire smoke. The wilderness here was thick, untamed.

Noon sun burned overhead. Birds sang from the tree line. Wind moved through the grass, steady and cool.

Felix had picked this spot deliberately.

They'd been drilling since dawn.

Jamie circled slowly, boots crushing grass, trying to hold the stance Felix had beaten into him over two weeks of this. Knees bent. Weight forward. Sword loose in his grip but ready. The weapon felt wrong. Too light. Too small. Felix had given him the spare, a backup blade meant for emergencies.

Still. It was steel.

Felix stood center of the circle Jamie was making, his own sword planted point-down in the earth, both hands resting on the pommel. His helmet sat discarded in the grass ten feet away. Sweat ran down his scarred face despite the breeze.

"In a sword fight, there's many factors at play, constantly working for you, or against you. Positioning. Calculated force. Patience. And, most importantly, your feet."

Jamie stopped moving. "My feet?"

"Have you ever danced with a woman?"

"Sure."

"Then you get the idea?"

Jamie frowned. "Not really."

Felix shifted his grip. "Footwork sets tone. Tone sets trajectory. Now, take a swing at me."

"What?"

"Swing at me."

Jamie looked at the blade in his hand. Looked at Felix. Back at the blade. "What if I hit you?"

"That's the goal, isn't it?"

"Fucking stupid if you ask me."

"Now, Jamie."

Jamie shrugged. Set his stance. The sword suddenly felt heavier now that he meant to use it with purpose. His heart kicked faster. Palms went slick.

"Go on. Make it sharp. Cut me with it."

Jamie charged.

Fast. Sword held low at his hip, point aimed at Felix's center. Felix moved.

One step sideways. Minimal. His sword came up and swatted Jamie's blade away. Metal rang across the hilltop. Then his other hand shot out, caught Jamie across the face with a backhand.

Jamie's head snapped. His legs tangled. Gravity took him. He hit ground hard on his back. His sword flew from his grip, landed in grass three feet away.

Stars burst behind his eyes.

Felix stood over him. "That wasn't very sharp."

Jamie groaned. His jaw throbbed. "Fuck off, you twat."

"I thought you wanted to learn how to fight, not joust."

"Shut up."

"No time for banter. Get up. Your head would be separated from your body by now."

Jamie pushed up on his elbows. His back ached where he'd landed. His jaw felt loose in its socket. "So will yours by the end of this if you're not careful."

Felix extended his hand.

Jamie swatted it away. Rolled to his side. Got to his knees. Stood without help. His legs shook but held.

"You want it all at once. That's your problem."

Jamie retrieved his sword. He turned. Felix had already assumed ready stance, blade raised, weight centered.

Jamie swung.

Steel met steel with a crash that shot up his arm to his shoulder. They separated. Jamie reset. Swung again.

Felix dodged. Simple pivot. His foot hooked Jamie's ankle.

Jamie went down. Blood ran over his lips now, copper on his tongue. His nose was bleeding. His eyes watered. His hands shook with more than exhaustion.

"Again."

Jamie spat mud. Pushed himself up. Anger now. Hot and sharp.

He stood. Wiped blood with his sleeve. Picked up his sword. His grip was too tight. His jaw clenched.

Felix watched. Waiting.

Jamie charged again.

This time he didn't just run forward. He remembered. Footwork. He came in at an angle, sword raised, and when he swung it was committed.

Their blades met. The impact jarred his arms. He held on. Pushed back. Felix gave ground. Just one step. But ground.

They separated. Jamie didn't wait. Swung again. Felix parried. The blades screamed. Once. Twice. Three times rapid, metal shrieking, both men moving now, feet working through grass in patterns.

Jamie was keeping up. He could feel the rhythm Felix had described, the conversation that happened in steel.

Felix attacked. High cut aimed at Jamie's head. Jamie raised his sword. Blocked it. Force drove him back two steps but he didn't fall. Didn't stumble. Found balance and came back in.

They clashed again. And again. The hilltop rang. Birds stopped singing. Wind carried the metallic echo down into valleys.

Jamie was soaked now. But he could see it. The pattern. The dance.

He saw the opening. Went for it.

Felix wasn't there.

The blade cut empty air. Jamie's momentum carried him forward. Off balance. Exposed. He knew what was coming but couldn't stop it.

Felix's elbow caught him square in the nose.

The world went white. Then red. Then black at the edges. Jamie's legs quit. He dropped to his knees. His sword fell from fingers that wouldn't close anymore. Blood poured from his nose.

Felix stepped back. Lowered his sword. His breathing was elevated now.

"Better."

Jamie knelt in grass. The pain was bright and immediate. But underneath the pain sat something else.

Pride.

He'd lasted longer. Made Felix work. Seen the pattern even if he hadn't been fast enough to exploit it.

"Get up. We've only begun."

Jamie lowered his hands. Blood covered his palms. His nose was crooked. Definitely broken.

He stood anyway.

Felix tossed him a rag. Jamie caught it. Pressed it to his face. The white cloth turned red instantly. He held it there until the worst of the bleeding slowed.

"You're learning."

Jamie lowered the rag. His face was a wreck. But he was grinning. Couldn't help it. "Again."

Felix smiled. Not the cold thing he wore for the world. Something genuine.

"Again."

They went back to their positions. The sun climbed higher. The birds resumed their songs. Wind kept blowing. On the hilltop, two men danced the oldest dance there was.

They trained through winter's very last gasp. The hilltop became their church. Dawn to dusk. Every day that weather allowed and most days it didn't. Felix was methodical.

Jamie's nose healed crooked. Felix didn't apologize. Just told him to be grateful it still worked.

"Vanity gets you killed. Pain teaches. Scars remind."

By the second week, Jamie could hold his stance for an hour without his legs trembling. His hands developed calluses where the grip rubbed. His shoulders stopped screaming when he raised the blade.

Felix added complexity. Combinations. Feints. The grammar of violence spoken in steel.

"Block high, counter low. Your opponent commits to one line, he opens another. Find it. Take it."

They drilled until Jamie's muscles knew the patterns without thought. Until his body moved before his mind caught up. Until the sword stopped being foreign and became familiar.

Felix was never gentle. Every mistake earned correction. A slap. An elbow. A sweep that put Jamie in the dirt. The bruises accumulated. His body became a map of his education, purple and yellow and green.

But he learned.

Rain came in the third week. Cold and steady. Felix didn't stop. Just handed Jamie his sword and walked to the hilltop.

"Rain makes footing bad. Learn to move anyway."

Grass became mud. Jamie slipped. Fell. Got up. Learned to plant his feet differently. Learned to read the ground.

Felix drilled him until falling stopped. Until his boots found purchase in slick earth.

Then came the first bounty where Jamie mattered.

A village south of Wolfpine. Three men wanted for robbery and assault. Twenty crowns each. Felix and Jamie rode in at dusk.

Felix dismounted and handed Jamie his bag. "Wait with the horses."

"What?"

"Wait. With. The horses."

Jamie opened his mouth to argue. Felix's expression suggested that would be unwise. Jamie stayed with the horses.

Felix disappeared into the tavern. Twenty minutes later he emerged dragging two unconscious men by their collars. A third stumbled behind him, hands bound, nose broken, looking like he'd made poor decisions and was now reconsidering them.

Felix dumped them at Jamie's feet. "Tie these two."

Jamie worked the rope. The men didn't wake. Felix had hit them hard enough to keep them quiet for hours.

They delivered all three to the magistrate in Wolfpine. Collected sixty crowns.

Jamie had carried rope. Felix had done everything else.

The second bounty went similarly. A horse thief operating near Rivermouth. Felix told Jamie to hold the horses outside town. Came back fifteen minutes later with the thief slung over his shoulder, unconscious, bleeding from his ears.

"Help me tie him."

Jamie helped. The thief woke up halfway through the binding process, took one look at Felix's scarred face, and went very still.

They collected ten crowns.

Jamie had held horses and tied an unconscious man. Felix had done the rest.

The third bounty was when the pattern became clear.

Two smugglers working the forest roads. Fifteen crowns each. Felix and Jamie tracked them to a camp.

Felix stopped a hundred yards out. Turned to Jamie. "Here."

He handed him a bag. Heavy. Full of supplies they'd need for the next week.

"And this."

Another bag. The bedrolls.

"This too."

His water skins.

"Don't forget these."

Extra rope. A cooking pot. Two pans that clanked together.

Jamie stood there buried under gear, arms straining, looking like a packhorse that had been poorly loaded by a drunk.

"Stay here. Don't move. Don't make noise."

Felix disappeared into the brush.

Jamie waited. Arms burning. Back screaming. He set the bags down as quietly as he could. Sat on a log. Listened to distant sounds of violence. A shout. A crash. Silence.

Felix returned ten minutes later, wiping blood from his knuckles. "Got them. Pick that up."

He pointed at the pile of gear Jamie had just set down.

Jamie stared at him. "You're joking."

"Do I look like I'm joking?"

Jamie picked it all up. They walked back to where they'd left the horses. The smugglers were tied to a tree, both unconscious, both bleeding from various places.

They collected thirty crowns.

Jamie had carried bags. Felix had done everything.

By the fourth bounty, Felix wasn't even pretending.

A camp of bandits north of the forest. Four men. Thirty crowns total.

Felix loaded Jamie down with every piece of gear they owned. Bags. Bedrolls. Water skins. Rope. The cooking supplies. His spare sword. The medical kit. A shovel they'd acquired somewhere. A lantern. Two weeks of dried meat wrapped in cloth.

Jamie could barely move. He looked like a traveling merchant who'd lost his cart and was trying to carry his entire inventory on his back.

"Stay here. Don't move. If you drop anything I'll make you carry double tomorrow."

Felix walked toward the bandit camp. Alone. Unburdened. Moving like a man heading to work.

Jamie stood in the brush, buried under gear, sweating despite the cold, and watched Felix's back disappear into the trees.

Fifteen minutes later Felix returned. Not a scratch on him.

"They're subdued. Let's go."

All four bandits were unconscious. Two had broken bones. One was missing teeth. The fourth had soiled himself.

They collected thirty crowns.

Jamie had been a pack mule. Felix had done the work.

Snow returned. The training didn't stop.

Felix made Jamie fight in snow up to his knees. Made him learn to move when every step cost effort.

"Your enemy won't wait for spring and butterflies."

Jamie's fingers went numb. His breath came in white clouds. But his sword arm stayed warm. The motion generated heat.

Between training sessions, they took bounties. Felix would load Jamie down with gear, point at a spot, tell him to wait. Then he'd disappear. Come back later with unconscious or terrified men in tow.

Jamie carried things. Felix did the fighting.

At night by the fire, Felix would talk through what he'd done. How he'd approached. Where he'd struck. Why he'd chosen that angle over another.

The first man saw me coming. I let him. He drew his sword. Committed to a high strike. I went low. Took his knee. He dropped. The second man tried to run. I threw my knife. Caught him in the thigh. He fell. The third surrendered."

Jamie listened. Absorbed. Learned through Felix's words what he wasn't learning through action.

His sword work improved. His footwork became solid. His combinations grew smooth. But he hadn't put steel into flesh. Hadn't felt a blade stick in bone. Hadn't watched a man's eyes go empty because of something he'd done.

Spring came. Mud season.

They took a bounty outside a village Jamie couldn't name. Five men wanted for robbery and assault. Forty crowns total.

Felix surveyed the area. Spotted a hill overlooking the target camp. Turned to Jamie.

"Up there. Watch."

He handed Jamie a spyglass. Old brass. Battered.

"What am I watching for?"

"Technique."

Felix walked down the hill toward the camp. Five men. Three were sleeping. Two were awake, sitting by a fire, playing cards with a deck that was missing most of the face cards.

Jamie put the glass to his eye. The world jumped closer. He could see Felix moving through brush, using cover, approaching from downwind so the horses wouldn't smell him.

Felix reached the camp perimeter. Stopped. Waited. Patient.

One of the card players stood. Stretched. Walked toward the tree line to relieve himself.

Felix moved.

Silent. Fast. He closed the distance before the man finished unbuttoning his pants. His hand came up. Something glinted. The pommel of his sword. It connected with the back of the man's skull. The man dropped without sound.

Through the spyglass, Jamie watched Felix drag the body into shadow. Watched him reset. Return to cover.

The second card player called out. "Oi! You fall in?"

No response.

The man stood. Walked toward where his companion had disappeared. His hand on his knife. Cautious now.

Felix let him get close. Then stepped from cover. The man saw him. Tried to draw. Too slow.

Felix's sword came up. The flat of the blade caught the man across the temple. He spun. Hit the ground. Didn't move.

Two down. Three sleeping.

Felix walked into the camp. No stealth now. Just approached the first sleeping man and kicked him awake.

The man's eyes opened. He saw Felix standing over him. His hand went for his weapon.

Felix stomped on his wrist. Bones cracked. The man screamed. Felix's fist shut him up. Two punches. Fast. Brutal. The man went limp.

The other two were awake now. Scrambling. One grabbed a sword. The other grabbed a knife.

Felix turned to face them. His sword still sheathed. His hands loose at his sides.

The man with the sword charged. Desperate. Wild.

Felix sidestepped. Minimal movement. His foot shot out. Caught the charging man's ankle. The man fell forward. His momentum carried him face-first into a tree stump. He lay there groaning.

The last man with the knife ran.

Felix let him take five steps. Then threw a rock the size of a fist. It caught the runner in the back of the head. The man stumbled. Fell. Felix walked over and kicked him in the ribs until he stopped trying to get up.

Five men down in under three minutes.

Jamie lowered the spyglass. His hands were shaking.

Felix tied all five. Stacked them by the fire. Waved up at the hill.

Jamie came down. They delivered the men. Collected eighty crowns.

That night Felix handed him the spyglass. "Keep it. You'll need it."

"For what?"

"Watching. Learning." Felix poked the fire. "You're not ready yet."

"For what? Carrying bags?"

"For killing."

"I know how to fight."

"Fighting and killing aren't the same thing."

"What's the difference?"

"One you can undo. The other you can't." Felix looked at him across the flames. "You'll kill when it's necessary. Not before."

Jamie wanted to argue.

But he didn't. Because Felix was right. He didn't know if he was ready.

So he kept training. Kept carrying bags. Kept watching through the spyglass while Felix did the work.

Felix added new skills. Tracking. Reading signs in dirt and grass. Understanding how men moved through terrain. Where they'd camp. How they'd post watch.

"See those branches? Broken recently. Someone pushed through here. Heavy. Probably carrying something."

Jamie learned to read the forest. To see what Felix saw.

They took more bounties. Each time Felix would point at a spot. Tell Jamie to wait. To watch. To learn.

Each time Jamie would set up on high ground with the spyglass. Would watch Felix work.

He saw Felix disarm a man with a sword. Saw him dodge a knife. Saw him take down three men in the time it took Jamie to blink.

And Jamie learned. Not through doing. Through observation. Through Felix's explanations afterward.

"The swordsman committed high. Left his ribs exposed. I went in low. Took his leg. He couldn't guard from the ground."

"The knife fighter was fast but predictable. Three strikes. All to center mass. I sidestepped the third. Countered to his elbow. He dropped the blade."

"The big one relied on strength. Slow. Telegraphed. I let him swing. Dodged. Struck while he was extended. Simple."

By April, Jamie could predict what Felix would do before he did it. Could see the openings. Could understand the choices. But he hadn't made any himself. Hadn't tested theory against reality. His sword work had become excellent. His footwork was solid. His strikes were clean. But all of it was practice. None of it was real.

They sat by their fire one night in silence.

Eventually, Jamie asked, "How much longer?"

"Until what, lad?"

"Until I'm ready."

Felix studied him across the flames.

"More than you were in the beginning."

The silence returned. It wasn't companionable.

Jamie exhaled through his nose. Of course, he'd asked and Felix had answered and the answer was what it always was: honest in ways that helped nothing. The feeling that followed was too small to have a name. Just the dull awareness that he'd wanted something Felix couldn't give him and had known it before opening his mouth.

Wind slipped between the trees. Embers climbed, brief and beautiful, then died.

In the dark, their horses shifted, restless with whatever animals know that men pretend not to.

ACT III

THE DRAGON & THE PRINCE

Enter PRINCE CORWIN, sword drawne, armour gleaming blacke.

PRINCE CORWIN. Come forth, vile flame, and meete thy fated end! By crowne and oath, thy raigne I shall suspend! I knowe thee, beast, thou art what Father taught: The face of feare, the monster to be fought!

A blast of fire. Enter THE DRAGON from the mist, ancient, vast.

THE DRAGON. Who dares disturbe the silence of my tombe? The steele-borne whelpes who ride on winges of doome? I see the blacke; I see the fathers hand; I see a sonne who doth not understande.

PRINCE CORWIN. Foule beast! Thou art the terror of this land!

He striketh. THE DRAGON breathes fire but doth not pursue. CORWIN shieldes, retreats.

THE DRAGON. Goe, boy. Tell thy king his blade hath fail'd. I doe not wish to kill what feare hath veiled.

Exit CORWIN, fleeing.

THE DRAGON alone. Always with swordes. Never with wordes. They make the monster first, then come in hordes.

Enter PRINCE LEO, cautiously, bearing no weapon, hands open.

PRINCE LEO. Great serpent, if thou art not fled nor felled, I come to heare what hath so long been held. I beare no blade; I bring no kingly writ; I onely wish to knowe the truth of it.

THE DRAGON. Ah, one not clad in wrath, but robed in thought. Come neare, young sage; let feare be overwrought. In all my yeares beneath this frozen throne, None came to aske. They came to claime, or moane.

PRINCE LEO. Art thou the scourge they name in royall hall? Or dost thou dreame beneath the mountaines thrall?

THE DRAGON. I dreame of peace, of skies unmarred by screames, Of quiet mindes, and young men brave with dreames. I am no plague; I am no demon sent, I am what's left when empire seekes a scent. They neede a foe to name, a beast to feare, That kinges may seeme more kingly standing here. So I become the monster in their lore, Though I have onely ever wisht for less, not more.

PRINCE LEO. Then speake, O wyrme, and I shall be thy quill; For knowledge borne of fire is nobler still.

They sit together as snow begins to fall.

THE DRAGON. The truest strength is not in steele or flame, But in the minde that askes before it came. Thou art the first to see me as I am, Not beast, but mirror to thy fathers sham.

SCENE 11

The cellar had no windows. Three layers of steel in the walls, Damien had said once, with the pride of a man describing his workshop. Three feet of stone above that, packed earth beyond, the weight of the entire castle pressing down from overhead. Sound went in and died there, absorbed by darkness and mass and the particular acoustics of despair. Men had screamed in this room. Their voices had gone nowhere. The walls kept their secrets.

A single torch burned in an iron sconce by the door, throwing orange light that barely reached the corners. The flame guttered in air that tasted of rust and piss and something older, something that had soaked into the stone over years of use. Blood lingered. So did fear.

Henry Beverley sat chained to a chair in the center of the room. Heavy iron manacles circled his wrists, bolted to the chair's arms with rivets the size of a man's thumb. His ankles were similarly bound. The chair itself was oak, ancient and solid, its legs sunk into grooves worn smooth by previous occupants who'd sat exactly where he sat now.

His head hung forward. Blood and sweat dripped from his scalp to the bridge of his nose, collecting there in fat drops before falling to his lap. His breathing was labored. Wet. Each inhale produced a rattle that suggested ribs had been broken and were working their way toward puncturing something vital. His beard was matted with dried blood. His clothes were torn. Someone had already been here before. Someone had started the work and left him to marinate in his injuries.

The door opened.

Torchlight from the stairwell spilled in, brighter than the single flame inside, enough to make Henry squint despite his swollen eyes. Two figures entered, casting long shadows across the floor.

Henry lifted his head. The effort cost him. His neck muscles trembled with the strain. His eyes were purple and swollen nearly shut but he could still see enough to recognize the taller figure, the one who moved with the unhurried grace of someone who owned time itself.

"Just who I imagined."

His voice came out thick and slurred, damaged by whatever beating he'd endured before this one. But there was defiance in it still. Pride. The kind that gets men killed but at least lets them die standing.

Damien crossed the floor without hurry. Behind him, Falstaff lingered near the door like a ghost who'd forgotten how to leave, pale and silent, clutching a leather-bound ledger to his chest as if the accounts it contained might protect him from what was coming.

The torchlight caught Damien's face. He was smiling. Not the performative smile he wore in court, not the political calculation he showed his brother. This was genuine. The smile of a man arriving home after a long journey.

"We need to know where your son is stationed. If he rallies

the northern houses, your daughter's marriage means nothing."

Henry's mouth split into a grin. Blood outlined his teeth, filling the gaps where several had been knocked loose. The grin widened. Became something unhinged.

"Peter? Oh... Heh... Ha-ha... Ha-ha-ha-ha-ha-ha..."

The laughter built. Gained momentum. It started as a chuckle, dry and bitter, then climbed in pitch and volume until it filled the cellar, bouncing off walls that had heard this sound before from other men in other chairs. The laughter of the doomed. The laughter of men who'd run out of choices and found freedom in having nothing left to lose.

Damien stood watching. Patient. His smile didn't falter. If anything, it deepened, as if Henry's breakdown was exactly the entertainment he'd been hoping for.

"Falstaff."

The councilman flinched. "Yes, My Lord?"

Henry's laughter had gone shrill now, cracking at the edges, threatening to break into something worse. Tears leaked from his swollen eyes. Whether from humor or pain or simple exhaustion was impossible to say.

Damien's voice dropped. Went flat and cold as winter iron. "Leave us."

Falstaff shifted his weight from foot to foot, a nervous dance that suggested his bowels were considering betrayal. "Your brother insisted supervision."

"My brother is not my concern."

Falstaff opened his mouth. Closed it. His fingers tightened on the ledger until the leather creaked.

"Sir—"

Damien looked at Falstaff with the attention a butcher gives meat, measuring where to make the first cut.

"Do we have an issue, Councilman?"

Henry's cackles morphed into a coughing fit. Violent. Wet. Blood sprayed from his mouth, misting the air in front of him, spattering across his lap in dark droplets. His body convulsed with each cough, the chains rattling against iron, the sound of a dog on a short leash.

Falstaff's face went whiter. The little color that remained drained away until he looked like a corpse that hadn't realized it was dead yet. His throat worked. His mouth opened but no sound came out.

"Good."

Falstaff left. His footsteps echoed up the stairwell, fast and panicked, the sound of a man grateful to be breathing and terrified he might not be for much longer. The door at the top opened. Closed. The sound of the bolt sliding home carried down, final as a coffin lid.

Damien crossed to the door and locked it from the inside. The bolt was new steel, thick as a man's wrist, sliding into brackets sunk deep into . The sound it made was definitive. No one was getting in. No one was getting out. Not until Damien decided otherwise.

He turned back to the room.

Henry had stopped coughing. His head hung forward again, chest heaving, each breath a struggle. Blood dripped from his mouth in a thin stream, adding to the pool in his lap.

Damien walked to the table against the far wall. The torch didn't reach this far. The table existed in shadow, its contents suggested more than seen, shapes that the mind filled in with its worst assumptions.

He lifted the torch from its sconce and brought it closer.

The light revealed what waited there.

Instruments. Tools. The vocabulary of pain arranged in neat rows like a surgeon's kit, each piece cleaned and oiled and ready for use. Knives of varying lengths and curves, some straight for cutting, some hooked for tearing, all sharp enough to split hair. Saws with teeth like sharks, serrated and cruel. Axes, small ones meant for fingers and toes, larger ones for limbs. A heretic's fork, four-pronged and evil, designed to be strapped under the chin and collarbone, forcing the victim's head up in permanent supplication or driving the prongs into flesh with every attempted movement.

And at the end of the table, a square cage the size of a man's fist. Inside it, a rat. Starving. Its ribs visible through mangy fur. Its eyes red with hunger and hate, fixed on Henry with the single-minded intensity of a creature that knew meat when it saw it.

"Do you know what I like about this room, Henry?"

Damien's voice was conversational. Warm. The tone a man uses discussing architecture with a friend over drinks.

"It's quiet. Compact, intimate. Contained. Most men, they get uncomfortable. Not me. I find it refreshing. But, as my father used to say, I'm an odd duck."

His finger moved over the knives. Hovering. Considering. Playing some private game of selection, eeny-meeny-miny-moe with instruments of torture.

He selected a blade. Held it up to the torchlight. The steel gleamed orange.

"What do you think, Henry? Am I an odd duck?"

Henry lifted his head. The effort cost him everything he had left. His neck trembled. His breathing went ragged. But he met Damien's eyes, and when he spoke, his voice carried the flat certainty of a man who'd made his peace.

"You waste your time."

Damien replaced the knife. Selected another. A straight razor this time, the kind barbers used, folded steel with an edge that could shave a man or open his throat with equal ease.

"I'm ready to meet the Gods. I'm ready to... see my Queen."

The words came out tired. Resigned. The voice of a man who'd run out the clock and was waiting for the final bell.

Damien looked at him. His expression carried something that might have been pity if you didn't know better. His head tilted slightly.

"Did you think you were going to die today?"

The question hung in the air. Henry's eyes widened slightly. Understanding began to dawn, terrible and complete.

Damien laughed. The sound was warm. Genuine. Rich with humor that came from someplace deep and honest. Worse than the torture itself because it suggested he was enjoying this on a level that had nothing to do with duty or information or even cruelty. This was joy. Pure and simple.

"Nay, old man. You will part with flesh."

The razor moved.

Fast.

Horizontal across Henry's cheek, starting just below his left eye, cutting clean through skin and fat, stopping short of the bone but not by much. The cut was precise. Calculated. Deep enough to scar but shallow enough to avoid major vessels. The kind of wound that came from practice, from understanding anatomy, from knowing exactly how much damage you could inflict without killing.

Blood welled immediately. Ran down Henry's face in thick streams. His mouth opened. The sound that came out was high and strangled, barely human, the squeal a wounded animal makes when it knows the predator is just beginning and there's nowhere to run.

"I promised my brother peace of mind, Henry."

Damien's voice hadn't changed. Still conversational. Still warm.

He leaned over Henry's shoulder. The razor hovered by his carotid artery. Close enough that Henry could feel the cold steel against his pulse. Close enough that one twitch, one flinch, one wrong breath would be the last thing he ever did.

"I intend to keep my promise."

Henry's good eye rolled back. His chest heaved. Blood ran from the cut on his face, dripping from his jaw, adding to the growing stain on his clothes.

"You spit on your father's legacy."

The words came out choked. Desperate. The last weapon of a disarmed man.

Damien smiled. Tossed the bloodied blade aside. It clattered across stone, skittering into shadow. He cracked his knuckles. Each joint popped with the sound of kindling snapping, dry wood breaking. He rolled his shoulders. Loosened his neck. The movements of a man preparing for physical labor.

"My father was unambitious. A pathetic consort with the blood of a cankerous whore and a pig-fucker."

His fist drove into Henry's stomach.

The impact was a wet thud. All the air left Henry's lungs in a rush. His body tried to fold forward but the chains held him upright, forced him to take it straight on. His mouth opened. His throat worked. Then he vomited.

The sick splashed across his lap, chunks and bile and blood mixing into a foul soup that stank of wine and terror. It ran down his legs. Pooled beneath the chair. The smell filled the small room, sharp and acidic, competing with the rust and fear that had been there first.

A slap. Open palm. Henry's head snapped sideways. Blood flew from his mouth, spattering the wall. His ear rang. His vision whited out. When it returned, Damien was closer, leaning in, his face inches from Henry's.

"Perhaps you two might've gotten on."

Another blow. Closed fist this time. To the jaw. Bone met bone. Teeth flew from Henry's mouth like dice scattered across a table. They met the floor with delicate clicks, white against gray. Blood poured from his lips, running down his chin in thick streams that wouldn't stop.

Damien stepped back. Wiped his knuckles on his pants. Examined the damage with the attention of a man checking his work. His hands were unmarked. He'd learned long ago how to hit without hurting himself.

"Where is he, Henry?"

Henry's head lolled forward. Blood and drool mixed. Dripped. His breathing was a wet rattle. When he tried to speak, the words came out thick and slurred through a mouth that no longer worked properly. Half his teeth were gone. His tongue was swollen. But he managed it.

"You know I won't give up my son. My fate has been decided. I'm an old man, Damien. I won't survive this."

He paused. Gathered strength. Lifted his head enough to meet Damien's eyes. What remained of his mouth pulled into something that might have been a smile if you squinted.

"But d'you know what?"

The smile widened. Blood outlined every remaining tooth.

Filled the gaps where teeth used to be. Made his grin look like a jack-o'-lantern's.

"Neither will you."

The words dropped like bricks down a well. Prophecy or curse or just the bitter hope of a dying man or perhaps all three. Either way, they sat between them, true or not, believed or not, spoken and heard.

The moment stretched.

Then came the knock.

Three sharp raps on the door. Apologetic. Urgent.

"My Lord, it's your brother."

Damien straightened. Brushed imaginary dust from his breastplate. Adjusted his collar. The movements of a man finishing one appointment and preparing for another.

He walked to the door without looking back at Henry.

Behind him, the old king sat alone in his chair, bleeding, the sound of his breathing wet and labored, laughing quietly to himself about something only he understood. Prophecy or madness. Perhaps both.

Damien climbed the stairs. Left the torch burning. Left the door unlocked. Henry wasn't going anywhere. The chains would see to that.

At the top of the stairwell, Falstaff waited, pale and shaking, the ledger still clutched to his chest.

"Your brother requests your presence. Immediately."

Damien walked past him. Behind him, Falstaff scurried to keep up, his breathing quick and anxious, the sound of a small animal trying to remain unnoticed by larger predators.

The door to Lionel's chamber was already open when Damien arrived.

The room beyond held centuries in its stones. Walls rose to vaulted ceilings where oak ribs met in patterns carved by men who had died believing their work would outlast kingdoms. Tapestries hung between tall windows, their threads depicting coronations and conquests in colors that had faded to the approximate shades of memory. The air was cool.

A candle burned on the desk near the window. Its flame bent sideways, wavering. The wax pooled at its base, white and soft, drowning the wick slowly.

His brother stood by the window itself, wine glass in hand, sunlight streaming through the leaded glass behind him. The light came through colored panes—red, gold, green—and painted him in fragments. Made the red liquid in his glass glow like something sacramental, like blood transmuted through ritual into something holy. He wore his crown. Midday, in his private chamber, donning it like armor. Like proof.

Below, in the courtyard, the sound of hammers carried up through the open window. Their voices rose in bursts, instructions, curses, laughter. Normal sounds. Life continuing outside these walls as though the room they were standing in didn't exist, as though power was something that happened elsewhere.

"I imagined this was important. It's barely noon, brother."

Lionel didn't turn. His back remained to the door, his posture rigid, one hand holding the wine glass, the other clenched in a fist at his side. His shoulders were drawn up. Tight. The muscles visible through the silk. His spine was straight. Too straight. The posture of a man who'd rehearsed this.

Damien stopped in the doorway. His hand rested on the doorframe, feeling the smooth oak beneath his palm, the slight give of wood that had stood for generations and would stand for generations more. Making Lionel come to him. Or issue an invitation like a proper host.

The silence stretched. The candle flame bent lower. Nearly horizontal now. In the courtyard, a man shouted instructions. Timber struck timber with hollow sounds. A wheel creaked. Someone laughed.

"You disobey me."

The words came out clipped. The tone of a man who'd run this conversation in his mind a dozen times and was determined to stick to the script he'd written.

Damien stepped inside, closing the door behind him.

"Brother?"

He measured his brother's silence. Calculated. Waited. Let the question sit there, unanswered, growing heavier with each second that passed.

The candle flame steadied. Became vertical again. Burned straight for three heartbeats. Then guttered. Nearly went out. A wisp of smoke rose, carrying the scent of burnt wick into air that had gone still.

"You put Falstaff in a very undesirable position," Lionel said. "Was it necessary?"

Damien didn't answer.

Lionel's grip on the wine glass tightened. His knuckles went white. The tendons stood out. The crimson liquid trembled slightly. Small ripples across the surface. Red waves.

"Are you the King?"

Lionel turned. His face carried the expression of a child who'd just learned to say no and was drunk on the power of it.

"I'm sorry?"

"Are. You. The. King?"

Damien shrugged. One shoulder. The gesture somehow more dismissive than any words could have been.

"Then why do you think you are?"

"Are you weary of me?"

"Father knew what you were. And so do I. I never loved you less for it."

The candle flame bent.

"What am I, brother?"

"Harsh." Lionel's tone was careful now. Political. Measured. The voice he used in council meetings when trying to convince rather than command. "In my experience, it's more effective contained than not."

"Your trust wanes?"

"No more than your loyalty."

Damien smiled. His eyes went cold.

"Why don't you do it?"

Lionel blinked. This wasn't how it was supposed to go. His prepared responses were useless now. He was improvising. "Do what?"

"Question him."

"It is not my duty."

The words came out automatic. Defensive. The response he'd been taught. The excuse he'd been given. The lie he'd been told and had chosen to believe because believing it was easier than acknowledging what it meant if it wasn't true.

"Or is it your delicate stomach?"

The candle flame bent again. This time it stayed bent. Horizontal. The smoke poured from it now, thick and gray, spreading across the desk in a low cloud that smelled of burnt wax and something acrid.

"It is not my duty."

"So, you're telling me what my duty is?"

"I'm simply guiding you."

"'Guiding' me?"

"Of course."

Lionel had found his footing again. Back on script. The familiar words gave him strength. He'd prepared for this part.

"And if I were to step off?"

"Then I would be inclined to correct you."

The light shifted again. The sun had moved. The colors on the floor changed. Red gave way to gold. Gold gave way to green. The patterns bled into each other at their edges, creating shades that had no names, that existed only in transition, in the space between defined things.

"Will this be an issue?"

Damien crossed the floor. Shoulders relaxed. Hands clasped behind his back. Expression neutral.

He stopped directly in front of Lionel. Close. Close enough to smell the wine on his breath. Close enough to see the fear in his eyes that the bravado couldn't quite hide. Close enough to see the pulse jumping in his throat—rapid, desperate, the rhythm of a heart that knew it was in danger but couldn't make the body move, couldn't trigger flight because flight would be admission.

He took the wine glass from Lionel's hand.

The gesture was smooth. Casual. The way you take a toy

from a child who's misbehaving.

Damien held the glass up to the window. Light passed through the red liquid. Refracted. Scattered. Painted his palm crimson. The shadow it cast on the floor between them was dark. Blood-colored. It lay across the stone like a stain.

"Where is this from?"

"Northbury. Lovely, isn't it?"

Damien threw the wine in his face.

The liquid hit Lionel full on. Splashed across his forehead, his eyes, his nose, his mouth. Ran down his cheeks in rivulets that followed the contours of his skull, that found channels and followed them, that moved like blood from a head wound. Soaked into his hair. Darkened it from gold to brown. Dripped from his eyelashes. From his nose. From his lips. The smell of it filled the space between them—grape and oak and something sweet that had turned sharp with age.

Lionel gasped. Sputtered. His hands came up involuntarily. Protective. Too late. His eyes squeezed shut. Wine dripped from his chin. Ran down his throat—down his exposed, vulnerable throat—and disappeared into his collar. The crimson liquid darkened the silk. Spread. Stained it wet and dark as blood.

Then Damien upended the glass over his brother's head.

Poured every remaining drop. Let it cascade over Lionel's crown—the physical crown, gold and jeweled and now soaked with wine that ran in thin streams through the metalwork, that followed engraved patterns meant to suggest divine favor and instead looked like wounds weeping. Let it soak into his hair. Let it run down his neck in red rivulets that followed the curve of his spine, that traced the vertebrae like a blade testing for gaps between bone, that disappeared beneath his collar and spread across his shoulders.

The wine pooled in his collar. Soaked through the expensive fabric. Ran down his chest. Ruined everything it touched.

Damien leaned in.

"Were you guiding me then?"

Lionel stood frozen. Wine dripping. Flushed with humiliation that went deeper than skin, that colored him from the inside out, that had seeped into his bones. When he finally opened his eyes, they were wet. Whether from wine or tears was impossible to say.

His hand went to his throat. Touched it. Felt the wetness there. The sticky slide of wine over skin. His fingers came away red.

"I could have your head."

"And your Kingdom would follow."

The hammering outside had stopped.

Damien set the empty glass on the table beside the window. He turned. Walked to the door. Nothing in his stride suggested what had just happened. No rush. No anger. No satisfaction. Just a man leaving a room he'd finished with.

He paused at the threshold. Looked back.

The candle on the desk guttered. The flame bent. Wavered.

Then went out.

"Good chat, brother."

Damien left.

The silence was enormous. The room felt larger to Lionel now that he was alone in it. The vaulted ceiling higher, the walls more distant, as though the space itself was retreating from him.

His shoulders began to shake. Small movements at first. Then larger. His chest hitched. His breathing went ragged.

He tried to remove the crown. His hands fumbled with it. The metal was slick with wine. It slipped in his grasp. Fell. Hit the floor with a sound that was both soft and terrible.

He walked to the window. His boots left wet prints on the stone. Red footprints. Like he was bleeding from his feet. Walking on wounds. Each step made a soft sound, wet fabric against cold rock, that echoed in the silence.

He swallowed. The motion hurt. Like his throat had been damaged. But it was just wine. Just humiliation. Just the understanding that the thing he'd thought made him safe—the crown, the title, the blood right—meant nothing when his brother decided it meant nothing.

The sunlight on the floor had hardened. Changed color. The

red had faded. The gold was yellow now. Sickly. The green had turned gray. The patterns had lost their beauty.

He stood at the window. Wine-soaked. Crown on the floor. The King of England, alone in his chamber, learning what every fool learns eventually: that authority without strength is just permission to be hated.

In the courtyard below, the hammers fell.

The timber rose.

The world kept turning.

And it was in that quiet that something twice as intoxicating—foreign, yet as familiar as the eastern sunrise; new, though older than the castle's very foundations—rose through Lionel's veins in place of wine: a moral awakening as awful as it was liberating.

SCENE 12

THE DEATH OF HENRY BEVERLEY

Henry waited in the same chair.

Blood had dried on his face in dark lines that followed the geography of his skull; the ridge of his cheekbone, the hollow beneath his eye, the channel that ran from temple to jaw where a blade had opened him. His breathing had steadied into something almost rhythmic, the wet rattle of broken ribs quieter now, controlled. He'd found some equilibrium between pain and consciousness and was maintaining it through will alone.

His wrists bore the circular bruises of iron. His hands had gone numb, then returned in waves of burning pins and needles. The body was still trying, still committed to keeping Henry Beverley alive even though Henry Beverley himself had made peace with alternatives.

Above him, faintly, came the sound of hammers. Distant. Rhythmic. The builders in the courtyard working on something.

Then the hammering stopped.

The silence that followed felt wrong.

Footsteps replaced it. Not Damien's. Henry knew that gait. This tread was different. More cautious.

The bolt slid back. Metal on metal. The rasp of iron that needed oiling.

The door opened.

Torchlight spilled in, more than the cellar deserved. It came around the shoulders of the men who entered, outlining them in crooked halos. The light was orange. Alive. It cast shadows that climbed the walls and bent across the vaulted ceiling.

Three men descended the stairs. Richardson came first—broad, square-shouldered, built like someone had gotten bored halfway through carving a statue. Behind him, moving with a stiffness that owed more to nerves than spine, came Lionel.

He wore his crown. Not the ceremonial one, but the simpler band.

There were others. Two knights in the Taylor livery, and between them a young man Henry had never seen before. He was all edges, this one. Hair the color of summer wheat, cropped close. Eyes pale and empty as morning ice, the kind that assessed meat and bone and the mechanical problem of separating one from the other. His jaw looked carved rather than grown. There was nothing remarkable about him except the absence of anything soft.

Sir William Rodham. Twenty years old, if memory served. A name that meant nothing to Henry beyond the certainty that he would remember it now.

Richardson crossed to the chair. His fingers—thick as sausages, scarred across the knuckles—worked the bolts that held Henry's arms. When the manacles released, returning blood burned like fire. He gasped.

Lionel stopped three paces away. Far enough that Henry couldn't reach him. Close enough that Henry could see the wine-stain dried at the base of the king's throat, dark against pale skin. The crown sat slightly askew.

"Where is your son, Henry?"

Henry lifted his head. The room tilted. His ribs screamed. Blood dripped from the cut in his cheek, half-dried, cracking when he moved. The world swam, then steadied.

He looked at Lionel and saw everything. The wine in his hair. The damp at his collar. The way his hands were clasped behind his back in concealment, hiding a tremor. The crown sitting askew like a drunk's hat. He looked at Lionel and saw a man who had been humiliated recently and was now seeking to restore himself through the suffering of someone weaker.

Henry laughed. A single broken huff that left blood on his lip.

"You Taylors are all the same. Thick, ugly, and entitled."

"Very well," Lionel said. He glanced at Richardson. No nod. Just a small tilt of his head.

The knights moved in. Hands seized Henry's arms and shoulders. The manacles came off his ankles with a wrench of iron. The chair was dragged back. Henry's feet hit ground that felt colder than he remembered. For a second his legs considered folding. Pride kept them locked. Because Henry Beverley had been many things—soldier, king, father, exile—but he had never been a man who needed carrying.

"Easy," Richardson muttered to the men hauling him, a warning to be careful with the property.

They marched him toward the stairs.

The climb was a study in small humiliations. Each step sent lightning through his ribs. His breath rattled. The walls pressed close. Stone scraped his shoulder when one knight misjudged the angle.

The air changed as they climbed. Less stale. More smoke and wet wool and something that might have been baking bread. Warmer near the top. At the top of the stairs, the castle opened around them, corridors stretching in multiple directions, walls rising to vaulted ceilings. Tapestries hung at intervals, showing men who'd made better—or worse—choices centuries ago, faces hewn in thread staring down without sympathy.

Servants flattened themselves against the walls as the procession passed. Their faces were carefully blank. Eyes down. The practiced neutrality of people who'd learned that survival meant being invisible when power moved through corridors. Lionel walked a half-step back, hands still clasped, crown still askew. He didn't meet Henry's eye when the older man stumbled and had to be yanked upright.

They reached the outer doors.

Heavy oak reinforced with iron bands. Two guards pulled them open. The wood groaned.

The world beyond was a smear of gray; low sky, ash-colored stone, mud that had forgotten what it meant to be dry. The courtyard had changed since Henry had last seen it. The scaffolding he'd heard being built now towered against the inner wall. Raw timber lashed together in deliberate geometry. Men had worked fast. Fear made for efficient carpenters. The wood was still fresh, still bleeding sap.

At its center stood the gallows. A crossbeam of thick oak, darkened where damp had begun to sink in. New rope hung from it, pale against the gray morning, hemp that hadn't had time to weather, a loop tied with skilled hands. Beneath it, a crude platform had been assembled from planks still oozing sap.

They dragged Henry through the mud.

His boots sank immediately. The earth clutched at his feet. Each step required effort, each lift producing a wet sucking sound that echoed across the courtyard.

The courtyard was not empty.

Somewhere to his left, a stablehand stopped mid-task, pitchfork frozen. Somewhere to his right, a laundry girl clutched a basket of linens, knuckles white. She was young. Fourteen, maybe. Too young to have seen this before.

Peasants and servants and guards clustered in loose rings around the gallows. Some had the decency to look away when they recognized Henry Beverley. Others watched openly, eyes bright, faces flushed with the light of spectacle.

It was not that they were cruel by nature. But cruelty seen from a distance with no risk of blood on your own hands looked a great deal like clarity, like justice, like the world finally making sense.

Margaret was already there. They'd dragged her from her chambers at dawn without explanation. Just the pounding on her door, rough hands pulling her from bed, no time to dress properly or bind her hair. The guards had said nothing during the walk through the castle corridors, their grip firm but not cruel, steering her toward the courtyard with the cold competence of men following orders they didn't question.

Henry saw her before she saw him. She came through the gate in a storm of silk and panic, her dress already muddy at the hem. Her hair was unbound—wrong, always wrong for Margaret in public. It fell in dark waves, tangled and wild. Her eyes were wide and raw, red-rimmed, wet.

Two knights flanked her. Their hands rested lightly on her arms, almost escort rather than restraint.

Margaret's eyes scanned the courtyard.

Then she saw Henry.

"No!"

She lunged forward. The knights held firm. For a wild moment it looked like she might drag them across the courtyard by sheer force of terror. Her feet scrambled in the mud, her whole body strained.

Then one tightened his grip. The other swept her legs—a kick behind the knees, physics applied correctly—and she dropped hard to her knees in the mud.

She struggled. Her hands clawed at the ground. Her dress soaked up mud, the silk darkening from blue to brown to black. The knights held her there, head forced up, hands gripping her shoulders with pressure that would bruise.

Lionel watched this with a face that might once have been kind. But that was gone now, burned away by wine and humiliation and the terrible clarity that came from understanding exactly how powerless you were.

The wine on his throat had cracked as it dried. His hands were steady now. His jaw was set. The moral awakening Damien had sparked in him was working quickly. Nothing reorganized a man faster than humiliation properly administered.

He looked at the knights holding Margaret.

"Do not allow her to look away."

The knights heard him. One shifted his grip to her jaw, forcing her head up until her neck strained and her eyes had nowhere to go but forward.

Margaret's breathing came in short, sharp gasps. Hyperventilating.

Richardson and Rodham brought Henry to the platform.

Up close, the timber smelled of sap and sweat and iron. The rope brushed Henry's cheek as they positioned him. New hemp. Rough.

The platform was three feet off the ground. High enough that everyone could see.

"Last chance, Henry."

Lionel's voice carried across the courtyard. Formal. Ceremonial. Offering mercy he had no intention of granting.

There was something almost weary in his voice, as if some small part of him still remembered being a different kind of man.

Henry looked at his daughter.

Margaret knelt in the mud fifteen feet away. Her face was tear-wet, lashes clumped, lips parted around a trapped breath. A bright smear of blood marked the side of her neck where a knight's grip had been too eager.

He looked at Lionel.

A boy in a man's costume. Wine-stained and desperate. Playing King.

Then Henry did the only thing left that was entirely his.

He spat.

The gobbet of blood and saliva hit Lionel's cheek just below the eye. It clung there, obscene and bright, a single red comet trailing down royal flesh.

The courtyard held its breath. Lionel didn't flinch. His jaw tightened—a muscle jumping, barely visible—but otherwise he remained still. The brutal education Damien had provided found a rail to run on.

"Very well," he said again, barely above a whisper.

He nodded.

Just once.

The rope went over Henry's head. Richardson's hands were surprisingly gentle as he positioned the noose, adjusted it so the knot sat just right against Henry's jaw, just behind the ear. Rough coils rasped against torn skin. Richardson tightened the knot with a jerk that made black spots dance. The noose bit into his windpipe. The world narrowed.

This was not the sophisticated machinery of cities, of trapdoors and calculated drops. This was cruder. More honest in its brutality.

Richardson and Rodham took the other end of the rope. They wrapped it once around their hands. Braced their feet in the mud. Tested the weight. Muscle corded in their arms.

Henry's feet left the planks as they pulled. His body lurched upward, jerked into the air. His boots dangled. His spine stretched. Fire lanced through his ribs. His breath became a strangled rattle. The rope dug in and his windpipe collapsed. Air stopped. His lungs screamed. The world blurred at the edges, colors bleeding out, replaced by encroaching darkness.

His body reacted without permission. His legs kicked. Frantic. Involuntary. His hands went to the rope. Clawed at it. Tried to get fingers under it. But the rope was tight and his fingers were weak and his body was dying.

He swung slightly. The rope creaked. New hemp stretching under his weight.

"Please." Margaret's voice. Broken. "Please—"

Her whole body was shaking. The knights held her steady. Kept her head up. Made her watch.

Lionel stepped closer to her. Mud sucked at his boots. He stopped beside her. Close enough that his shadow fell across her face.

"Rodham."

Lionel's voice was flat. Empty.

The young knight moved.

He drew the knife from his belt. A nine-inch blade with a snake-skin-wrapped hilt. The edge caught the gray light. Very sharp.

Henry hung before him, chest heaving against the rope, body thrashing with the last dregs of survival instinct. His eyes bulged, veins standing out in his temples. His face had gone from red to purple to something darker. The cut on his cheek had reopened. Blood ran freely now.

Rodham's face showed nothing.

He stepped in close. Positioned himself. Then, with one smooth motion, he drove the blade up and in beneath Henry's ribs on the left side.

The angle was precise. Practiced. He'd been taught where to put it. The sound was wet. Steel entering flesh. Parting it.

For a moment, nothing happened.

Then Rodham twisted the blade. Opened the wound wider. Drew it down and across.

Henry's abdomen distended monstrously. His intestines, no longer held, began to slide.

They came out slowly at first. A bulge.

Then they spilled. Slid out in a slick pour as gravity took over. There was a smell—sharp, metallic—that crawled into throats and stayed there.

Henry's guts hit the mud beneath him in a thick trickle. Coiled against his boots. Pink intestines. Gray stomach. Dark liver. All of it still connected, still attached to a body that was somehow, impossibly, still alive.

The crowd reacted. Not as one. In jagged, incoherent bursts. A peasant woman clapped a hand to her mouth; a muffled keening trapped behind her palm. One guard turned away and retched into his helm. Another leaned forward, fascinated, pupils huge. The stablehand dropped his pitchfork. A child somewhere began to cry.

Margaret tried to turn her head. The hand on her jaw forced it back. Her eyes squeezed shut. The knight's thumb and forefinger found her eyelids. Pried them open. She watched her father die, watched the way his body twitched and writhed, the way the rope bit deeper with every movement, the way his hands clawed at nothing. Watched his legs kick weakly at a sky that had never promised him anything. Watched the rope creak. Watched the timber hold.

She watched his face turn from purple to black. Watched his tongue push past his lips, swollen and dark. Watched his eyes bulge further, further.

She watched his entrails steam in the cold.

The sound of her breath became shuddering gasps. Each one sounded like something breaking.

Lionel didn't watch Henry.

He watched her. Watched Margaret. Watched the moment something in her eyes changed.

He nodded to the knights holding her.

They released her.

Margaret collapsed forward onto all fours. Her palms sank into the mud. Her whole body shook. Her sobs tore through her like someone was ripping emotion out by the handful.

She gasped for air. Each breath felt insufficient.

Lionel stepped close enough that his shadow fell across her. "You think me credulous?"

She didn't answer. He looked at the guards.

"Lock her in her chambers." A murmur ran through the onlookers. "Watch the windows."

Two knights stepped forward. Each took one of Margaret's arms. Their grips were firm but not brutal. They hauled her upright. Her legs obeyed without her fully realizing it. The body had its own instincts for survival.

She swayed. Found balance.

Her dress was ruined. Mud climbed from hem to waist. Her hair hung in tangled ropes. Her face was a mess of tears and dirt.

She twisted once. Just enough to look back.

Her father hung from the rope, still now. Finally still. His body had stopped fighting. His hands dangled limp at his sides.

His innards lay in the mud in a glistening heap, cooling quickly, steam still rising.

His eyes were open. Staring. Seeing nothing.

Above him, the new gallows loomed against the slate sky. Raw timber. New rope. The smell of sap and death mixing into something that would haunt Margaret Beverley for the rest of her natural life.

The knights pulled her away. She walked with them. Had no choice. Her boots sucked in the mud with each step. Left prints. Proof she'd been here.

Lionel turned away first.

He walked back toward the castle with measured steps, each footfall a small argument against the tremor still buzzing at the edges of his muscles. The crown on his head felt heavier than it had that morning. Not because it had changed weight, but because he finally understood fully what it cost to keep it.

Behind him, in the courtyard, Henry Beverley hung from new timber. Dead. Finally. Completely.

And somewhere, high above, the hammers started up again.

Distant at first. Then louder. The builders returning to work. Timber rang. Iron struck. Men shouted instructions. Normal sounds. Work sounds.

The courtyard began to empty. Guards returned to their posts. Servants returned to their tasks. The laundry girl picked up her dropped basket and walked away without looking back. The stablehand retrieved his pitchfork and went back to mucking stalls.

Work resumed.

SCENE 13

THE WARRINGTON LAKE BRAWL

The tavern sat at the edge of the lake like something that had grown there rather than been built. Wood and aged cobblestone weathered to the same gray. A roof that sagged in the middle. Windows so small and high they might as well not have existed.

Felix and Jamie hitched their horses outside. The animals were tired, flanks dark with sweat, breath still heavy from the ride. Wolfpine was hours behind them now. The sun had climbed to its apex, hung there burning, the kind of oppressive noon heat that made sweat run down your spine and pool at the small of your back, that made leather stick to skin and metal too hot to touch barehanded.

"Why are we here?" Jamie asked.

"A pint."

Inside, the air was thick with smoke and the smell of old beer and older men. The tavern was dim despite the hour, as though the building itself rejected daylight on principle. What illumination existed came in thin blades through cracks in the walls, through gaps in the roof where repairs had been promised and forgotten, through the half-open door that let in a single shaft of dust-laden sunlight that died a few feet past the threshold. Tradesmen clustered at tables. Loud. Drunk. Souls that started at dawn and didn't stop until unconsciousness or violence intervened, whichever came first.

Jamie took a table near the back, out of the way, positioning himself where he could see the room. Felix walked to the bar.

The bartender was fifty-something, maybe older. Thick hands scarred from years of breaking up fights and cleaning broken glass. A face that suggested he'd been handsome once, before life and liquor had worn him down to something merely functional, something that poured drinks and took bits and asked no questions because questions got you killed in places like this.

He dried his hands on a rag that had been white once and was the color of old dishwater now.

"Two ales," Felix said.

The bartender looked him over. Started at the helmet and worked down. The black armor that caught what little light there was and threw it back darker. The sword at his hip. The way Felix stood—loose but ready, the stance of someone who'd been in more fights than the bartender had served drinks.

He tried a smile. Tried a joke to break the tension his instincts were screaming at him.

"Never known a man to wear his helmet while he drinks."

Felix just looked at him. Said nothing. The smile died on the man's face like a candle in wind.

"Couple shillings, then."

Felix set down two bits hard enough that they rang off the wood, sharp little sounds that carried in the quiet that had formed around him. Then he turned his back on the bartender and crossed to Jamie's table.

He sat. Removed his helmet with slow deliberation. Set it on the table between them like a third presence, like something with weight beyond metal.

Jamie opened his mouth. "What are we—"

"Get off me!"

The voice cut through the tavern noise like a knife through cloth. Young. Female. Frayed at the edges with fear that was trying very hard to sound like anger.

Jamie's head snapped around.

Four men crowded a table near the center of the room. A girl was pinned between them and the wall, trapped in the small geography of their bodies and their intentions. Sixteen, maybe seventeen. Her dress torn at the shoulder, the fabric hanging loose in a way that suggested rough hands and rougher treatment. Face flushed. Eyes wide. Breathing fast.

One man had his hand clamped on her arm. Another laughed at something the third had said, a sound that had nothing to do with humor and everything to do with power. The third man leaned in close, speaking words Jamie couldn't catch but could interpret from the way the girl's face went pale.

The fourth had one eye. The other socket was just a dark pit, unashamed and uncovered, a charcoal absence that stared as effectively as the real one. Emptiness where an eye should be, and somehow that made it worse, made it harder to look away from.

"Is it the bloke with one eye?" Jamie asked, his voice low.

"Hush," Felix said.

The bartender arrived with the ales, moving quickly, efficiently, a man who wanted this transaction done. He set the mugs down carefully, his eyes flicking once to the girl, to the men surrounding her, then away again with the practiced speed of someone who'd learned long ago that seeing too much got you involved and being involved got you dead.

He retreated back to his bar. Not his problem. Didn't dare make it his problem. Couldn't afford to.

The one-eyed man stood. Slowly. His chair scraped stone, the sound cutting through the ambient noise like a bell tolling.

He was looking straight at Felix.

Something shifted in Felix's posture. A tightening across his shoulders that Jamie had learned to read. Felix's hand went still on his mug.

Robert Montague. Robert the Mean. The epithet was less creativity than it was a warning. been cashiered from a company for what he'd done to prisoners, once outside Bordeaux where Felix had ridden past a farmhouse and seen the aftermath of Robert's work, where the bodies had been arranged in ways that suggested someone had been conducting experiments in how long fear could keep a heart beating. Three mercenary companies had expelled him for conduct too brutal even for men whose profession was killing, which was less a moral stance than a practical concern about what his presence did to their ability to get hired again.

"You," he said.

His voice was loud enough to reach every corner of the tavern, loud enough to be heard over the drunken conversations and the scrape of chairs and the background hum of men avoiding their lives. Conversations thinned. Died. Heads turned. The room slid toward silence in the way rooms do when violence is incoming and everyone wants to see it but no one wants to be in arm's reach when it lands.

Montague was big. Early thirties. Built like someone who'd spent his life lifting heavy things and breaking harder ones, whose body had been forged in labor and violence until the two became indistinguishable. A worn leather patch covered the ruined socket now, the strap buried in greasy dark hair that hung past his collar. Scars crossed his face in pale ridges—blade scars, burn scars, the kind that suggested a history of pain survived and lessons learned the hard way.

He looked like Felix. Not in features. Not in coloring. But in the way his body advertised its history, in the map of violence written on skin and bone, in the understanding that came from having killed men and having nearly been killed in return and having survived both often enough that the distinction stopped mattering.

"The Black Rider, isn't it?" he called, and his smile widened. "I thought as much."

He came over. His men stayed where they were, but their attention had shifted entirely. The girl slipped out of the gap his standing had created, quick and low and smart, gone through the door before anyone bothered to notice she was no longer there.

The big man pulled out a chair uninvited and sat, turning it slightly so he could see both Felix and the room. The smile stayed in place. A friendly shape stretched over something that wasn't friendly at all.

"You're a legend, mate. I've heard the stories." He leaned in, elbows on the table, the posture of old friends catching up over drinks. "I'm a fan, actually. What brings you here?"

"Traveling a lot these days."

"Is that right?"

"Yourself?"

"Wee pint, is all."

Felix's gaze flicked toward the now-empty table where the girl had been, where torn fabric still lay on the bench. "And the girl?"

The man shrugged, the gesture dismissive, careless. "I've had better."

Felix lifted his ale. "I'll drink to that."

They clinked mugs. Drank. The ale was warm and bitter, but it did its job. Wet the throat. Bought time. Established terms.

The man set his down, wiped his mouth with the back of his hand, leaving a wet streak across his knuckles. He belched. Grinned. "Would you like a swing at her, then?"

"The whore in Wolfpine earlier tided me over," Felix said. Convincing enough. "Bit bitey, though."

The man laughed. Loud and too at ease. His men laughed with him from across the room, perfectly synchronized, like trained dogs responding to a whistle only they could hear.

"If I may," Montague said, the laughter dying as quickly as it had come, "what's a man like you doing in Warrington?"

"Hunting."

"Is that right?" The smile stretched further, pulling tight at the corners, becoming something harder. "From the Watch to skinning foxes by a campfire, are you?"

"I didn't mean foxes, mate."

The tavern went still.

Completely, absolutely still.

Sound bled out of it like water from a cracked cup. The drunk conversations stopped. The laughter died.

Montague's smile stayed fixed in place. His men across the room stopped their performance. Their attention snapped to Felix like hounds sighting movement in the brush, like predators recognizing another predator and understanding that the hierarchy was about to be determined.

The shift from buffoonery to readiness took less than a heartbeat. From drunk fools to killers.

The girl's absence felt less like luck and more like instinct now. She'd known. Had read the room better than any of them.

"When I heard Tobias' best man tuck and ran from Northbury, I couldn't believe it," Robert said. "Yet—here we are."

"Yes," Felix grinned. "Here we are."

"No longer with the crown, then?"

"Are you disappointed?"

"On the contrary." The man's single eye was very bright now, fever-bright, the gleam of someone who'd found what they were looking for and was savoring the moment before taking it. "Though I'd rather kill one of Taylor's dogs than that of a chewed-up stray."

They acknowledged each other across the scarred wood of the table. The space between them felt like the only real thing in the room, like everything else was backdrop, scenery, props for what was about to happen.

Jamie's fingers found the knife at his belt.

The man's hand moved toward his sword.

Felix kicked the table.

It came up like a breaking wave, all the weight and momentum of oak and iron fittings driving upward, catching Robert square under the ribs and lifting him backward. Chair and man went over together in a crash of wood and flesh and surprise. The man's back hit the floor hard enough to drive air from lungs.

One of his men across the room was already moving, hand disappearing under his coat, reaching for whatever he kept there.

Felix's arm flashed to his boot and snapped forward, steel crossing the room in a blink and ending in the man's throat.

Felix didn't watch him fall. Was already over the overturned table, sword drawn in one smooth motion, the blade singing as it cleared the scabbard. He closed on the remaining two men before they'd fully registered that their companion was dead.

Steel met steel with a crack that shook dust from the rafters, that made Jamie's teeth ache. The two remaining men came at Felix from opposite sides, trying to hem him in, trying to use numbers to compensate for skill.

He pivoted, turned their angles into problems for them instead of him, made their advantage his opening. They got in each other's way, had to pull strikes that would have made their ally plural.

Jamie pressed himself against a support pillar and watched, frozen in that useless half-crouch of men who haven't yet decided whether they're spectators or participants, whether they're brave enough to matter or smart enough to survive.

One swung high, a wild cut aimed at Felix's head. Felix ducked under it, felt the blade pass close enough to stir his hair, and rose into the man's guard. His elbow drove upward, caught the man square in the nose. Cartilage crumpled with a wet pop that carried in the sudden quiet. The man reeled backward, hands flying to his face, blood pouring between his fingers.

Felix's sword went into his gut while his hands were still up. Quick and businesslike. No flourish. Just steel finding flesh and doing what steel did. The man folded around the blade. Felix pulled it free. Let him drop.

The last man came in wild and desperate, all fear and adrenaline and no technique. Felix felt him more than saw him—that sixth sense that came from decades of violence, from fighting in the dark and the mud and the chaos where seeing didn't matter as much as knowing.

He turned. Dropped low. The blade skimmed through the air where his head had been, close enough that he heard it cutting nothing, then buried itself in the floorboards with a solid *thunk*.

The man jerked on the hilt, tried to wrench it free. It was stuck. Really stuck. Three inches of good steel wedged in old hardwood.

Felix's sword slashed across the back of his ankle. Just above the boot. Where tendon connected to bone. Where cutting meant a man stopped walking and started dying.

The tendons parted. The man shrieked—a sound that wasn't human, wasn't language, just raw animal pain—and crashed down. His hands left the sword hilt. Found his ruined ankle instead. Too late. Always too late.

Felix's follow-up cut to the throat was almost merciful. Ended the screaming. Let the man find silence.

Three down.

The overturned table shifted. Groaned. Then heaved aside like a lid being thrown from a coffin.

Robert the Mean rose.

Jamie had heard the name before, muttered in Eli's tavern by men who went quiet after saying it, who looked at their drinks rather than at each other while the story got told. Something about a woman and a scythe and hours of screaming in a farmhouse where Robert had been left alone with prisoners. The kind of story that didn't get embellished because the truth was sufficient.

The nickname wasn't colorful. It was accurate.

His face was red. Breathing hard. All the tavern charm was gone now, burned away like fog under sun. What stood there was just bulk and rage and the promise of violence delivered with interest.

He charged.

No technique. No strategy. Just forward momentum and bad intentions.

The impact drove Felix backward into a support beam. The sound of his back hitting wood was loud. Solid. Robert followed through, forearm across Felix's throat, pinning him there like an insect to a board. Felix's boots scraped for purchase on the floor. Found none. His hands came up, trying to create space, trying to breathe.

"I must say I'm impressed, Ryder," Robert said.

His voice was disturbingly calm. Conversational. Like they were still drinking ale and discussing nothing important. Like his men weren't dead at his feet. Like Felix's face wasn't going red from lack of air.

"But it's time to go home," Robert said, his breath hot and foul. "Except you haven't got a home anymore, do you?"

Robert drew his sword one-handed. The blade sang free of its scabbard.

It came up in a vicious arc meant to open Felix from skull to breastbone, meant to split him like firewood. Felix got his own sword up barely in time, the blades meeting with a sound that was part scream and part prayer. The force of it rattled down his arms, made his shoulders scream.

Robert kept pressing. Weight and strength and simple brutal momentum turning every clash into a slow defeat. This wasn't a duel. Wasn't even really a fight. It was a dismantling. Piece by piece.

They traded blows. Felix blocked. Parried. Tried to create distance. Robert closed it. Again. Again. Relentless.

Felix's breath came ragged now. His arms shook. Muscle fatigue setting in. He was strong and skilled and seasoned by decades of war and survival.

Robert was just stronger.

A boot snapped up, caught Felix's wrist with perfect timing. Pain exploded. His fingers opened involuntarily. His sword flew, skittering across the floor, spinning, coming to rest far out of reach against the far wall.

Robert raised his blade for the finishing stroke. Big. Overhand. Both hands on the grip.

Felix dove sideways. Threw himself. The sword came down where he'd been, bit deep into the wall, splinters exploding outward. Robert snarled, yanked the blade free with a wrench that sent splinters flying.

Felix kicked out from the ground, desperate, hooking Robert's ankle with his boot. The big man's feet went out from under him. He hit the floor hard, cursing, his sword spinning away.

Felix didn't waste the opening. Couldn't. He crawled hard for his own sword, fingers splayed, lungs burning, everything burning. His hand closed around the grip. Relief flared hot in his chest—

Robert was already up.

Standing. Breathing hard but standing. His sword recovered and lifted. The tip pointed down at Felix's chest. Executioner's position.

Felix rolled onto his back, trying to bring his own blade up, but the angle was wrong and his body was too slow, too tired, too broken from the impact and the blood loss and the simple accumulated weight of fighting men who were bigger and younger and fresher. He could see how this ended. Saw the cut landing. Felt the sureness of it settling over him like cold water, like acceptance, like the understanding that came when fighting stopped being about winning and became about how you died.

The sword began to fall.

It never hit.

Robert's face changed first. Confusion rippled across it, then something like surprise, mouth opening around words that wouldn't come, single eye going wide with the understanding that something had gone very wrong.

He looked down.

Steel jutted from his stomach. A long blade, driven clean through from behind, the point protruding from flesh and leather and mail, wet and red in the dim light. Blood ran down it in a steady curtain, dripped from the tip, pooled on the floor between his boots.

The sword slid back out. Robert crumpled forward like a puppet with cut strings, landing hard at Felix's feet, face hitting stone with a crack.

He didn't move after that.

Jamie stood behind him.

He held the dead man's sword in both hands. Knuckles white. Arms shaking slightly. The blade was red from point to guard, blood running down it in thin streams that dripped from the crossguard onto boots that would never be clean again.

His face had gone pale, freckles standing out like fresh scars against skin that looked waxy, bloodless. But his eyes were clear. Fixed. Almost bright. Focused with an intensity that suggested he was seeing everything and nothing, that he was present and absent in the same moment.

His first kill.

Something shifted in his expression. Moved behind his eyes. Not horror. Not guilt. Not the things you'd expect to see in a boy who'd just driven a sword through a man's spine. Something else. Something harder. A grim, crooked satisfaction, small but unmistakable, like hunger finding food, like thirst finding water, like a question being answered that he hadn't known he was asking.

"I'm thinking we split this one," he said.

Felix pushed himself to his knees. Slow. Everything hurt. His throat throbbed where Robert's grip had crushed it. His ribs screamed. But he was alive.

Because Jamie had acted.

He stared at Jamie. At the blood on his hands. At the sword he held like he'd been born with it. At the body cooling at his feet.

"Took you long enough," Felix rasped.

Jamie looked down at the sword in his hands. Turned it slightly, watching light move along the blade, feeling the weight, the balance, the way it sat in his grip as if it had always belonged there, as if all the months of training had been leading to this moment, to this weight, to this particular piece of steel.

"And I'm thinking this one belongs to me now," he said.

The tavern was empty. Had been for a while. The patrons had scattered the moment steel started singing, had fled through the door and the back rooms and anywhere that wasn't here. The only sounds were the tick of cooling metal, the drip of blood finding cracks in the floorboards, the labored breathing of two men who'd survived something they shouldn't have.

Felix retrieved his sword from where it had fallen. His helmet too. Checked himself for wounds that needed immediate attention. Found none that did.

He slid the helmet on. The world narrowed to two iron-rimmed circles.

"We should go," he said.

Jamie didn't argue.

Outside, the sun was too bright after the tavern's dim. Punishing. The lake beyond lay flat and blue, its surface undisturbed, reflecting the sky like a mirror, pretending nothing had happened twenty feet away, pretending the world was clean.

Their horses stood where they'd left them, patient and uninterested in human violence. They'd probably seen worse.

Felix mounted. Pain flared across his ribs, shot down his neck, settled into his bones like an old friend. Jamie swung into his saddle. The new sword hung from his belt, its presence a constant weight against his hip. Heavy. Real. His. Earned.

They rode away from Warrington Lake at an unhurried pace. Behind them, the tavern sat quiet, holding new story that would spread in slightly different versions up and down the roads for years, each telling embellishing differently until no one remembered what was true and what wasn't and it stopped mattering.

Jamie's hands were steady on the reins.

Felix glanced over once. Just long enough to see the change written on Jamie's face and recognize it the way one old soldier recognized another. Something had died in that tavern and something else had been born and the two would never meet again.

He said nothing.

The sun climbed toward afternoon. The day grew hotter. The road stretched ahead, empty and waiting. The lake fell away behind them. The tavern became a memory, then a story, then less than that.

And Jamie rode south with blood on his hands and a new sword at his hip and the understanding that he'd found something in that darkness that had been waiting for him all along.

SCENE 14

BY THE FIRE

Night settled over the camp in layers. The light went first, bleeding out of the sky in shades of gray and purple until only the treeline remained visible as a jagged black edge against darkness. Then the temperature dropped. Cold air slid down from the hills, moved through the pines, settled into the low ground where they'd made camp. Sound went last. The birds stopped. The wind quieted. What remained was the fire and the silence pressing in around it.

The fire had burned low. Just coals now, glowing red and orange at their centers, darkening to black at the edges where the heat had died. They threw enough light to see by but not much farther than the circle of stones they'd built to contain them. Beyond that, darkness. Complete. The kind that made you forget there was a world past the firelight.

Jamie sat cross-legged on the far side with a piece of parchment balanced across his knee. The quill in his hand hovered over the page, suspended in that space between wanting to write and not knowing what words would matter. The ink bottle sat wedged in the dirt beside him, cork pulled loose, the sharp chemical smell of it cutting through the smoke and pine resin that hung in the cold air.

Felix watched him from across the fire. His back rested against a fallen log, the wood rough and cold through his coat. A bottle of whiskey sat against his thigh, half-empty now, the glass catching firelight and throwing it back in amber. He'd been drinking since the sun went down. The measured kind. The kind that warmed without clouding, that kept the edges soft without blurring what needed to stay sharp.

Jamie wrote a line. His hand moved across the parchment with deliberate strokes. Then stopped. He stared at what he'd written. Scratched it out. The quill made harsh sounds against the paper, ink smearing where he crossed through words he couldn't make true. He tried again. Wrote two words. Stopped.

The only sound was the scratching of quill on parchment and the fire breathing and the occasional shift of wind through the trees overhead.

The horses moved in the darkness beyond the firelight. Their shapes were invisible but their presence announced itself in small sounds. Tack creaking. Hooves shifting in dirt. One of them stomped once, hard, then settled. The other nickered softly. A question or a comment. Then quiet.

The silence stretched. Held. Jamie's quill stayed frozen above the page.

Then he spoke, eyes still on the parchment. "Did it ever get easier?"

Felix lifted his gaze from the coals. His face was half in shadow, half painted orange by the dying light. "Did what get easier?"

"Killing a man."

Felix's thumb tapped against the bottle neck. Once. Twice. A small rhythm while he considered the question or considered how to answer it or considered whether answering mattered. He took a drink. Long. Slow. Let the whiskey burn down his throat and settle warm in his chest. Set the bottle back against his leg.

"It isn't meant to be," he said.

Jamie's hand stayed frozen, quill hovering, ink gathering at the tip but not falling. "Killing for crowns," he said. His voice had gone flat. "You almost make it sound like duty."

Felix shifted his weight against the log. The leather of his coat creaked. The sound loud in the quiet. "It's the work that's left to me."

Jamie didn't argue. Didn't push. Just let it sit there between them. The fire cracked softly. A coal split down the middle, showed a heart of bright red underneath, then darkened as air hit it. The night leaned closer. The cold came with it.

Finally, Felix nodded toward the parchment. "What is that you're writing?"

"A letter."

"To who?"

"A girl."

"Her name?"

"Lillian."

Felix inclined his head. "Pretty."

Jamie set the quill down. His fingers curled around it once, holding on like it might escape, then released. He looked at the fire now instead of the parchment. Stared into the coals.

"Her father couldn't pay the levy," he said. "Same as mine. Richardson gave him a choice."

He paused. Breathed. Continued.

"They took her from the house. Her father barely looked at her when they put her on the horse. Just stood there. Didn't move. Didn't say anything. They rode off and he went back inside before they'd cleared the gate."

An owl called once from somewhere in the trees. The sound carried across the darkness. Then nothing.

Felix kept his eyes on the boy's face. Jamie wasn't crying. Wasn't shaking. He was doing something worse. Staring at the letter with the look of a man who'd convinced himself it didn't matter. That writing wouldn't change anything. That she was already gone and pretending otherwise was just delaying the inevitable acceptance.

Felix knew that look. Had seen it in mirrors. In other men's faces right before they gave up. Death of resolve. The moment when fighting stopped being about winning and became about just waiting for the end.

Men broke quietly. This was how it started.

"I'm going to kill him," Jamie said.

Felix studied him across the fire. The words had landed without rage. Without heat. Just a statement delivered in the same flat tone you'd use to say you were going to fix a roof or shoe a horse. Truth accepted and carried forward.

"Do you have a plan?" Felix asked.

"No."

Felix let out a slow breath through his nose. Set the bottle down in the dirt beside him. Leaned forward slightly. "We'll need a plan," he said. Sharp enough to cut through the quiet before it swallowed the boy whole. "Something to get you inside the gates. Past the guards. Close enough to matter."

Jamie blinked. His head came up. He stared at Felix across the fire. "Really?"

"Your bloody letter won't get you far," Felix said. "Guard'll use it to light his pipe. You need access. You need a reason to be there that doesn't get you killed before you're three steps past the gate."

Jamie kept staring. Processing. "How?"

Felix shrugged. A small movement. Casual. The gesture of a man discussing something inconvenient but manageable. "Way in's always there. You just don't see it until you've no choice but to look."

Jamie looked back at the parchment. At his own handwriting. At the words he'd written and crossed out and tried again. His jaw shifted. Something flickered behind his eyes. A thought forming. Faint. Half-visible. A coal catching breath and glowing brighter.

Then his gaze drifted. Away from Felix. Away from the fire. Somewhere inward. Back through time and distance to a memory that hadn't mattered when he'd first seen it but was—

A flyer.

Damp.

Tacked crooked to a post outside Ed's shop in Wolfpine. The paper warped from rain. Ink half-run in places. A cracked crown crest at the top. A list of towns running down the page. Dates beside each one. Performances scheduled. The last line at the bottom: *Taylor's End*.

Performance at the castle.

By royal invitation.

He hadn't thought twice about it then. They'd been focused on corpses and crowns and cake and leaving before Ed got on another roll. The memory had slipped beneath the surface with everything else that didn't immediately threaten to kill him.

But now it rose.

Clean. Clear. Complete.

Jamie sat up straighter. His breathing changed. Quickened.

"The only ones who've been inside the castle this past year," he said. His voice quiet but gathering certainty. "The only ones who got past the gates without being questioned."

Felix looked over. Waited.

"Shakespeare," Jamie said.

Felix blinked. "What?"

"His men. Theatre companies." Jamie's words came faster now as the pieces locked together. "Barnaby Oddfellow's troupe. They're touring. Ending at Taylor's End. Inside the castle. Performing for the King."

Felix tensed. A small tightening around the eyes. A man hearing the name of a place he'd spent twenty-four years avoiding.

Jamie didn't notice. He was leaning forward now, hands on his knees, eyes bright with the first real hope Felix had seen in him since Wolfpine.

"They come through every couple years," Jamie said, his breath visible in the cold air, white vapor dissipating. "Barnaby tried for Shakespeare's company in London years back. Didn't make it. Started his own troupe instead. They do the touring circuit. Small towns. Cut-down versions of the big plays. Half-length Romeo and Juliet. Shortened comedies. The kind of thing poor folk can afford and nobles will still watch when they're bored."

Felix rubbed a hand over his jaw. The stubble rasped under his palm. "And Lionel fancies himself a patron."

"Exactly." Jamie nodded. Fast. Certain. "He built that stage after Shakespeare performed there in the nineties. Had carpenters working on it for months. Everyone in Taylor's End talked about it. He calls the performers his guests. Treats them like visiting dignitaries. If Barnaby's troupe is scheduled to perform inside the hall, if we can get to Northbury before they leave—"

Felix closed his eyes. Just for a moment. Long enough to steady something old and unwelcome that was shifting in his chest. The name of the place. The memory of what it had been. What it still held. What returning there would cost.

He opened his eyes. Looked at Jamie. At the boy who didn't know the castle he wanted to infiltrate was the same castle Felix had fled from twenty-four years ago with a newborn in his arms and blood on his hands.

Jamie stood. His breath came quick, visible in the cold, white clouds that hung briefly then vanished.

"This could work," he said. Half to himself. Half to Felix. Half to the darkness that surrounded them. "This could actually work."

Felix didn't answer. Just watched the boy. The resolve rekindling in real time. The doubt burning away. The future pulling him forward with a level of force that couldn't be stopped even if you wanted to stop it.

And beneath all that observation, Felix felt the pull too. Felt it in his chest and his gut and his bones. Two months of circling England. Two months of taking bounties and moving and staying ahead of the past and telling himself he was helping the boy without committing to anything that would bring them too close to the place he'd sworn never to see again.

All of it had been delay. Postponement. Running cosplaying as moving forward.

Northbury lay on the road he'd spent half his life avoiding. The road that led to Taylor's End. The road that led back to the castle where the woman he'd loved had died.

Jamie had finally said the one thing that turned them around. Had found the path that Felix had known was there but hadn't wanted to acknowledge. Had made returning inevitable.

"In the morning, then," Felix said.

Jamie nodded. Sat back down. Picked up the quill with steady hands now. Finished the letter. Folded the parchment when he was done. Creased it twice. Laid it beside his bedroll where he could see it. A promise made tangible. A reason to keep moving forward.

He settled onto his back. Pulled his cloak over his shoulders. Stared up at the thin slice of sky visible through the branches overhead. Stars had come out. Cold points of light in the black. His breathing slowed. Deepened.

Felix stayed awake. Watched the fire collapse into itself. Watched the coals darken and die. Felt the cold move in as the heat faded.

He looked at Jamie. At the boy's face gone slack with sleep. At features that carried echoes Felix couldn't ignore even when he wanted to. The blonde hair that caught what little light remained. The shape of his jaw. The way his mouth relaxed when he wasn't holding himself so tightly controlled.

Felix had seen that face before. In different circumstances. In a different time. On a woman he'd loved and lost and spent twenty-four years trying to forget because remembering made the running harder.

He pushed the thought away. Reached for the bottle. Found it empty. Set it aside.

The night deepened around them. The fire went out completely. Just ash now. Gray and cold. The darkness moved in to fill the space where light had been. The horses shifted and settled. The wind changed direction. Brought the smell of water and stone down from the hills.

Felix stayed awake while Jamie slept. Stayed with the weight of what morning would bring settling onto him. The journey to Northbury. The theatre company. The slow work of getting inside the castle. Getting close to Lillian. Creating the conditions that would let Jamie try the rescue he was going to try regardless of whether it was smart or survivable.

The boy would attempt it. Would walk into that castle and go for the girl they'd taken from him. Would probably die doing it.

Felix knew this. Had known it since the moment the plan formed. Had known it before that. Had known it since the day he'd found Jamie in the cannibal camp and realized protecting him was impossible but necessary anyway.

The only question was whether Jamie died alone or whether Felix died with him.

The answer had been decided twenty-four years ago. Was being decided now. Would keep being decided until one of them or both stopped breathing.

Felix leaned his head back against the log. Let his eyes close halfway. Rest without sleep. The quiet that came when choices were made and waiting was all that remained.

By morning the fire would be ash and the path toward Northbury would be waiting. Open. Clear. Irreversible.

The way to Taylor's End. The way home. The way back to everything Felix had spent his life running from.

The night held them both. Kept them. Let them rest in the small space they'd carved from wilderness and time.

And the world turned toward dawn with the same indifference it had shown every dawn before. Carrying them forward into whatever waited. Recording nothing. Promising less.

SCENE 15

BARNABY ODDFELLOW

Northbury appeared in the morning light like a place that had given up on being seen. Fog sat low over the town, thick and wet, clinging to the ground the way regret clung to old decisions. It muffled sound. Dimmed color. Made the whole place feel provisional, temporary, a sketch of a town rather than the thing itself.

Jamie had been here before. Years ago. He remembered it differently. Livelier. More. But memory had a way of flattering the past, of adding warmth and noise and life that probably hadn't been there to begin with. What remained now was small. Narrow roofs hunched against each other for warmth or protection or the simple comfort of not being alone. Windows shuttered. Chimneys barely smoking, as though embarrassed to announce their presence. No people. No movement. Just fog and frost and the hollow sound of hooves on hard ground.

They rode side by side down the main street. Their horses'

hooves struck earth that had frozen overnight, each impact producing a dull thud that echoed and died quickly in the dampened air. Nothing stirred. No vendors setting up stalls. No dogs slinking through alleys looking for scraps. No shopkeepers unlocking doors or sweeping steps. Just the fog swallowing everything and the faint ghost of their passage behind them.

The town felt held. Waiting.

They stopped in front of a darkened storefront near the end of the street.

A wooden sign hung crooked from two rusted chains above the door. The wood was old. Warped. The paint had peeled in long strips that curled away from the grain, revealing gray wood underneath. What letters remained were faded but still legible:

Barnaby Oddfellow's Traveling Stage Co.

The sign swayed slightly in the breeze. The chains creaked. A sound that suggested both movement and decay, traveling and barely alive.

Jamie dismounted first. His boots hit the ground. Cold shot up through his legs. He looked at the sign. At the peeling paint. At the rust eating through the chains. At the dark windows that suggested no one had been inside in days or weeks or longer.

Felix swung down a moment later.

They stood there. Looking at the storefront. At the sign. At what remained of Barnaby Oddfellow's theatrical ambitions.

"This is promising," Felix said.

Jamie said nothing. Just turned his attention to a poster nailed to a wooden post beside the shop. The paper was cheap. Damp. The edges curled. The ink had run in places where rain had gotten to it.

The image was something between ambitious and tragic. Someone had attempted to draw a dragon. Had failed. What remained was a bloated lizard-thing breathing what was clearly meant to be flame but looked more like steam or possibly fog. Thick. Formless. Unthreatening. A prince stood nearby—at least Jamie assumed it was a prince based on the crown someone had sketched above his head—thrusting a sword in the general direction of the dragon without any apparent conviction that the weapon would do anything useful.

Above the image, in shaky hand-lettering that suggested either haste or incompetence or both:

THE DRAGON AND THE PRINCE — A GRAND EPIC

Jamie stared at it. Felix stared longer. His face showed nothing. Just studied the poster with the kind of attention you gave to things that defied immediate categorization.

After a long moment, Felix spoke. "We should try for the leads."

Jamie turned to look at him. "We're not here to act. We need access. That's it. In and out. In fact, we'd be better off limiting our time onstage, especially because—"

"I have an idea," Felix said, already moving toward the door.

Jamie let out a quiet sigh.

The door opened with a creak that suggested pain. Old hinges protesting movement. Wood scraping against a frame that had warped over time until opening and closing had become an act of violence against the building's structural integrity.

Inside, the air was stale. Dead. It smelled of mildew and old paint and something else Jamie couldn't quite name. Disappointment, maybe. The particular scent of dreams that had died slowly over years rather than all at once. The smell of a place that had never seen better days and had stopped pretending it might.

The room was dim. What light existed came through warped windowpanes in thin shafts that cut through the gloom at odd angles. Dust hung suspended in those beams, each particle drifting slowly, caught between descent and suspension, auditioning for a role in a play that would never be performed.

The space was small. Cramped. A desk sat near the front, buried under loose parchments and old scripts and what looked like costume pieces that had been cannibalized for parts. Shelves lined the walls, sagging under the weight of more scripts, more fabric, more evidence of theatrical ambition that had curdled into something closer to hoarding.

At the desk sat a man who looked as though life had compressed him for convenience. Barrel-shaped torso. Short arms. Legs Jamie couldn't see but assumed were proportional to the rest. Pallid skin. Thinning hair combed over a scalp that showed through in places. Two beady eyes set deep in a face that had learned to expect disappointment and was rarely surprised.

Barnaby Oddfellow, presumably.

He was writing something on a curled sheet of parchment. His quill moved with a certain intensity that suggested whatever he was writing mattered deeply to him and to no one else. He didn't look up when the door opened. Didn't acknowledge their presence. Just kept writing.

"We're closed," he said. His voice carried the flat resignation of someone who'd said those words too many times to bother inflecting them with meaning.

Jamie and Felix stood just inside the doorway. Jamie glanced at Felix. Felix's face showed nothing. Just waited. Patient. The way you waited for small men with small authority to finish performing whatever ritual made them feel important.

Jamie stepped forward. Cleared his throat. "Are you the director?"

Barnaby sighed. A long, theatrical exhalation that suggested the question had caused him physical pain. He set his quill down with exaggerated care. Capped it. Placed it precisely parallel to the edge of his desk. Then, finally, looked up.

His expression made it immediately clear he regretted acknowledging their existence.

"Lord," he said. Not quite a prayer. Not quite a curse. Something between. "How can I help you lot?"

Jamie felt Felix's presence behind him. Large. Still. Waiting. He forced himself not to look back. "We were hoping to audition."

Barnaby's eyes narrowed. Suspicious. The look of a man who'd been disappointed before and had learned to spot it coming. "Part of the Union, are you? I sent for talent months ago. Heard nothing back. Typical."

"No, sir."

"Then what are you?"

Jamie hesitated. The absurdity of the situation hit him again. Two killers standing in a failed theatre asking to pretend to be actors so they could infiltrate a castle and murder a knight. The plan sounded more insane every time he thought about it. "Just a pair of dreamers."

Barnaby's eyes closed briefly. Whether from pain or prayer or the simple exhaustion of dealing with idiots remained unclear. When he opened them again, his expression had shifted. Gone harder. More pragmatic.

"Well, casting has concluded," he said. Then, after a pause, eyes narrowing further: "Unless you're actually actors?"

"Yes, we—" Felix started.

"Travelers, more like," Barnaby cut in. His gaze moved between them. Assessing. Dismissing. He gestured vaguely at the sagging beams overhead, at the building that was slowly collapsing around them. "Do either of you happen to be adept at carpentry?"

Jamie blinked. "Sorry?"

"Carpentry!" Barnaby's voice carried the exasperation of someone explained something obvious to someone stupid. "We are desperately scarce in that department. The stage is held together with hope and spite. Mostly spite." He looked Jamie up and down. "You look like a strapping young lad. Strong back. Good hands. Carpentry?"

Jamie had no idea what to do with that. Behind him, Felix's silence felt dangerous.

"I suppose I could—" Jamie started.

"Splendid." Barnaby was already making notes on his parchment. Scribbling. Not looking up. "And you." He raised his gaze. Way up. Had to crane his neck back to meet Felix's eyes. His quill froze midair. "The big fellow."

"I'd like to audition," Felix said. His voice was flat. Empty. The tone that preceded violence.

Barnaby's attention returned to his parchment. Safer there. "Casting is closed, my large friend. I do apologize. But I can certainly jot you down for our subsequent tour, which will be—" he checked another sheet, squinted at faded ink, "—next fall. Yes. Next fall. Wonderful."

Felix took a single step forward.

Just one.

The floorboards groaned. Not a small sound. Not the usual creak of old wood under weight. This was deeper, the sound wood made when it was being asked to bear more than it was designed to handle and was considering surrender.

The inkpot on Barnaby's desk rattled. The quill rolled. A stack of scripts piled precariously on the corner of the desk swayed, tipped, and fell. They hit the floor in a soft cascade of paper and failure. Dust shook loose from the rafters overhead. Drifted down through the shafts of light. Settled on everything.

Barnaby froze. His hand hovered over the parchment. His eyes went very wide. His throat moved. Swallowed. The sound was audible in the sudden quiet.

Felix leaned in. Not close. Not touching. Just enough to occupy Barnaby's entire field of vision, to make it clear that the desk between them was furniture and furniture could be moved or removed or ignored entirely if necessary.

"I'd like to audition," Felix said again.

The room held its breath. Even the dust seemed to pause its descent. Waiting.

Barnaby's pupils had dilated. Pure Mammalian response. The part of his brain that still remembered being prey recognizing something large and dangerous and very close. His hand trembled slightly as he set the quill down. Carefully. Deliberately. The movement of someone trying very hard not to make any sudden gestures that might be interpreted as threat or flight.

"Well," he whispered. His voice cracked halfway through the word. "Let's see what you've got."

Felix straightened. Stepped back. The pressure in the room eased. Barnaby sucked in air like he'd been holding his breath and hadn't realized it.

Jamie watched this unfold with the detachment of someone who'd seen Felix intimidate people before and knew exactly how it would end. There was something almost routine about it now. Felix entered a space. The space adjusted. People recalibrated their expectations. Everyone moved forward with a clearer understanding of where they stood.

Barnaby was looking at them differently now. Not as dreamers or travelers or idiots who'd wandered in off the street. As something else. Something that required careful handling.

He cleared his throat. Tried to reassemble some dignity. Failed. Tried again.

"Right," he said. His voice steadier now but still thin. "An audition. Yes. Of course." He shuffled through papers on his desk. Looking for something. Not finding it. Looking again. "We're currently preparing The Dragon and the Prince. Grand epic. Very... ambitious. We'll be performing at several towns along the route to Taylor's End, culminating in a royal performance at the castle itself."

"Taylor's End," Jamie said, attention sharpening. Careful to keep his voice neutral. Interested but not too interested. "Inside the castle?"

"Indeed." Barnaby had found what he was looking for. A script. Tattered. Stained. He held it up like evidence. "King Lionel is a great patron of the arts. Built his own theatre. Invites companies to perform regularly. We are honored to have been selected."

Selected, Jamie thought, probably meant they were the only company desperate enough to accept whatever Lionel was paying.

"And you need actors?" Felix asked.

"We need... many things," Barnaby said. He was looking at Felix with a mixture of fear and calculation. The fear was genuine. The calculation was professional. A theatre director's instinct recognizing that a man Felix's size could be useful in certain roles. "What experience do you have?"

"Enough," Felix said.

"That's wonderfully vague." Barnaby set the script down. Folded his hands on the desk. Tried to project authority he clearly didn't feel. "What roles have you played?"

"Soldiers, mostly."

"Ah. Yes. Well." Barnaby's eyes traveled up and down Felix's frame. Taking in the height. The breadth. The way he stood. "I suppose we could use you as the dragon."

Silence.

Felix stared at him. His expression didn't change. But something in the quality of his stillness shifted. Became more focused. More dangerous.

Jamie cleared his throat. "Perhaps something with fewer... scales?"

Barnaby blinked. Looked between them. Realizing he'd made an error. "Of course. Of course. I merely meant... the physicality of the role requires someone of substantial... that is to say..." He trailed off. Regrouped. "We have a guard. Several guards, actually. They serve the prince. Protect him from the dragon. Very heroic. Noble. Would that interest you?"

"Yes," Felix said.

"Wonderful." Barnaby was writing again. Making notes. His hands had stopped shaking. "And you." He looked at Jamie. "Carpentry, was it?"

"I'd also like to audition," Jamie said.

Barnaby paused. Set his quill down. "For?"

"The prince."

Barnaby's eyes narrowed. "Have you any experience with theatre?"

"No."

"Can you project your voice?"

"When necessary."

"Do you understand the concept of dramatic irony?"

"No."

Barnaby leaned back in his chair. It creaked ominously. "This is highly irregular."

"We'll work cheap," Jamie said.

That changed things. Barnaby's expression shifted. The calculation overtaking the skepticism. theatre companies lived on tight margins. Performers who worked cheap were performers you hired and competence was what you worried about later.

"How cheap?" Barnaby asked.

"Passage to Taylor's End," Jamie said. "Food. A place to sleep. That's it."

Barnaby stared at him. Trying to understand the angle. Trying to figure out why two men would work for almost nothing just to travel with a failing theatre company to perform in a castle. His eyes moved to the sword at Jamie's hip. To Felix's armor. To the way they both stood. Alert. Ready. Men who'd seen violence and weren't afraid of it.

Something like understanding moved across his face. Not complete understanding. Just the vague awareness that these men had reasons he didn't want to know about and wouldn't beg after.

"Very well," he said finally. "You'll report tomorrow at dawn. We depart for Snakewater in three days. Then Taylor's End." He picked up his quill again. Started writing. Dismissing them. "If you're not here at dawn, I'll assume you've reconsidered."

Jamie nodded. "We'll be here."

"I'm certain you will be," Barnaby said, not looking up, his tone suggesting he was already regretting this decision but couldn't quite bring himself to reverse it.

Jamie turned toward the door. Felix followed. They stepped out into the fog and the cold. The door closed behind them with the same pained creak it had opened with.

They hesitated, silent, watching the quiet, foggy street and the still-sleeping town.

"The dragon," Felix said finally.

Jamie almost smiled. "He didn't mean it as an insult."

"Didn't he?"

"He's desperate. Desperate men make poor choices."

Felix looked at him. "We're desperate men making poor choices."

"Yes," Jamie said. "But ours might work."

They moved to their horses. Mounted. Sat there in the saddles for a moment, looking back at Barnaby Oddfellow's Traveling Stage Company. At the peeling paint. At the terrible poster. At the doorway they'd just walked through and would walk through again tomorrow.

This was the plan. This was their way into Taylor's End. Into the castle. Close enough to Lillian to matter.

It was insane. Fragile. Built on the cooperation of a failed theatre director and the assumption that no one would look too closely at two new guards in a production of a play about a dragon and a prince.

But it was what they had. And what they had would have to be enough.

"Dawn," Felix said.

"Dawn," Jamie agreed.

They turned their horses. Rode back the way they'd come. The fog swallowed them. The town returned to its silence. And somewhere behind them, in a cramped office that smelled of mildew and disappointment, Barnaby Oddfellow added two names to a cast list and wondered what exactly he'd just agreed to.

SCENE 16

THE TERRACE

The terrace was the prettiest part of her prison.

White stone columns rising twenty feet, their capitals carved with roses and thorns. The sun came in slanted now, late afternoon, painting everything gold and amber. Vines had climbed the supports over years, thick green stems spiraling upward with the patience of things that grew and didn't care about human time. Red blooms hung heavy on the stems, nodding in the breeze. Petals fell. Drifted down into the manicured gardens below. The gardens where everything was trimmed and ordered and arranged according to Lionel's vision of how beauty should present itself.

Below the terrace, the kingdom stretched out in perfect geometric patterns. Hedges cut into straight lines. Paths meeting at right angles. Flower beds arranged by color and height. Order imposed on nature through violence so consistent it looked peaceful.

Margaret sat on a low bench carved from the same white stone as the columns. Her hands were folded in her lap. Her back straight. Her face still.

A guard stood outside the archway leading back into the castle. His spear tapped stone. Once. Announcing. "His Majesty."

Lionel stepped onto the terrace.

He wore a black-and-gold cloak that caught the afternoon light and reflected it back in sharp points. His hair had been trimmed recently. His stubble shaped. Rings gleamed on every finger. A king dressed for apology the way other men dressed for court.

Margaret didn't rise, nor did she bow or even so much as turn her head. She simply sat there, hands folded, back straight, looking at the gardens.

Lionel stopped a few paces away, just far enough to maintain the fiction of giving her space.

"Margaret," he began, as if speaking to a frightened child prone to bolt, "I believe I do owe you an apology."

She lifted her eyes to him.

They were clear. Flat. Absent of redness.

Lionel faltered. The words he'd prepared caught in his throat. He'd expected emotion, anger, tears, something he could react to.

"I never meant for it," he said, though the words stumbled slightly. "Your father forced my hand. His insubordination left me no choice. I had to make an example. Still, my decorum..."

Margaret said nothing.

"I would have spared you the sight. I can imagine you—"

"No."

Lionel blinked. "I'm sorry?"

"You cannot imagine it."

A muscle jumped under his eye. "I am attempting to mend what was broken between our families. You are safe here. Protected. The past is behind us, Margaret."

Her gaze drifted away from him and back to the gardens. To the hedges trimmed to perfect lines, the ornamental pond that sat still and polished and reflected nothing but sky. Beauty arranged by force. Order maintained through constant correction.

"My father is behind us," she said. Her voice quiet. Empty. "The past isn't."

Lionel shifted his weight. Uncomfortable. The rings on his fingers caught sunlight. Threw it back. He didn't like being uncomfortable. Didn't like feeling off-balance in a conversation he'd initiated. "Hatred clouds judgment, my dear."

"There is no hate in my heart." She looked back toward the horizon. "I only wait."

"For what?"

"For my brother."

Something shifted beneath Lionel's carefully constructed exterior. Just a flicker. Gone before it could be named. But there.

"Your brother fled." He cleared his throat. "My scouts have found no trace of him. He is likely dead. The wilderness—"

"He lives," Margaret said, quiet as snow falling, certain as stone. "He is strong and stupid and mad and he has an army and he will kill you."

Lionel squared his shoulders. Adjusted his posture. His mouth opened. Closed.

"The thing about boys who lose everything, Your Grace," Margaret said, "is they stop being boys."

"You are speaking dangerously—"

"I speak fact. My brother will come. He will walk through those gates and you won't see him for what he is until it's too late. And when he stands over you, when your crown is in the dirt somewhere and your blood runneth as black as your heart, you will remember this communication. You asked how I felt, Your Grace. This is how."

She rose and walked inside.

Lionel sat alone on the terrace. The whole world spread out below him, the kingdom arranged just so. Everything in its place, in order.

But the ground suddenly felt a little less solid. The light a little less bright.

And the future, most certainly, less guaranteed.

SCENE 17

Damien fastened the oiled coat across his chest in the courtyard behind the castle, where the stones ran black with rain. The garment hung heavy on his shoulders, hooded and long, the fabric darkened to the color of char. Lightning split the sky above the northern hills, throwing the battlements into brief, skeletal relief. His horse—a black destrier, tall and silent—stood waiting, its breath steaming in the cold.

He mounted without speaking. The guards at the postern gate didn't ask where he was going. They never did.

He rode north into the countryside, into the rain. The storm moved with him, thunder rolling low across the fields. Lightning struck again, closer this time, illuminating the road in jagged white. The hood shadowed his face entirely. From a distance, he might have been nothing—a shape, a rumor, something the rain conjured and would take back when it was done.

The hut crouched low in the reeds like something

half-drowned. By the time Damien arrived, the rain had lessened to a cold drizzle, the sky hanging low and gray above the marsh. The light was dying. Water beaded on the oiled fabric of his coat. His boots sank into the mud without sound, each step swallowed by the wet earth. The air smelled of rot and standing water and something older—peat, perhaps, or the smell of things that had been buried and forgotten.

The door—if it could be called that—hung crooked on leather hinges, and through the gap he could see the flicker of a tallow candle inside. No smoke rose from the chimney. The reeds pressed close around the hut, as though trying to reclaim it.

He didn't knock.

The old woman sat facing the door, her hands folded in her lap. She wore black, layers of it, stained and worn thin at the elbows. Her hair was white as fish-bone, braided tight against her skull. Her eyes were milk-clouded, nearly sightless, but they fixed on him the moment he entered, as though she'd been watching the door for years.

"Long have I waited."

Her voice was dry, accented, the consonants hard and strange. Romanian. Damien stood in the doorway, his shoulders filling the frame. Water dripped from the hem of his coat onto the warped floorboards. He didn't remove his hood.

"What took, child?" she asked.

He stepped inside. The hut smelled of smoke and rot and something sharper—herbs, perhaps, or old blood. Jars lined the walls, filled with murky liquids, animal bones, twisted roots. An icon hung above her cot, the paint peeling: the Virgin, her face long and severe, holding a child wrapped in red. The candle guttered in its dish, throwing shadows that climbed the walls like vines. The flame bent toward him as he moved, as though drawn by his presence.

Damien closed the door behind him. The latch clicked softly. The room seemed smaller with him in it, the walls pressing inward.

"You know why I come," he said.

He moved to the center of the room, his head nearly brushing the rafters. The floorboards groaned beneath his weight. He didn't sit. The candlelight carved his face into planes of shadow and bone. His eyes, dark and unblinking, settled on her.

The old woman smiled. Her teeth were brown, uneven, jagged.

"Thou comest for the boy."

"Tell me what you know."

She tilted her head, birdlike, as though listening to something he couldn't hear. Her hands trembled in her lap, not from fear but from age, from too many years holding too much weight. The tremor moved up her wrists, into her arms. Outside, the wind moved through the reeds with a sound like breathing.

"I brought him into the world," she said. "These hands pulled him from the dark. Beneath his tongue lay the sign—three drops, black as pitch, turned bright as stars. Yellow-haired, blood-slick. Eyes green as spring grass, eyes that see into the bone of a man. Death followed him from the womb, but death wouldn't take him. Death turned its face away."

Damien took a step closer. The floorboards groaned. His shadow fell across her, swallowing the candlelight. She didn't flinch.

"Where?"

She laughed—a wet, rattling sound that caught in her throat.

"Why dost thou hunt a ghost?"

Damien's hand rested on the pommel of his knife. His fingers curled around the grip, slow and deliberate. The leather was cold beneath his palm.

"Ghosts don't bleed," he said.

The old woman's breath quickened. Her hands began to tremble harder now, clutching at the fabric of her skirts. The candle flame dipped and swayed, casting her face in and out of darkness.

"He is the one the earth will not forget," she whispered. "The true king."

"There is no true king."

"Thou art wrong!"

Her voice cracked on the last word, rising to something almost like triumph. Damien crouched before her, his knees creaking. The oiled coat spread around him like wings. He brought his face level with hers, close enough that he could see the milky film across her eyes, the broken veins in the whites. Close enough to smell the sourness of her breath.

"I care not what you believe, witch," he said. "Where was the bastard taken? What was he named?"

She stared at him, and for a moment her face softened, as though she pitied him. Her clouded eyes seemed to focus on something behind him, or beyond him—something he couldn't see.

"Already thou art a corpse. Died the night thy hands closed upon thy father's throat."

"The boy, you crone."

She closed her eyes. Her lips moved, soundless at first, then forming words in a language he didn't recognize. Romanian, perhaps, or Latin, or something else. The candlelight dimmed, as though the flame itself recoiled from the words. When she opened her eyes again, they were wet with tears that traced clean lines down her weathered cheeks.

"I see him," she said, her voice rising, trembling with ecstasy. Her body began to rock, forward and back, her hands twisting in her lap. "I see him even now! Hair like wheat, blood like fire! The weight of crowns in his very bones! He will break thee! He will bury thee! He will..."

Her expression flattened into something unreadable, her tone dropping into cold fact.

"He will kill thee."

Damien stood. Water still dripped from his coat, pooling at his feet. Outside, the wind had died. The reeds were silent.

"You understand what I must do?" he asked.

She stopped. Her mouth hung open. She stared at him, and then she smiled again, wider this time, her brown teeth bared like an animal's.

"Swine," she said.

Damien stood motionless.

"Swine," she said again, louder now. "Swine, swine, swine..."

Her voice rose, filling the small space until it pressed against the walls. The word became a rhythm, a curse, a prayer. Damien moved behind her, his boots silent on the warped floor. Something slid into his hand with a soft, practiced click. She didn't turn. She kept chanting, rocking back and forth, her hands clawing at her skirts. Her fingers left dark streaks in the fabric.

"Swine, swine, swine, swine!"

He placed his hand on the crown of her head, steadying her. His palm covered her skull completely. The chanting grew louder, frantic, joyful, as though she were welcoming something long-awaited.

"Swine, swine, swine, swine!"

The blade entered the base of her skull with the ease of a key into a well-worn lock. She stopped mid-word. Her body went slack, her head lolling forward against his hand. Damien withdrew the blade and stepped back. Blood ran down her neck, dark and slow, pooling in the hollow of her collarbone before spilling onto her black dress where it disappeared into the fabric like water into earth.

Damien flexed his wrist. The blade slid back into his sleeve, leaving his hand empty again.

The candle flame steadied. The shadows stopped moving.

He didn't look at the old woman again. He stepped out into the marsh, into the gathering dark, and the reeds closed behind him like water.

Damien's quarters sat in the north tower, where the stone held the cold even in summer. The room was spare—a bed he rarely used, a table, two chairs, a wooden tub in the corner. No tapestries. The blade on the mantle. Documents covering his desk like fallen leaves.

He entered and bolted the door.

The candles had burned low. He lit two more from the hearth and set them on the desk. The light fell across the parchments—some official, others older, brittle, written in hands long dead. Birth records. Guard rotations. Kitchen inventories.

Testimony from servants who'd worked the castle in 1578.

His eyes moved across the pages.

One document lay separate, weighted by stone. An illustrated account from the royal physician, dated *November 1578*. The illustration showed a woman kneeling beside a bed—dark hair braided tight, foreign features, hands pressed to a prone belly. Beneath, in cramped Latin: *Obstetrix Valachiae—midwife, Romanian, summoned by order of the Queen. Departed before dawn. No record of payment.*

His finger traced the edge of the parchment.

He crossed to the corner. The tub sat there, wide and shallow. Filled nearly to the brim with blood, pig's blood, still warm.

He removed his coat. His shirt. His boots.

He stepped in.

The blood rose to his waist as he sat. He leaned back. Warmth pressed against his ribs. His breathing slowed. His jaw loosened. One hand drifted beneath the surface, fingers spreading, then closing. He exhaled.

His shoulders eased.

The candles flickered. The room silent except for liquid settling against wood.

He closed his eyes.

Yellow-haired. Green-eyed. Twenty-four.

South.

A tremor ran through him—brief, involuntary. His head tilted back against the rim. His breathing steadied into something almost still.

He sat.

The candlelight moved across the surface, bronze and black.

After a time, he opened his eyes.

SCENE 18

PERCIVAL MCGUIRE & TEDDY IVANOVICH

The rehearsal hall was a barn that had been asked to pretend otherwise.

Someone had hung velvet curtains along the far wall—burgundy, moth-eaten, sagging in the middle like a drunk leaning against a lamppost. Candles had been placed in holders that looked borrowed from a church and never returned. The floor was still hay-strewn in the corners, and the air held the faint memory of livestock, though the animals themselves had been relocated or perhaps simply died of embarrassment.

Barnaby Oddfellow stood at the center of it all, arms folded, watching two actors murder a scene.

The actors in question were named—according to the call sheet pinned near the door—Mortimer Slade and Humphrey Vole. Mortimer was meant to be the Dragon. Humphrey, the Prince. What they were actually doing defied easy categorization. Mortimer moved like a man trying to remember where he'd left his keys. Humphrey delivered his lines with all the conviction of someone reading a ransom note aloud for the first time.

"Come forth, vile flame," Humphrey intoned, "and meet thy fated end." He thrust his wooden sword in Mortimer's general direction. The thrust had all the menace of a man pointing at a menu item he wasn't sure he wanted.

Mortimer responded by raising both arms and producing a sound that was presumably meant to be a roar. It came out closer to the noise a cat makes when you step on its tail. He waved his arms. The motion suggested less ancient terror and more vigorous disagreement with a street vendor's prices.

Jamie stood against the side wall, arms crossed, watching this unfold with a horrified fascination. Beside him, Felix was motionless. His face showed nothing. But Jamie had learned to read the nothing on Felix's face, and this particular nothing contained multitudes of judgment.

"By crown and oath," Humphrey continued, voice cracking on the word 'oath' like a boy entering puberty mid-sentence, "thy reign I shall suspend!"

Mortimer hissed. Actually hissed.

"*Stop*." Barnaby's voice cut through the barn. "Stop. Please. For the love of everything sacred, stop!"

Mortimer and Humphrey froze mid-gesture, caught in poses that would have looked absurd even in context. Out of context, they looked like men who'd been cursed by a witch with a sense of humor.

Barnaby approached them slowly. His short legs carried him across the hay-strewn floor with the deliberate pace of a man walking toward a grave he'd been asked to dig himself. He stopped. Looked up at Mortimer. Way up. His expression contained the particular exhaustion of someone who had seen too much and been paid too little.

"Mortimer," he said. "The Dragon is an ancient creature. Wise. Terrible. Capable of incinerating armies with a single breath." He paused. Let that settle. "You are playing him like a man who has just realized he's left the stove on."

Mortimer opened his mouth to protest. Barnaby held up a hand.

"And *you*." He turned to Humphrey. "The Prince. Noble. Brave. A warrior who has trained his entire life for this moment." Another pause. "You're delivering his battle cry like you're asking a shopkeeper if they have any more in the back."

"I was trying for understated," Humphrey offered.

"You achieved it. In fact, you achieved it so thoroughly that the understatement itself is embarrassed." Barnaby's hands came together in a gesture that was half prayer, half plea for death. "There is a difference between restraint and absence. One is a choice. The other is a void. You, my friend, are currently a void."

From somewhere near the back of the barn, Jamie heard a small laugh. Sharp. Musical. Like someone who'd been trying not to and had failed.

He turned. Found the source.

She was leaning against the wall near what passed for wings; a dirty-blonde girl in peasant clothes, rough linen that suggested work rather than costume. Knuckle gloves made of hide covered her hands, the leather worn smooth in places, cracked in others. A scar ran beneath her right eye, thin and pale.

She was watching the stage. Or had been. Now she was watching Jamie.

Her eyes held his. A half-smile played at her mouth—knowing, amused, as if she'd just caught him doing something he shouldn't and was deciding whether to tell. Then she winked. A single deliberate gesture that conveyed both flirtation and accusation in equal measure.

Jamie looked away. Looked back at the stage. Tried to pretend his neck hadn't gotten warm.

Barnaby had dismissed Mortimer and Humphrey with a wave that suggested he'd already forgotten their names and was happier for it. He consulted a curled sheet of parchment, squinting at ink that had probably been legible once.

"Percival McGuire," he called out, "and Teddy Ivanovich."

The names hung in the air like bad smells. Jamie felt Felix's eyes on him. The names had been Jamie's idea, scrawled on the signup sheet in a moment of panic when the registrar asked for something official. He'd meant them to sound distinguished. Continental. They sounded like a cheese merchant and his foreign creditor.

Neither moved.

"Percival McGuire and Teddy Ivanovich," Barnaby repeated, louder, the way you'd call for a dog that was pretending not to hear. "For the Dragon and Prince roles. If you exist, now would be an opportune moment to demonstrate it."

Jamie pushed off the wall. Walked toward the makeshift stage. His boots sounded too loud on the floor. Every step felt observed, catalogued, judged. Behind him, Felix followed. The floorboards groaned under his weight, adding their own commentary.

Barnaby looked up from his parchment. His eyes traveled from Jamie to Felix. Then up. Way up. The journey took several seconds.

"Ah," he said. "You."

"Us," Jamie agreed.

Barnaby's expression cycled through several emotions in quick succession: regret, resignation, and something that might have been indigestion but was probably just despair. He handed Jamie a tattered script.

"You'll read the Prince. Page four. The confrontation scene." He turned to Felix. "Mr. McGuire. You'll be The Dragon. Same page. Try not to terrify anyone."

Felix took his script. Said nothing. His silence had a quality to it that made Barnaby take a small step backward, a movement that seemed involuntary, the body's wisdom overriding the mind's politeness.

Jamie looked at the page. The words swam.

"Whenever you're ready, Teddy," Barnaby said. There was a slight emphasis on the name. A testing. An acknowledgment that he knew it wasn't real and was choosing not to press.

Jamie cleared his throat. Found the line. Opened his mouth.

"Come forth, vile—" His voice cracked. Not dramatically, like Humphrey's. Just cracked. A dry splinter of sound that died before it reached the back wall. He stopped. Tried again. "Come forth, vile flame, and meet thy—" He stumbled over 'thy.' The word felt foreign in his mouth, something borrowed that didn't fit.

Somewhere behind him, he heard that laugh again. The girl. Watching.

"Fated," Barnaby supplied, his voice flat as old bread. "Fated end."

"—fated end," Jamie finished. The words came out wrong. Hurried. Like he was trying to get through a door before it closed.

He tried the next line. Got through it. The one after that, too. But something was missing—the thing that made words mean something beyond their dictionary definitions. He was reciting. Not speaking. Not believing. Just... producing sounds in the correct order and hoping that would be enough.

It wasn't enough. He could tell by Barnaby's face. By the way the small man's shoulders had begun to slump. By the increasingly frequent glances toward the ceiling, as though help might descend from the rafters.

Finally, Jamie reached a line that felt almost possible. "By crown and oath, thy reign I shall suspend." He said it with something approaching conviction. Not much. But something. A small flame of actual emotion flickering beneath the stilted words.

Barnaby's eyebrows rose a fraction. "Better," he said. Not praise. Just acknowledgment that things had improved from terrible to merely bad. "Hold that. Whatever that was. Hold it." He turned to Felix. "Now you."

Felix hadn't moved during any of this. Had stood with the script in his hand, unread, as though the words on the page were irrelevant to whatever was about to happen.

Now he stepped forward. Just one step. But something changed.

Jamie saw it happen. Had seen it before, in different contexts, but never quite like this. Felix's shoulders shifted. Dropped slightly. His spine straightened, but not rigidly—it was the straightening of something that had been coiled and was now extending. His chin rose. His eyes changed. Not the color. The depth. As though whatever usually lived behind them had retreated, and something else—something older, stranger, less human—had taken its place.

When he spoke, his voice filled the barn. Not loud. That was the unsettling part. It wasn't loud at all. But it reached everywhere, settled into corners, made the candle flames shiver in their holders.

"Who dares disturb the silence of my tomb?" The line landed like thunder. "The steel-born whelps who ride on wings of doom?"

The barn went quiet. Not silent—there was still the distant sound of horses outside, wind against the walls, the small creaks of old wood—but the people in it had stopped making noise. Stopped breathing, some of them.

Felix moved. Slowly. The movement of something that had no need to hurry because nothing in the world could threaten it. He raised one hand, fingers slightly curved, and the gesture somehow suggested claws without being claws, suggested fire without showing flame.

"Always with blades," he continued, and now his voice held something like sorrow, ancient and weary, the grief of centuries compressed into five syllables. "Never with words."

Jamie realized he'd taken a step back. Hadn't meant to. His body had simply decided, without consulting him, that distance was wise.

Barnaby Oddfellow stood frozen. His mouth had fallen open slightly. His eyes had gone wet—not crying, not yet, but close. The look of a man who had spent years watching mediocrity parade itself as art and had just been ambushed by the genuine thing.

"I dream of peace," Felix said, and now he was looking directly at Jamie, or through him, or at something Jamie couldn't see, "of skies unmarred by screams. Of quiet minds. And young men brave with dreams."

The last word hung in the air. Faded slowly. Like smoke from an extinguished candle.

Silence. Complete. The kind that followed something that couldn't be followed.

Then, from the back of the barn, a single clap.

Jamie turned. The girl—the blonde with the scar and the knowing eyes—was applauding.

Others joined. Mortimer and Humphrey, looking somewhat ill, as though they'd just been shown how unnecessary they were. A few stagehands. Someone who might have been a costumer. The applause built, spread, became something close to an ovation; small, provincial, happening in a converted barn that smelled of hay and regret, but genuine.

Felix blinked. The thing behind his eyes retreated. He looked around at the clapping people with an expression Jamie had never seen on him before: confusion. Pure and unguarded. As though he'd gone somewhere else during the performance and had only just returned to find everyone staring.

Barnaby approached him. Had to tilt his head back to meet Felix's eyes. There were tears on his cheeks now, actual tears, trailing into the creases of his face.

"Where," he said, voice thick, "where did you learn to do that?"

Felix said nothing. Because there was nothing to say. He hadn't learned it. That was the point. That was the thing that made it terrifying.

"You—" Barnaby had to stop. Compose himself. Wipe his face with a sleeve that had seen better days. "You have something. I don't know what to call it. Instinct. Truth. The thing you can't teach because it's either there or it isn't, and most of the time it isn't, and you spend your whole life watching people pretend they have it when they don't, and then—" He gestured helplessly at Felix. "Then this."

Felix's mouth twitched. Almost a smile. So brief Jamie might have imagined it. A crack in the armor, there and gone.

Barnaby turned to Jamie. The tears were still drying on his

cheeks, but his expression had shifted to something more complicated. Kinder perhaps, but also pitying.

"And Teddy," he said. "Your performance was..." He paused. Searched for a word. Found one. "Inspiring."

Jamie stared at him. "Inspiring."

"Yes," Barnaby nodded. "You inspired me. To remember that not everyone is born with talent, and yet they try anyway. There's something noble in that. Something almost heroic." He patted Jamie's arm. The gesture was meant to be comforting. It felt like a diagnosis.

Jamie opened his mouth. Closed it. There was nothing to say to that that wouldn't make things worse.

"And don't fret about the Prince," Barnaby added, almost as an afterthought. "We've a proper boy from Ashford joining us at first light. Loud voice, good posture. You'll stay with carpentry, Ivanovich, where you might actually prove yourself useful."

Jamie absorbed that. It wasn't a demotion. It wasn't a promotion. It was... the truth. The work that had always made more sense in his hands than words ever did.

"We leave for Snakewater at dawn," Barnaby continued, already moving away, already thinking about other things. "Get your things. Get some sleep. The road is long, and the accommodations are..." He waved vaguely. "Present."

He disappeared into the backstage gloom, trailing broken dreams and artistic disappointment like a comet trailing dust.

Jamie stood there. Felix stood beside him. Neither spoke.

Across the barn, the blonde girl caught Jamie's eye. She was still smiling. Still watching. She mouthed something—two words, he thought, though he couldn't quite read them—and then she turned and vanished through a side door, leaving only the memory of her amusement behind.

SCENE 19

The caravan smelled of sawdust and old paint.

Jamie sat on a wooden crate that had once held stage props and now held his weight with a grudging tolerance that suggested it might change its mind at any moment. The interior of the wagon was cramped, cluttered with the debris of traveling theatre: costume pieces draped over hooks, masks staring from shadows, a collection of wooden swords that looked like they'd been through more battles than most actual weapons.

Across from him, on an identical crate, sat the blonde girl.

She was staring at him. Had been staring at him since the wagon lurched into motion half an hour ago. Not speaking. Not looking away. Just... watching. With those knowing eyes and that half-smile that seemed permanent, etched into her face like the scar beneath her eye.

Jamie had tried ignoring it. Had studied the ceiling planks. Had counted the masks on the wall (seven). Had examined his own hands as though they contained secrets worth learning. None of it helped. Her attention was a physical thing, a weight against his skin.

Finally, he snapped.

"Staring problem, do you?"

Her smile widened. When she spoke, her voice carried an accent—Irish, he thought, the vowels rolling differently than English ones, musical in a way that seemed intentional. "Problem implies I'm not enjoyin' myself. I'm enjoyin' myself quite a lot, actually."

"Glad someone is."

"You're not? Shame." She shifted on her crate. Crossed her legs. The movement was casual, but Jamie noticed how her eyes never left his face, cataloguing reactions. "Most people find me delightful company."

"Most people haven't been trapped in a box with you for thirty minutes."

"An hour, by the time we reach Snakewater." Her smile became something closer to a grin. "Plenty of time to become friends. Or enemies. Depends on how the conversation goes."

Jamie leaned back against the wagon wall. The wood creaked. "You're weird. You know that?"

"At least I am who I say I am."

The words landed in the space between them. Stayed there. Jamie felt something cold move through his chest—not fear, exactly, but its first cousin. The girl's expression hadn't changed. Still smiling. Still amused. But her eyes had sharpened.

"I don't know what you're talking about," he said.

"Of course not." She examined her gloved hands, as though the conversation had become secondary to something far more interesting happening with her fingers. "Teddy Ivanovich. That's a name, that is. Sounds like something you'd make up if someone asked you for a fake name and you panicked."

"It's real."

"It's real because you're sayin' it. Doesn't make it true." She looked up. Met his eyes. "You were almost convincing right then. You should use that on stage. Audiences adore a liar."

Jamie said nothing. There was nothing to say that wouldn't dig the hole deeper.

The wagon hit a rut. Everything rattled. A mask fell from its hook and landed face-up on the floor, empty eyes staring at the ceiling.

"Miranda Quinn," she said finally. "Carpentry. Backstage work. The invisible labor that makes the visible labor possible."

"A girl in carpentry?"

Her eyebrow rose; a single, eloquent arch. "A boy with opinions?"

"I just meant—"

"You meant what you meant. Most people do." She didn't seem offended. If anything, she seemed pleased, as though his predictability was a kind of gift. "I'm good with my hands." She held them up. Turned them over. The gloves were worn thin at the knuckles. "Always have been. My da taught me. Said there was no point having a daughter if she couldn't build her own coffin when the time came."

"Bit grim."

"Irish. We're born grim. Come out the womb already disappointed by the shite weather."

The wagon rattled on. Light came through gaps in the wood, thin and gray, the color of a sky that couldn't decide if it wanted to rain.

"Where's your father now?" Jamie asked. He wasn't sure why. Didn't usually care about other people's histories. But there was something in the way she'd said 'was' that made him curious.

Miranda was quiet for a moment. Longer than he'd expected. When she spoke, her voice had lost some of its edge.

"Gone," she said. "Went out hunting one morning. Never came back. Like he'd walked into the forest and the forest had decided to keep him."

"I'm sorry."

"It was years ago." She shrugged. "I waited. For a while. Kept thinking he'd come through the door, tell me it had all been some mistake, some adventure taken longer than expected. But doors don't work that way, do they? People leave and they don't come back, and after a while you stop expecting them to."

She looked at him. Something in her expression had shifted. The armor was still there—the wit, the sharpness, the knowing smile—but behind it, just for a moment, was someone else. Someone that still waited for doors to open even though they knew better.

"You know what that's like, do you?" she said. "People leaving. Not coming back."

"Yeah," Jamie said. "I know what that's like."

Miranda nodded.

Then the wagon lurched again, harder this time.

"We're stopping," Miranda said. Her voice was back to normal; light, quick, that musical Irish lilt restored. "Snakewater. This should be fun."

"Fun?"

"Fun in the way that stepping in something unpleasant is fun. You look down, you say 'well, that's happened,' and you move on." She stood. Stretched. Her joints popped. "It's a gambling town. Full of people who've bet wrong and are looking for someone to take it out on. Smile at the wrong person, you'll lose teeth. Smile at all, you'll lose teeth. The teeth situation is precarious generally."

She moved toward the wagon's rear door. Paused. Looked back at him.

"Whoever you are," she said, "whatever you're doing here, be careful. This isn't the kind of place to fuck about."

Then she was gone, out the door and into whatever waited beyond.

Jamie sat for a moment. Let her words settle. Then he followed.

SCENE 20

Snakewater announced itself by smell before sight.

The air changed as they descended toward the town—grew heavier, wetter, thick with something organic and wrong. Marsh rot. The particular stench of water that had stopped moving and started decaying, of vegetation breaking down into slime, of things dying in shallow pools and being absorbed back into the mud.

Then the town itself emerged from the haze.

It was built on stilts. Had to be. The ground was more water than earth, a maze of channels and pools that caught the fading light and held it, oily and still. Wooden walkways connected buildings that leaned against each other like drunks too tired to stand alone. Everything was crooked. Everything sagged. The whole place looked like it had been assembled in a hurry by people who didn't expect it to last and had been proven right.

The sun was already low, though it couldn't be much past

midday. Something about the geography—the surrounding hills, the perpetual mist rising from the marsh—made Snakewater a place where daylight arrived late and left early, as though even the sun didn't want to see what happened here.

Jamie stepped down from the wagon. His boots sank slightly into the soft ground. Around him, the rest of the company was disembarking, voices too loud, movements too quick—the nervous energy of people entering unfamiliar territory and trying to pretend they weren't afraid.

Felix materialized beside him. Silent. Watchful. His eyes moved across the town with the slow deliberation of someone cataloguing threats.

"Something's wrong," Jamie said. Quiet. Meant only for Felix.

"Yes."

They stood together, watching.

People were watching back.

Men lined the main walkway—if it could be called that—leaning against posts, sitting on crates, standing in doorways. They weren't doing anything. That was the problem. They were just... present. Observing. Their eyes followed the theatre company with the attention you gave to something you were measuring. Calculating. Deciding what it was worth and how hard it would be to take.

Jamie caught one man's gaze. Held it. The man didn't look away. Didn't blink. Just stared, his expression flat and empty, as though Jamie were a piece of furniture that had momentarily confused him by moving.

The women were different. The few he could see moved quickly, eyes down, following paths that seemed designed to avoid attention. One passed within a few feet of him—young, pale, carrying a bundle of something wrapped in cloth—and she didn't look up. Not once. Her shoulders were hunched. Her steps were small. She moved like someone trying to take up as little space as possible, to exist so quietly that the world might forget she was there.

From somewhere nearby came the sound of metal on stone.

Rhythmic. Deliberate. Jamie turned toward it.

A blacksmith's forge stood at the edge of the main square—if the muddy clearing surrounded by gambling dens could be called a square. The smith was outside, working a blade against a whetstone. But he wasn't working. Not really. The strokes were too slow. Too careful. He'd sharpen, pause, hold the blade up to what passed for light, turn it, examine it. Then sharpen again. The same motion. Over and over. Like a ritual. Like a threat being polished.

The sound cut through the ambient noise of the town. The splash of footsteps on wet wood. The distant calls of marsh birds. The low murmur of voices from inside buildings. All of it faded, and what remained was that scrape of metal on stone, patient and persistent, the sound of something being made ready.

Jamie watched the smith. The smith watched him back. Neither spoke.

Nearby, Barnaby was shouting directions, organizing the company, trying to impose order on chaos. His voice seemed thin here. Swallowed by the marsh air. The words reached Jamie's ears but lost their meaning somewhere along the way.

Jamie shouldered a crate of timber from the wagon—set pieces they'd need to rebuild the stage in whatever passed for a square here.

Miranda appeared at his elbow. He hadn't heard her approach.

"Lovely, isn't it?" Her voice was low. No irony in it this time. "Really makes you feel welcome."

"Is it always like this?" Miranda rested a hand on the rolled backdrop beams—her department more than anyone's—and tapped a loose dowel with a carpenter's instinct for what might break under strain.

"I've never been." She was scanning the buildings, the walkways, the watching men. "But I've heard stories. The kind that make you choose a different route, if you can." She glanced at him. "We couldn't. Snakewater's the only stop between here and Taylor's End that has anything like an audience. Barnaby needs the money."

Here we are, Jamie thought. In a town that felt like a trap that hadn't quite closed yet. Where the men watched like predators and the women moved like prey. Where the sun left early and the dark came on fast and no one seemed surprised by any of it.

Felix hadn't moved. Was still standing where Jamie had left him, a dark shape against the gray sky, watching the smith, watching the men, watching everything with eyes that missed nothing.

Jamie thought about the castle they were trying to reach. About Richardson. About the mission that had brought them here, to this muddy, rotting corner of nowhere.

Somewhere in the town, a door slammed. The sound echoed across the marsh, flat and final. The smith kept sharpening.

Scrape. Pause. Turn. Scrape. Pause. Turn.

Night would come. Jamie could feel it pressing in from the edges, eager to arrive.

In Snakewater, he suspected, night was when the real business happened.

He followed the company toward whatever passed for lodgings, and the watching eyes followed him, and the sound of that blade against stone followed him too, and none of it stopped even after he'd passed out of sight.

SCENE 21

THE ROYAL COUNCIL

The chamber was cold despite the candles. The light they cast was thin. Yellow. It made the shadows deeper rather than chasing them away, pooled in the hollows of old men's faces, caught the gold thread in Lionel's robes and made it look like something dying.

The table ran the length of the room. Black stone, polished by generations of hands and elbows, cold to the touch even in summer. Twelve chairs flanked it, high-backed, carved with the Taylor crest. Eleven were occupied by men in ceremonial robes, lords and advisors who had served the crown longer than Lionel had been alive. The twelfth held Damien.

He sat at the far end, opposite Lionel, his black armor absorbing candlelight rather than reflecting it. The gold trim at his collar and cuffs caught occasional flickers, small sparks in all that darkness. His hands rested on the table. His face was still. He hadn't spoken since the meeting began. Hadn't needed to.

Lord Falstaff stood at the table's midpoint, sheaves of parchment spread before him. His robes were the deep burgundy of his station, trimmed with ermine gone yellow with age. His hands trembled slightly as he sorted through reports. Old hands. Liver-spotted. Hands that had signed treaties and death warrants and letters of condolence for forty years.

"The latest dispatch arrived this morning, Your Grace." Falstaff's voice carried the particular weight of bad news delivered too many times. "Our scouts confirm that Peter Beverley's forces have grown. Significantly."

Lionel sat at the head of the table. His robes were black and gold, heavy on his shoulders, damp at the collar. His fingers rested on the surface. He watched them. Watched the way they'd begun to tap without his permission. A rhythm. Nervous. Uncontrolled.

He stilled them. Pressed flat.

"How significantly?"

"Three times what he commanded a fortnight ago, Your Grace. Perhaps more." Falstaff turned a page. The parchment whispered against itself. "He's rallied the Strays. Mountain men in Harthfell who've never bent the knee."

"Three times." Lionel heard his own voice from a distance.

"Nearly two thousand men, Your Grace."

The chamber was silent. Eleven old men sat in their carved chairs and said nothing. Their eyes moved between Falstaff's reports and Lionel's face.

Lionel's throat felt tight. "And where are they now?"

"That is the difficulty, Your Grace." Falstaff set down one sheaf and lifted another. "He was last confirmed in the foothills four days past. A substantial encampment. Cookfires. Latrine trenches. Signs of long occupation."

"Was."

"Our forces arrived to find it abandoned. The fires still warm." Falstaff looked up. "He knew we were coming. Moved into the mountains before we arrived."

The candles flickered. A draft from somewhere. The flames bent sideways, recovered, bent again.

"Two thousand men don't vanish."

"In Harthfell they do, Your Grace. The mountains have hidden armies before. The passes are narrow. The forests thick. A man who knows the terrain—" Falstaff trailed off.

Lionel's hands were shaking now. Visibly. Before he could attempt to hide it, the tremor had traveled up his arms, into his shoulders, settled in his chest where his heart had started in on his ribs.

"We'll send more men. A larger force. Enough to—"

"We've no men to spare, Your Grace." This from Lord Ashworth, seated halfway down the table. "The northern garrisons are committed. The harvest levies have been called. If we strip the borders—"

"Then *strip* them." Lionel was half-standing, palms flat on the table, arms trembling with the effort of holding himself upright, looking like a man thrice his age. "Strip them bare. I want Peter Beverley's head on a pike before—"

A sound.

Small. Barely audible. But Lionel heard it the way a wounded animal hears the snap of a twig.

Lord Wynn sat two chairs to Lionel's left. Old. Gray-bearded. A man who had served three kings and survived them all by knowing when to nod and when to stay silent. But now his mouth had betrayed him. A soft exhalation through his nose. A sound that might have been a sigh or might have been a chuckle. His lips pressed together too late, suppressing something that had already escaped.

Lionel turned his head. Slow. The motion of something mechanical.

"Something amuses you, Lord Wynn?"

His voice didn't sound like his own. Flat. Dead. The voice of a man who had passed through terror and come out somewhere else entirely.

Wynn's face went pale. "Your Grace, I meant no—"

"You laugh."

"A cough, Your Grace. The hour is late and I am old and—"

The candleholder was right there. Iron. Heavy. Meant to

hold a single taper, weighted at the base to keep it upright. It sat at Lionel's elbow where it had sat throughout the meeting, its flame guttering in the drafts, casting shadows across his hands.

He grabbed it before he knew he was going to.

The candle fell. Rolled across the table trailing smoke.

Lionel was already swinging.

The iron base caught Wynn across the temple. The old man's head snapped sideways. His chair tipped. He went down hard, one arm tangled in his robes, the other coming up too late to shield his face.

"Your Grace!"

Falstaff's voice. Or someone's voice. The sound had gone strange, muffled, as though the chamber had filled with water. All Lionel could see was Wynn on the floor, Wynn's eyes, the fear in them that mirrored his own fear, that had *laughed* at his fear, that had seen his weakness and found it amusing.

He swung again. Missed. The iron struck stone and the impact jarred up his arm. He swung again. Connected. Wynn's hands came up and the candleholder smashed through his fingers. Bone cracked. Blood spattered. Wynn screamed. The sound was high and thin.

"Please—" Wynn was trying to crawl. Trying to get under the table. Away. Anywhere. His broken fingers left red smears on the black stone floor. "Your Grace, I beg you, I have children, I have—"

Lionel followed. Grabbed the back of Wynn's robes. Hauled him out from under the table. The old man weighed nothing. Fear made men light. Fear made everything light except the iron in Lionel's hand, which had grown heavier with each ugly, awkward swing, which wanted to fall, which fell now across the back of Wynn's skull with a sound like nothing Lionel had ever heard.

Wet. Final. The particular music of something ending that should not have ended.

Wynn's body jerked. Once. His hands clawed at the stone, fingers scraping, leaving marks. Then he was still.

Lionel stood over him. Breathing hard. The candleholder

hung from his grip, its iron base dark with blood that caught the remaining candlelight and gleamed. His robes were spattered. His face was spattered. He could feel it cooling on his skin, could taste copper in his mouth though he hadn't been struck, though none of this blood was his.

The chamber was silent.

Eleven men sat frozen in their chairs. No one had moved. No one had tried to stop it. It had happened too fast, erupted and ended in the space of seconds, and now they sat with their hands on the table and their mouths open and their eyes fixed on the body of their colleague spreading blood across the floor.

Falstaff's parchments had scattered. They lay in the pooling red, ink bleeding, reports on troop movements and supply lines dissolving into evidence of something else entirely.

At the far end of the table, Damien sat exactly as he had throughout. Still. Watchful. His face was expressionless beneath the weight of his armor.

But his mouth twitched.

Just once. A flicker at the corner of his lips. There and gone so fast that anyone watching might have imagined it. A smirk. Small. Private. The expression of a man watching something he'd expected finally come to pass.

Lionel, out of breath, hair strewn, faced the council, though his gaze was elsewhere, somewhere far removed.

"This council is adjourned."

He let the candleholder fall.

No one moved as he walked toward the door. His boots left prints in Wynn's blood, marking his passage, marking what he'd done, marking the very moment when an idiot king became something worse.

The door opened. Closed.

In the chamber, eleven men looked at each other across the ancient table, and the remaining candles guttered, and the blood spread slowly toward their feet, and no one said a word.

Falstaff lowered himself into the nearest chair. His face was gray. His hands shook worse than Lionel's ever had.

"God help us," he whispered. "God help us all."

At the far end of the table, Damien rose. His armor made no sound as he moved. He walked to where Wynn's body lay and stood over it for a long moment, studying the ruined skull, the broken fingers still curled in supplication, the particular devastation that fear and iron could accomplish together.

Then he stepped over the corpse and followed his king.

His footsteps echoed down the corridor like a promise.

SCENE 22

COSTUMES

The sun bled out across the marsh in shades of rust and rot. Last light caught the standing water and turned it to hammered copper, beautiful in the way that poisonous things are sometimes beautiful. The company had made camp on the only dry ground they could find, a slight rise at the edge of town where the mud conceded to something that could be called soil.

Miranda was helping unload the costume wagon when Felix appeared beside her, though most of what she touched wasn't silk or sequins but the collapsible stage braces shoved under the costume trunks.

She hadn't heard him approach. Never did. For a man his size, in armor that weighed more than she did, he moved like smoke.

"You smell like a horse fucked a grave," she said without looking up.

"And yet you keep following me."

"Someone has to make sure you don't get lost." She hauled a trunk off the wagon bed, let it drop, straightened with her hands on her hips. "At your age, the mind goes first."

Felix grunted. It might have been a laugh. Hard to tell with him. He stood watching the sun die over Snakewater, his scarred face catching the red light, turning the old wound into something that looked fresh. Raw. The burn tissue at his neck glistened.

"Charming town," he said.

"Isn't it? I've already been propositioned twice."

"Only twice?"

"The night is young." She wiped her hands on her breeches. They came away muddy. Everything in Snakewater came away muddy. "That blacksmith's been staring at me since we arrived. The one with the whetstone."

Felix didn't look at the smith. He looked past him, at the shadowed walkway behind the forge, the upper balcony, the dark-handled door half-open two buildings down. Whatever had his attention wasn't the man with the whetstone.

"I noticed."

"'Course you did. You notice everything." She turned to face him fully. The last of the light was fading now, shadows pooling in the hollows of the town, creeping up from the water like something hungry. "So what's the play, old man? We perform tomorrow and move on? Or does Snakewater have other plans for us?"

Felix was silent for a moment. His jaw worked. That thing he did when he was thinking thoughts he wouldn't share.

"Stay close tonight," he said finally. "Keep your knife where you can reach it."

"I always keep my knife where I can reach it."

"I gathered that." He looked at her then, and it was in the way he rarely did, with something behind his eyes that might have been respect or might have been worry or might have been both tangled together in ways that couldn't be separated.

Then he walked away. His armor didn't make a sound.

Miranda watched him go. The marsh breathed around her,

insects beginning their evening chorus, water moving beneath the boardwalks with a sound like whispered secrets. The blacksmith was still at his forge. Still sharpening. The scrape of metal on stone carried across the twilight like a promise.

She touched the knife at her belt. Felt its weight.

"Fucking strange," she muttered.

Night came on fast.

SCENE 23

EYES IN THE NIGHT

The stage leaned like a dying animal, its stilts crooked, its boards swollen from years of marsh moisture and neglect. Barnaby insisted the show must go on, even as the platform sagged under its own weight. Snakewater gathered for it anyway. Not with curiosity, but with the stillness of creatures who had crawled out of the reeds to watch something bleed.

Men stood in a loose semicircle, arms crossed, shoulders hunched. Women slipped behind them quickly, heads down, moving like shadows trying not to be noticed. Children were absent. Not a single small face peering from behind a skirt or doorway. That was the first sign something was wrong. Towns this poor always had children underfoot, hungry for spectacle. Their absence made the whole square feel abandoned in spirit, even with forty people present.

The air smelled of marsh rot and woodsmoke layered over something deeper. Something almost sweet and organic. The odor of vegetation that had died but refused to finish the job. Every breath carried the damp heaviness of a place that didn't want outsiders inhaling its air for long.

Jamie crouched behind the stage with a hammer in one hand and a fistful of bent nails in the other. The platform above him groaned with every footstep. The boards were warped. The joints were wrong. He'd spent the last hour trying to reinforce struts that should have been replaced entirely, driving nails into wood so soft with damp that they sank without resistance.

"Hand me the rope."

Miranda was beside him, her sleeves rolled past her elbows, her hands black with pitch. She'd been working the rigging for the dragon puppet, such as it was. A system of pulleys and counterweights that was supposed to make the beast descend from the heavens. In practice, the beast was a patchwork of canvas and salvaged cloth that looked like laundry hung to dry, and the descent was more of a controlled fall.

She passed him the rope without looking. Her eyes were on the crowd.

"They're not talking," she said.

Jamie followed her gaze. Thirty people, maybe forty, arranged in that loose semicircle. They should have been murmuring. Commenting. Shifting weight, scratching, coughing. The small sounds that crowds make when they gather. But these people were silent. Still. Watching the stage with the flat attention of men appraising livestock.

"Maybe they're just quiet folk."

"Quiet folk murmur. They cough. Whisper. Shift." Miranda's voice tightened. "Look at their hands."

Jamie looked. The men in the front row had their arms crossed or their hands in their pockets or their fingers hooked through belt loops. Casual postures. Relaxed. But their weight was forward. Balanced on the balls of their feet. Ready to move.

She'd said the same thing once in Rivermouth. That time, she was right.

"Shit," he said.

"Yeah."

Above them, the stage creaked. Thomas walked across the boards carrying a torch meant to represent the dragon's fire. Old Morris followed with the crown. He didn't look like himself. Face pale. Breath shallow. Eyes unfocused, moving like someone half-absent from his own body. Humphrey was somewhere in the wings, struggling into the chorus robes that had been patched so many times they looked like quilts.

The Ashford boy Barnaby had promised that morning stood center stage. He was playing the Prince. Seventeen years old, recruited three towns back when their last juvenile lead drank himself blind and fell off a bridge. He had good posture. Strong jaw. A face that might have sold tickets in a proper theatre.

But his hands were shaking. Jamie could see it from twenty feet away. The scroll he held trembled like a leaf in wind.

"Here in this quiet cell of dust and page," the boy began, his voice thin, swallowed by the marsh air before it reached the back row, "I trace the wordes of every ancient sage..."

No one in the crowd reacted. No lean forward. They just watched, silent, their faces catching the last of the daylight.

From somewhere nearby came the sound of metal on stone. Rhythmic. Deliberate. The blacksmith was at his forge on the edge of the square, visible through a gap between buildings. He sat on an overturned crate, working a blade against a whetstone. The scraping cut through the boy's recitation, louder than his voice, more insistent. He wasn't even looking at the stage. Just sharpening. Scrape. Pause. Turn. Scrape.

The Ashford boy faltered. Lost his place. Found it again.

"Beyond these walles, the kingdome spreads its weight, ore simple folke who labour, watch, and wait..."

Jamie turned back to his work. The hinge on the trap door was bent. He'd been trying to straighten it for ten minutes. The metal was rusted through in places, flaking orange under his fingers. He worked the claw of his hammer into the gap and pulled. The hinge bent further in the wrong direction.

"*Fuck.*"

"Let me." Miranda took the hammer. She had a different grip, a different angle. The metal groaned and shifted. Not fixed, but functional. Maybe. "That'll hold until act three. After that, we pray."

Jamie's hands worked faster than his mind. Carpentry had always done his thinking for him.

"We should be praying now."

She almost smiled. The expression died before it reached her eyes.

On stage, the boy had reached the entrance of the Dragon. The pulleys groaned. The canvas beast descended from its position above the backdrop, jerking and swaying, one wing already torn free of its frame. It looked like a corpse dangling from a broken gallows. It spun lazily, ridiculous, tragic.

Mortimer Slade stood beneath it, wrapped in his patchwork cloak, arms raised in what was supposed to be menace. He was sixty years old. His knees cracked when he walked. His voice had been a ruin since before Jamie joined the company.

"WHAT MORTAL DARES APPROACH MY—"

The roar cracked. Broke. Became a cough. Mortimer doubled over, hacking into his sleeve, the cloak slipping from his shoulders. Someone in the wings scrambled to retrieve it. The canvas dragon swung overhead, its rigging tangled, spinning slowly in circles.

Children would have laughed, had there been any.

Adults didn't.

They simply watched.

The blacksmith kept sharpening.

Jamie found himself scanning for Felix. Found him at the edge of the square, thirty feet from the nearest spectator, standing with his back to a listing wall. He wasn't watching the stage. He was watching the crowd. His arms hung loose at his sides. His weight was centered. His eyes moved in slow sweeps, cataloging faces, registering positions, tracking the small movements that preceded larger ones.

The crowd had noticed him too. Or rather, they had noticed something without knowing what. There was a gap around Felix. An empty space that no one stood in, no one walked through. The spectators flowed around him like water around a stone, unconsciously maintaining distance, giving him room they didn't know they were giving.

Felix's eyes met Jamie's for a moment. Held. And Jamie felt, briefly, as though Felix wasn't guarding the stage at all. As though he was waiting for something. Then his gaze moved on.

On stage, the Ashford boy was trying to recover the scene. His voice had found a register somewhere between speaking and shouting, too loud for the intimacy the scene required, too soft to carry authority. He gestured with hands that wouldn't stop trembling. His feet shuffled on boards that groaned under his weight.

"Father, the dragon is not what you feare. It is your feare itself that brought it here."

Somewhere in the crowd, someone spat. Not out of impatience. Something territorial. Something claiming.

The play lurched forward. Scenes blurred together. The King bellowed lines that should have thundered and came out thin. The Queen wept tears that might have been real, from frustration if not grief. The Dragon descended twice more, each time tangling worse in its rigging, until Mortimer abandoned the puppet entirely and simply stood beneath it, delivering his lines to an audience that had stopped pretending to care.

No one left. That was the wrong thing. In any other town, by the second act, the disinterested would have drifted away. Gone home. Found other entertainment. But Snakewater stayed. Every person who had gathered at the start remained at the finish, watching, silent, their faces catching the light of the torches that had been lit as the sun went down.

The play ended. The Ashford boy delivered his final lines to no one in particular, his voice hoarse, his hands still shaking. The cast assembled for a bow that nobody had requested. They held the pose for three seconds. Five. Ten.

No applause. No murmur of appreciation. No bits thrown. Just silence, and the scrape of the blacksmith's whetstone, and the slow dispersal of bodies that moved away without hurry, without urgency, without any visible communication between them. One moment the crowd was there. The next it was thinning. The next it was gone, absorbed back into the rotting buildings and darkening alleys, leaving the company alone in a square that had never wanted them.

"Well," Barnaby said from somewhere behind the stage. His voice was too bright. Forced. "That was... that was something. Tough crowd. Every town has them. We'll... regroup tomorrow. Yes. Regroup."

No one answered. The cast was already stripping costumes, faces grim, movements quick. They wanted off this stage. They wanted inside. The light was going fast now, the sun already below the treeline, shadows pooling in the square like dark water rising.

Jamie started on the stage. There was no saving most of it. The boards would rot in a week. The stilts were already listing. But the hardware could be salvaged. The hinges. The pulleys. The ropes. He worked quickly, Miranda beside him, their hands moving in a rhythm that didn't require speech.

"Pass me the mallet."

She passed it.

"The pins on the left side."

She pulled them.

Thomas helped for a while, then disappeared toward the wagons. Jamie didn't see him join the others leaving the square. Old Morris carried an armload of costumes and didn't come back. Humphrey stood at the edge of the square, staring at nothing, until someone called his name and he wandered off into the gathering dark.

The blacksmith was still at his forge. Still sharpening. The blade caught the last of the light, a thin bright line in all that shadow. He hadn't moved. Hadn't spoken. Just sat there, patient as stone, working the edge with the same steady rhythm he'd maintained throughout the performance.

Scrape. Pause. Turn. Scrape.

"We should go," Miranda said. Her voice was different now. Quieter. The wit had drained out of it, leaving something else underneath. "We should get inside."

Jamie nodded. They gathered the last of the tools. The hammers and mallets. The coils of rope. The bucket of nails, half of them bent, salvaged from the stage they'd just torn down. The boards themselves they left where they fell. No one was coming back for them. No one was coming back here at all if they could help it.

Felix materialized beside them. Jamie hadn't heard him approach. Never did.

"The lodge is this way." His voice was flat. Giving nothing. "Stay close. Don't stop."

They walked. The three of them plus whatever remained of the company, trailing through Snakewater's narrow streets in a loose column. The buildings leaned overhead. The boardwalks groaned beneath their feet. Somewhere in the dark, water moved. Somewhere further, a door slammed.

Jamie couldn't tell whether the blacksmith was still at his forge, or if the dark had swallowed him whole.

Behind them, growing fainter but never quite disappearing, the sound of the whetstone continued.

Scrape. Pause. Turn. Scrape.

The marsh-lodge appeared ahead. Damp. Sagging. Candlelight flickering behind warped shutters. It looked like something that had grown rather than been built, something that had risen from the swamp and might sink back into it at any moment.

Barnaby was at the door, ushering people inside, counting heads, his ledger clutched to his chest, his smile rehearsed.

"Everyone in. Quick now. Long day tomorrow. Rest up."

Jamie paused at the threshold. Looked back toward the square, though it was invisible now, swallowed by the dark and the mist that had begun to rise from the water.

The whetstone had stopped.

He didn't know why that was worse than the sound continuing.

Miranda's hand found his elbow. Pulled. "Come on."

He went inside. The door closed behind them. The marsh breathed outside, patient and vast, and somewhere in the dark the blacksmith finished his work and set down his blade and waited for whatever came next.

The company settled into the lodge. Bodies arranged on pallets. Voices lowered to murmurs. Candles guttered in the drafts that crept through the walls.

No one spoke about the performance. No one spoke about the crowd. No one spoke about the silence that had followed them through the streets or the feeling, shared but unvoiced, that something had been watching them since they arrived and hadn't stopped watching yet.

Sleep came eventually. For some.

Jamie lay in the loft and stared at the ceiling and listened to the marsh breathe and waited for something he couldn't name.

The night had just begun.

Somewhere below the floorboards, something moved.

Jamie couldn't sleep. The lodge was too cramped. Too warm. The air thick with bodies and breath and the particular heaviness that settles over places built on drowning ground. Every sound seemed magnified. Rats in the thatch. Water slapping the stilts below. The distant calls of marsh birds that didn't sound quite like birds.

Then a sound that didn't belong; a weight shifting, boards complaining under someone who meant to be quiet. A voice, low and slurred with something that wasn't drink: *"Hold still, you fucking—"*

Miranda's voice answered, furious and strangled: *"Get off—"*

Jamie was moving before he decided to. He slid across the loft boards on instinct, barefoot, silent, the planks slick with damp. He found the gap between two warped boards and peered down just in time to see the man's hand clamped over Miranda's mouth, her body pinned, her legs kicking for leverage.

Moonlight came through the warped walls in thin slices. Enough to see shapes. Enough to see the figure crouched over Miranda's pallet, one hand clamped across her mouth, the other pinning her shoulder to the straw. Big. Broad. Moving with the efficiency of someone who'd done this before and expected to do it again.

Miranda's legs kicked. Her fingers clawed at the hand on her face. She wasn't screaming because she couldn't, but her eyes caught moonlight and they were wild with fury. The look of something trapped that intended to make its captor bleed.

That's when he dropped.

The fall was eight feet. He landed wrong, ankle twisting on the uneven floor, pain flaring up his leg. Distant. Happening to someone else. The man looked up. His face was shadow, but his posture changed. Irritation. A professional interrupted.

Jamie hit him low.

They went over together in a tangle of limbs and curses. The floor was slick with marsh damp. Jamie's hands slipped as he tried to find purchase, tried to get an arm around the man's throat the way Felix had taught him. The man was huge. Mass and muscle packed onto bone in ways that spoke of war.

An elbow caught Jamie across the temple. The world tilted. Stars burst behind his eyes. He tasted copper and felt his grip loosen, felt the man twist free and rise, felt a boot catch him in the ribs with force enough to lift him off the ground.

He slammed against the wall. The planks shuddered. Above, voices rose. Players waking. Confused.

"*What's happening—*"

"*Who's there—*"

The man stood over Jamie. Breathing hard. Hand going to his belt. Steel whispering against leather.

"Bloody kids." Low. Disgusted. "Always getting in the way."

The blade came up. Moonlight caught its edge.

Jamie watched it rise. Understood he was going to die here. In this rotting lodge. In Snakewater. With the marsh breathing outside and the company waking above and none of it mattering because the blade was at its apex and nothing stood between him and its descent.

The cookpot caught the man across the back of the skull. A sickening, sodden *crunch*. Cast iron meeting bone. The man staggered. The blade dropped. His knees buckled and he went down in stages. Posture first. Balance second. Everything else after.

He landed face-first on the damp floor. Didn't move.

Miranda stood behind him. Cookpot in her white-knuckled grip. Chest heaving. Hair wild around her face. Her shift was torn at the shoulder. Her feet bare. Blood on her face that wasn't hers. Her eyes held fury with nowhere left to land.

She looked at Jamie. He looked at her.

Above them, chaos. The loft erupted with movement, voices rising and overlapping.

"Someone's hurt—"

"What's happened—"

Barnaby's voice cut through, commanding: "Everyone stay calm! Stay where you are!"

No one did. Bodies descended from the loft. Someone stumbled over the man on the floor and screamed. Someone shouted about murderers. About Snakewater. About how they never should have stopped here.

The door crashed open.

Cold marsh air flooded the lodge. Figures in the doorway. Jamie couldn't count them. Three. Four. More moving behind. Their silhouettes were wrong. Too big. Too still. They didn't move like actors.

"Everyone out!" A voice Jamie didn't recognize. Hard. Accustomed to obedience. "There's been an incident. Outside. Now. Move."

The company obeyed. Too confused to question, too frightened to resist. They stumbled into the night in sleeping clothes, barefoot, shivering. Jamie tried to follow Miranda but the press of bodies separated them. Someone's elbow caught his ribs. Someone's foot came down on his twisted ankle.

Outside, the marsh breathed. Mist clung to the boardwalks. Torchlight flickered somewhere distant. The company huddled in front of the lodge, clutching themselves against the cold, and the men who'd ordered them out stood in a loose perimeter. Watching. Waiting.

"Where's Thomas?"

"He was right behind me—"

"*What about Old Morris?*"

Names called into darkness. People who should have been there weren't. The confusion deepened. Voices overlapping. Fear spreading like rot through wet wood.

Jamie found Miranda at the edge of the group. She was shaking. Cold or shock or both. Her hand found his and gripped. He gripped back.

"Something's wrong," she whispered.

He nodded. Words wouldn't come.

Through the mist, movement. Shapes in the dark, half-glimpsed. The boardwalks groaning under weight that came and went. Jamie thought he heard voices. Low. Urgent. The sound of something being dragged. A muffled protest that stopped too quickly.

The marsh swallowed it all.

Then Felix emerged from the fog.

He moved through the company without speaking. His armor caught torchlight. His face was stone. His eyes passed over Jamie and Miranda and didn't pause. He walked to the lodge door, looked inside at the body, and stood for a long moment.

When he turned, his expression hadn't changed.

"Everyone back inside. The situation is handled. Return to your beds."

No one moved.

"*Now.*"

They moved. They always moved when Felix used that voice. Bodies shuffling toward the lodge, stepping around blood on the floor, climbing back into the loft, lying on pallets that felt like traps.

Jamie tried to catch Felix's eye as he passed. Felix didn't look at him.

Miranda squeezed his hand once and didn't let go.

"Get some sleep," she said. The words came out flat. "Tomorrow, we leave this shithole."

She lay down against the wall and Jamie followed, lowering himself beside her with care. The pallet was narrow. Their shoulders touched. She stayed rigid for a long moment, then shifted just enough to make space, her back warm against his chest.

The lodge settled around them. Breath. Boards. The soft, restless movements of people pretending to sleep.

Jamie closed his eyes. His ankle throbbed. His ribs burned. His head felt stuffed with wet wool. Miranda didn't move.

Sleep took him anyway.

Dawn came gray and wet.

Jamie woke to movement. People rising. Belongings gathered. The company preparing to leave Snakewater as fast as wagons could be hitched.

He climbed down from the loft. His ankle protested. His ribs ached. His head felt wrong in ways he couldn't name.

The body was gone. The floor had been scrubbed.

But the faces were wrong.

Jamie stood in the center of the lodge and turned slowly. The people packing bags. Rolling pallets. Pulling on boots. He knew these faces. Had traveled with them for days. Eaten with them. Rehearsed with them.

These were not those faces.

The man stuffing a costume into a trunk had a scar across his knuckles. No Morris. No Thomas. Their pallets were bare; neatly arranged, too neatly, as though someone had staged them instead of slept in them. Jamie had never seen him before. The woman coiling rope by the door moved with her weight forward, balanced on the balls of her feet. Actors moved differently. Actors performed even when they weren't performing. This woman moved like she expected attack.

He counted again. Fifteen faces he didn't recognize. The troupe had numbered nineteen when they arrived.

Where were the others?

Barnaby emerged from a back room. Harried. Distracted. Clutching his ledger.

"Ah, Jamie. Good. Help with the wagons, will you? We're behind."

"Where's Thomas?"

Barnaby didn't look up. "Who?"

"Thomas. The messenger in the second act."

"Oh, him." Barnaby waved a hand. "Had to make some changes after last night. Some of the company found Snakewater disagreeable. Can't blame them. We've picked up some new faces. Good people. Quick studies."

"In the middle of the night?"

"theatre waits for no one." Thin smile. Brittle. "The wagons. Please."

He walked away. Jamie watched him go.

Across the room, Miranda pulled on her boots. She looked up. Caught his eye.

She'd noticed too.

Jamie looked toward the door. Felix stood outside, overseeing the loading. His back to the lodge. His posture relaxed. His armor caught weak morning light.

He didn't look like a man who'd done something monstrous.

He looked like a man who'd been waiting for this moment a very long time.

Jamie picked up his pack. Walked toward the wagons. The new faces parted to let him pass. Polite. Deferential. The courtesy of soldiers pretending to be something else.

The marsh breathed around them. Mist rose from the water. Snakewater watched with hollow eyes and rotting teeth, and if it knew what had happened in the night, what had been swapped and stolen and spirited into the dark, it said nothing.

The marsh always kept its secrets.

That was what it was for.

ACT IV

THE LAMBE BLEEDETH SWIFTER
THEN THE WOLFE

A C T U S   Q U A R T U S ,   S C A E N A   Q U I N T A

Enter KING ALFRED and QUEENE EVELYN. Enter PRINCE CORWIN, helm removed, head bowed.

KING ALFRED. What, fled? My sonne, the rider of our name, Returneth not with glorie, but with shame?

PRINCE CORWIN. The beast was vast, its fire beyond my steele— No mortal blade could make the monster kneele.

KING ALFRED. Then we shall raise an armie. We shall burne The mountaine downe until the creature learne That kinges are not defied, that crownes doe not retreate!

PRINCE LEO entering. Father, I beg thee: heare me ere you speake of defeat. I journeyed to the mount and met the wyrme; I found no monster there, but something firm And olde and wise and patient as the stone. It seekes not warre; it onely wants alone. The dragon is no scourge, it is a glasse That showes us what our pride hath let to passe. If we but leave it peace upon its throne, The beast will leave our kingdome safe, unknowne.

KING ALFRED. Thou treate with monsters? Thou, of royall blood? Wouldst have me bowe to what I've sworne to flood With steele and fire and all a kinges disdaine? This court is not for boyes who parle with bane.

PRINCE LEO. Father, the dragon is not what you feare, It is your feare itself that brought it here.

KING ALFRED. Silence! I am King, and kinges are cleare: We doe not aske; we take; we persevere. The beast shall die, though all our armies fall; There is no roome for truth in kingly hall.

QUEENE EVELYN watches, hands clasped, silent. LEO lookes about the court; the smiling lords, the flowered spring, the hard eyes.

PRINCE LEO aside. The court is but a den of smiling wolves, Where springtimes face the winters heart absolves. They speake of honour; what they meane is pride. My father rules a kingdome that hath lied So long it knowes not truth from what it feares, And I am exile now, though none have saide the wordes these yeares.

Exeunt severally.

SCENE 24

THE QUEEN

1577

The roses were dying.

It was the wrong time of year for them anyway; late autumn, the air carrying that particular cold that preceded the real cold, the warning shot before winter's siege. But someone had planted them here in the queen's garden, in soil that faced south and caught what sun there was, and they had bloomed against all reason. Now they were paying for it. Petals blackened at the edges. Stems gone brittle. The last of the red deepening toward something closer to dried blood.

Anya stood among them in a dress the color of winter sky. Pale blue. Almost gray. The kind of color that made her hair look like something impossible: gold in a kingdom of gray stone, summer caught and held past its season, brightness that had no business surviving in a place this cold. She was nineteen years old. She had been queen since birth; the last of the Taylor line, the trueblood heir to a dynasty that stretched back to 1420.

She had been married for two of those years to a man who had been chosen for her.

Felix watched her from the colonnade.

He was not supposed to be watching. He was supposed to be standing guard at the eastern gate, where the king's men rotated in shifts and the hours passed in silence and nothing ever happened. But his relief had come early—a young soldier eager to prove himself, willing to take the extra time—and Felix had found his feet carrying him here, to this garden, to this colonnade, to this precise angle of observation where he could see her without being seen.

This was the fifth time this week.

He knew he should stop. Knew it the way you know fire burns, the way you know water drowns, the way you know that some doors, once opened, cannot be closed again. She was the queen. The true queen, not by marriage but by blood, by lineage, by the unbroken chain of Taylors who had ruled this kingdom since before the histories were written. Her husband was king only because she had made him so. Tobias of Ashford, third son of a minor lord, elevated beyond all expectation or merit because someone had decided Anya needed a husband and he was available and adequately groomed.

The whole court knew what Tobias was. They whispered it in corridors and laughed about it in taverns and pitied the queen who had to share his bed. Weak, they said. Spineless. A man who flinched from decisions and deferred to advisors and spent more time with his ledgers than his sword. Not stupid—never that. Tobias had a mind for numbers, for logistics, for the small calculations that kept a kingdom fed and funded. But a king needed more than arithmetic. A king needed presence. Command. The thing that made men follow and enemies hesitate.

Tobias had none of it. And everyone knew. Including his wife.

Felix was everything Tobias was not.

This was the thing he tried not to think about. The thing that made his presence in this garden so dangerous, so presumptuous, so close to treason that the line had become invisible. He was eighteen years old. He had been knighted at fifteen by King Aldric himself for actions in the border wars, a cavalry charge that had turned a rout into a victory, his sword arm working until the steel was slick and his horse was screaming and the enemy line broke because he refused to let it hold. He bore the scars of that day and a dozen others. His body was a map of service, of duty, of the particular kind of courage that didn't think about consequences until the fighting was done.

He was everything a king should be. And he was nothing. A knight. A servant. A man whose bloodline meant nothing, whose name would vanish when he died, whose only legacy would be the battles he'd fought for other men's glory.

He had no right to watch her. No right to want her. No right to stand in shadows and memorize the way her fingers touched dying roses, gentle and sad, as though she were saying goodbye to something only she could see.

"You're not very good at hiding."

Her voice carried across the garden. She hadn't turned. Hadn't looked toward the colonnade. But she knew. Of course she knew.

Felix stepped from the shadows. There was no point in pretending.

"Your Grace—"

"Don't." The word came soft but carried edges. "Not here. Not when it's just us and the dying flowers and the cold." She turned. Her eyes found his. "Do you know what I was thinking about? Just now, before you made noise with your breathing?"

"No."

"I was thinking about my father. He fought six wars. Won five. The one he lost, it was because he was betrayed by men he trusted, and even then, he killed eleven of them before they brought him down. Eleven men. With a sword in one hand and a dagger in the other and arrows in his chest." She looked down at her own hands: small, pale, uncalloused. "That blood is in me. Over a century of warriors and conquerors and men who shaped this kingdom with iron and will. And what did I do with it? I married Tobias."

"You didn't have a choice."

"Everyone has choices. I made mine." Her jaw tightened. "I was seventeen. I was told the kingdom needed stability. I was told Tobias was kind, which he is, and clever, which he also is, and that kindness and cleverness were what the realm required after Aldric's wars. I was told—" She stopped. Breathed. "I was told many things. And I believed them. Because I was young and I thought the people who advised me wanted what was best. And now I am nineteen and I sleep beside a man who's afraid of thunderstorms, and I wonder what my father would say if he were still here to see what his line has become."

The silence held. Felix watched her.

"He'd ask why no one was bleeding," he said quietly. "Why we're wasting good weather."

Anya's shoulders moved. A breath that wasn't quite a laugh.

"And then he'd ask what the banker was doing in his chair."

That broke her. The laugh came out of her like something she'd been holding underwater, sudden and loud and real. She covered her mouth with her hand but it didn't help. Her shoulders shook. She turned away, then turned back, and Felix was smiling now too, that rare, unguarded thing she almost never saw, and for a moment they were just two people in a dying garden laughing at something terrible and true.

"It's what he'd say."

"*Stop it.*" She wiped her eyes with the heel of her hand, still half-laughing. "You're horrible."

The laughter faded. But something remained in its wake, warm and conspiratorial.

"Tobias isn't—" Felix started, then stopped. He didn't know how to finish. Wasn't sure he cared to.

"Tobias isn't cruel," she finished. "He doesn't beat me. Doesn't shame me publicly. Doesn't keep mistresses, at least none that I've discovered, though I suspect that's more cowardice than fidelity. He's perfectly adequate in all the ways that don't matter and completely absent in all the ways that do." She crossed her arms against the cold. "Do you know what he said to me last night? We were in bed. I was trying to... it doesn't matter what I was trying to do. And he patted my hand. Patted it. Like I was a dog that had done a trick. And he said, 'You're very patient with me, Anya. I know I'm not what you hoped for.'"

She laughed. This time it was hollow. Bitter.

"He knows. That's the worst part. He knows exactly what he is and what he isn't, and he's made peace with it! He's *comfortable* in his inadequacy. He's built a whole life in the space where a real man should be, and he's fine there." She looked at Felix, her eyes traveling across his face, his shoulders, the sword at his hip, the scars visible above his collar. "And then there's you."

"I'm no one."

"You're the opposite of no one. You're everything he should have been and isn't. You're what I thought I was marrying, before I understood what 'kind' and 'clever' really meant." She stepped closer. The distance between them halved. "You stand in doorways and watch me when you think I can't see. You never say anything. And I spend half my days wondering what you're thinking and the other half angry at myself for caring."

"You shouldn't care."

"I know."

"This is dangerous."

"I know that too."

"If anyone found out—"

"They'd kill you." She said it simply. The way you'd say the sun rises in the east. "They'd say you seduced me, or enchanted me, or forced me. They'd never believe I came to you willingly. That I wanted you. That I lay awake at night thinking about your hands and your voice and the way you look at me like I'm something precious instead of something useful." Her voice had dropped. Barely above a whisper now. "They'd take your head. And I'd have to watch. And then I'd spend the rest of my life in that bed with Tobias, being patted like a dog, and I'd know that I once had a chance to feel something real and I let it die because I was afraid."

The wind came then, carrying the smell of winter and

woodsmoke and the last green things surrendering to the frost. It caught her hair, lifted it, sent gold streaming like a banner no one had given her permission to fly.

"I'm not afraid," Felix said.

"I know. That's why I keep coming here." She reached up. Touched his face. Her fingers were cold against his cheek, tracing the scar there, small and white, earned in a battle she'd never seen. "You're not afraid of anything, are you?"

"I'm afraid of this."

"Of me?"

"Of what I feel when I look at you." His hand came up, covered hers, pressed her palm flat against his face. "I've fought men who wanted to kill me. I've charged cavalry lines. I've done things that should have ended me a dozen times over. None of it scared me. But *this*—" He turned his head slightly. His lips brushed her palm. "This terrifies me."

"Good." Her voice was rough. "It should. It terrifies me too."

"What are we doing?"

"I don't know." She stepped closer still. Almost no space between them now. He could smell her, rosewater and something else, something warm beneath it, the last trace of summer hidden in a woman the winter was trying to claim. "But I know that I'm the last of my line and I'm supposed to produce heirs and all I've produced is emptiness. I know that my husband pats my hand and calls me patient and has no idea that patience is just another word for dying slowly." Her other hand found his chest. Pressed flat against his heart. "And I know that you're here. And you see me."

Felix closed his eyes. Opened them.

"I love you," he said. "I've loved you since the first time I saw you, in the great hall, when you were receiving petitioners and you spent twenty minutes listening to a farmer complain about his neighbor's goats. You didn't have to listen. You could have dismissed him in seconds. But you listened, and you asked questions, and you actually cared about his goats, and I thought—" He almost laughed. "I thought, that's what a ruler is supposed to be. That's what a hundred and fifty years of Taylor blood looks like when it's undiluted. And I've loved you every day since. Through every shift at every gate. Through every glimpse across every courtyard. Through every night I lay awake telling myself to stop, knowing I never would."

Anya's eyes were wet. She didn't wipe them.

"Say my name," she whispered.

"Anya."

"Again."

"Anya."

She kissed him. Four years of wrong marriage and wrong touches and wrong everything, channeled into a single point of contact. Her mouth on his. Her hands climbing to his neck, his hair, pulling him down to her. His arms wrapping around her waist, lifting her slightly, pulling her close until there was no space at all, until he could feel her heartbeat against his chest, racing to match his own.

The roses watched. Blackened. Dying. Keeping secrets.

When they finally broke apart, both of them were breathing hard. Anya's lips were swollen. A strand of her hair had come loose, fallen across her face—gold against flushed skin, bright against the gray afternoon. Felix reached up and brushed it back, tucked it behind her ear. The gesture was tender in a way that surprised him. He hadn't known he had tenderness in him. He'd thought war had burned it out.

"Tomorrow," she said. "Same time. Same place."

"And after tomorrow?"

"I don't know." She smiled. It was the first real smile he'd ever seen from her—not the court smile, not the queen smile, but something private and fragile and entirely her own. For a moment, the warmth trapped behind her eyes broke through. She looked like what she was: sunlight that had been locked in a stone tower, finally finding a window. "But I know I want to find out."

She stepped back. Smoothed her dress. Touched her hair. Became the queen again in stages, composing herself with the practiced efficiency of someone who had learned to hide everything she felt.

"If we do this," Felix said, "there's no going back."

"I know."

"It will change everything."

"I know that too." She held his gaze. "I've spent four years not changing anything. Being patient. Being adequate. Being the queen everyone expected me to be." Her chin lifted. For a moment, he saw it—the ghost of Aldric, the Lionheart, the blood that had conquered kingdoms. "I'm done being what they expect."

She walked away. Her hair caught the last of the dying light, held it, carried it with her like something stolen. Her shadow stretched behind her, long and thin, reaching toward something neither of them could name.

Felix stood in the garden until the cold became real cold, until the roses were just shapes in the darkness, until the first stars appeared above the castle walls. He touched his lips. Tasted her there. Tasted ruin. Tasted joy.

They were the same thing, he realized. They had always been the same thing.

He walked back to his post. Relieved the young soldier who'd been covering for him. Stood in the darkness with his hand on his sword and his heart full of something that would either save him or destroy him.

In her chambers, Anya dismissed her maids. Sat before her mirror. Looked at her own face—the Taylor face, the golden Taylor hair that had marked her line for generations—and saw someone new looking back. Someone who still had light in her. Someone the cold hadn't killed yet.

In his study, Tobias bent over his ledgers, adding columns, checking figures, unaware that the foundation of his borrowed crown had just developed a crack that would eventually swallow everything.

The garden kept its secrets.

But gardens, like people, don't keep them forever.

SCENE 25

PETER BEVERLEY & THE STRAYS OF HARTHFELL

1602
One week earlier

Peter Beverley stood at the edge of the camp, his back to the wind, watching the man's mouth move. The words came out in pieces—executed, public, the square, your father—and Peter heard them the way you hear stones dropping into a well. Distant. Final. Each one falling further than the last.

The camp spread behind him across a shallow ridge: forty men, maybe fifty, huddled around fires that fought the wind and lost. Tents snapped against their stakes. Horses stamped and steamed. The sky was the color of old iron, pressing down on mountains that had never learned to kneel.

"Say it again," Peter said.

The messenger—a boy, really, sixteen if he was lucky, wearing clothes that had been someone else's before the someone else stopped needing them—swallowed hard. "Your father, my lord. Henry Beverley. Executed three days past in the capital. By order of the crown."

"Which crown?"

"The—" The boy hesitated. "King Lionel's crown, my lord."

"Lionel." Peter tasted the name. Let it sit on his tongue like something sour. "The little man."

"My lord?"

Peter turned. Looked at the camp. At his men, who had stopped what they were doing to watch. At the three Taylor soldiers tied to the post near the eastern fire—prisoners taken in a skirmish two weeks prior, kept alive for leverage that no longer mattered. "And my sister? Margaret?"

"Still married, my lord. To the king."

Peter walked toward the prisoners.

They were bound to a thick wooden post that had been driven into the frozen ground, hands behind their backs, rope at the wrists, ankles, throats. They'd been there two days. Their lips were blue. Their eyes followed Peter with the dull attention of men who had stopped hoping for rescue and started hoping for speed.

"Names," Peter said.

The one on the left—youngest, maybe twenty, a beard that couldn't decide if it wanted to exist—spoke first. "Corporal Thomas Ainsley, Third Company of the—"

"I didn't ask your bloody rank." Peter stopped in front of him. Close enough to see the frost in his eyebrows. "I asked your name."

"Thomas. Just Thomas."

"Just Thomas." Peter looked at the other two. "And you?"

"William Marsh," said the middle one. Older. Harder eyes. A man who'd seen enough to know what was coming and had decided to face it standing.

The third said nothing. His head hung forward. He might have been unconscious. He might have been praying. Didn't matter.

Peter turned and walked back toward the fire where his captains waited. Dunbar was there—grizzled, gray-bearded, missing two fingers on his left hand from a fight he never talked about. Beside him stood young Cormac, who wasn't young anymore but had earned the name at fifteen and never shaken it. A few others. Hard men with hard faces, watching their lord with the careful attention of soldiers who sensed something shifting.

"My lord," Dunbar said. "The prisoners. If we're to ransom them—"

"We're not."

Peter walked past them. To the weapons rack near his tent. To the bow that hung there—yew and sinew, unstrung, made for him by a craftsman in Edinburgh who'd died of plague two winters past. He took it down. Found the string. Bent the bow against his thigh and strung it with the practiced ease of someone who'd done it a thousand times.

"My lord?" Cormac's voice. Uncertain.

Peter selected three arrows from the quiver. Examined each one. Set two in his belt. Nocked the third.

"We're not ransoming them."

"My lord, if we kill them, we lose any chance of—"

"Of what?" Peter turned, the bow hanging loose at his side, arrow already nocked. "Of negotiating? Of trading away another one of my siblings? Of playing the game as it's meant to be played?" He smiled. "That was my father's game. I intend to show them mine."

No one spoke.

Peter walked back toward the prisoners.

He stopped fifteen feet from the post. Raised the bow. Drew.

Just Thomas opened his mouth to speak.

The arrow took him through the throat.

The sound was small. Wet. A truncated gurgle, a spray of red against the frost, and then Thomas was sagging against his ropes, hands still bound, legs kicking once, twice, then still. The whole thing took perhaps three seconds.

Peter was already nocking the second arrow.

William Marsh had time to say *"Christ—"* before the shaft punched through his left eye and buried itself in the post behind him. His body jerked, went rigid, and slumped.

The third prisoner finally lifted his head. He'd been praying after all. His lips were still—

Thwack.

The arrow took him through the open mouth.

Silence.

The wind blew. The fires crackled. Somewhere a horse whinnied, high and nervous. Fifty men stood frozen around the camp, staring at their lord, at the three bodies that had been breathing thirty seconds ago and were now leaking steam and blood into the mountain air.

Peter lowered the bow. Unstrung it. Walked back to the weapons rack and hung it in its place with the same unhurried precision he'd used to take it down.

"Dunbar."

The old captain's voice came out rough. "My lord."

"We break camp within the hour. Alert the men, ready the horses."

"Where to, my lord?"

"Harthfell."

A pause. The kind of pause that contained entire arguments, compressed and discarded. "The mountains, my lord? In winter?"

"The Strays live there. Year-round. If they can survive it, so can we."

"The Strays don't take kindly to visitors, my lord—"

"Then we'll be the exception." Peter pulled on his gloves. Leather, lined with fur, the fingers worn smooth from use. "The Taylors have my sister. They have the capital. They have the treasury and the army and the legitimacy, such as it is. What they don't have is Harthfell. Now, what we don't have is a choice, and what *I* don't give is a fuck. Alert the men, ready the horses, Captain. It is an order."

Peter looked around the camp. At the men who were still staring at him, still processing what they'd seen.

"If anyone would like to stay behind," he said, "now would be the time."

No one moved. No one spoke.

"Very well." Peter smiled again. This time there was something almost genuine in it—dark, sharp, the smile of a man who'd remembered what he was capable of and found he still didn't mind. "One hour. Pack light. We hike until we find them or they find us."

He walked toward his tent.

Behind him, Dunbar exchanged a look with Cormac. The look said many things: *Did you see that?* and *God help us* and *Fuck*.

The wind scattered their silence across the frozen ridge.

The mountains ate sound.

That was the first thing Peter noticed, two days into the climb. The world grew quieter the higher they went—no birds, no beasts, no rustle of leaves because there were no leaves, only stone and ice and the wind that carved them both into shapes that looked like intention. Each footstep fell into a void. Each voice sounded like something stolen from a larger silence that would eventually take it back.

They lost two horses the first day. A trail that looked solid gave way beneath the lead animal's hooves, and horse and rider both went down the cliff in a tangle of screaming and dust. The rider was Simmons, a farrier's son from Dunkirk who'd joined Peter's company six months prior. He'd been twenty-two.

Peter didn't pause. Didn't eulogize. Just nodded at the cliff as though Simmons had been a message and he'd received it and kept climbing.

The second horse broke its leg on loose scree. Cormac cut its throat before it could scream, and they left the carcass for whatever lived up here that was hungry enough to eat frozen meat.

By the third morning, the men were too tired to be afraid.

That was when they found the Strays.

Rather, that was when the Strays let themselves be found.

The pass opened onto a small plateau, a flat stretch of rock and ice bounded by walls of granite that rose into fog. Peter's company spread across it in loose formation, forty-three men left from the original fifty, breath pluming white in air that felt thin and sharp in the lungs.

The figure emerged from the fog like something coalescing from the mountain itself.

He was tall. Broad. Wrapped in layers of hide and wool and battered metal that looked like it had been salvaged from a dozen different wars. His face was scarred—one long mark that ran from his left temple to his jaw, twisting his mouth into a permanent quarter-smile that had nothing to do with amusement. His eyes were gray. Pale gray, almost colorless, the shade of ice over deep water.

He stopped thirty feet from Peter's line. Stood there. Said nothing.

Behind him, more shapes materialized from the fog. Two. Five. A dozen. They carried weapons—axes, spears, bows with arrows already nocked—and they moved into position without sound, without signal, with the coordination of something that had practiced this a thousand times.

"Lord Garran Morrow," Peter said.

"You know my name."

"I know many names. Yours was worth learning." Peter kept his hands visible, away from his weapons. "I am—"

"Peter Beverley, otherwise known as Mad Peter. Son of Proud Henry. Brother to Lady Margaret." Garran's voice was low, deliberate, each word placed like a stone in a wall. "We know who comes into our mountains. We knew when you broke camp. We knew when you started climbing. We've known you were here for two days."

"And yet you let us climb."

"Wanted to see if you'd make it." The quarter-smile twitched. "Most don't."

"We lost two."

"Two." Garran nodded slowly. "Better than most. Your people can walk, at least. Doesn't mean they can fight."

"I didn't come to fight."

"No? Then what did you bring forty soldiers into my mountains for? The view?" Garran gestured at the fog, the stone, the shapes that continued to emerge from both. Twenty men now. Thirty. "If it's a fight you're avoiding, you've chosen a strange way to show it."

Peter looked at the growing assembly of mountain fighters. They'd spread into a loose semicircle—behind Garran, beside him, and now, he realized, above him too. Figures on the granite walls. Crouched on ledges. Perched in crevices that shouldn't have been able to hold a man. Bows trained downward. Spears ready.

His men had noticed. He could feel them tensing, hands drifting toward weapons, breath quickening. Dunbar was muttering something under his breath that might have been a prayer or might have been a curse.

"Impressive," Peter said.

"You're standing in a killing ground, Beverley. There are more than fifty arrows trained on your men right now. One word from me, and you're all meat for the crows—assuming the crows come this high, which they don't, so you'd just freeze where you fell and wait for spring to rot you."

"A charming description."

"Is it?" Garran stopped ten feet from Peter. Close enough to see the individual scars on his face, the old wounds layered over older wounds. "Tell me why I shouldn't."

Peter held his gaze. Didn't blink. Didn't shift. The wind cut between them, carrying ice crystals that stung the face and blurred the edges of everything.

"Because you hate the Taylors more than you hate me."

Silence pressed down on the plateau like another layer of fog.

"Go on," Garran said.

"You've been pushed back for three generations. Every time the crown needs land, needs resources, needs a place to dump its criminals or build its forts, you're the ones who pay. The western valleys were yours, once. The timber rights along the Kell, yours. The mining claims in the Southholds, yours. I could go on. I have a list. But you know it better than I do, because you've been keeping it longer."

"Pretty words. You rehearse them on the climb?"

"Some of them. The rest I'm making up as I go." Peter allowed himself a small smile. "The Taylors drew and quartered my father three days ago. This is two months after he yielded. They've married my sister to their insipid boy king and put her in a cage she'll never leave. They think they've won. They think me beaten, broken, fucking about the English countryside like a headless chicken—"

"And what concern is it of mine?"

The words landed flat. No malice. Just the honest question of a man who had watched his mother die and learned that other people's grievances were rarely worth bleeding for, who had stopped expecting the world to be fair a long time ago.

"Your father's dead. Your sister's caged. These are *your* wounds, young man. Not mine. I've seen a hundred men climb into these mountains with their anger and a hundred reasons why I should die for them. Give me one reason this is different."

Peter felt the weight of fifty arrows. Felt the silence pressing down. Felt, for the first time since he'd started climbing, the genuine possibility that this ended with his body freezing on a plateau no one would ever find.

He breathed. Steadied.

"Because I'm not asking you to die for me. I'm going south with or without you. I'm asking if you want to come."

Garran studied him. The pale eyes moved across Peter's face, his posture, the way he stood in the center of a killing ground with fifty arrows aimed at his heart and spoke as though he were delivering a speech in a throne room. He inhaled deeply. Straightened. Looked past Peter at the exhausted soldiers behind him, the horses they'd managed to keep alive, the supplies that wouldn't last another week.

"What do you want?"

"An alliance."

"With what?"

"With two thousand Strays." Peter's voice didn't change, but something behind it hardened. "You have at least sixty here with arrows notched. Then you give me two thousand more spread out across the hills, in the villages, in the borderlands. Men who lost fathers in the last war. Brothers. Sons. Men who've been waiting for someone to give them a reason to sharpen their blades and remember what they're for."

"And you're that reason?"

"I'm the inciter. The Taylors—that's the reason." Peter took a step forward. Into Garran's space. Into the killing ground's dead center. "They think they ended the Beverley line when they murdered my father. They think Margaret's children will be Taylor children, Taylor heirs, the bloodline absorbed and forgotten."

"So," Garran said, clearing his throat, "you want us to die for your revenge."

"I want you to fight for your own. I don't care about your mountains. I don't care about your customs or your dragon gods or whatever the *fuck* it is you lot do up here in the cold. What I care about is ending the people who desecrated my father and imprisoned my sister. You have your own reasons to want them ended. Different reasons, yes, but the target's the same."

The wind shifted. The fog swirled. For a moment, it thinned enough to show the true scale of what surrounded them—not fifty Strays but a hundred, maybe more, scattered across the plateau and the walls above it, a small army that had materialized from stone and ice and patience.

"Theatrics aside, what's in it for my people?" Garran asked. "Besides the pleasure of your company."

"Land. Lots." Peter said it flatly. "The western valleys. Returned. The timber rights along the Kell. Returned. The mining claims in the Southholds—"

"I said what's *in* it, Beverley, not what you'll promise—"

"Then don't take my promise. Take my rage." Peter's jaw tightened. "I'm not asking you to trust me, Lord Garran. I'm asking you to believe that I intend to burn the Taylors to ash before I die. Believe that, and the land will follow, because there won't be anyone left to take it from you."

Garran was quiet for a long moment. The fog closed back in,

shrinking the world to a small circle of stone and bodies.

"There's a blood-debt," he said finally. "Between my people and the crown."

"I've heard."

"Thirty years ago. A village called Carran's Hollow. Two hundred people. The Taylors came in winter—said we'd been raiding, which was true enough, but raiding's been the way of things for generations, and nobody died over it until them. They killed everyone. Men, women, children, animals. Burned the buildings. Salted what they couldn't burn. Left the bodies for the crows that don't come this high." He looked at Peter. "Two hundred. My mother was one of them. I was six. Hiding in a grain cellar, listening to her scream."

Peter said nothing. There was nothing to say.

"So." Garran exhaled slowly. "You want to end the Taylors. That's your hatred. Mine's older. Been sitting in my chest for thirty years, and I've learned to live with it because there was never a way to let it out." He tilted his head. "You're offering me a war."

"I'm offering you a way."

"Same thing." Garran turned. Looked at his people—the hundred-odd fighters who'd emerged from the mountain like a nightmare made flesh. "If we move with you, Beverley, we move to end kings. Not to make new ones. Not to trade one crown for another. To end them. The whole bloody idea of them. You understand?"

Peter held his gaze.

A hundred arrows. A hundred men who would put every one of them through his chest if he answered wrong. The fog pressing down. The wind cutting between them. And somewhere beneath all of it, the truth he would never speak aloud: that he had not climbed into these mountains to end kings. He had climbed here to become one. He would burn the Taylor dynasty to ash and build his own on the ruins, and Garran Morrow and his two thousand Strays would help him do it whether they understood the terms or not.

But that was a truth for later. For after. For when the arrows were pointed somewhere else.

"Aye," he said. "That's the point."

Garran smiled. It was the first real expression Peter had seen on his face: cold, sharp, the smile of a man who'd finally found something worth killing for after thirty years of waiting.

"Then we have an understanding." He extended his hand. "Welcome to Harthfell, Beverley. Try not to die before we reach the lowlands. I'd hate to waste the trip."

Peter clasped his forearm.

"I'll do my best."

"See that you do." Garran released him. Turned to his people. Raised one hand in a gesture that might have meant stand down or might have meant prepare—Peter couldn't tell, and suspected that was intentional. "We move at dawn. The pass to the south is clear for another three days before the storms close it. After that, we're committed." He looked back at Peter. "You and I have much to discuss, Beverley."

"I look forward to it."

"A liar." The quarter-smile returned. "But a useful one. Rest."

He walked away into the fog. His people followed—melting back into the stone and ice, disappearing as completely as they'd appeared, until Peter's company stood alone on the plateau with nothing but the wind to prove anyone had been there at all.

Dunbar appeared at Peter's elbow. His face was pale beneath the weathering.

"My lord," he said. "Did we just ally with them, or did we just become their prisoners?"

Peter looked at the fog. At the empty walls. At the killing ground that had chosen, for now, not to kill.

"Ask me again in a week."

He walked toward what passed for shelter. Behind him, his men began to make camp, moving with the shell-shocked efficiency of soldiers who'd just learned something new about the war they were fighting.

The mountains watched. Patient. Ancient. Keeping their

own counsel.

In a week, the Strays would descend from their passes.

In a week, everything would change.

But that was a week away, and Peter Beverley had learned—in a camp on a frozen ridge, with three arrows and three bodies and the echo of his father's death still ringing in his skull—that weeks were made of days, and days were made of moments, and moments were the only currency that mattered anymore.

He'd spend them well.

Or he'd spend them all.

SCENE 26

THE ROAD TO TAYLOR'S END

They left Snakewater before the town had properly remembered how to breathe again.

Morning sat low over the fields, a thin gray light laid across hedgerows and ditches, The road itself was more suggestion than construction, a rut of churned mud and old stone that wandered between bare trees and patient cattle. The wagon creaked along it at the pace of a tired thought.

Jamie sat on the front bench beside the driver, hands tucked beneath his thighs for warmth, scalp stinging in the air. Felix had taken one look at the lice comb in Snakewater and pointed at Jamie's hair with the same tone he used for battlefield orders. Four minutes later his curls were on the tavern floor and a boy with a chipped razor had revealed the shape of his skull to the world.

He felt it now with every little gust, the newness of it; the skin tight across bone, the small shivers that chased each draft.

He kept catching himself reaching up for hair that no longer existed. A man who had spent his life disappearing into crowds had, with one practical decision, turned his head into a lantern.

The wagon groaned as it hit a rut. Miranda shifted beside him on the bench, shoulder knocking his arm. She had wrapped herself in her cloak, the hood pulled forward, dark hair tucked away. Only her face was visible and even that, this morning, felt like something she had borrowed rather than owned.

Snakewater still clung to her, not in the obvious ways. No bruises bloomed on her throat now. Felix—Percival to her, that was—had given her extra salve for those, and the swelling had gone down. Her clothes were whole. Her voice had returned. The rough Irish lilt sat back in her sentences like it had always been there.

The difference lived in the way she sat. Closer. Not exactly folded in, not broken, yet something in her had turned inward. When she leaned against him, she made it look casual, as if she only wanted the better view. The weight of her arm on his made that lie transparent.

"You are very shiny," she said at last. "The sun is going to use your head as a looking glass."

"I look like an egg."

"A handsome egg." She smiled and straightened, as if the word had slipped out before she could fuss with it. "Besides, it suits you. Less to grab if someone decides to throw you off a wall."

"Comforting."

"You asked."

She had nearly been dead two nights ago. The mind took time to convince itself that had not become the permanent state of things.

Felix rode ahead of the wagon on a black horse that still carried the stiffness of ship travel in its gait. Jamie watched him for a while. Snakewater had cost him something. Whether that cost lay in what almost happened, or in what had been required after, Jamie could not yet say.

The road bent around a clump of hawthorn and then stopped. The wagon shuddered to a halt so abruptly that Jamie's teeth clicked together. Felix's hand shot up in a flat palm. The new men tightened their reins. Somewhere at the rear a horse snorted and stamped.

"Stay," Felix called without looking back. His voice carried no strain, only instruction.

Jamie stood on the bench to see.

The deer lay square in the center of the road as if it had specifically chosen that place to die. A young stag, not yet impressive, soft antlers still in velvet. One hind leg lay at an unnatural angle, bone pressing pale against skin. The animal's flank rose and fell in short, shallow bursts.

Blood had seeped into the mud beneath it, darkening the rut in a starburst. The tracks said it had tried to drag itself off the path, then failed and settled into this waiting.

Miranda followed his gaze, squinted, then let her attention slide away.

"Poor thing," she murmured, not unkindly. "It will make the wolves happy."

Felix, staying mounted, flicked two fingers at one of men riding a few horses back.

He was bald. Not shaved like Jamie, but bald in the way a man is when his hair has abandoned the effort and retreated. The skull beneath carried a scatter of pale scars like faint, raised rivers. His eyes had a washed-out quality to them. No malice lived in them. No anger either. Simply absence.

He swung down from his horse and crossed to the stag, boots sucking in the mud, and knelt beside it. One hand rested on its neck for a moment. Perhaps he was feeling for something. Pulse, breath, weight. Perhaps he was just steadying it.

His knife appeared without flourish. One second his hand lay empty at his belt. The next, steel glinted against the air. No one, later, would be able to say they had seen him draw.

The cut itself was small, almost neat. A single passing of the blade where neck met jaw, quick and precise. Blood came in a sudden sheet, hot and bright, steaming in the cold air. The stag jerked once, entire body seizing, then relaxed. The breath left it in a long shudder.

When the twitching stopped, he wiped the knife on the animal's flank in one smooth stroke, then folded it away. The knife vanished as quickly as it had appeared.

He took the forelegs and dragged the carcass from the road. He didn't look around to see who watched. The act existed in its own self-contained space, one small chore among many.

Jamie realized he had been holding his breath. He let it out slowly. His heart had stepped up its pace, not with fear exactly, more with the awareness of something incongruous. Plenty of men knew how to kill animals. Farmers, hunters, butchers, blacksmith. The motion had a different manner when done by someone who had spent years cutting throats that argued with the process.

Behind him, one of the older players made a half-hearted joke about venison for supper. Another complained about the delay and his aching posterior. The wheel at the back of the wagon squeaked in a small, fretful rhythm.

Miranda watched the hedgerows. Her attention had jumped ahead to the castle. When the road cleared and the wagon rolled forward again, she seemed to shake off a small part of herself and tuck it back where she kept her courage.

"Percival was right about the hair," she admitted. "You would have been scratching yourself bloody by now."

Jamie let his eyes travel once more to the bald fellow, now back in his saddle, expression unchanged. The man's gaze swept the treeline in the same quiet, unhurried way it had considered the dying animal. Nothing lingered in him. No triumph, no distaste. Only a readiness that made the space around him feel frigid.

He pressed his hands under his thighs again and watched the castle grow.

Wind slid across his scalp, cool and clean. The spring fields on either side of the road stirred in low ripples. Miranda hummed something under her breath, an Irish tune that had survived more empires than this one. Felix raised his hand once more, signaling some minor adjustment in formation that no one questioned.

The stag lay in the ditch behind them, blood soaking into the countryside, already being forgotten. Jamie knew he would remember that small, neat cut long after the bruises on Miranda's throat had faded. Some actions made sense only in hindsight. Others announced themselves with the clarity of a knife in open air.

SCENE 27

"You are gleaming again," Miranda said. "I could use you as a looking glass to fix my hair."

"You fixed it three times already."

"It is the first thing they will see. Might as well make it worth seeing."

The portcullis ahead was raised, the teeth of it framed in the arch like a second, suspended jaw. Men watched from the murder holes, nothing visible but the suggestion of helmets and the darker oval of eyes. A Taylor banner hung over the entrance, the gold fluttering against black.

Sound changed inside the tunnel. The shuffle of hooves and wheels echoed off stone, amplified and thrown back. The courtyard beyond spread wide and hard, flagstones worn by generations of drills. Barracks lined one side, stables the other. A well sat near the center, its rope freshly coiled, the bucket still dripping from someone's morning drawing. The air smelled of hay, old smoke, and hot iron.

Just inside the gate, iron spikes had been driven into the stone. Henry Beverley's head occupied the middle one.

The features had collapsed inward as flesh shrank, but the structure remained. Jaw, cheek, the familiar slope of a nose that had once been broken and healed slightly askew. The hair was still thick, braided roughly back for execution. Crows had taken the eyes. The empty sockets stared at nothing and everyone.

Jamie looked once, fully, and then put it away. The image settled in the same locked drawer where he kept Rowan's hopeless gaze and Lillian's scream when they dragged her away. He kept his expression neutral.

"Kneel," Barnaby whispered.

Jamie went down on one knee. The rest of the troupe followed in a staggered tide, like a wave hitting sand at slightly different times. Miranda knelt at his side, hand touching the ground a second longer than necessary to steady herself. The stone was cold even through worn leather.

Boots approached. Three sets, the rhythm clean and confident.

Jamie kept his gaze lowered, lifting it only as far as the line of their boots, letting his view build slowly. Polished leather. Spurs. The harder, heavier set of greaves.

King Lionel stopped in front of them.

He wore the crown Damien had chosen for him, a modest circlet that tried to pretend it had never seen blood. His doublet was rich without being ostentatious. His face had been carefully maintained, the beard trimmed close, the hair glossed and arranged.

The thing that struck Jamie was not the costume but the eyes. Lionel's gaze was quick and restless, never lingering too long, as if he were afraid that if he stared at anything for more than a few heartbeats, he might discover what he didn't want to know.

Behind him stood Richardson, in full armor, a solid wall of a man whose expression had absorbed the courtyard's indifference. On the king's other side waited Sir Rodham, shorter, neater, his posture too precise to be easy.

"Mr. Oddfellow," Lionel said, and the words came out warm, almost relieved. "I trust your journey was seamless."

Barnaby bowed his head. "It was, indeed, Your Grace."

"Quite a crew you have brought."

"Thank you, Your Grace."

Lionel flicked his fingers, granting permission, and Barnaby and the others rose. Jamie followed, careful and unhurried, settling his weight so that his body looked relaxed rather than poised.

Lionel's eyes moved along the line of faces. He was counting, lips shaping silent numbers. The habit of tallying something he understood, perhaps, in a world where everything else had been handed to him.

"Your letter suggested a fuller company."

"We have nineteen in all, Your Grace," Barnaby replied.

"Eighteen."

"Yes, Your Grace."

"Yes?"

"We have nineteen, Your Grace."

Lionel's brow drew together. "I count eighteen."

Jamie heard the space open before anyone else moved to fill it.

"He has a nervous problem," he blurted.

The courtyard's attention swung to him. Guards on the walls leaned a fraction closer. Even the horses seemed to listen.

"Sorry?" Lionel asked.

"Our nineteenth, Your Grace," Jamie said. "It's his condition. Strangers agitate him. He works best onstage, with a script. Outside of that, he finds crowds difficult. He thought it wiser to let him gather himself in the wagon."

"I see," Lionel said.

"Actors," Jamie added, with a small, apologetic lift of one shoulder. "You can imagine."

Richardson's voice cut in, harsh and deep. "He *will* kneel to his king—"

"I will allow it," Lionel said without taking his gaze off Jamie.

"These are travelers, men of the arts. We can allow them a moment to adjust. Taylor's Castle is notorious for overwhelming outsiders at first sight."

"He wanted you to know he is honored," Jamie continued, immediately unsure why. "And very eager to perform."

Lionel's mouth twitched at that, amusement or vanity or both. "That is very pleasant to hear." His attention sharpened. "And you are, my good man?"

"Teddy, Your Grace."

Lionel motioned for more.

Of course he did.

"Ivanovich," Jamie said, the syllables tumbling out before he could stop them. He wondered, dimly, why he hadn't chosen something shorter. Something English. "Teddy Ivanovich."

Lionel tested the name quietly to himself, like a line of verse he couldn't quite place. Jamie held his face still, thinking of all the ways a bad name could get a man remembered.

Then something else caught Lionel's eye. He looked past Jamie, toward the wagons.

"And your elusive friend?" he asked. "The shy one. Does he have a name, or shall we whistle when we need him?"

Jamie opened his mouth and, for a heartbeat, had nothing.

"He does not go by a name, Your Grace," he said at last, careful now. "Not while on tour. He believes the character should remain unbroken from the moment we leave one town until we arrive at the next."

A vibration traveled through the nearest wagon, canvas shivering, a weight shifting inside.

From within, two quick knocks sounded against the wood, spaced evenly.

"He wants you to know he's preparing, Your Grace," Jamie relayed,

Lionel laughed, brief and bright. "A true artist! I confess I am enamored. We shall have to find a way to coax him out without breaking him."

Behind Lionel, Margaret had taken her place at an open window overlooking the courtyard, hands resting on the sill, weight tilted slightly forward. The gown she wore was a deep green the color of river water before rain. Her dark hair fell unbound around her shoulders, a small defiance someone would comment on later in careful tones.

From her height the men below looked like pieces on a board, moving into positions someone else had chosen years ago. Lionel in his careful velvet. Richardson and Rodham bracketing him like punctuation. Two lines of players in road-stained clothes trying to look smaller than they were.

One of them drew her eye and refused to let go.

He stood a little behind Barnaby, near a woman whose posture carried the memory of tavern stages. His head had been shaved to the scalp, the bare skin catching light. The lack of hair did nothing to soften the sense of something coiled in him. His face belonged to a craftsman or a soldier, not a fool. His eyes lifted once, as if against his own judgment, and met hers.

Margaret had never seen him before. She knew that. Yet something in the line of his jaw, the way he held his shoulders in the presence of crowns, the quiet, measuring attention in his gaze, clicked into place with an old, uncomfortably private part of her. The part that still remembered standing at windows in Harthfell, watching her father ride out and her brother come back bloody, both convinced the world could be bent into fairness if they only pushed hard enough.

She didn't smile at once. The first expression was curiosity, then wariness, then something like relief that startled her. Only after that did the corners of her mouth tilt. Not the public smile she used for court, that bland, gracious arrangement everyone recognized. This one was smaller, meant only for him, designed to vanish if anyone looked up from the courtyard.

He stared longer than prudence allowed.

"Your Grace?" Richardson said quietly near Lionel's elbow. "He has not finished answering."

Jamie snapped his gaze back down, heart giving one hard knock against his ribs in reproof.

"Apologies, Your Grace," he said. "Travel dust. I was woolgathering."

Lionel seemed amused rather than offended. "Let us hope you are less distracted under the lights," he said. "I can hardly contain my excitement. The court has been in want of proper diversion for months."

High in the eastern tower, Damien Taylor watched the same scene from a different angle.

His chamber window afforded a view of the courtyard and the gate tunnel, the whole apparatus of welcome and denial. He stood beside it in his shirtsleeves, the morning cold sliding in against his bare forearms, hair still damp from a basin wash. Behind him, the bed was unmade, sheets twisted.

A young man lay across them, shirtless, propped on one elbow. Edmund Vane, merchant's son from the Kell, eyes the soft brown of polished walnut. He watched Damien with the languid satisfaction of someone who had eaten well and anticipated seconds.

"Those the players?" Edmund asked. "They look poorer than usual. Perhaps it is the new fashion."

Damien didn't answer.

From his height the troops of the yard, the king and his escorts, the newcomers, all arranged themselves in patterns he had memorized since boyhood. This was his board, not Lionel's, no matter whose head wore the crown. He knew the height of every wall, the angle of every arrow slit, the time each guard shift changed.

One man disrupted the familiar picture.

The shaved head helped. The light struck the skull and made him easy to track. Damien watched him kneel, rise, speak. Watched the slight delay before he gave a name. Watched the moment his attention caught on something above and refused to let go.

Yellow hair, the mind supplied automatically, though only the barest stubble showed against the skin. Not the full, bright mane he had imagined all his life, but the color was there in the short growth, pale and insistent.

Green eyes.

The air in the chamber seemed to thin.

The memory didn't belong to him, yet it had shaped him. A midwife's voice in a room he had not entered, carried to him through years of whispered repetition and careful omissions. *Yellow haired, green eyed, death will follow him from the womb. The child who kills kings. The boy the queen birthed while the world burned.*

He had always been half convinced it was a story Anya's enemies told to stain her; a superstition wrapped in guilt. The other half had kept him awake most nights of his youth, cataloguing every blond boy in the kingdom.

The one below spoke, the words too distant to hear, but Damien saw the slight narrowing of Lionel's eyes, the quick adjustment of Barnaby's stance when the answer didn't come fast enough. Saw the queen at her window, leaning forward a breath more than necessary.

"Come back to bed," Edmund said behind him. "You can watch your brother's pets later."

Damien stepped away from the window. The decision felt like it took years and no time at all.

"Leave," Damien said.

The laughter died, confusion sliding into its place.

For a moment Edmund looked as if he might push. The silence in the room, which was not quite silence at all, advised against it.

He put on his shirt. Fumbled with the laces. Collected the rest of his clothing with as much dignity as speed allowed. Left.

Damien stood very still in the sudden quiet, shirt unbuttoned at the throat, bare feet cold against the rushes. He didn't return to the window at once. Instead, he crossed to the mirror that hung above his desk, the glass slightly warped from an old, imperfect casting.

His reflection stared back at him, stretched and compressed in small betrayals.

He buttoned his shirt slowly, each fastening deliberate, watching his fingers move. When he reached his throat he paused, thumb resting against the hollow there. For a moment he imagined a knife in another man's hand, a single neat cut where skin met bone. The castle below, the brothers, the crown, the careful scaffolding of his power, all reduced to the distance between steel and artery.

He let his hand fall.

Only then did he return to the window. The boy was still in the yard. Still speaking. Lionel was laughing now, some comment about quarters and food and how terribly hungry real art made a man. Margaret had retreated a step from her window, enough to pretend she had merely passed by.

Damien watched the shaved head move among the others.

In the courtyard, the formalities shifted into something looser.

Lionel clapped his hands together, pleased with his own hospitality. "You must be ravished after the journey," he said. "We have prepared food in the lower hall. Your quarters are ready. Clean, warm." He craned his neck toward the wagon where Felix hid. "And private, of course!"

Two measured knocks answered from inside.

"Brilliant," Lionel marveled, a short burst of laughter escaping him. "Mr Oddfellow, you must tell me how you manage them. I can barely get my own servants to sit still, and here you have men climbing into boxes for your art."

"They are certainly easier to direct than nobles, Your Grace."

"Have you seen 'The Siege of Northbury' performed since they rewrote the third act? The new ending with the fire? Remarkable. I wept, I'm not ashamed to say."

Barnaby's eyes lit in a way Jamie recognized. Whatever danger they were in, a man like Barnaby couldn't help accepting an invitation into his favorite territory.

"We saw a version in the capital before winter," he replied. "The staging lacked conviction. Too much smoke, not enough fear."

"Exactly," Lionel said, delighted. "Exactly. The smoke is only convincing if the actors remember they are meant to be breathing it. Otherwise, one might as well wave incense. Come, you must tell me your opinion on the Ashford cycle. My brother finds it dreadfully tedious, but I think it speaks to something essential in the northern character."

The king and the player fell into step together as the party began to drift toward the inner archway. The two of them started talking in earnest, names of playwrights and favorite monologues and half-remembered productions spilling out with the ease of old friends.

From the outside, with his crown and his careful clothes, Lionel looked like a man in command. Listening to him argue about whether comedy needed blood to matter, Jamie saw something else: a boy who had found, in theatre, a vocabulary for the courage he didn't possess and the tragedies he was not brave enough to live through himself.

Miranda leaned close enough that he could feel her breath on his neck. "He loves the sound of words," she whispered. "That is something, at least."

Guards closed in at the edges as they moved across the yard, a polite escort that felt a shade heavier than courtesy. Somewhere behind them a stable hand began to haul the wagon toward its assigned place. Felix remained inside, either listening or already somewhere else in his mind, plotting routes through corridors he had not yet walked.

Jamie's glance lifted once more to the upper stories.

Margaret had stepped back from the window, a shadow now rather than a shape. Even so, he felt her attention on him like a faint pressure.

In the tower, unseen, Damien watched them all like a man who had finally spotted the flaw in his own reflection.

Jamie followed the king into the castle he had come to burn, bare scalp cold, stomach steady, hands empty. On either side of him walked men who thought they knew what this visit would be.

They didn't.

SCENE 28

THE FATES WE CHOOSE

The chamber was too quiet.

Felix stood in the center of it and let the silence press against him. Stone walls. A narrow bed. A window that faced the gardens. Someone had left a basin of water on the table and a cloth folded beside it, the small courtesies extended to guests who were not quite trusted.

He had not asked for this room. Barnaby had arranged quarters, and one of the stewards had led Felix here through back corridors while the rest of the company followed Lionel into the lower hall. No one had questioned his absence. The story about nerves had held.

The bag sat where he had dropped it, canvas worn thin at the seams, armor wrapped inside. He didn't open it. The smell of the road clung to his clothes, Snakewater fog and horse sweat and something older underneath, something that belonged to the years before the road became the only place he knew how to live.

He crossed to the window.

The gardens spread below in neat rows, hedges trimmed to angles that pleased no one in particular. Gravel paths wound between them. A fountain stood dry at the center, basin cracked, stone darkened where water had pooled and evaporated summer after summer. Rose bushes lined the southern wall, bare this time of year, thorns catching the weak afternoon light.

Twenty-four years since he had looked at those roses.

Spring had come early in 1578.

The roses were already blooming when they should have been buds, red and white crowding the branches as if the flowers knew something the gardeners did not. Felix walked the gravel path with his hands loose at his sides, armor catching the afternoon sun. He was nineteen. The scar that would later split his face from brow to jaw had not yet happened. His hair was dark and full, and when he smiled it was the smile of a man who still believed cleverness could outrun consequence.

He knew she was there before he rounded the hedge. The stillness she carried when she did not want to be found. The faint displacement of garden air that meant someone was sitting where they should not be sitting, thinking what they should not be thinking.

Anya sat on the bench beneath the oak, hands folded in her lap, posture so still she might have been waiting for a painter who would never arrive. Her dress was gray, the color she wore when she wanted to disappear into sky. Her blonde hair fell loose around her shoulders. She only wore it down when she had stopped caring who saw.

That was the first wrong thing.

"You are brooding, your grace," he said.

She did not turn. "I am thinking."

"The dangerous kind or the merely destructive kind?"

"Must there be a distinction?"

"With you? Always."

He circled the bench and stood before her, blocking the roses. Her eyes lifted to his face with the weariness of someone who had known he would come and wished he had not and was grateful anyway. The shadows beneath them were new. He catalogued them alongside the tension in her jaw, the white-knuckled grip of her own fingers, the particular angle of her shoulders that meant she had not slept.

"How long have you been out here?"

"Does it matter?"

"It matters if you have been freezing yourself into marble for my benefit."

"Not everything is for your benefit."

"Tell me."

"There is nothing to tell."

"Anya."

"There is nothing—"

"You are sitting in the garden you hate, wearing the dress you wear when you want to be invisible, and you have not insulted me once in nearly a minute." He crouched in front of her, bringing his face level with hers. "Something is wrong. I would prefer you tell me what it is before I begin guessing, because my guesses will be worse."

Her eyes met his. This close he could see the fracture lines, the places where the mask had been applied too hastily that morning and was already beginning to slip.

"I am with child."

The words arrived simply. Felix heard them. Understood them. Felt the ground reorganize itself beneath his feet.

He did not move.

"How long?"

"Two months. Perhaps more."

He reached for her hands. She let him take them—her fingers cold, trembling slightly, the hands of a woman who had been holding something too tightly for too long. He pressed them between his palms and felt her exhale, a small release of breath she probably did not know she had been holding.

"Does he know?"

"Not yet." Her voice steadied. "He will not suspect. He visits my chambers often enough that the timing will seem ordinary."

The word landed wrong. Felix turned it over, examined it. Ordinary. A child conceived in secret, raised in plain sight, wearing another man's name. His child. Hers. Hidden inside a marriage she had not chosen; beneath the architecture of a duty she had never been allowed to refuse.

"When you say the timing—"

"I mean what you think I mean." She met his eyes. "I have been careful. I am always careful. He will believe what he needs to believe."

Something cold moved through Felix's chest. Not jealousy—he had made his peace with that particular demon the first time he kissed her, knowing whose bed she would return to after. Something else. The knowledge of what she was carrying, and what it would cost her to carry it, and how little of that cost he would ever be permitted to share.

"And when the child comes?"

"It will be the heir." She said it simply, the way she said everything that hurt too much to say any other way. "Taylor blood. The only blood that matters."

"And mine."

Her hands tightened in his. For a moment her composure wavered, something raw flickering behind her eyes. "And yours."

He lifted her hands to his mouth and pressed his lips against her knuckles.

"I could take you away from here."

"No."

"I know people. Ships that leave without manifests, places where names mean nothing—"

"Felix." Her voice was gentle, which was worse than if she had been angry. "You know why I cannot."

He did know. He had always known. The Taylor line, one hundred and fifty-seven years unbroken. The kingdom balanced on the point of a needle. Aldric's legacy and the legacy before him, the whole grinding machinery of succession that had made her a queen before she was ever allowed to be a woman.

"What I know," he said carefully, "is that you are sitting in a garden telling me you are carrying our child, and in the same breath telling me nothing will change."

"Because nothing can."

"Says who?"

"Says everyone. Says history. Says the particular configuration of power that keeps my husband on his throne and my family name above the gates." She pulled one hand free and touched his face. Her fingers found the line of his jaw, traced it. "Says me, Felix. Because I am the only one who can."

He caught her wrist. Held it. Did not let go.

"This is not a fate you chose."

"None of it was chosen. That does not make it any less mine." Her thumb brushed his cheekbone, the touch so light it barely registered. "This child will be everything. The only part of us that survives intact. The only thing I can give you that will last longer than we do."

"I don't want something that lasts. I want—"

"I know what you want." Her voice broke, just slightly, in the place where she kept the things she couldn't afford to say. "I know exactly what you want. And I cannot give it to you. I cannot give it to either of us. All I can give you is this."

She placed her free hand against her stomach. A gesture so small it would have meant nothing to anyone watching. Between them, it meant everything.

Felix released her wrist. He stayed crouched on the gravel, looking up at her, this woman he had loved since he was old enough to know what love cost and too young to understand he would pay it anyway.

"I will protect this child," he said. "Whatever happens. Whatever it costs."

"I know you will."

"I will protect you."

"You cannot."

"Watch me."

She smiled then, finally, a real smile, cracked through with grief. She leaned forward and pressed her forehead to his, their breath mingling in the small space between.

"I love you," she said, very quietly. "I have loved you since before I knew I was not supposed to. That is the only truth I have left. Do you understand?"

He closed his eyes. Her skin warm against his. The smell of her, rose water and something underneath that was only hers.

"I understand."

"No." She pulled back, and her eyes were dry now. "But you will. Eventually."

She stood. Smoothed her dress. Became the queen again in small adjustments of posture and expression.

"I will see you at dinner," she said. "You will stand along the wall with the other knights. You will not look at me more than courtesy requires."

"And if I do?"

"You will not."

She was right. He would not. He had learned, by then, the particular discipline of looking at her only when looking was permitted. The way a starving man learned to walk past bread without reaching for it.

She walked back toward the castle, hair golden against the gray stone. He watched her until she disappeared through a doorway. Then he stayed on his knees in the garden for a long time, listening to the fountain that did not run, watching the roses bloom too early into a spring that would not last.

The roses were bare now.

Felix stood at the window and counted the thorns. A useless exercise. The kind of thing a man did when the alternative was thinking about what came next.

The machinery of the next few days was already in motion, gears turning, weights shifting, everything moving toward the moment when masks would come off and steel would speak. Twenty-four years he had waited. Twenty-four years of blood and road dust and the slow patient work of becoming the man who could walk back into this castle and finish what had started in a garden when a woman told him she was carrying his child.

He had promised to protect the child.

He had not been able to protect her.

The memory of her forehead against his. The smell of rose water. The cracked smile that contained more grief than any tears could have.

Eventually, she had said. *You will understand eventually.*

He understood now. He wished he didn't.

He turned from the window. The bag sat on the floor, armor wrapped inside.

He sat on the edge of the narrow bed and listened to the silence.

The roses would bloom again in summer.

Felix wouldn't be here to see them.

SCENE 29

DOGS

The corridors were different at night.

Jamie moved through them with a bundle of bedsheets pressed against his chest. He hadn't been able to sleep. The castle sat too heavily around him, all that stone and silence pressing down like a hand on the back of his neck. He needed to walk. To learn the shape of the place. Felix had taught him that much without ever explaining why it mattered.

The torches had burned low in their sconces. Shadows pooled in doorways and along the joints where wall met floor. His footsteps echoed and returned to him changed, as if the castle were repeating his movements back in a language he didn't speak.

He turned a corner and stopped.

To his right, a doorway opened into a small antechamber. Torchlight moved within, steadier than the corridor sconces, and in that light stood something that seized the eye before the mind could catch up.

A statue.

Nearly seven feet of pale stone. A figure in armor, one hand resting on a sword pommel, the other held loosely at his side. The face was handsome in the way powerful faces were handsome; not beauty exactly, but the assumption of it. The chin lifted. The gaze fixed on something beyond the room, beyond the castle, beyond the reach of whoever stood at the statue's base looking up.

Jamie stepped into the chamber. The bedsheets hung forgotten against his hip.

He studied the stone face. The sculptor had caught something true in the set of the jaw, the slight forward lean of the shoulders. Hunger, maybe. Or the memory of hunger in a man who had learned to dress it as something nobler.

"'Among men, there are lions...'"

Jamie turned sharply. His heart knocked once against his ribs.

Damien Taylor stood in the doorway.

He had not been there a moment before. Jamie would have sworn to it. Yet he stood now as if he had always been standing there, hands clasped behind his back, head tilted in mild curiosity.

"'...there are wolves... and there are dogs.'" Damien stepped into the chamber, hands clasped behind his back. "'What separates them is merely their resolve.'"

"Who said that?"

"You're looking at him." Damien stopped beside Jamie, close enough that their shoulders nearly touched. "The statue. It's of my father."

Jamie looked back at the stone face.

"It's incredible."

"Why are you here?"

"My lord?"

"It's late," Damien said warmly. "With your journey, I surmised you'd be more shadow than man."

"*Oh.*" Jamie shifted the bedsheets in his arms, suddenly

aware of how foolish they made him look. "Caught my eye, is all."

"It's all right. I too suffer from a restless soul. A cursed affliction, but also a gift. The night is kinder to the mind."

Damien moved closer to the sculpture, studying it the way a man might study his own reflection in uncertain light. "Truthfully, I used to hate this statue. When I was younger, I was convinced it watched me." He paused. "Now it comforts me."

"Were you close with him?"

"My father?" Damien's mouth moved into something that was not quite a smile. "Hardly. But we saw each other."

He turned then, and his attention settled on Jamie with a focus that felt like pressure.

"Where are you from?"

"Wolfpine, my lord."

"Charming."

"Thank you, my lord."

"It's my understanding that you are a man of carpentry."

"That's correct, my lord."

"Not one for the costumes, then."

"My father taught me how to use my hands." The words came out before Jamie could stop them. He felt the small flinch of grief that always followed when he spoke of Rowan without meaning to.

"I see that. We could use an extra pair."

"My lord?"

"Our moat. The timber frame needs reinforcing before the rains come. The men could use help. If it's no trouble."

"Not at all, my lord."

"Tremendous. The crown thanks you." Damien turned toward the corridor. "Perhaps a tour?"

"I couldn't, my lord

"Nonsense. The pleasure is mine." He gestured toward the darkness beyond the doorway. "Shall we?"

The great hall was empty at this hour.

Moonlight fell through the stained-glass windows and painted the floor in fractured bands of black and gold, the colors of Taylor rendered in light instead of cloth. The windows themselves were old—older than the current wing, Damien had said as they passed beneath the threshold—and the glass had warped in places, bending the moonlight into shapes that shifted when Jamie moved. Their footsteps echoed in the vaulted space and came back to them from the distant ceiling, doubled and strange. Jamie felt small in a way that had nothing to do with the architecture.

"Here we are." Damien stopped near the center of the hall, turning slowly as if seeing it for the first time. His shadow stretched long across the flagstones, merging with the dark bands thrown by the windows. "When I was a boy, my father and I would walk through the castle at night. After the servants had gone to bed. After my mother." He paused on the word, let it settle. "I learned every corner. Every passage. The places where the stone had cracked and no one had thought to mend it. The rooms that had been sealed for generations." His gaze moved upward, tracing the ribbed vaulting. "But this room was always my favorite."

"Why?"

"Because it remembers." Damien gestured toward the walls. "Everything else in this castle serves the living. This room serves the dead."

Jamie's gaze moved along the walls. Portraits hung at intervals, faces watching from gilt frames. Lords and ladies. Kings. The accumulated weight of a dynasty preserved in oil and canvas. Some of the faces shared Damien's coloring—the dark hair, the angular jaw—while others seemed to belong to different bloodlines entirely, absorbed through marriage or conquest. A few of the older portraits had darkened with age, the varnish gone amber, the features retreating into shadow as if the subjects were slowly withdrawing from the world of the living.

One portrait drew him forward. Larger than the others. A man in ceremonial armor, crown resting on dark hair, the same face he had seen rendered in stone moments before. But the painter had caught something the sculptor had missed—or perhaps chosen to show what the sculptor had been wise enough to hide. A coldness in the eyes. A mouth that knew how to smile without warmth, and perhaps favored so.

King Tobias Taylor II, read the plaque beneath.

"Is this him again?"

"Guilty." Damien had followed him, standing close enough that Jamie could feel the warmth of his presence without turning. "My father commissioned it himself. He wanted something that would last longer than stone."

"Stone lasts a long time."

"Stone can be broken. Canvas can be burned. But the *idea* of a man—that is what endures. That is what he understood."

Jamie studied the painted face. The artist had rendered the armor in exacting detail, each plate and joint, each rivet catching light from some unseen source. But the face itself seemed almost unfinished by comparison. As if the painter had been afraid to look too closely.

"Your father," Damien said. "Is he well?"

The question came from nowhere. Jamie felt a cold flash of panic move through his chest that he had to strangle before it reached his face. He thought of Rowan. Of the last time he had seen him, standing in the doorway of their cottage with the morning light behind him, his hand raised in farewell. He thought of the years since. The silence. The not knowing that was worse than knowledge.

"Well enough," he heard himself say. "Last I saw him."

"And when was that?"

"Some time ago." Jamie kept his eyes on the portrait, afraid of what his face might betray. "We don't keep regular contact."

"A shame." Damien's tone offered nothing; no sympathy, no judgment, no indication of whether he believed the lie. "A father and son should understand each other. Even when understanding is... difficult."

In the lower corner of the portrait, barely visible in the dim light, Jamie found an inscription. 1578. G.G.

"The year I was born."

The words left his mouth before he considered them. A small offering of coincidence, nothing more. But Damien's attention sharpened beside him, a shift so subtle Jamie might have imagined it. A slight turn of the head. A pause in his breathing. When Jamie glanced sideways, Damien's expression had not changed, but something *behind* it had.

"It was completed after the Northbury incident," Damien said. "Before my time. I've been told the painter spent six months at court. Refused to leave until he had captured my father exactly as he wished to be seen."

"What happened to him?"

"Who?"

"The king."

"Took ill." His voice had flattened, emptied of the warmth it had carried moments before. "Three years past."

"I'm sorry."

Damien said nothing. His gaze remained fixed on the portrait, on the painted face of the man who had raised him, and for a moment something complicated moved behind his eyes. Grief, perhaps. Or something darker that wore its clothing. His hands, clasped behind his back, shifted against each other.

Then it was gone.

"He was not an easy man," Damien said finally. "But he was my father. And this kingdom was his life."

He turned from the portrait, and when he looked at Jamie again, the earlier ease had returned.

"We carry our fathers with us, whether we wish to or not. Their lessons. Their failures. Their silences."

He began walking toward the far end of the hall, where another doorway waited in shadow.

"Come. There's more to see."

The theatre took Jamie's breath in a way he hadn't expected.

They entered through a side door—Damien producing a key from somewhere on his person, the lock turning with an oiled whisper that suggested frequent use—and emerged into a space that seemed to belong to a different building entirely. A different world, perhaps. The corridor behind them had been stone and shadow and the particular dampness of old castles at night. This was something else.

The ceiling vaulted upward into darkness, the upper reaches lost where the candlelight couldn't follow. Rows of seats descended toward a stage framed by columns carved with figures Jamie couldn't identify; gods or monsters or the strange hybrid creatures that lived in the space between. Everything gleamed. Polished wood the color of chestnuts. Brass fixtures held candles that no one had bothered to light, their wicks black with old char. Velvet upholstery the color of wine covered each seat, deep and rich.

The smell hit him next. Beeswax and dust and something underneath that might have been perfume or might have been the ghost of it, the olfactory memory of a hundred performances attended by women who could afford to smell like flowers in winter. The air itself felt different here—warmer, thicker, as if the room had been sealed against the drafts that plagued the rest of the castle.

"Who paid for this?"

His voice came out smaller than he intended. The acoustics swallowed it, then returned it changed, softer, as if the theatre were teaching him how to speak within its walls.

"The bank."

Jamie followed, and with each step the scale of the place impressed itself more deeply upon him. The seats on either side watched like empty faces, row after row of them, hundreds of velvet mouths waiting to be filled. He tried to imagine this room full of courtiers and nobles arranged by rank and favor, musicians tuning instruments in the gallery above, the rustle of silk and the murmur of anticipation before the curtain rose. The whispered cruelties, the political calculations disguised as appreciation for art, the way power arranged itself even in spaces designed for entertainment.

He'd grown up in Taylor's End. He'd seen the castle from a distance his entire life, had watched its towers catch the morning light while he hauled water or mended fences or did the thousand small tasks that comprised a life lived in the shadow of wealth. He'd known, in the abstract way that poor people always knew, that the world inside those walls was different from his own.

He hadn't understood how different.

"It's stunning." He meant it.

"It does its job," Damien murmured.

The words landed flat, almost dismissive, and Jamie glanced at Damien's profile. The Prince's expression hadn't changed—that mild, interested look he wore like a mask over whatever actually moved behind his eyes—but something in the tone suggested contempt. For the theatre? For the brother who used it? For Jamie's obvious awe?

He couldn't tell. Within every gesture seemed to live three meanings, and two of them were designed to mislead.

They reached the front of the house. The stage rose before them, boards worn smooth by generations of footsteps, the grain of the wood visible even in the low light. How many plays had been performed here? How many lies told in the service of entertainment? How many truths dressed up as fiction so they could be spoken aloud without consequence?

"Where does the king sit?"

Damien pointed to an elevated chair in the center of the front row. Throne-like. Positioned so that whoever sat there would be seen as clearly as the players on stage—perhaps more clearly, given the angle of the surrounding seats. A man could watch a play from that chair, but he couldn't do so privately. Every reaction would be visible. Every laugh, every frown, every moment of boredom or delight catalogued by the courtiers arranged behind him.

It occurred to Jamie that this was the point. The king didn't come to the theatre to watch. He came to be watched watching.

"Personally, I prefer the gallery," Damien said. "The view is better. But my brother is quite the devotee."

Jamie stared at the empty stage. The boards held no answers. They'd witnessed too much to offer anything as simple as truth.

"She would love this."

The words escaped before he could stop them. A door he hadn't meant to open, swinging wide and naked.

"Who?"

Jamie felt the question land. The weight of it. He shouldn't have spoken. Shouldn't have given Damien anything to hold, any thread to pull. Felix had warned him about this—the way powerful men collected information the way other men collected bits, storing it away at little cost until it could be used to advantage.

But the words were out now. He couldn't call them back.

"An old friend of mine." He kept his voice steady. Forced himself to meet Damien's eyes. "She was taken."

"I'm sorry."

The sympathy in Damien's voice sounded genuine. That was the worst part. Jamie couldn't tell if it was performance or something real, and the uncertainty made him feel more exposed than an obvious lie would have.

"The Snakewater Savages." The lie came easily. He'd practiced it on the road, turning it over in his mind until it fit his mouth like a familiar food. "Have you heard of them?"

"I have."

"Nasty lot."

"I wasn't aware they were active near Wolfpine."

The observation slid in like a knife; casual, almost offhand, but edged. Jamie felt it catch against the fabric of his story, testing for weakness.

"Nor were we."

The silence that followed had a nasty texture to it. A weight that pressed against Jamie's chest and made the air feel thicker than it had a moment before. He could feel Damien studying him, weighing the story against whatever instinct had been triggered by the inconsistency. The Snakewater Savages operated in the marshlands to the east. Wolfpine sat in the opposite direction, nestled against the foothills. The geography didn't fit.

But Damien didn't press. That was almost worse. A man

who pressed could be deflected. A man who simply watched
and waited and stored things away for later use was something
else entirely.

"Have you ever loved a woman, my lord?"

Jamie didn't know why he asked it. Deflection, perhaps. A
way to shift the weight of the conversation onto safer ground.
Or perhaps something else; a genuine curiosity about the man
standing beside him, this Prince who spoke of his father's statue
with something that sounded like contempt and his brother's
theatre with something that sounded like hate.

Damien's expression didn't change. "My mother, I suppose."

The answer landed strangely. *Suppose*. As if love were a hy-
pothesis rather than a certainty. As if the Prince wasn't entirely
sure what the word meant or whether he'd ever truly felt it.

"I never knew mine." Jamie looked at the empty stage rather
than at the man beside him. The boards held nothing, but they
were easier to face than Damien's careful eyes. "But sometimes
I *feel* her. Is that mad?"

"Not at all."

"I just hope she's well. Cared for. Happy." He paused. The
next words came harder, dragged up from somewhere deeper
than he usually allowed himself to visit. "Wherever she is."

Damien's hand came to rest on Jamie's shoulder. The touch
was light, almost fraternal, the gesture of a brother comforting
another. But something in it made Jamie's skin want to pull
away. A wrongness he couldn't name. The sense that the gesture meant something different to the man giving it than it did
to the man receiving it.

"I'm sure she is," Damien said. "And she'd be proud. Believe
me."

Jamie made himself smile. "I hope so."

They walked back through the corridors the way they'd come.
The torches had burned lower still, some guttering toward ex-
tinction, others already dead and smoking in their sconces. The

castle felt different now; not smaller, but more present. More aware. As if it had been listening the whole time and had finally decided to pay attention.

Jamie catalogued the route as they walked. Left at the tapestry of the hunt. Right at the suit of armor with the dented helm. Straight through the gallery where moonlight fell in silver rectangles across the floor. The information settled into his mind automatically, the habit of survival he'd learned on the road with Felix. Know your exits. Know your path. Know which doors lock from the inside and which lock from the outside.

He didn't know why the knowledge felt more urgent now than it had an hour ago. Something had shifted. Some balance had tipped. The castle that had seemed merely large and cold when he arrived now felt like something else entirely.

They were nearly back to the players' quarters when the sound came.

Low. Deep. A rumble that seemed to rise from beneath the floor and pass through the walls and fade into a silence that felt thicker than before. Not thunder—the sky had been clear when they entered the theatre. Not footsteps—nothing human moved with that weight. The sound came from somewhere below them, or around them, or everywhere at once, a vibration that Jamie felt in his chest before his ears had finished processing it.

Jamie stopped walking. His hand moved instinctively toward a sword he wasn't wearing, fingers closing on empty air where a hilt should have been.

"What was that?"

Damien hadn't stopped. Hadn't, as far as Jamie could tell, reacted at all. His stride remained even, his shoulders relaxed, his hands still clasped behind his back in that posture of casual authority he wore so easily.

"Dogs," he said, without turning around.

The word fell flat. Final. A door closing on a room Jamie wasn't meant to enter. He stood in the corridor and watched Damien's back recede into the darkness, and for a moment he considered pressing. Asking what kind of dogs made a sound like that. Asking why a Prince would keep animals in the basement of a castle. Asking any of the questions that pressed against the inside of his skull like water against a dam.

He didn't ask.

After a moment, Jamie followed.

The rumble didn't come again. But the silence it left behind had a different quality than the silence that had come before—heavier, somehow, and more deliberate. As if the castle were holding its breath.

As if something beneath them were doing the same.

The candles had burned to nubs by the time Jeffrey Spires lost his fourth hand of the night.

"Horseshit." He threw his cards on the table. The other players exchanged glances—the kind of glances men exchange when someone's been pushing it all night and they've decided together, without speaking, not to push back. "Deal again."

"Game's over, Jeffrey."

"I said deal again."

The men at the table collected their coins and stood. Jeffrey watched them go with the unfocused hostility of a man who'd been drinking since sundown. He muttered something under his breath. Laughed at his own joke. Reached for the bottle in front of him and found it empty.

Eli polished a glass behind the bar and said nothing.

Jeffrey had been coming to Taylor's Ale more often lately. Before, he'd kept to his shop, his woodwork, his quiet routines. A private man. The kind who nodded when you passed him in the street but didn't stop to talk. He'd raised his daughter alone after his wife died, and people respected that, the way they respected anyone who carried weight without complaint.

Now he came in three, four nights a week. Laughing too loud. Buying rounds he couldn't afford. Telling stories that went nowhere and laughing at the ends of them anyway. Acting like a man with nothing on his conscience. Acting like everything was fine.

Eli watched him, watched the way his hands shook when he reached for his cup, the way his eyes skittered away from anyone who held his gaze too long, the way he flinched, sometimes, at sounds that weren't there—a door closing, a voice raised in the corner. The universal language of guilt was written across his body in a language Eli had learned to read years ago while tending bar, while watching men drink themselves toward truths they couldn't face sober.

Two months ago, Jeffrey Spires had stood in front of his own shop and watched his daughter be dragged away by the King's Watch. Eli had heard the story from three different people. How Jeffrey had looked at his feet. How Lillian had screamed for him, screamed his name, screamed *father* until her voice broke, and Jeffrey Spires had not moved. Had not spoken. Had simply stood there while they put her on a horse and rode away.

The glass in Eli's hand creaked. He loosened his grip. Set it down carefully.

The tavern emptied in stages. Farmers first, stumbling home to whatever warmth waited for them. Then merchants, counting their coins, pulling their coats tight against the cold that crept under the door. Then the drunks who had to be shown out.

Jeffrey was among the last. He sat swaying on his stool, staring at the grain of the bar like it held some secret he was trying to decode. His face was slack. His eyes were wet and red.

"Closing," Eli said.

Jeffrey looked up. He'd been avoiding Eli's gaze all night. Eli had noticed.

"One more."

"*Closing.*"

His tone held little room for debate. Jeffrey's mouth opened, then closed. For a moment he looked like he might say something. Eli waited. Let the silence stretch.

Jeffrey pushed himself off the stool and made for the door without another word.

Eli watched him go.

The tavern was empty now. Quiet in the way only empty

rooms can be quiet, the silence rushing in to fill the space where noise had been. The fire had burned down to embers. The smell of spilled ale and woodsmoke hung in the air. Somewhere outside, a dog barked once and went still.

Eli finished polishing the glass in his hand. Slow strokes. Even pressure. The same motion he'd made ten thousand times. He held the glass up to the dying firelight, checked for smears, found none. Set it on the shelf with the others.

He hung his rag on its hook.

Then he reached beneath the bar and retrieved a small knife from the shelf where he kept it wrapped in oilcloth. Not a sword. Not a cleaver. Just a knife, the kind you'd use to cut rope or pare fruit or open letters. A blade the length of his hand, honed sharp enough to part hair. He'd owned it for years. Never used it for anything that mattered.

He tucked it into his belt, beneath his coat where it wouldn't show.

The last candles guttered in their holders. Eli blew them out one by one, moving through the darkness by memory, by the map of this place he'd built over decades of nights exactly like this one. When the last flame died, the only light came from the embers in the hearth, orange and low, painting shadows on the walls.

He stood there for a moment. Breathing. Letting the decision settle into his bones.

Then he crossed to the door.

Outside, April had remembered it was still winter.

The cold hit him like a hand across the face; the bitter, biting cold of the small hours, the kind that came down from the mountains and settled into the valley like something with weight. His breath plumed white in front of him. The mud of the street had frozen into ruts and ridges, hard beneath his boots.

The full moon hung fat and pale above the rooftops, bathing everything in light the color of bone. The road gleamed with it. The frost on the storefronts glittered. The world looked carved from silver and shadow, still as a painting, still as death.

Two in the morning, maybe three. The witching hour, his mother would have called it. The hour when the veil between worlds wore thin and things that should stay buried climbed up into the light. Eli didn't believe in any of that. He was a businessman. He believed in what he could see, what he could touch, what he could do with his own two hands.

And he believed in debts.

The street was empty. Every window dark. Every door closed. Taylor's End had pulled itself indoors and shuttered its eyes, and the silence that remained was the silence of a held breath, of a world waiting for something to happen. Even the dogs had stopped barking.

Eli put on his cap, locked the door behind him, and started walking.

Jeffrey was ahead of him by forty yards, weaving along the wooden porches that fronted the storefronts. His boots scraped the planks, loud in the silence, arrhythmic, the graceless percussion of a man too drunk to walk straight. He stumbled once, caught himself on a post, stood there swaying for a moment, then pushed off and kept moving. His breath clouded around his head. His shadow stretched long and strange in the moonlight, rippling across the frozen mud.

He didn't look back.

Eli followed at a distance. Matching his pace to Jeffrey's, staying far enough back that his footsteps wouldn't carry, close enough that he'd never lose sight. The wooden porches gave way to packed earth, then to the narrow lane that wound toward the eastern edge of the village where the craftsmen kept their shops.

The cold worked into his fingers, his ears, the space between his collar and his neck. He didn't feel it. He was thinking about Lillian. About the way Jamie and her used to look at each other. About the sound of her screaming as his brother's men took her away.

Jeffrey turned off the main lane. He stepped into the alley between the chandler's shop and the old grain store; a narrow cut between buildings, barely wide enough for two men to pass.

Eli heard him fumbling with his trousers. The sound of piss hitting frozen dirt.

He closed the distance in silence.

The alley was dark. The buildings on either side rose up and blocked the moonlight, leaving only a thin stripe of silver at the far end. The cold was deeper here, trapped between the walls. Eli's boots found the frozen ground without sound.

Two shapes in the darkness now. One still, one swaying. Silhouettes against the deeper black.

Jeffrey turned. Squinted. His hands were still at his trousers. *"The fuck are you doing, mate?"*

Eli went in fast.

The first blow took Jeffrey in the stomach, just below the ribs. A short, hard thrust that Eli felt all the way up his arm, the resistance of cloth and flesh, then the give, then the wet heat spreading across his knuckles. Jeffrey's eyes went wide. His mouth opened around a sound that never came.

Eli pulled the blade free and went in again.

The second blow caught him in the chest. The third in the side. Jeffrey's hands came up—too slow, too drunk, too late—and Eli was already inside his guard, already working, the knife rising and falling in short vicious strokes, the wet percussion of metal finding meat.

Jeffrey grabbed at Eli's shirt. His fingers scrabbled for purchase, found it, lost it. He tried to say something—a word, a name, a plea—but all that came out was a bubbling sound, like water running through a blocked drain.

His legs folded.

He went down into the frozen mud and the piss and the dark with a muted thud. Eli stood over him for a moment. Breathing hard. His hand was hot and wet. Steam rose from the blade in the cold air.

Jeffrey Spires looked up at him. His eyes were still open. His mouth was still working, trying to form words, trying to understand. Then the light behind his eyes went out, and he was just a shape on the ground, just a problem that had been solved.

Eli squatted and wiped the blade on Jeffrey's coat. Tucked it back into his belt.

He looked down at the body. At the man who'd sold his daughter to save himself. At the spreading dark stain that the moonlight turned to silver.

He felt nothing.

Eli turned and walked out of the alley the way he'd come.

The street was empty. The moon hung where he'd left it, fat and pale and indifferent. The cold had not relented. His breath still plumed white. The world looked exactly as it had five minutes ago, as if nothing had happened, as if nothing had changed.

He walked back to the tavern. Let himself in. Washed his hands in the basin behind the bar, watching the water turn pink, then red, then clear again. Dried them on a clean rag.

Then he climbed the stairs to his room, took off his boots, and lay down in the dark.

In the morning, someone would find Jeffrey Spires in the alley between the chandler's shop and the old grain store. There would be questions. There would be talk. His brother might send men to investigate, and the men would ask around, and no one would know anything, because no one had seen anything, because the kind of man who killed Jeffrey Spires was the kind of man who knew how to move through the world without being seen.

Nothing was ever said about Jeffrey Spires again.

SCENE 30

PREPARATIONS

The sun was doing something it had no business doing in March.

Jamie felt it across his shoulders, through the rough-spun shirt he'd borrowed from the castle stores, working its way into the muscles that had already begun to complain. He stood knee-deep in the timber frame of the moat's outer wall, hammer in hand, the smell of fresh-cut oak and stagnant water filling his nostrils. Around him, a dozen men worked in various stages of undress, their voices carrying across the site in the rhythm of labor, grunts and curses and the occasional bark of instruction.

The moat itself stretched forty feet across at this point, its water the color of old copper, thick with silt and whatever else had accumulated over generations of castle life. The timber frame they were reinforcing ran along the inner edge, a lattice-work of beams and braces designed to keep the earthen walls from collapsing into the water. Most of the wood was old. Soft in places.

Jamie drove another nail into the crossbeam. The wood accepted it grudgingly, fibers splitting around the iron. His palm was blistered where the hammer handle had rubbed the skin raw. He'd stopped noticing an hour ago.

"You've got an audience."

Miranda's voice came from above. She sat on the stone lip of the moat wall, legs dangling, a half-eaten apple in one hand. She'd been watching him work for the better part of the morning, offering commentary that ranged from helpful to deliberately unhelpful depending on her mood.

"I've got several," Jamie said without looking up. "The guards change every hour. I've started naming them."

"Not the guards." Miranda took a bite of her apple. Chewed. Swallowed. "Higher."

Jamie straightened. His back protested. He shielded his eyes against the sun and looked up at the castle walls.

Margaret Beverley stood on the eastern rampart.

She was too far away to see clearly, but the shape of her was unmistakable—the dark hair, the green dress that shimmered around this hour, the particular stillness of a woman who had learned to stand in one place for long periods without appearing to wait. She wasn't looking at the moat work. She was looking at Jamie. When she saw him looking back, she smiled.

It was a small thing. A private thing. The kind of smile that existed only in the space between two people and vanished the moment anyone else tried to see it.

Jamie looked away.

"There she goes again." Miranda's voice had acquired an edge. "The king's wife, watching the carpenter."

"She's not watching me."

"She's definitely watching you."

"She's watching the work."

"She's watching you *do* the work. There's a difference." Miranda bit into her apple again. "Must be nice. Having royalty make eyes at you while you're covered in sweat and moat water."

"She's not making eyes."

"She's making something." Miranda examined her apple as though it had personally offended her. "Third time today. Fourth if you count breakfast. Which I do, because I was there, and I saw her look at you over the rest of the company like you were something she wanted to bottle up and spread on toast."

"Interesting choice of analogy."

Jamie drove another nail. Harder than necessary. The wood cracked.

"Like you said, she's the king's wife."

"She's the king's prisoner," Miranda said. "Doesn't mean she can't look. All the more reason, actually."

"Looking gets people killed."

"So does breathing, eventually." She tossed the apple core into the moat. It landed with a small splash and floated there, slowly spinning in the current. "I'm just saying. If I were locked in a tower with Lionel Taylor for company, I'd be looking too."

Jamie raised an eyebrow. Her cheeks blossomed.

"At anyone," she added. "At anything, really. At the shape a shadow made on a wall, if it meant I didn't have to think about what waited for me at night."

Jamie said nothing. He found another nail. Positioned it. Swung.

"All I'm saying," Miranda continued, "is that she smiles at you different than she smiles at other people. I've been watching."

"Well, I haven't noticed."

Miranda smirked and stood up. "Liar."

She walked away.

Jamie looked up at the rampart again.

Margaret had vanished.

The cells beneath Taylor's End had been carved from living rock.

They sat three levels below the main keep, accessible only through a series of corridors that narrowed as they descended, the ceilings dropping until even a man of average height had to duck. No natural light reached this far. The torches in their iron sconces were the only illumination, their flames bending in drafts that came from nowhere and led to nowhere, the castle breathing through passages no one had mapped in generations.

The smell was old moss and old water and old despair. Guards had developed the habit of not breathing through their noses down here, inhaling only through their mouths, as though that might keep some essential part of themselves clean.

Lillian sat on the bench in the corner of her cell. She had learned, in the two weeks since they moved her here, to keep her back against the wall. The bench was the only furniture. The floor was too cold to sit on for long, and standing made her knees ache in ways she didn't want to think about. So, she sat. And she waited. And she watched the torchlight flicker through the iron bars that separated her from the corridor beyond.

They'd given her a shift to wear. Gray. Shapeless. Garment designed to erase the person inside it, to turn a woman into a function rather than a fact. She'd torn the hem on the first day, using the strip of fabric to tie her hair back from her face. A small rebellion. The guards had noticed. They'd said nothing.

Her hands were rough now in ways they hadn't been before. The scullery had done that—three months of scrubbing pots and hauling water and kneeling on cold floors until her knees bled through her stockings. She'd been good at it, in the mechanical sense. Good at disappearing into the work, letting her body perform the motions while her mind went somewhere else. Somewhere he couldn't reach.

The head cook had complained that she worked too quietly. *Unnatural*, he'd called it. *Like she's not really there.*

She'd smiled at that.

That was what had gotten her moved to the cells. Not the smile specifically, but what came after. The under-steward who'd cornered her in the pantry. The pot of boiling water she'd thrown at his face. The way she'd stood there afterward, watching him scream, feeling nothing at all except a dim satisfaction that some part of her still knew how to fight back.

They'd called it acting out. She called it survival.

Footsteps in the corridor. She heard them before she saw anything. The particular cadence of boots on stone, two sets, one heavier than the other. She pulled her knees closer to her chest. Made herself small. Not out of fear. Out of strategy. Men looked at small women differently than they looked at large ones. They underestimated. And underestimation, she had learned, was the only weapon she had left.

Sir William Rodham appeared in the torchlight.

He was beautiful the way poisonous things were sometimes beautiful. Golden hair that fell in waves to his shoulders. Blue eyes the color of shallow water over sharp rocks. A face assembled from all the right pieces in all the right proportions, the kind of face that made women trust and men envy.

He smiled when he saw her.

"Good evening, lamb."

Lillian said nothing. She'd learned that too. Silence made them angrier than words, but anger made them careless, and carelessness was something she could use.

Rodham produced a key from his belt. The lock clicked. The door swung open on hinges that someone kept deliberately oiled—she'd noticed that detail the first night, turned it over in her mind until she understood what it meant. Oiled hinges meant quiet openings. Quiet openings meant visits no one was supposed to hear. Meant this had happened before. Meant it would happen again. Meant the whole machinery of this place had been calibrated to allow for men like him, had been designed with small darknesses built into its architecture, spaces where screaming didn't carry and morning never came to account for the night.

"I've been thinking about you." He stepped into the cell. The space shrank around him. His shadow fell across her like something with weight. "Kept wondering whether you were thinking about me too."

She didn't move. Didn't flinch. Kept her eyes on a point just past his shoulder, focusing on the wall behind him, on the crack that ran from floor to ceiling like a seam in the rock.

"Nothing to say?" He crouched in front of her. This close, she could smell him—wine and perfume and the particular musk of a man who had never been refused anything in his life. "You had plenty to say to Aldous. That poor under-steward. He'll wear the scars for years."

"He deserved them."

"There she is." Rodham's smile widened. "There's my lamb."

His hand came up. Touched her face. She shuddered.

"I like you," he said. "Most of the women they send down here are already broken by the time I get to them. Crying. Begging. Offering whatever they think I want to hear. It's rather bored me." His thumb traced her cheekbone. "And then arrives a girl who throws boiling water at a man twice her size, watches him burn, and feels nothing."

"I felt something."

"Oh?"

"I felt glad."

His eyes flickered with delight.

"You are a *marvelous* little lamb," Rodham leered. "I believe you're destined to be one of my favorites."

"Sir William."

The voice came from the corridor. A voice like winter arriving—not the first frost, but the deep cold that came later, the cold that killed silently, that you didn't feel until you were already dead. Rodham's hand froze. His expression cycled through several emotions in quick succession—annoyance, terror, calculation, terror again—before settling into something almost neutral. He turned.

Damien Taylor stood in the doorway. He wore no armor tonight. Just a dark doublet and darker trousers, the clothes of a man who had been preparing for bed when something interrupted him. His feet were bare. His hair was loose around his shoulders. But none of that diminished him. If anything, the informality made him more frightening. A man in armor was a man prepared for war. A man in bedclothes who still radiated that particular kind of cold authority was something else entirely.

The temperature in the cell seemed to drop. Not seemed—did. Lillian felt it on her skin, felt the nauseating physiological warmth Rodham's sadistic anticipation had brought with him curdle and retreat. She pressed harder against the wall without deciding to. Some part of her—the animal part, the part that had kept her alive—recognized what had just walked into the room. Recognized that Rodham, for all his venom, was merely a snake. And snakes fled when winter came.

"My lord." Rodham's voice had gone small. "I didn't expect—"

"On your feet."

Rodham rose so quickly he nearly stumbled. Damien stepped into the cell. His eyes moved from Rodham to Lillian to the space between them, cataloguing everything, missing nothing. His expression didn't change, but something behind it shifted—the microscopic adjustment of a man filing information away for later use.

"I was merely—"

"Silence." Damien's voice remained flat. "Do you imagine no one notices, William?"

Rodham's face had gone pale beneath the torchlight. "M'lord, I can explain—"

Damien's hand came up and across in a single motion, palm connecting with Rodham's cheek with a sound like a branch breaking. The knight's head snapped sideways with a yelp. He staggered. Caught himself against the wall with one gauntleted hand, steel scraping rock, the other shielding his face.

"You are not to touch another woman in these cells. If I am to even suspect otherwise, I will have you stripped of your knighthood and sent to work the border garrisons until your hair turns white and your teeth fall out, and that is if you're lucky. Do you understand?"

Rodham's wiped his mouth with the back of his hand and stared at the red smear as though he'd never seen his own blood before.

"Y-yes, m'lord."

"Good." Damien turned away from him. Dismissed him as completely as if he'd ceased to exist. "Leave us, Sir Rodham."

Rodham left. His footsteps echoed down the corridor, faster than they'd been on approach. The sound faded. Disappeared.

Damien stood in the center of the cell, looking at Lillian. Whatever she'd expected—fear, perhaps, or a different kind of threat—didn't arrive. Instead, Damien's expression mellowed.

"Are you hurt?"

The question caught her off guard. She heard herself answer before she'd decided to speak.

"No."

"Lovely." He nodded once. The gesture was almost professional. "I apologize for William. As knight, he proves moderately useful— generally speaking, of course—but his appetites demand stern management."

"He's done this before?"

"He has," Damien said, "but you knew that already." He glanced down the corridor where Rodham had fled tail-down, then lowered himself to her eye level, leaving three yards between them. "It won't happen again."

"How can you be certain?"

He didn't blink. "It won't."

She studied his face. The angles of it. The careful blankness that concealed whatever actually moved behind his eyes. He reminded her of something, though she couldn't quite place what—a cat, perhaps, watching a mouse from a distance, deciding whether the effort was worth the meal.

"Why are you here?"

"Because I have questions." He moved to the bench and sat down beside her, just close enough to make the space feel intimate rather than threatening. "Questions you might be able to answer."

"I'm a scullery maid. I don't know anything worth knowing."

"A scullery maid who was brought here from Taylor's End. You grew up in the village. You know the people there. The families, the children who've come and gone. Is that accurate?"

Something cold moved through Lillian's chest. She kept her face still. Kept her body still. Kept everything still except her heart, which had begun to beat faster in ways she couldn't control.

"I know some of them."

"I'm looking for a boy." Damien's eyes hadn't left her face. "Blonde hair. Green eyes. Would be about your age, perhaps a bit older. Handsome, I suspect, for a commoner."

Lillian's throat tightened. She swallowed against it. "There are a lot of blonde boys in the village, my lord."

"This one is no other boy." Damien leaned forward slightly. "This one would be different. Perhaps he's brave. Clever. Perhaps he possesses a certain quality that can't quite be named."

She thought of Jamie. *Of course, she thought of Jamie.* The way his hair caught the sun. The way his eyes changed color depending on whether he was angry or sad or tired or trying not to laugh. The way he'd looked at her the night before Richardson's men came. The way it had felt when he kissed her on the ridge.

"I don't know anyone like that," she mumbled, looking away.

"Are you certain?"

"Yes."

Damien nodded slowly. "What's your name?"

"Lillian."

"*Lillian.*" He let the word sit on his tongue. "Lovely. It suits you. Are you kin to Jeffrey Spires?"

"Yes."

"I remember now."

"Remember what?"

"He owed debts to the castle. Considerable ones. It's my understanding you were all he had left to offer."

Emotion flashed across her grime-coated face. Rage. Excitement. Grief. "Have you seen him?"

"Myself? No. Though I suspect if I had, I'd have put my blade in him. It takes a particular brand of coward to surrender his own daughter to settle his delinquencies. The transaction of savages. I would have never let it stand." He paused. "I want you to know, Lillian, that I am sorry. For all of it."

The apology sat between them, unexpected and strange. She didn't trust it. She knew better than to trust it. But she felt it land anyway, somewhere beneath the place where she'd learned to stop feeling things. That was the danger of him, she realized. Not the cruelty or the wrath—those she could navigate or at least understand. It was this. The careful kindness. The performed humanity. The way he made you want to believe him even as some deeper instinct screamed from behind a momentarily locked door.

"What do you want from me?"

"A truth," he said simply. "A truth about a boy from Taylor's End. A boy who might be very important, who might change everything."

"I don't know any 'important' boys—"

"Think harder."

"I've told you—"

"You've told me nothing," he snapped. "There is a boy. And you know him. I saw it in your eyes the moment I described him. The way your breathing shallowed and your heart began thumping like an ensnared rabbit's. Tell me his name."

"There's no one—"

"His *name*, Lillian."

"I don't—"

"Tell me, and I'll make certain Sir William never touches you again. Tell me, and I'll have you moved to better quarters. Tell me, and perhaps I'll let you leave this castle altogether when this is over." His voice had dropped to something almost intimate. The voice of a confessor rather than an inquisitor. "A name. That's all. One small word—"

"*Jamie.*"

The name fell out with the clumsy thud of a trout meeting dock.

Damien had gone still. His face showed nothing. His body showed nothing. But something behind his eyes had changed: a light coming on in a dark room, a mechanism clicking into place.

"Jamie."

She wanted to take it back. Wanted to reach into the air and grab the word and stuff it back into her mouth where it belonged.

But words didn't work that way.

Damien stood. Cleared his throat. "Thank you, Lillian."

"I didn't mean to—"

"You've done me a service tonight." His voice was warm again. Almost kind. "As promised, I'll have your new quarters prepared. A proper bed. Real food. Perhaps even a window, if it can be arranged. You've earned it, Miss Spires."

He was already walking toward the door when he paused. Turned his head just enough to catch her in his peripheral vision.

"Your father is dead, by the way. Found this morning behind the chandler's shop." He adjusted his sleeve. "I thought you should know."

Then he was gone.

His footsteps faded down the corridor, growing softer until they disappeared entirely, leaving Lillian alone in the cell with the torchlight and the silence and the terrible weight of what she'd done settling onto her shoulders like a shroud.

The castle was full of people who knew where Damien was.

Lionel had asked three of them. A steward near the kitchens, busy with inventory, who had paused mid-count to bow and answer. A guard at the eastern stair, standing at attention, who had not quite met the king's eyes when he spoke. A page crossing the gallery with an armful of linens, who had nearly dropped them in his haste to be helpful. Each had offered the same answer in different words: The prince is in his chambers, Your Grace. Has been since morning.

Lionel accepted this. He had no reason not to. Damien kept strange hours. Damien worked when others slept and slept when others worked and maintained a schedule that answered to no one, least of all his brother. If the servants said he was in his chambers, then he was in his chambers. The servants always knew.

Lionel climbed the stairs to the eastern tower with a question he'd been meaning to ask for days. Something about the theatre troupe. Something about seating arrangements for the upcoming performance, or perhaps the order of the entertainments, or the particular requests Barnaby Oddfellow had made regarding stage access. He couldn't quite remember now. The details had blurred together the way details always did when he tried to hold too many of them at once, when the machinery of kingship presented him with decisions that all seemed equally important and equally beyond his capacity to judge.

Damien would know. Damien always knew. That was the arrangement they had settled into years ago, though neither of them had ever spoken it aloud. Lionel wore the crown. Damien carried the weight of it.

The stairs wound upward in a tight spiral, the steps worn smooth by generations of feet. Lionel counted them without meaning to. Thirty-seven from the landing to the door. He had counted them as a boy, racing Damien to the top, and he counted them still, though the races had ended long ago and he could no longer remember who had won more often.

The door to his brother's chamber stood closed.

Lionel knocked. The sound was small against the heavy wood, swallowed almost immediately by the thickness of the walls. He waited. Listened for footsteps, for the creak of a chair, for any indication that someone had heard and was coming to answer.

Nothing.

He knocked again. Harder this time. The door rattled slightly in its frame.

Still nothing.

Perhaps Damien had gone out. Perhaps the servants had been mistaken, or perhaps he had left through some other exit while they weren't watching. There were passages in this castle that only certain people knew about. Damien knew them all.

Lionel tried the handle. It turned.

The room was empty.

Afternoon light fell through the window in a single bright column, catching dust motes that turned in the air like something thinking. The quality of the light was different up here than in the lower chambers. Cleaner, somehow. Less filtered by the accumulated weight of the castle below. Lionel stood in the doorway and watched the dust move and felt, for a moment, as though he had stepped into a space that existed outside the normal flow of time.

The bed was made. Servants' work, precise corners, pillows arranged just so against the headboard. The coverlet was pulled tight across the mattress without a single wrinkle. Whoever had made it had taken care. Had perhaps taken more care than usual, smoothing away any evidence of whatever had disturbed the linens before.

The desk held papers in neat stacks. Correspondence, perhaps. Reports. The endless documentation that Damien accumulated and organized and used in ways Lionel had never quite understood. A quill lay beside an inkwell, both positioned at precise angles to the edge of the desk. Even Damien's disorder, when it existed, had a kind of order to it.

A water basin sat on the stand near the window, cloth folded beside it. The water had been used recently. Lionel could see the faint ripples still settling on its surface, disturbed by some vibration in the floor or the walls or perhaps only by the door opening behind him.

He stood in the doorway for a long moment, uncertain.

He had never entered this room without invitation. Had never thought to. Even as boys, when they had shared nearly everything else, Damien's private spaces had remained private. There was something in his brother that required solitude the way other men required food or water. A door closed against the world. A place where no one else could follow.

The space felt private now in ways that extended beyond the usual privacy of chambers. Something in the arrangement of objects. The careful placement of each thing in relation to every other thing. The sense that someone had thought about where everything should go and had reasons for those decisions that wouldn't be shared with anyone who happened to wander in.

Lionel should leave. Come back later. Find Damien somewhere else and ask his question about the theatre, about the seating, about whatever it was he had climbed thirty-seven stairs to discuss.

He stepped inside.

His footsteps sounded different in here. Softer. More tentative. As though the room itself were absorbing the noise, keeping it from traveling too far. He walked toward the window without quite meaning to, drawn by the light, by the view of the courtyard below where tiny figures moved about their business.

The chair by the window held something.

A shirt.

Lionel stopped walking.

Fine linen, cream-colored, draped across the seat as though someone had removed it quickly and forgotten to retrieve it. Or as though someone had left in haste and the shirt had been the last thing on either of their minds. The fabric caught the light from the window and seemed almost to glow against the dark wood of the chair.

Lionel looked at it.

The shirt was too large for Damien. He could see that immediately, though he couldn't have said how he knew his brother's measurements well enough to judge. The shoulders were broader. The sleeves longer. The cut was fashionable in a particular way, a thing a young man might wear if he wanted to be noticed at court, or what merchant's son with ambitions might commission from a good tailor, spending more than he should because appearance mattered when you were trying to climb.

Lionel looked at the shirt for a long moment.

He looked at the bed. At the precise corners and the tight coverlet and the pillows arranged just so. At the slight depression in the center of the mattress that the servants' work had not quite managed to smooth away.

He looked at the window. At the water basin with its recently disturbed surface. At the cloth folded beside it, which now that he looked more closely seemed damp at one corner, as though someone had used it to wash and left it to dry.

He looked at the shirt again.

The dust motes turned in the light. They moved slowly, almost meditatively, following currents of air that Lionel couldn't feel. He watched them for what might have been seconds or minutes. Time had gone strange in this room. Time had stopped behaving the way time was supposed to behave.

The castle sounds continued below. Voices, footsteps, the ordinary machinery of a household in motion. The clatter of something in the kitchens. The bark of a sergeant drilling men in the yard. The endless background noise of a world that didn't know or care what was happening in this particular room at this particular moment. Somewhere a door closed. Somewhere else, someone laughed. The laugh traveled up through the stones and arrived muffled, transformed into something that didn't quite sound like laughter anymore.

Lionel's face did something complicated.

Not quite a frown. Not quite anything else. The expression of a man whose thoughts had run up against something unexpected and couldn't find a way around it. His brow drew together slightly. His mouth opened, then closed. His jaw worked as though he were chewing words he couldn't bring himself to speak.

His hand lifted toward the shirt. Stopped halfway. Hung in the air for a moment, fingers slightly curled, reaching for something he didn't actually want to touch.

The hand returned to his side.

He stood very still. The stillness of a man who had walked into a room expecting one thing and found another. The stillness of a man who was trying to understand what he was looking at and finding that understanding kept sliding away from him, kept refusing to resolve into anything he knew how to hold.

The shirt lay on the chair. Cream-colored. Fine linen. Too large for Damien. The shirt of a young man with broad shoulders and long arms and reasons to be in this room that Lionel couldn't name and didn't want to name and was naming anyway, somewhere in the back of his mind where the thoughts he didn't choose to think went on thinking themselves regardless.

He turned.

He walked out of the room.

He closed the door behind him with care, as though there were someone sleeping inside who might be disturbed by noise. His hand lingered on the handle for a moment longer than necessary. Then he let go.

His footsteps echoed on the stairs as he descended. Thirty-seven steps from the door to the landing. He didn't count them this time. He didn't think about racing or winning or the brother who had always been faster, smarter, better at the games they played as children.

His expression, if anyone had been watching, showed nothing at all. Or perhaps showed too much of nothing. The particular blankness of a man holding something he didn't know how to set down. The careful emptiness of a face that had been arranged to reveal precisely what its owner wanted revealed, which at this moment was nothing, nothing at all, nothing that could be read or interpreted or used.

A servant passed him on the stairs. Bowed. Murmured something respectful. Lionel nodded in response, the gesture automatic, and kept walking.

He didn't look for Damien again that afternoon.

He didn't mention what he had seen.

The question about the theatre, about the seating arrangements, about whatever small matter had brought him to the eastern tower in the first place, went unasked. It didn't seem important anymore. It didn't seem like a thing that mattered, measured against the weight of a cream-colored shirt draped across a chair in an empty room.

Lionel returned to his own chambers and sat by his own window and watched the courtyard below and said nothing to anyone for a very long time.

The afternoon had turned warmer than the morning promised.

Jamie worked the outer frame of the moat wall, driving nails into crossbeams that had softened with age and damp. His shirt stuck to his back. Sweat ran down his temples and collected at his jaw, dropping onto the wood below. He had stopped wiping it away an hour ago. The effort seemed pointless when more would follow.

The other workers had spread out along the timber frame, each man focused on his own section. The sounds of labor filled the air in irregular rhythms. Hammers striking. Wood groaning. The occasional curse when a nail bent or a plank split. No one spoke more than necessary. The heat had taken the conversation out of them.

Jamie reached for another nail and felt the skin of his palm protest. The blisters had opened sometime before noon. He had wrapped them with strips torn from an old rag, but the cloth had soaked through with blood and sweat and now offered more irritation than protection.

He positioned the nail. Raised the hammer.

"You're bleeding."

The voice came from above. He looked up.

Margaret Beverley stood at the edge of the moat wall, silhouetted against the afternoon sky. She wore a dress the color of moss. Simple by court standards. Her hair was pulled back from her face. Her hands hung at her sides, empty, uncertain what to do with themselves.

Jamie lowered the hammer. "It's nothing."

"It doesn't look like nothing."

He glanced at his palm. The rag had gone red. She was right. It didn't look like nothing.

"I've had worse."

"That's not the reassurance you think it is."

He didn't know what to say to that. He stood in the timber frame with his hammer in one hand and his bleeding palm in the other and looked at the queen's sister and waited for her to tell him what she wanted.

She didn't. Not immediately. She looked at him the way she had looked at him from the window, from the rampart, from across the courtyard during the arrival. Studying. Cataloguing. Trying to fit him into some framework she had built in her mind and finding that he didn't quite match.

"I've seen you before," she said.

"I've seen you too."

"No. Before that. Before you came here." She paused. Her brow drew together slightly. "I don't know where. I don't know when. But I know your face."

Jamie felt something cold move through his chest. The feeling of being recognized when being recognized was dangerous. But her expression held no accusation. Only confusion. Only the particular frustration of a memory that refused to resolve.

"I have that kind of face," he said. "Common. Forgettable."

"You don't." She said it simply, without flattery. A statement of fact. "Would you walk with me?"

The question hung in the air between them. The other workers had not stopped their labor, but Jamie could feel their attention shifting, the peripheral awareness of men who had noticed something unusual happening at the edge of their worksite.

"I'm meant to be here until evening."

"I know." She glanced at the moat, at the timber frame, at the men who were pretending not to watch. "I'm asking anyway."

He should say no. He knew he should say no. There were a hundred reasons to say no, and Felix would have listed all of them if he were here, would have explained in that quiet, precise way of his exactly how much danger lived in a simple walk with a woman whose husband wore a crown.

"All right," Jamie said.

He climbed out of the timber frame. His boots squelched in the mud at the base of the wall. He set the hammer down on a pile of planks and wiped his hands on his trousers, which accomplished nothing except to smear the blood across the fabric.

Margaret watched him. When he reached her level, she turned and began walking toward the castle's eastern wing without checking to see if he followed.

He followed.

The queen's garden occupied a walled courtyard behind the kitchens, accessible through an archway that had been carved with figures worn smooth by centuries of weather and hands. Margaret walked through the archway without hesitation. He came after, ducking slightly beneath the low stone lintel, and found himself in a space that felt separate from the rest of the castle. The noise of the courtyard faded. The bustle of the kitchens receded to a distant clatter. Even the light seemed different here, filtered through the branches of trees that had been allowed to grow wild.

The garden had been beautiful once. Jamie could see that in the bones of it. The paths had been laid with care, pale stones fitted together in patterns that wound between flower beds and around a central fountain. The fountain itself was dry, its basin cracked, moss growing in the seams where water had once collected. The flower beds held more weeds than flowers. The hedges that bordered the paths had lost their shape, growing in directions no gardener had intended.

They walked in silence for a while. The path curved around the dry fountain and continued toward the far wall, where a bench sat beneath a tree whose branches had grown heavy with neglect, drooping toward the ground like arms too tired to hold themselves up.

"You're not what I expected," Margaret said.

"What did you expect?"

"I don't know. Someone who looked like a player. Someone who smiled more easily." She glanced at him over her shoulder. "You look like you're waiting for something bad to happen."

"Maybe I am."

"Are you?"

He considered the question. Considered all the things he couldn't tell her.

"I think everyone in this castle is waiting for something bad to happen," he said. "The ones who aren't are the ones who haven't been paying attention."

She stopped walking. Turned to face him. The afternoon light fell across her face and showed him things he had not noticed from a distance. The shadows beneath her eyes. The tension in her jaw. The particular quality of tiredness that came not from lack of sleep but from something deeper, something that sleep couldn't touch.

"My father is dead."

The words arrived without preamble. Jamie felt them land.

"I know," he said. "I'm sorry."

"Are you?" She studied him. "You didn't know him."

"I didn't have to know him to be sorry you lost him."

Something moved across her face. Not quite gratitude. Not quite suspicion. Something between them, something that couldn't decide which way to fall.

"They put his head on a spike," she said. "At the gate. I see it every time I cross the courtyard. Every time I look out my window. They put my father's head on a spike and they expect me to smile at dinner and make pleasant conversation and pretend that everything is normal."

"I'm sorry," he said again. It was inadequate. He knew it was inadequate. But it was the only thing he had to offer.

"You keep saying that."

"Well, I keep meaning it."

She looked at him for a long moment. The silence stretched between them, filled with the small sounds of the neglected garden. Wind in the branches. Birds in the hedges. The distant clatter of the kitchens, muffled by walls and distance.

"Why do I feel like I know you?" she asked.

"I don't know."

"It's not just your face. It's something else. Something in the way you stand. The way you look at me." She took a step closer. "Like you understand something you shouldn't understand. Like you've lost something too."

Jamie's throat tightened. He thought of Rowan. Of Lillian. Of the village that had been his whole world until the world decided to take it from him. He thought of his mother, whoever she had been, wherever she was now, whether she was alive or dead or something in between.

"Everyone's lost something," he said.

"That's not an answer."

"It's what I got."

She was close enough now that he could see the individual strands of hair that had escaped her careful arrangement, curling against her temples in the humidity. Close enough that he could smell whatever she had used to wash, something faintly floral, almost lost beneath the green smell of the overgrown garden.

"I don't know why I asked you to walk with me," she said. "I don't know why I'm telling you any of this. I don't tell anyone anything." She paused. Her eyes searched his face. "But you feel safe. I don't know why. You shouldn't feel safe. Nothing here is safe. But you do."

Jamie didn't move. He didn't trust himself to move. The distance between them had shrunk to something that felt dangerous, charged with a tension he didn't know how to name or navigate.

"I'm not safe," he said quietly. "I'm the least safe person in this castle. If you knew what I was, what I came here to do, you would run."

"Would I?"

"You should."

"That's not the same thing."

Her hand came up. Touched his face. The gesture was tentative, exploratory, the touch of someone who had forgotten how to reach for another person and was trying to remember. Her fingers found his jaw, traced the line of it, settled against his cheek.

He should pull away. He should step back, apologize, return to the moat and his hammer and the safe anonymity of labor. He should do any of the hundred sensible things that Felix had trained him to do when situations became complicated.

He didn't.

"You're shaking," she said.

"I know."

"Why?"

He couldn't answer. He didn't have words for what was happening inside him. The collision of grief and longing and fear and something else, like the moment when a key slides into a lock and you realize the door was never as closed as you thought.

She kissed him.

Or he kissed her. Later, he wouldn't be able to say who moved first. One moment they were standing apart, her hand on his face, his heart beating too fast. The next moment there was no distance at all, just the press of her mouth against his, soft and uncertain, the kiss of two people who didn't know each other and understood each other anyway.

It lasted only a moment. A few seconds, perhaps. Long enough for Jamie to feel the warmth of her, the trembling that matched his own, the desperation that lived beneath her careful composure. Then she pulled back.

Her eyes were wide. Her breathing had changed. She looked at him as though seeing him for the first time, or as though seeing something in him she had not expected to find.

"I shouldn't have done that," she said.

"No."

"I'm married."

"I know."

"To the king."

"I know."

She stepped back. Put distance between them. Her hand rose to her mouth, touched her lips as though checking to see if they had changed.

"I don't even know your name," she said. "Teddy Ivanovich is not your real name."

"How do you know?"

"Because it's bloody ridiculous!"

Jamie swallowed. Breathed.

"Jamie," he said. "My name is Jamie."

She nodded slowly. The name seemed to settle into her, finding a place to rest.

"Jamie," she repeated. "I'm Margaret."

"I know who you are."

"Do you?"

She turned and walked away. Her footsteps made soft sounds on the overgrown path.

Jamie stood alone in the neglected garden with the taste of her still on his lips and the weight of everything he had not told her pressing down on his chest. The fountain sat dry and cracked beside him. The hedges grew wild around him. The trees drooped their heavy branches toward the ground.

He touched his mouth. His fingers came away with nothing. No evidence. No proof. Just the memory of warmth and the knowledge that something had happened that could not be unhappened.

He stayed in the garden for a long time after she left.

When he finally returned to the moat, the other workers glanced at him with questions they didn't ask. He picked up his hammer. Found a nail. Drove it into the wood with more force than necessary.

The afternoon wore on. The sun moved across the sky. The shadows lengthened.

And somewhere in the castle above, a woman with her father's head on a spike outside her window touched her lips and tried to understand what she had done.

The corridor outside Damien's chamber still carried the faint sweetness of lavender water. Edmund's scent. The smell of something that had been allowed to exist for a few hours before necessity arrived and ended it.

Damien stood at the window, watching nothing.

The courtyard below was dark. The torches had burned low. Somewhere a dog barked twice and then stopped, chastened by the silence or the cold or both. The castle settled around him in small groans, the sounds a body makes when it's tired of holding itself upright.

He'd walked back from the cells slowly. Let the corridors stretch. Let the silence accumulate between each footstep until the weight of it felt almost physical. Lillian's voice still sat in his ears. The way she'd said the name. Jamie. Two syllables. Nothing remarkable in the sound of it. A common name. A peasant's name.

And yet.

He crossed to the mirror above his desk. The glass was old, slightly warped, and his reflection bent in places that made his face unfamiliar. He'd looked into this mirror a thousand times. Had watched himself grow from boy to man in its imperfect surface. Had learned to arrange his features into whatever expression the moment required—amusement, interest, cold authority—and had watched the glass confirm each performance.

Tonight, the glass showed him something else.

He looked at his face. The angles of it. The dark hair that fell across his forehead. The eyes that people called handsome without understanding what they were actually seeing. He searched for something in the arrangement of features—some quality that would justify the architecture, some truth hiding beneath the surface that would explain why he was here and not somewhere else, why he wore silk instead of rags, why servants bowed when he passed.

The glass offered nothing back.

Jamie.

The name moved through him like nausea. He didn't know why. The boy was real. That much was certain now. Years of half-believing in a ghost, of cataloguing blonde children in marketplaces and village squares, of telling himself the whole thing was superstition and knowing it wasn't. And now a name. A face. A body working his moat, walking his corridors, standing in front of his father's statue with green eyes that held something Damien couldn't identify.

He'd seen it in the courtyard. The way the boy looked up at the castle. Not with awe—that would have been comprehensible, even expected. Something else. Something that suggested he was seeing the place as it actually was, stripped of the pageantry and the stone, reduced to whatever truth lay beneath.

Damien pressed his palm flat against the mirror. The glass was cold. His reflection disappeared behind his hand, and for a moment there was only darkness where his face had been.

Better. Easier. The absence of something was always simpler than its presence.

The door groaned.

He didn't turn. He knew the pattern of that entrance, the particular shuffle, the apologetic weight distribution of someone who'd already decided they were intruding. But the footsteps that followed were wrong. Too light. Too many.

He turned.

Two women stood just inside the threshold. Country-pretty, both of them. One kept adjusting her bodice with nervous hands, laughter escaping in small, inappropriate bursts. The other had the dull-eyed patience of someone who'd learned to calculate crowns against dignity and found the math just acceptable.

Behind them, half-hidden in the doorway's shadow, Lionel watched.

Damien understood immediately. The shirt Edmund had left. The way Lionel's gaze had lingered too long at dinner. The particular quality of concern that lived in his brother's face whenever he encountered something he couldn't explain—a mixture of fear and determination that usually preceded catastrophe.

This was rescue. Or what Lionel imagined rescue looked like.

"My lord," the bolder woman said. She stepped forward. Offered a smile that had probably worked on a hundred men. "Your brother thought—"

"Out."

Damien's voice was level. The room absorbed it; let it settle into the stones.

The women exchanged a glance. They didn't move.

"Your Grace said you might need—"

"I said out."

Still, they hesitated. Damien watched them calculate. They were accustomed to men who refused and then relented, who protested and then surrendered, whose resistance was performance rather than policy. They'd learned to read the difference between *no* and *not yet*.

"At once, I say!"

The women fled. Skirts whispered against the rushes. One stumbled on the threshold, caught herself, vanished into the corridor with the other close behind.

The door hadn't finished swinging shut before Lionel stepped inside.

He was smiling. That hopeful, uncertain expression he wore whenever he wanted approval and suspected he wouldn't receive it. The smile of a boy who'd brought home a wounded bird and couldn't understand why no one was praising him for the kindness.

Damien crossed the distance before Lionel could speak.

His hand found his brother's chest and drove him backward, slamming him against the wall. His fingers closed around Lionel's throat, not in rage, not in passion, but with the precise pressure of someone who understood exactly where the line was between discomfort and unconsciousness, between warning and murder.

Lionel's breath stopped. His hands flew up, pawing at Damien's grip with the frantic uselessness of a man who'd never learned to fight.

Damien's face hovered inches away. Close enough to see the fear pooling in his brother's eyes. Close enough to watch his pupils dilate.

"You will never," he said, each word delivered separately, carved from the silence, "attempt something like that again."

Lionel tried to speak. Managed only a thin wheeze.

"I was—"

Damien's fingers tightened. Lionel made a sound. High and thin and nothing like a king. His knees buckled. Tears spilled down his cheeks, cutting tracks through the powder he'd applied that morning. His feet scraped against the floor, seeking purchase, finding none.

Damien leaned closer.

"You think me broken? You think I require your correction? That I might be mended through the same blunt machinery that governs your own appetites?"

Lionel's vision was going white at the edges. Damien could see it—the way his eyes lost focus, the small tremors beginning in his hands.

"You have spent your entire life believing that you understand the people around you. That your crown grants you insight. But you have never understood anything. Not the castle. Not the court. Not the men who serve you or the women who endure you." His voice dropped. "And you have certainly never understood me."

A sob escaped Lionel's throat. The sound of a man realizing, for the first time, that he was alone in a room with someone he'd never actually met.

"I have *watched* you," Damien hissed. "Every day. Every stumble. Every performance of authority you mistake for the thing itself. I have seen you clearly since we were children." He let the weight of it settle. "And you—"

He released his grip. Lionel collapsed. He gasped like a man pulled from deep water, hands pressing against his throat, tears streaming unchecked.

Damien stood over him.

"—have only just begun to see me."

Lionel stared up at his brother. The horror in his face wasn't fear of violence. It was something deeper. The recognition that every interaction they'd ever shared, every confidence, every moment of brotherly affection Lionel had treasured, had been observed from behind glass. Catalogued. Found wanting. Damien had been watching him fail for twenty-two years, and Lionel had never once noticed.

"Say nothing of this. Not to your men. Not to your priests. Not to anyone."

Lionel nodded. The motion was frantic. Pathetic. The eager compliance of a dog that had finally learned what teeth were for.

Damien turned away.

He walked back to the window. To the dark courtyard below. To the reflection in the glass that showed him nothing he wanted to see.

Behind him, Lionel scrambled to his feet and fled the room without closing the door.

Damien didn't watch him go.

The silence returned.

He stood at the window and let the darkness settle around him. His hands hung loose at his sides. His breathing was even. Nothing about his body suggested that anything had happened, that his brother had just crawled away weeping, that the women had fled like he was plague made flesh.

The mirror waited behind him. He could feel it there—that warped glass, that imperfect surface—watching him the way it always watched. Waiting to show him whatever he was willing to see.

He didn't turn.

Jamie.

The name sat in his chest like something swallowed. Two syllables. A common name. A peasant's name. Belonging to a boy with yellow hair and green eyes who was sleeping somewhere in this castle right now, dreaming whatever dreams peasants dreamed, carrying in his blood a story he didn't know.

Damien had hunted that story for years. Had built his entire philosophy around the certainty that legitimacy was fiction, that blood meant nothing, that crowns were just metal shaped to fit heads that happened to be nearby when the shaping occurred. And now the boy was here. *Real.* Named.

Something in Damien had cracked at the sight of him, cracked somewhere deep and dark in the place where he kept the things he didn't examine, the questions he didn't ask, the truths he'd decided weren't worth the cost of acknowledging. The boy had looked at his father's statue like he was seeing through it. Like the stone was transparent and something else waited behind it, something true, something that couldn't be carved or commissioned or controlled. Damien had never looked at anything that way. Had never been able to. His eyes only saw surfaces. Arrangements. Mechanisms.

The boy saw through.

And Damien, standing in his chamber with his brother's terror still fresh in the air and the smell of lavender fading, felt something he hadn't felt in years.

Envy.

Not for the crown the boy might claim. Not for the blood that made him legitimate in ways Damien could never be. Something simpler. Something worse.

The boy didn't *know* what he was. Didn't know the weight of it, the cost of it, the way carrying it would bend him into shapes he'd never chosen. He walked through the world with the lightness of someone who belonged to himself. Damien had never belonged to himself. Not once. Not for a single moment. He'd been his father's project, and later his shame, since birth, shaped and molded and refined into whatever instrument the family required until it didn't. Every gesture was calculated. Every word was weighed. Every relationship was leverage waiting to be applied.

The boy was free.

And tomorrow Damien would have to decide what to do about that.

He turned from the window. Crossed to the mirror. Made himself look.

The glass showed him what it always showed: a face arranged into whatever expression the moment required. Tonight the expression was nothing. Blank. A canvas waiting for someone to paint something on it.

He raised one hand. Pressed his palm flat against the glass, covering his reflection.

The cold seeped into his skin. He let it.

When he finally pulled his hand away, the glass was fogged where his warmth had touched it. For a moment, his face was obscured; just a shape, an outline, something that could have been anyone.

Then the fog faded. The face returned. And Damien stood alone in his chamber with a name lodged in his chest and the first crack in his foundation spreading somewhere he couldn't see.

The candle guttered. The silence held. And somewhere in the castle below, a boy named Jamie slept without dreaming, unaware that his existence had just broken something that would never heal.

SCENE 31

LONG LIVE KING LIONEL

1599

The bedchamber smelled of dying.

Not death, not yet, but the slow surrender to it. Sweat gone sour in sheets unchanged for weeks. Herbs burning in braziers that did nothing but make the air thick and sweet in a way that turned the stomach. The particular staleness of a room where windows stayed shuttered because the man in the bed had decided that daylight was for people who still believed in tomorrow.

Damien stood at the foot of that bed and watched his father rot.

Tobias II had been a formidable man once. Now the flesh hung loose on bones that seemed to shrink with each passing day. His skin had gone the color of old parchment, stretched tight across his skull, and his eyes—always small, always calculating—had sunk into hollows that made them look like bits pressed into dough.

He was forty-seven years old. He looked eighty.

"You're still here," Tobias said. His voice came out wet, thick with the fluid that had been collecting in his lungs for months. The physicians called it consumption. Damien called it justice delayed. "Thought I told you to leave."

"You did."

"And yet." Tobias's hand lifted from the coverlet—a gesture that had once commanded armies, dismissed servants, struck sons across the face. Now it trembled like a leaf in wind before dropping back to the bed. "Still here. Hovering. Like a vulture waiting for the carcass to stop twitching."

Damien said nothing. There was nothing to say. He had learned that lesson young—that silence was the only defense against a man who used words the way other men used knives. Every response was ammunition. Every emotion was weakness. Every moment of genuine feeling was an opening through which Tobias would drive the blade.

Twenty years of that education. Twenty years of learning what happened when you let someone see what hurt you.

"Your brother was here earlier," Tobias continued. "Brought me wine. Held my hand. Wept a little." The wet sound in his chest might have been a laugh. "Good boy, Lionel. Soft, but good. He'll make a fine king."

There it was.

"The council's decision, then."

"My decision." Tobias's eyes found his, and for a moment the dying man vanished and the king returned: cruel, sharp, enjoying the wound he was about to inflict. "Crown goes to Lionel. Ceremony's tomorrow, if I last that long. If I don't—" He shrugged, the motion small and painful. "Makes no difference. It's done."

"But I'm the eldest."

"You are."

"And the strongest. The smartest. The brav—"

"The bravest?" Tobias's laugh became a cough, wet and rattling, and for a long moment he couldn't speak. When he recovered, there was blood at the corner of his mouth. He didn't wipe it away. "Is that what you think? That you're *brave*?"

Damien's hands had curled into fists at his sides. He uncurled them. Breathed. Counted to five the way he'd learned to count when he was small and his father's voice had made him want to run and hide and never come out.

"Give me a reason," he said.

"What?"

"A reason." The word came out harder than he intended. He softened his voice, made it reasonable, made it the voice of a man asking a simple question rather than a son begging for something he would never receive. "You're passing the crown to a boy who can barely dress himself without help. Who cries when the hunting dogs bring down a stag. Who's spent more time in brothels than in council chambers. I want a reason."

The moment stretched. In the braziers, the herbs crackled and spat. Somewhere in the castle, a door closed. The wind moved against the shuttered windows with a sound like fingernails on wood.

Tobias' lips peeled back from teeth that had gone yellow and loose. "All right. I'll give you a reason."

He pushed himself up on his elbows, the effort visible in every line of his body, in the tremor of his arms, in the fresh sweat that broke across his forehead. But he did it. Forced himself to look at Damien from something like his full height.

"Your mother was a whore."

Damien didn't flinch. He'd heard this before. A hundred times. A thousand. Every time Tobias wanted to remind his sons what they were, where they came from, how little they deserved the name they carried.

"She'd fuck anything that paid," Tobias continued, his voice finding strength in cruelty. "Did, too. Half the garrison, probably. Definitely the butcher's son—you remember him? The one with the lazy eye? She let him put it in her for a lamb shank." The laugh again, wet and horrible. "A fucking lamb shank. That's what your mother was worth."

"You've told me."

"I'm telling you again." Tobias coughed. "Both of you came

out of that. That's what you are. Whore's sons." He paused, let the words land. "But you—"

He stopped. Coughed again. Spat something dark into a cloth beside the bed.

"*You*," he continued, "are worse. Do you know why?"

"Tell me."

"Because you're a bloody fairy. That a good enough reason for you?"

The silence that followed was absolute.

There was no version of this where he was enough. No performance adequate to earn his father's approval. No accomplishment sufficient to overcome the fundamental fact of what Tobias believed him to be. He had spent twenty years trying to be worthy of a man who had decided his unworthiness before he drew his first breath.

Enough.

The word didn't come from anywhere he recognized. Didn't feel like his own voice, his own thought. It simply arrived, fully formed, with the weight of something that had been waiting a very long time to be heard.

Enough.

He walked around the side of the bed.

"What are you doing?"

Damien didn't answer. He sat on the edge of the bed, the mattress depressing under his weight, his hip settling against his father's wasted thigh. This close, he could smell the rot beneath the herbs. Could see the individual hairs in Tobias's eyebrows, gone white and wild with age.

"Damien!" Tobias snapped. "What are you—"

The pillow was in Damien's hands.

He didn't remember picking it up. Didn't remember making the decision. One moment he was sitting on the bed, and the next the pillow was pressing down over his father's face and his arms were rigid with effort and somewhere underneath the feathers and linen Tobias II was making a sound that wasn't quite a scream.

The first seconds were chaos.

Tobias's hands flew up, the hands that had struck him so many times, that had gripped his collar and shaken him until his teeth rattled, that had slapped his face in front of servants and lords and anyone else who happened to be watching. They clawed at Damien's wrists, at his forearms, nails dragging furrows in the skin that would scar.

Damien pressed harder.

His father's body convulsed. The legs kicked beneath the coverlet, tangling in the sheets, struggling for purchase on a mattress that offered none. The sounds coming through the pillow were muffled but audible; wet, desperate, the sounds of a man whose lungs were already failing trying to draw breath through obstruction.

Tears ran down Damien's face.

He didn't sob. Didn't shake. The tears simply arrived, tracking down his cheeks and dripping from his jaw onto the pillow, onto his own hands, mixing with the sweat that had broken out across his palms. He cried the way a wound bleeds: without volition, without control, his body responding to damage while his mind stayed perfectly still.

Thirty seconds.

Tobias's struggles weakened. The hands that had been clawing now simply gripped, fingers locked around Damien's wrists with strength that was fading by the heartbeat. His legs still kicked, but the movements were slower, less coordinated, the frantic scramble of earlier becoming something more like a twitch.

Damien watched his own hands. They were steady. White-knuckled around the pillow, veins standing out along the forearms, but steady. The body knew what to do even if the mind was somewhere else entirely.

Forty-five seconds.

A sound escaped from beneath the pillow. A whimper, perhaps, or a plea. The sound of a man realizing that his son was going to kill him and there was nothing he could do to stop it.

Damien pressed harder.

One minute.

The hands on his wrists had gone slack. They still gripped, but reflexively now, without intention. The body beneath him had stopped convulsing and started simply moving—small, involuntary spasms that rippled through the muscles, the nervous system firing random signals as it began to shut down.

Damien felt something give way inside himself. His face was still wet with tears, but the tears had stopped coming. His eyes were dry now. Fixed on the pillow. On the shape of his father's face beneath the fabric.

One minute fifteen seconds.

The legs had gone still. The hands had fallen away from his wrists, dropping to the mattress with a soft sound that seemed louder than it was. The only movement now was a faint tremor in the torso, the last signals from a brain that was dying.

Damien didn't look away.

One minute thirty seconds.

Stillness.

Tobias II was dead.

Damien held the pillow in place for another twenty seconds. Then thirty. He had read somewhere that it took longer than people thought, that consciousness could return if pressure was released too soon, that the body could restart itself through sheer animal persistence.

He wasn't taking any chances.

Two minutes.

He lifted the pillow.

His father's face stared up at the ceiling with eyes that had gone fixed and wide. The mouth was open, frozen in the act of trying to breathe. There was blood on the lips—the coughing had ruptured something in the final moments—and the tongue protruded slightly, swollen and dark.

Damien looked at that face for a long time.

He had imagined this moment. In the dark hours, in the private spaces of his mind where no one else was allowed, he had imagined what it would feel like to watch his father die. He had expected satisfaction. Or relief. Or at least the absence of pain, the lifting of a weight he'd carried so long he'd forgotten what it felt like to stand straight.

He felt nothing.

The tears had dried on his cheeks. His hands had stopped shaking. His breathing was steady.

He stood.

His reflection caught in the mirror across the room: a tall young man in dark clothing, face expressionless, eyes that had changed somehow in the last two minutes. He couldn't have said what was different about them. Only that the person looking back at him was not quite the same person who had entered this room.

He straightened his doublet. Adjusted his collar. Ran his fingers through his hair, smoothing the strands that had fallen across his forehead during the struggle.

When he was presentable, he walked to the door. Opened it. Stepped into the corridor where two guards stood at attention, where servants waited at discreet distances, where the entire machinery of a kingdom continued to turn without any awareness of what had just happened in the room behind him.

"The King is dead," Damien said.

His voice was calm. Clear. The voice of a prince delivering news that was sad but expected, that required solemnity but not surprise.

"Fetch my brother. Fetch the physicians. Fetch the council."

He paused. Let the weight of the moment settle.

"Long live King Lionel."

SCENE 32

FEAST

The great hall of Taylor's Castle had been built to humble men. Vaulted ceilings rose into shadow, their heights lost to torchlight that couldn't reach them. Banners hung from iron fixtures, crimson and gold, the Taylor crest repeated in silk until it became less symbol than atmosphere; a reminder, woven into every surface, of who owned the air you breathed. The long table stretched the length of the room like a spine, heavy oak blackened by generations of feasts, its surface scarred and polished and scarred again until the wood held the memory of every meal ever consumed upon it.

Tonight it held enough food for a village. Roasted capons glistening with fat. Trenchers of bread soaking in meat drippings. Wheels of cheese the size of shields. Towers of fruit—apples and pears and something exotic, oranges perhaps, brought from God knew where at God knew what cost. Wine flowed from pitchers that never seemed to empty, dark and red, catching the torchlight like liquid garnets.

No one was hungry.

The troupe entered through the eastern doors, led by Barnaby with his showman's stride and theatrical bow. Behind him came the others in careful procession: the bald man with his unsettling stillness, the woman who played queens, the boy who played princes, the musicians clutching instruments like talismans against whatever waited in this room.

Miranda walked near the back, close enough to Teddy to feel the tension radiating off him like heat from a forge. She had known something was wrong since they arrived at the castle. The way Teddy's easy warmth had calcified into something brittle and careful, a performance of calm that fooled everyone except her.

And Percival. The old man still hadn't left the room assigned to him. Three days now, and Miranda had been sliding food under the door like he was a prisoner rather than a guest.

Now, entering the great hall without him, she felt his absence like a missing tooth.

"Friends! Performers! Welcome!"

King Lionel's voice rang through the hall, too loud, too bright, a torch thrown into a room that needed no more light. He stood at the head of the table in robes of purple velvet, a crown that looked too heavy for his head, his face arranged into an expression of generosity that couldn't quite hide the fear beneath it.

"We are honored—truly honored—to host the Band of Oddfellows in our humble hall." He gestured expansively at the feast, at the banners, at the castle that was anything but humble. "Please. Eat. Drink. Tomorrow you will perform for the court, but tonight—tonight you are our guests."

Barnaby bowed with flourishes that made his cape swirl. "Your Grace is too kind. The Band of Oddfellows are humbled by such hospitality."

"Nonsense, nonsense." Lionel waved a hand, wine already sloshing in his goblet. "Art must be celebrated. My father always said so. Didn't he, brother?"

The question was directed at the figure seated to Lionel's right.

Damien Taylor had not moved since the troupe entered. He sat with one hand curled around a wine glass he had not drunk from, his posture relaxed in the way that predators are relaxed: still because movement was not necessary yet, patient because the kill was already certain. His eyes had found Jamie the moment the doors opened and had not left him since.

Jamie had not noticed. Or was pretending he had not.

"Father said many things," Damien said. "Most of them to hear himself speak."

Lionel's smile flickered. "Well, *yes*, but he appreciated—"

"He appreciated himself." Damien's gaze finally moved from Jamie to his brother. "And those who reflected him back as he wished to be seen."

The silence that followed was brief but total. Miranda felt it press against her skin like humidity before a storm. Then Lionel laughed—too loud, too long, too forced—and gestured for the wine to be poured, and the moment passed into the general noise of a feast beginning.

But something had shifted. The air held a charge now, a tension that had not been there before. Miranda watched the other guests—minor nobles, courtiers, a few merchants wealthy enough to buy their way to the table—and saw them register it too. Smiles went fixed. Conversations turned careful. Everyone in the room had suddenly remembered that they were eating in the presence of something dangerous.

The feast continued. Wine flowed. Voices rose and fell in the careful rhythms of courtly conversation. Barnaby held forth on the history of his troupe, though much of it was untrue. Lionel listened with apparent fascination, laughing at jokes that were not funny, praising stories that were not true, performing the role of gracious host with the desperate energy of someone who knew the performance was failing.

Damien said nothing. Watched everything.

Then, halfway through the second course, he spoke again.

"I've arranged entertainment."

The doors at the far end of the hall opened. Three women entered, dressed in gowns that suggested wealth without quite achieving it; the kind of finery that came from brothels rather than noble houses, silk that had been worn by too many bodies, jewelry that caught the light a little too eagerly.

Courtesans. Professional ones, by the look of them. The kind who knew how to move through a room full of powerful men without quite belonging to it.

But there was a fourth figure behind them.

Lillian.

Of course, Miranda didn't know her—had never seen her before this moment—but she knew immediately that this girl mattered. Something in the way Teddy's stillness deepened. Something in the cruel satisfaction that flickered across Damien's face, there and gone in an instant, a crack in the mask that revealed the furnace beneath.

She was young. Pretty, in the wan way of someone who had not eaten properly in weeks. Her dress was borrowed—too large in the shoulders, cinched awkwardly at the waist—and her hair had been arranged by hands that didn't care about her comfort. She walked with the careful steps of someone who had learned that sudden movements brought pain.

The moment she saw the hall, the banners, the faces turning toward her, her left hand rose to her collarbone, fingers pressing against the hollow of her throat in a gesture so small, so instinctive, that no one else seemed to notice.

But Jamie noticed.

Miranda saw the recognition move through him like a current, not of her face, which he had clearly known already, but of that gesture. That specific press of fingers against skin. Something from before. Something private. A habit she had carried from childhood, perhaps, or a nervous tell he had memorized in some village neither of them would ever see again.

His hand moved beneath the table. Not to a weapon—there was no weapon—but to his own thigh, pressing hard enough that his knuckles went white. Anchoring himself. Holding the mask in place through pain.

"A gift from my brother's dungeons," Damien said, and his voice was silk wrapped around broken glass. "The Lady Lillian. Formerly of some village or other. Currently a guest of the crown."

He gestured, and the courtesans guided Lillian to a seat at the far end of the table—not quite among the guests, not quite among the servants. A deliberate nowhere. A position engineered to humiliate.

The two courtesans settled on either side of her, bracketing her with their professional warmth, their painted smiles, their hands that touched her shoulders and hair with familiarity she clearly had not invited.

Jamie didn't move.

Miranda watched him not move. Watched the effort it cost him to keep his eyes on his plate, to keep his hands steady, to keep breathing at a rate that suggested calm rather than the fury she could feel radiating off him like heat.

He knows her. He knows her and he's watching Damien destroy her and he can't do anything about it.

"She's been cooperative," Damien continued, addressing the table at large but watching only Jamie. "Quiet. Obedient. A model servant, really. I confess I've grown rather fond of her. There's something rather restful about a woman who understands her position. Who doesn't pretend to be more than she is."

The word *fond* hung in the air.

Lillian's face had gone white. Her eyes were fixed on the table in front of her, on the plate of food she clearly couldn't eat, on anything except the faces watching her. Her hand had dropped from her throat, but Miranda could see it trembling in her lap.

"She reminds me of the girls back home," one of the courtesans said, playing her role with professional ease. "Same frightened look. Same skinny arms. Give her a few weeks in a proper house and she'd learn to smile, I expect."

Laughter scattered through the hall. Nervous. Obligatory. The sound of people who knew they were witnessing cruelty and had decided that participation was safer than objection.

"Perhaps," Damien said. "Though I find her silence refreshing. So many women feel compelled to fill every moment with chatter. Lillian understands the value of keeping one's mouth shut." He paused. "Mostly."

More laughter. Thinner this time.

Jamie's breathing had changed. Miranda couldn't have said how she knew—the difference was invisible, inaudible—but she felt it. The boy she had traveled with for weeks had vanished somewhere behind his eyes, and something else had come forward.

Damien smiled. The expression was beautiful and empty, a mask crafted to suggest warmth while containing none.

"Tell me," he said, and now his attention shifted fully to Jamie, a spotlight finding its target, "you're with the Band, aren't you? The one who carries props and runs errands."

Jamie looked up. His face was composed—neutral, polite, the expression of a servant addressed by a lord—but Miranda could see what it cost him.

"Yes, my lord."

"Teddy, was it?"

"Yes, my lord."

"And where do you come from? Originally?"

"Wolfpine, my lord."

"Ah, yes. Wolfpine." Damien's finger traced the rim of his wine glass, a lazy circle that drew the eye. "Teddy the carpenter from Wolfpine. I remember now." He glanced at Lillian, then back at Jamie. "She's from a village too. Our guest. A place called—what was it?"

"Taylor's End," Lillian whispered. Her voice was barely audible, roughened by weeks of disuse or weeping or both.

"That's right. A local. How could I forget?" He smiled at his own charade, a private joke that amused only him. "I'm told she had a friend there. A young man she quite fancied."

Jamie's expression didn't change. "Is that so, my lord?"

"She spoke of him. In her more—how should I say—*unguarded* moments." Damien's eyes had gone half-lidded, lazy, a cat watching a mouse it had already caught. "Some talk of yellow hair. Green eyes. A heroic name. Jamie, I believe it was."

Ripples spread through the room; not visible, not audible, but present. A shifting of attention. A holding of breath. The sense that something important had just happened, even if no one could quite identify what.

"Common name," Jamie said. "Half the boys in the north are called Jamie."

"Is that so?" Damien chuckled and glanced around the table, inviting the room to share in his amusement. "Forgive me, I confess I haven't brushed up on such statistics. It seems our friend Teddy here is something of an expert on the demographics of name commonality when he's not digging ditches or sawing planks."

"Don't need to be an expert," Jamie shot back through a clenched jaw, heat climbing in his neck. "It's common knowledge."

"Oh, I'm not refuting you," Damien returned, palms up in a placating gesture. "You know, Teddy, I find myself warming to you. Most servants flinch when I look at them. But you don't, do you? I mean, it's admirable, really. Whatever training produced you, it was certainly thorough."

The compliment was worse than the accusation. Miranda watched Jamie absorb it, watched him calculate the correct response, watched him choose.

"My lord is kind."

"My lord is curious." Damien's voice dropped. "So, if I were to ask our guest whether you reminded her of this Jamie, she wouldn't recognize you?"

Jamie shrugged. Damien turned to Lillian.

"Lillian. Look at this young man. The one with the Players. Have you seen him before?"

Lillian's head came up. Her eyes found Jamie's face, and Miranda saw the recognition flash through them: instant, instinctive, impossible to hide. A drowning woman seeing rescue and knowing, somehow, that the rescue was a trap.

"I..." Her voice cracked. "I don't..."

"Take your time, darling." Damien's tone was patient, encouraging, the voice of a confessor coaxing sin from a penitent. "We're in no hurry. Look closely. Search your memory. Perhaps he merely *resembles* your lost friend. Perhaps the similarity is coincidental."

The silence stretched. Lillian's eyes moved over Jamie's face—his jaw, his cheekbones, the color of his hair visible even in torchlight. Her lips parted. Her throat worked.

"He's..." She swallowed. "He *looks* like... someone I knew."

"Someone you knew." Damien nodded slowly. "Yes. I thought he might." He turned back to Jamie, and now the mask had slipped slightly, revealing something beneath that was worse than cruelty: certainty. "Strange coincidences seem to follow you, don't they? The company arrives at Taylor's Castle with a boy from Taylor's End in tow. The prisoner in our dungeon recognizes him. And yet he claims to be no one. A prop boy. A northern peasant with a common name."

"I am what I am, my lord."

"Yes. I believe you are."

He held Jamie's eyes for a long moment.

Then he looked away. Reached for his wine. Took a sip.

"Music," he said. "I think we should have music. Lionel, brother, have the minstrels play something lively. Our guests look far too serious."

"Yes!" Lionel's voice was too loud, too eager, the relief palpable. "Yes, excellent idea. Music! Something cheerful!"

The minstrels in the corner struck up a melody—bright, fast, inappropriate to the atmosphere but no one was willing to point that out. Conversation resumed with the forced energy of people escaping a flood, words tumbling over each other in the rush to fill the silence Damien had created.

Miranda watched Jamie's hands reappear above the table. They were trembling slightly. He picked up his wine, drank deeply, and set the goblet down carefully, as if the gesture itself might pass for composure.

Lillian had lowered her head again. The courtesans flanking her had gone quiet, sensing that whatever game was being played had moved beyond their understanding. Their hands no longer touched her shoulders. Even professional cruelty had limits.

And Damien sat at the head of the table, watching everything, touching nothing, the wine in his glass still barely tasted, his beautiful face arranged into an expression of mild interest that fooled no one.

The feast continued.

The music helped. Not much, but enough. It gave people something to focus on besides the tension still crackling through the air, something to tap their feet to, something to hide behind when conversation faltered.

Miranda didn't eat. Couldn't. Her stomach had closed itself against food the moment she understood what she was seeing. Not a feast but an interrogation; not hospitality but a trap closing slowly around someone she had begun to think of as a friend.

She watched Jamie make his way through the motions of eating. Small bites. Mechanical chewing. His eyes stayed down, fixed on his plate, but she could see them moving beneath his lowered lids, tracking Damien's position, Lillian's status, the guards stationed at each door.

The feast wound toward its conclusion with agonizing slowness. Desserts were served—honeyed fruits, almond pastries, something involving cream and spun sugar that looked more like architecture than food. Lionel made a toast to the Players, to the performance tomorrow, to art and beauty and the eternal traditions of the Taylor court. His words ran together, wine-slurred and desperate, a man trying to end a nightmare through the sheer force of forced cheerfulness.

Damien didn't speak again.

When the last plates were cleared and the musicians' melody faded into silence, the guests began to rise. Movement broke the spell that had held the room. Conversations resumed at normal volume. Laughter—real laughter, not the performative kind—emerged from corners where people had found genuine connection despite everything.

Miranda rose with the others. Found Jamie in the shuffle of bodies heading toward doors.

"Walk with me," she said.

Her hand closed around his wrist, fingers pressing harder than she intended, and she pulled him toward a side corridor before he could object.

The noise of the hall faded behind them. Torchlight gave way to candles, then to shadows as they moved deeper into the castle's maze of passages. Miranda didn't know where she was going—didn't care. Away. Somewhere Damien's eyes couldn't follow. Somewhere the air didn't taste like blood waiting to be spilled.

She stopped in an alcove where a window slit let in starlight, a narrow vertical gash in stone that offered a view of courtyard and sky. Turned to face him.

Jamie looked younger in this light. The shadows carved hollows under his eyes, emphasized the tension in his jaw, made him look like what he was—a boy playing a part in a drama too large for him, pretending to courage he was not sure he possessed.

"Your name isn't Teddy," Miranda said.

Jamie's expression didn't change. "Miranda—"

"Don't." Her voice cracked on the word. "Don't lie to me. Not now. Not after that." She gestured toward the hall they had left, toward everything that had happened there. "I watched your face when they brought her in. I watched you pretend not to know her. I'm not stupid, Teddy, or whatever your bloody name is."

He was quiet for a long moment. The starlight caught his face, turned his features silver and shadow.

"Jamie," he said finally. "My name is Jamie. Teddy was... a precaution."

"A precaution." She let the word sit between them. "And the girl? Lillian?"

"We grew up together. In Taylor's End."

"And he knows. Damien. He knows who you are."

"He knows *something*. Suspects more." Jamie's voice had gone flat, exhausted. "By tomorrow he'll be certain."

"What about Percival? The old prick who's been hiding in his room for three days?"

Jamie's mouth opened. Closed. The acceptance of his own predicament moved across his face.

"That's Felix," he said quietly. "His name is Felix."

"*Felix.*" She threw her hands up. "Christ. Is anyone in this troupe who they say they are?"

"Barnaby is. The musicians are. *You* are." He paused. "I didn't want to drag you into this. Any of you. We needed cover to get into the castle. A theatre troupe. Something that wouldn't draw suspicion."

"Cover." She scoffed. "So we're what? Props? Scenery for whatever the hell you're actually doing here?"

"We came to get her back," Jamie said. "That's all. Lillian. They took her from the village. Sold her to settle her father's debts. Felix said he could help me find her, get her out. That was supposed to be it. Get in, find her, leave."

"Supposed to be."

"I didn't know it would be like this." His hands opened and closed at his sides. "I didn't know Damien would—I didn't *know* any of this. Felix doesn't tell me things. He moves pieces around and expects me to follow."

Miranda studied him. The exhaustion in his face. The tremor in his hands. The animal desperation of someone who had walked into something much larger than they understood.

"You really didn't know?"

"*No.*" The word was hollow. "I thought we were rescuing my friend. That we'd be gone by now."

"And instead?"

Jamie didn't answer.

The silence stretched. Miranda's breathing was audible now, sharp and fast, the rhythm of someone fighting to stay in control.

"He wants to kill you," she said. "Damien. You understand that, don't you? Whatever game he's playing, however long he lets it run—"

"Probably."

"And you're just—what—accepting that?"

"I'm not leaving without her. Can't."

"And me? The rest of us? What happens to us when this all falls apart?"

"You should leave," Jamie said flatly. "Tomorrow, before the performance. Tell Barnaby you're ill. Get out of the castle and don't look back."

"That's your answer? Run?"

"It's the only one I have."

Miranda stood there for a long moment, her shoulders tight, her hands still gripping her elbows. The anger hadn't left her face, but something else had joined it. Something that looked almost like decision.

"If I stay," she said slowly, "and if there's a chance to help—"

"Miranda, don't be stupid—"

"Shut up! I'm not saying I forgive you. And I certainly don't trust you. But that girl in there..." She paused. Swallowed. "No one deserves what they're doing to her. And if you're stupid enough to try to save her, maybe you shouldn't have to do it alone."

Jamie's mouth curved; not quite a smile, but close.

She slapped him. Hard.

"Ow!"

"Don't ever lie to me again."

"I won't."

"You stupid, selfish, lying, short, beautiful boy. If I die tomorrow, I will haunt you for the rest of my days."

She turned away. Started walking toward wherever the corridor led.

"Miranda."

She stopped. Didn't turn back.

"Thank you," Jamie said. "For seeing. For asking."

She stood there for a moment. Then she walked on, leaving him alone in the starlight, a boy who had come to rescue a girl and found himself trapped in something much larger than rescue.

Jamie listened to her footsteps fade.

SCENE 33

1578
24 years earlier

The bells had stopped three days ago.

Taylor's Castle held its breath in the manner of all stone things asked to contain grief; rigid, cold, letting the silence pool in its corridors like standing water. The banners flew at half-mast. The kitchens served meals that no one ate. In the great hall, the throne sat empty while King Tobias locked himself in chambers that smelled of wine and unwashed linens, and the court walked softly, spoke in murmurs, and waited for permission to resume being alive.

In the nursery, a candle burned.

Felix stood at the window with the infant against his chest. The boy was three weeks old, small enough to fit in the crook of one arm, light as promise. Outside, the kingdom of Taylor's End spread below the castle in a patchwork of thatched roofs and smoking chimneys, the river cutting through its center like a scar that had healed silver. Northbury was ash somewhere beyond the horizon. Anya was ash somewhere in the royal crypt. The world had ended and continued anyway.

The baby stirred. Felix shifted his weight, adjusted the swaddling with fingers that knew how to hold swords, how to snap necks, how to sign death warrants. Now they learned this: the particular pressure needed to soothe an infant's spine.

"Shh," he said. The sound came out rough, unpracticed.

The boy's eyes were open. Green, like his mother's. Like hers had been before they'd closed forever in a bed soaked with childbed blood while Felix stood outside the door and listened to her screaming and couldn't enter because he was only the knight-commander, only the man who'd sworn to protect her, only the man who—

He stopped the thought. Pressed his lips to the crown of the boy's head.

Somewhere in the castle, glass shattered. Tobias's voice rose through stone and timber, the words indistinct but the fury unmistakable.

Felix's jaw tightened.

He turned from the window and walked to the cradle—carved oak, trimmed in gold, fit for a prince—and lowered the boy into its silk-lined basin with a care that felt foreign in his soldier's hands. The baby's fists curled and uncurled. His breathing steadied.

"Sleep," Felix said. "While you still can."

Miles below the castle, in a cottage at the eastern edge of Taylor's End where the street became a goat path and the goat path became the moors, Ruth wrung blood from a rag into a basin already pink with it.

"Hold still."

"I'm holding."

"You're not." She pressed the cloth to Rowan's knee and he hissed through his teeth. The wound gaped beneath her hands—arrow-torn, half-healed wrong, now reopened from the journey. The stitches she'd sewn two days ago had burst somewhere on the road. "You tore them."

"The cart hit a stone."

"The cart hit *fifty* stones. You tore them when you tried to walk."

Rowan's face was gray in the candlelight. He lay on the bed that took up most of the cottage's single room, his leg propped on folded blankets, his hands gripping the mattress edge hard enough to whiten his knuckles. He was twenty-five years old. He had served the crown for ten of those years. He had taken seven wounds in battle and walked away from all of them.

This was one he would not walk away from.

Not properly.

Not ever.

"There's bone showing," Ruth said.

"I know."

"If it festers—"

"It won't."

"You don't know that."

"I know you won't let it."

Ruth looked at him. The words sat between them, simple and heavy as the truth they carried. She was not his wife. She was not his woman in any official sense. She was the healer's widow from three streets over who'd started bringing him soup when his cough wouldn't clear last winter, and then started bringing other things—herbs, bandages, sharp words when he needed them. She'd never left.

"You're an idiot," she said.

"Been called worse."

"By better people, I hope."

A sound escaped him that might have been a laugh if there'd been any breath behind it. Ruth pressed the cloth harder and he stopped laughing.

The days passed in fragments.

Felix returned to the nursery each evening after his duties released him—standing at the door until the nursemaids cleared, then entering with the silence of a man who'd learned to move without sound. He lifted the boy from the cradle. Held him to the window. Watched the lights of Taylor's End flicker and dim as the town surrendered to sleep.

He didn't speak. Words felt dangerous. Words could be over-heard, remembered, repeated. But he looked at the boy's face in the candlelight and saw Anya looking back at him—the shape of the brow, the set of the mouth, the green eyes that held the world with a stillness that wasn't quite peace.

Mine, he thought. The word was a blade in his chest.

On the fifth night, he hummed. A low sound, half-re-membered from somewhere in his own childhood, a melody without words. The boy's eyes fluttered closed. His breathing slowed.

Felix stood there for a long time, humming to his son in a dead queen's nursery, and let himself feel the weight of what he'd done.

In the cottage, Rowan slept and woke and slept again. The fever came on the third day—low, persistent, enough to blur the edges of his thoughts but not enough to drag him under entirely. Ruth fed him broth. Changed his bandages. Slept in the chair by the fire because he thrashed too much to share the bed.

"You were calling out," she said on the fourth morning.

"Was I."

"Names." She poured water into a cup, held it to his lips. "Men you served with, I think. The ones who didn't come back."

Rowan drank. Said nothing.

"You called for someone named Felix."

His eyes found hers. Something moved behind them—not quite fear, not quite guilt. Something closer to a door closing.

"Old friend," he said.

"He hasn't come to see you."

"He's busy."

"He's your commander. You took an arrow for him at Northbury."

"I took an arrow for the queen." The words came out sharper than he intended. He softened. "Felix has the kingdom to man-age. Tobias is—" He stopped. Drank more water. "He's busy."

Ruth watched him for a moment. Then she took the cup and

turned to the basin, and her silence said everything her words did not.

Tobias found Felix in the armory on the sixth night.

The room was cold, lit by a single torch that threw shadows across the racks of swords and the hanging mail. Felix stood at the workbench, running a whetstone along the edge of a blade he didn't need to sharpen, the motion repetitive, meditative. He heard the door open. Didn't turn.

"The boy's sleeping," Tobias said.

"He usually does, at this hour."

"You'd know."

Felix's hand stilled on the blade. Then it resumed its motion. "I check on him. As I check on all matters of the castle's security."

"Security."

Tobias's laugh was a wet, ugly thing. He'd been drinking. Felix could smell it from ten feet away, could hear it in the loose roll of his words.

"That what you call it?"

"What would you call it, Your Grace?"

Footsteps. Tobias moving closer. The torch flame guttered in the disturbed air.

"*Guilt.*"

Felix set down the whetstone. Turned. Tobias stood three feet away, swaying slightly, his face bloated with drink and grief and something blacker. He wore no crown. His clothes hung on him as if they'd been made for a larger man. Six days of mourning had aged him ten years.

"I served your wife faithfully," Felix said. "As I've served you."

"You know what the servants say? What they whisper when they think I can't hear? Guess."

"Servants whisper many things, it's all they've—"

"Guess!" Tobias bellowed.

Felix shook his head. "I don't know what they whisper, Your Grace."

"They say she loved you." The words came out choked. "They say you were in her chambers. Night after night. They say—"

"They're wrong."

"Are they?"

The silence stretched. In the corridor outside, a guard's footsteps passed and faded.

"Ask me what you want to ask," Felix said.

Tobias's hand shot out in a shove that landed in the center of Felix's chest and drove him back half a step. The whetstone clattered to the floor. Neither man looked at it.

"Is he mine?"

Felix could have lied. Should have lied. The lie was *there*, waiting on his tongue. A good lie. A survivable lie.

He said nothing.

Tobias read the silence. His face changed—collapsed, really, like a building crumbling from its base. For a moment, he looked like a man who'd just been told his own death date. Then the grief curdled into something else.

"You fucked my wife."

"Tobias—"

"You fucked my wife, and now she's dead, and that thing in the nursery—" His voice cracked. "That thing isn't mine. Is it. *Is it.*"

Felix's hands had risen, palms out, the gesture of a man gentling a spooked horse. "Whatever happened between Anya and me—"

"'Whatever happened.'" Tobias's laugh was a sob. "*Whatever happened.* You're standing here, in my castle, and you're telling me whatever happened—"

"—the boy is *innocent.*"

Tobias went still.

"The boy," Felix continued, "is three weeks old. He doesn't know his mother is dead. He doesn't know his father—" He stopped. Started again. "He doesn't know *anything*, except that the world is cold and loud and frightening, and the only kindness he's received is from the hands that feed him and the arms that hold him. Whatever you do to me—whatever I deserve—he deserves none of it."

For a long moment, Tobias just stared at him. The torch crackled. Somewhere in the castle, a door slammed.

"Deserves," Tobias said finally. "You want to talk to me about what people deserve." He stepped closer. His breath was sour with wine. "My wife is dead. My kingdom is in mourning. My own Watch Commander was putting his cock in her while I—" He couldn't finish. "And you want to talk about what your little bastard deserves."

"He's your heir."

"He's *your* heir," Tobias snarled. "You think I'm stupid? You think I can't see it? The way you look at him. The way you hold him. The way you—" Tobias's hand found Felix's collar, twisted. "I should have you killed. I should have you dragged to the courtyard and—"

"Then do it."

Felix's voice was quiet. Steady. He didn't resist the grip.

"Please, do it," he said again, and he meant it. "But leave the boy out of it. Raise him as your own. Let him believe he's your son. Give him the life he was born to have and take whatever vengeance you want from me. I won't fight it."

Tobias's grip tightened. His knuckles were white against the dark wool of Felix's collar.

Then something shifted in his face. Something worse than rage.

"You think I'd raise another man's bastard? You think I'd let that *thing* sit on my throne? Carry my reign?" He released Felix with a shove. "I'll tell you what I'll do. I'll wait until you're gone—executed, exiled, I don't care—and then I'll take that boy to the cliffs myself. I'll hold him over the edge. And I'll let go."

Felix's blood went cold.

"You won't."

"Won't I?" Tobias smiled. It was the most terrible thing Felix had ever seen on a human face. "Try me. Give me a reason. Stay in this castle one more night and see what a grieving father is capable of."

Tobias stumbled off and vanished into the corridor.

Felix stood where he was, hands limp at his sides, his face gone white.

When Tobias's voice returned, it came from nowhere and everywhere at once, striking the stone walls and making Felix flinch where he stood.

"One more night, Ryder!"

The corridor was dark.

Felix walked without seeing. His hands were shaking. He couldn't make them stop.

I'll hold him over the edge.

The nursery door appeared. He pushed through it before the guard could speak.

Inside, the candles had burned low. The nursemaid was gone; dismissed hours ago, probably asleep in her quarters. The cradle sat in its alcove by the window, and in the cradle, the boy slept with his fists curled against his chest.

Felix stood over him.

I'll let go.

The decision wasn't a decision. Some things were inevitable. Some choices had already been made before you knew you were making them.

He reached into the cradle.

The boy weighed nothing.

Felix wrapped him in a second blanket, then a third, pulling the wool tight against the cold that waited outside these walls. The infant stirred, made a small sound of protest, then settled against Felix's chest with a sigh that broke something in him.

"I'm sorry."

The corridor stretched before him, torch-lit and empty. He moved through it like a ghost—past the guard station where two men played dice and didn't look up, past the gallery where Tobias's ancestors watched from their frames with painted eyes, past the chapel where Anya's tomb waited fresh and white and impossible.

He didn't stop. Couldn't stop.

The stairs to the east wing were narrow and steep, meant for servants rather than knights. Felix took them two at a time, one arm cradling the boy, the other trailing against the wall for balance. At the bottom, a door opened onto a corridor that led to the kitchens, and beyond the kitchens, a gate that the cooks used for early-morning deliveries.

He was almost there when he saw her.

The girl was young, maybe fifteen, carrying a basket of linens down the corridor with the hunched posture of someone who'd learned to make herself small. She froze when she saw him. The basket tilted. A sheet slipped out and puddled on the floor.

Felix stopped.

The boy in his arms made a soft sound. The girl's eyes dropped to the bundle. Widened.

Neither of them moved.

"You shouldn't be here," the girl said finally. Her voice was barely a whisper.

"No."

"That's—" She stopped. Swallowed. "That's the Little Prince."

Felix said nothing. His hand had drifted to the hilt of his sword without his telling it to. He watched her eyes track the motion. Watched her understand.

The silence stretched.

"I've seen you," she said. "In the queen's chambers. Late at night."

His grip tightened.

"I never said anything." The words came out in a rush, tumbling over each other. "I never—I wouldn't—" She was shaking now, the basket trembling in her hands. "Please. I have a mother. Sisters. I wouldn't tell anyone. I won't tell anyone."

Felix looked at her. She was young and terrified and completely in his power, and if he killed her, no one would ever know. The body would be found in a day or a week, and it would be one more mystery in a castle full of mysteries, and he would be long gone.

He could do it. He knew how.

The boy stirred against his chest. Made a sound like a question.

Felix's hand fell from his sword.

"Go to bed," he said.

The girl stared at him.

"Go to bed," he said again, "and forget you saw me. Forget you saw any of this. When they ask—and they will ask—tell them you were asleep. Tell them you heard nothing. Tell them the truth: you know nothing."

"I don't—"

"If you speak of this, I'll know." The lie came easily, worn smooth by years of commanding men. "If you speak of this, I'll come back. And I won't come alone."

She believed him. He could see it in the way her face went pale, in the way she clutched the basket like a shield.

"Yes, Sir."

"Go."

She went. Her footsteps faded down the corridor, and then Felix was alone with his son and the silence and the weight of what he was about to do.

The stable was dark.

Felix saddled his horse by feel—the leather familiar beneath his hands, the motions automatic. The boy lay in a nest of straw and blankets, quiet for now, his green eyes tracking the shadows that moved across the rafters.

"Not much longer," Felix murmured. "Just stay quiet. Can you do that for me?"

The boy blinked.

Felix cinched the saddle, checked the girth, led the horse to the mounting block. The night air was cold and wet, the smell of rain coming from the west. In the castle above, the windows glowed with the amber light of dying fires. No alarms yet. No bells.

He mounted. Settled the boy against his chest. Wrapped his

cloak around them both.

"Let's go."

The road to Taylor's End was mud and darkness.

Rain began halfway down the hill, light at first, then harder, driving needles of cold into every gap in Felix's clothing. The boy cried—a thin, reedy sound that cut through the noise of hooves and weather—and Felix hunched over him, using his body as a shield.

"I know," he said. "I know. Almost there."

Lightning split the sky, silent and white, and Felix counted in his head without thinking. One. Two. Three. Then the thunder came, rolling in from the mountains long and low. An old habit from the northern campaigns. In Taylor's End, the storms came wrong: the flash first, silent as a held breath, then the sound catching up seconds later. Something about the valley and the way it swallowed noise. The men used to joke about it. God showing you what he'd done before you heard the blow land.

The lights of the town appeared through the rain, scattered and dim. Felix counted streets in his head, turned left at the tanner's shop, right at the well, left again at the shrine to some saint whose name he'd never learned. The cottage materialized from the darkness: a low stone building with a thatched roof and a pen of huddled goats, smaller than he remembered, simpler.

He dismounted. Tied the horse to the fence. Walked to the door.

Knocked.

Nothing.

He knocked again, harder. The sound was swallowed by the rain. Inside, no light moved. No voice answered.

"Rowan." He kept his voice low, urgent. "Rowan, open the door."

From the direction of the castle, carried on the wind: the first faint toll of a bell.

Felix's stomach dropped.

He tried the door. Locked. He circled the cottage, rain

streaming down his face, the boy wailing against his chest. The back door was simpler; rough planks held together with iron bands, no lock, just a latch. He lifted it. Pushed through.

Inside, the cottage smelled of herbs and woodsmoke and the sharp tang of healing salves. A fire burned low in the hearth, casting orange light across a room he'd never seen. A table. A chair. A shelf of bottles and dried plants. And standing by the bed, turning at the sound of his entrance with a basin in her hands and a look on her face that said she'd been expecting trouble since the day she was born:

Ruth.

She didn't scream. That was the first thing Felix noticed. Women usually screamed when armed men burst into their homes in the middle of the night. Ruth just set down the basin and said:

"Who the hell are you?"

"I need to see Rowan."

"Rowan's sleeping."

"Wake him."

"No."

The word landed like a slap. Felix stood there, rain dripping from his cloak, his son crying against his chest, and this woman—this small, sharp-eyed woman he'd never met—looked at him like he was a beggar who'd wandered into the wrong house.

"I don't have time for this," he said. "The castle—"

"I heard the bells." Ruth crossed her arms. "I also heard the rain, and I hear that baby screaming, and I see a man in the king's livery standing in my kitchen with a bundle that looks an awful lot like the thing the whole town's been talking about for three weeks." Her eyes narrowed. "So unless you want to tell me what a knight of the realm is doing stealing the Little Prince in the middle of the night, you can turn around and walk back out the way you came."

Felix's hand twitched toward his sword. Ruth's eyes tracked the motion.

"You won't," she said.

"Won't what."

"Kill me. You're here because you're running, and you need help, and you think Rowan will give it to you. Yes?"

The baby's cries had faded to whimpers. Felix felt the small body trembling against his chest.

"Wake him," he said again.

"I told you. No."

"He's my friend."

"He's a crippled soldier who can barely stand to piss." Ruth's voice hardened. "You haven't visited once since he came back from Northbury. Not once. He took an arrow in the knee defending your dead queen, and you couldn't be bothered to climb down from your castle and see if he was alive. Now you show up with a stolen prince and expect him to—what? Shelter you? Raise your bastard?" She shook her head. "No."

"The king will kill this child."

"Not my concern."

"It should be. If I'm caught here—if they find the boy—Rowan will hang beside me. Is that what you want?"

Ruth's face flickered. The first crack in her armor.

"Then leave," she said. "Take the child somewhere else."

"There is nowhere else." Felix stepped closer. The firelight caught his face, the exhaustion and the fear he'd been holding back for hours finally breaking through. "Listen to me. The king believes this boy is mine. He may be right. It doesn't matter. What matters is that Tobias has promised to throw him from the cliffs if I don't disappear. Tonight. Now." He let the words land. "Rowan is the only man in this kingdom I trust. The only man who would die for a child he'd never met just because it was the right thing to do. If you care about him—if you know him at all—you know I'm telling the truth."

Ruth said nothing.

The fire crackled. The bells from the castle grew louder, joined now by shouts, distant but unmistakable. The alarm spreading.

"They're coming," Felix said.

"I know."

"I don't have time to argue with you."

"Then don't." Ruth uncrossed her arms. "Write him a letter. Explain what you need. Leave the child and go."

"He needs to hear it from me."

"He can't." She gestured toward the bed, toward the shape beneath the blankets that Felix now realized hadn't moved since he entered. "The fever took him two days ago. He's been in and out since then. I gave him something to help him sleep, and he won't wake until morning no matter how much noise you make."

Felix looked at the bed. At Rowan's face, slack and pale in the dim light, the face of a man fighting something he couldn't see.

"He doesn't know I'm here," he said.

"No."

"He won't know I came."

"Not unless I tell him."

Felix turned back to Ruth. She stood between him and the door, arms at her sides now, watching him with eyes that saw too much.

"You'll tell him," he said.

"Will I?"

"You have to. If you don't—if he wakes up and finds a baby with no explanation—"

"I'll handle it."

"You don't understand. Tobias will send men. They'll search every house in Taylor's End. If they find the boy here—"

"Then they'll find him. And I'll tell them I don't know where he came from. I'll tell them someone left him on our doorstep. I'll tell them—"

"They won't believe you."

"They might."

"They won't." Felix stepped toward her, and something in his face must have changed, because for the first time, Ruth took a step back. "You're a witness. You've seen me. You've seen the child. You know where he came from and who brought him. The moment Tobias's men ask you a single question, everything falls apart."

Ruth's back touched the wall.

"Don't."

Felix didn't answer. He was looking at the boy in his arms, at the small face that had finally gone calm, at the green eyes that watched him with a trust he didn't deserve.

"I don't have a choice," he said.

"Everyone has a choice."

Lightning flooded the cottage, silent and white.

"No." *One.* "Not everyone."

Ruth opened her mouth.

Two.

Felix moved.

Thunder swallowed the night.

The letter took longer than it should have.

Felix sat at the table with a quill and parchment he'd found in a drawer, his hands still unsteady, his mind racing to find the words that would make this right. The boy lay on the bed beside Rowan's sleeping form, wedged between pillows so he wouldn't roll, his cries faded to hiccups and then to silence.

Rowan,

I'm sorry to leave like this. My mother took ill, and I have to go to her. She may not last the week.

This morning, someone left a baby on your doorstep. I don't know whose he is or where he came from, but I couldn't leave him out in the cold. He's small and quiet and no trouble at all.

I know this is a terrible thing to ask of you. I know you're barely healed. But I also know you're a good man, and this child deserves a chance at life.

His name is Jamie.

I'll come back if I can. If I can't...

Please take care of him. Please take care of yourself.

Yours,

Ruth

Felix read it twice. The handwriting was wrong, too angular, too precise, but it would have to do. In the morning, Rowan would wake to find the woman who'd cared for him gone and a child in her place, and he would believe because he would want to believe, because the alternative was too terrible to consider.

He folded the letter. Set it on the table where Rowan would see it.

Then he crossed to the bed, bent over his son one last time, and pressed his lips to the boy's forehead.

"Be good," he whispered. "Be brave. Be nothing like me."

The boy's eyes fluttered open.

Green eyes.

Anya's eyes.

Felix turned away before they could see him cry.

The rain had stopped.

Felix rode through the gates of Taylor's End as the first gray light of dawn touched the eastern hills. Behind him, the cottage sat silent in the mud, holding its secrets. Ahead, the road stretched toward exile, toward anonymity, toward whatever life remained for a man who had betrayed his king and killed an innocent woman and abandoned his son to a crippled soldier in a goat-farmer's house.

He didn't look back.

Rowan woke to silence.

The fever had broken sometime in the night, leaving him weak and hollowed-out but clear-headed for the first time in days. He lay still for a long moment, blinking at the ceiling, trying to remember what day it was and why his knee had stopped screaming.

"Ruth?"

His voice came out as a croak. He tried again.

"Ruth. Water."

Nothing.

He pushed himself up on his elbows—the motion sending a wave of dizziness through his skull—and looked around the cottage. The fire had died. The chair by the bed was empty. The door to the back was closed.

"Ruth?"

Panic crept up his throat. He swung his legs over the side of the bed, hissing as his knee protested, and made himself stand. The world tilted. He grabbed the bedpost. Waited.

When he could see straight, he hobbled across the room, checking every corner, every shadow. The basin by the fire was cold. The kettle was empty. The pile of bandages she'd been using to dress his wound sat neatly folded on the shelf, untouched since yesterday.

She was gone.

Rowan sank into the chair by the table, breathing hard. His hands were shaking. She'd left, walked out in the middle of the night without a word, without an explanation, without even—

A sound.

Small. High-pitched. Coming from the bed.

Rowan turned.

There, nestled between the pillows where he'd been sleeping, was a baby.

The letter was on the table. He found it when he went looking for answers, when he tore the cottage apart searching for some sign, some clue, some reason why Ruth would have left and where she would have gone.

He read it three times.

Then he read it again.

His name is Jamie.

The boy was awake now, watching Rowan with eyes that seemed too old for his tiny face. Green eyes. Calm eyes. Eyes that held no accusation, no expectation, only a kind of patient trust that made Rowan's chest ache.

"Jamie," he said.

The boy blinked.

Rowan looked at the letter again. At the handwriting that didn't quite match Ruth's usual scrawl. At the story that didn't quite make sense.

He was a soldier. He'd survived ten years in the king's service by knowing when something was wrong, by trusting the instinct that said this was a lie even when the lie was too pretty to question.

But the boy was real. The boy was here. And somewhere out there, Ruth had made a choice that had cost her everything.

"All right," Rowan said. His voice cracked on the word. He cleared his throat and tried again. "All right, then. Jamie. Let's see what we can do."

He reached down with hands that had held swords and shields and dying friends, and he lifted his son into his arms.

In Taylor's Castle, the world was ending.

Tobias stood in the center of the nursery, surrounded by guards and servants and advisors who pressed against the walls like they were afraid to breathe. The cradle was empty. The window stood open. The candles had burned down to nubs.

"Find him," Tobias said.

His voice was quiet. That was the worst part—quieter than anyone had ever heard it, quiet like the moment before a blade finds flesh.

"Your Grace—"

"Find him." Tobias turned. His eyes were red-rimmed, his face a mask of something that had moved past rage into territory none of them recognized. "Find Felix. Find my son. Bring them back to me."

"The Commander's quarters are empty, Your Grace. His horse is missing. We believe—"

"I don't *care* what you believe! Tobias picked up the nearest object, a silver rattle, and hurled it at the wall. It struck with a whip-crack that made every guard present flinch. "I want riders on every road. I want men at every gate. I want Felix dragged back here in chains, and I want him to watch while I—"

The air suddenly left him.

His brow fell in on itself. Tears rose, hot and unbidden, tracing clear paths through the grime of his state.

"Leave me." The command came out shattered.

"Your Grace—"

"*Leave me.*"

They did. The door closed. Sharp, strained sobs filled the room.

Tobias walked to the cradle and stood over it for a long time. His hands gripped the carved wooden edge until his knuckles went white.

Then he turned and walked to Felix's quarters.

The letter was on the desk.

Your Grace,

By the time you read this, I will be gone.

I will not ask your forgiveness. I know there is none to give. What I did with Anya—what we did—was a betrayal of everything I swore to uphold. You trusted me with your kingdom, your queen, your honor, and I broke that trust in the most unforgivable way.

Jamie is my son. I know it. I think you know it too.

I could not leave him to your mercy. Not after what you said. Not after what you promised.

If you want vengeance, you have every right to it. Hunt me. Find me. Take my head and hang it from the castle gates. I won't run. I won't hide. But I will not let you touch him.

He is innocent. Whatever sins his father has committed, he bears none of them.

I hope, someday, you understand.

Felix

Tobias read the letter once. Then again. Then a third time.

Then he folded it very carefully, placed it in his breast pocket, and walked to the window.

The town of Taylor's End and England beyond it spread before him—his kingdom, his birthright, his father's legacy and his father's fathers before that. For thirty years, he had ruled it. For thirty years, he had trusted the wrong men and loved the wrong women and made choices that had led him here, to this room, to this moment, to a future without an heir and a past stained with betrayal.

The rage came back. Slow at first. Then faster.

"Traitor," he whispered.

The word felt good. Felt right.

"Traitor!"

This time it filled the room, echoing off the walls and the ceiling in a way that felt like permission.

By the time the guards returned, he had made his decision.

Felix was dead. The boy was dead. Both of them had died in the night, murdered by bandits on the road, their bodies never recovered. The official story would be grief and tragedy. The private story, the one Tobias would carry in his chest like a lodged blade, would be betrayal and revenge deferred.

He would wait. He would watch.

And if Felix or his bastard ever surfaced again, he would finish what should have been finished tonight.

In a cottage at the edge of Taylor's End, a soldier learned to hold a child.

Not the way he'd held weapons, not with precision, not with force. With patience. With fear. With a tenderness that surprised him every time he felt it rising in his chest.

The boy cried through the first night and the second. On the third, Rowan discovered that humming helped, a wordless tune he didn't remember learning, something from a life before soldiering, before blood, before the wound that would never fully heal.

He named him Jamie. The letter had said to. He didn't question it.

Winter came, and with it, the fever.

Not for Rowan—his knee had settled into the dull ache that would be his companion for the rest of his days. For the boy. A cough that started small and grew until his tiny chest rattled with every breath.

Rowan walked three miles through snow to find a healer. Paid her in bits he couldn't spare. Sat by the bed for four days while the fever burned and broke and burned again.

On the fifth morning, the boy opened his eyes and smiled at him.

Rowan wept. He couldn't remember the last time he'd wept

for anything.

By spring, Jamie was crawling.

He moved through the cottage like a determined little storm, grasping table legs and chair rungs, pulling himself up and falling down and pulling himself up again. Rowan followed behind, cushioning falls, catching small hands before they found the fire, learning a vigilance that had nothing to do with battlefields.

The goats watched from the yard with what looked like judgment. Rowan ignored them.

First steps: a Tuesday in late summer.

The boy stood at one end of the cottage, Rowan at the other, arms outstretched. Between them, six feet of packed earth floor that might as well have been a canyon.

"Come on, then," Rowan said. "You can do it."

Jamie wobbled. Took a step. Took another. Fell forward into Rowan's waiting hands with a squeal of triumph.

"There you go." Rowan's voice came out thick. "There you go, lad. That's it."

That night, he carved a small wooden horse from a piece of kindling. Put it in the boy's hands while he slept. In the morning, Jamie woke clutching it like treasure.

First words: "*Da.*"

Not father. Not Rowan. Just "Da," spoken with absolute certainty as the boy reached up from his breakfast.

Rowan set down his spoon. Looked at the child, at the green eyes and the yellow hair and the stubborn set of the jaw that reminded him of someone he couldn't quite place.

"That's right," he said. "Da."

He didn't correct him. Didn't explain. Some truths were better than others.

At seven, he started asking about soldiers.

The men from the castle passed through Taylor's End sometimes—patrols, tax collectors, the occasional messenger. Jamie watched them with a hunger Rowan recognized. The same hunger he'd felt at that age, watching his father's friends return from campaigns with stories and scars.

"Were you a soldier, Da?"

They were at the edge of the moors, Rowan teaching him to track rabbits. His knee ached in the cold. It always did now.

"I was."

"Did you fight in battles?"

"A few."

"Did you kill people?"

"When I had to."

Jamie absorbed this. Processed it. Filed it away in whatever part of a child's mind stored such information.

"Will you teach me?"

"Someday," he said. "When you're ready."

By ten, Jamie could handle a practice sword.

Not well: his form was sloppy, his footwork a disaster. But he had the instinct. The way he moved, the way he watched, the way he anticipated Rowan's attacks a half-second before they came.

"You've got a talent for this," Rowan said one evening, breathing hard, his knee screaming from an hour of drills.

Jamie beamed. "Can we go again?"

"Tomorrow." Rowan lowered himself onto the bench by the cottage door, rubbing his leg. "Tomorrow, you'll learn to hold your guard properly. Tonight, you'll learn mercy."

Jamie brought him water without being asked. Sat beside him on the bench. Watched the sun go down over the moors.

"Da?"

"Hmm?"

"Why does the castle watch us?"

Rowan followed his gaze. On the hill above Taylor's End, the castle loomed against the darkening sky. In one of its towers, a light flickered.

"That's what they're for."

It wasn't an answer. Jamie knew it wasn't an answer. But he didn't push.

Some questions waited for their own time.

At twelve, he got into his first real fight.

A boy from the market had said something and Jamie had hit

him. Then hit him again. Then kept hitting until three grown men pulled him off.

Rowan found him sitting in the alley behind the tanner's shop, knuckles bloody, face streaked with tears and fury.

"What did he say?"

Jamie shook his head.

"Jamie. What did he say?"

"He said I was no one. That I came from nowhere. That my father was a traitor and my mother was a filthy harlot."

He couldn't finish. Rowan sat down beside him in the mud, ignoring the protest from his knee.

"Listen to me." He waited until Jamie looked at him. "You come from somewhere. You come from *this*." He pressed his fist to his own chest, his eyes fierce. "And whoever your mother was, whoever your father was, they trusted me to raise you. And I damn well have."

Jamie wiped his nose with the back of his hand. "What if they were right?"

"About what?"

"About me being no one."

Rowan took the boy's face in his hands. Calloused palms against tear-streaked cheeks.

"You listen to me. You are *not* no one. You are Jamie Campbell, and you are my son. And you are going to be something."

The boy stared at him. Then he leaned forward and pressed his forehead against Rowan's chest, and his shoulders shook.

At seventeen, Jamie discovered books.

He'd learned to read years earlier—Rowan had taught him, laboriously, from an old infantry manual and whatever scraps of text they could find—but now he devoured them. History. Philosophy. Poetry. He walked three miles every week to borrow from the old schoolmaster, returning with his arms full and his mind fuller.

"What's this one about?" Rowan asked one evening, squinting at the spine.

"A war from a thousand years ago. Two kingdoms fighting over a woman."

"Sounds about right."

"You've heard of it?"

"Men don't need much excuse to kill each other. A woman's as good as any."

Jamie was quiet for a moment. Then: "Did you ever love anyone? Before me?"

"Once," he said. "A long time ago."

"What happened?"

"She went away."

Jamie waited for more. Rowan didn't give it.

He started noticing girls that year. Or rather, they started noticing him.

The baker's daughter. The farrier's niece. The red-haired girl who sold eggs at the market and always gave him an extra when her father wasn't looking.

Rowan watched from a distance, amused and faintly terrified. The boy was handsome. Had a presence. A gravity. People were drawn to him without knowing why.

"You're going to break hearts," Rowan said one evening, after Jamie had spent an hour helping the widow Martins repair her fence while her three daughters watched from the window.

"I wasn't—"

"You were. And you didn't even notice. That's the dangerous part."

Jamie looked at his hands. "Is that bad?"

"It's not good or bad. It just is." Rowan handed him a cup of cider. "Just remember: a woman's heart isn't a toy. And the ones you don't notice are the ones who'll remember you longest."

Jamie considered this. "Speaking from experience?"

"Speaking from wisdom."

At nineteen, Jamie found the fights.

Behind the Ale & Comfort, in a pit surrounded by men with money to lose and filled with boys with none to, Taylor's End's young and restless beat each other bloody for bits and glory. Eli Richardson ran the operation, kept it clean, kept it fair, kept the castle's men looking the other way with regular payments and occasional favors.

Jamie's first fight lasted twelve seconds. The other boy was bigger, stronger, meaner. He came in swinging like he meant to kill. Jamie sidestepped, dropped his weight, and drove his shoulder into the boy's midsection. They went down together. Two punches later, it was over.

He collected his winnings—three bits, enough for a month of bread—and walked home with blood on his knuckles and something new and incredible burning in his chest.

He went back the next week. And the week after.

By the end of his first season, no one in Taylor's End would fight him anymore.

"You're going to get yourself killed."

Rowan stood in the doorway of the cottage, his arms crossed, his face set in the expression that meant this wasn't a discussion.

Jamie was wrapping his hands with strips of cloth. "I'm careful."

"You're nineteen. You don't know what careful means."

"Eli watches out for me."

"Eli watches out for his purse."

Jamie pulled the wrapping tight with his teeth. "It's good money, Da."

"There's other ways to make money."

"Not for someone like me."

Rowan's arms dropped to his sides.

"What's that supposed to mean?"

"It means I don't have a name."

Rowan said nothing. His hand found the doorframe, and he stepped aside.

"Be home before midnight."

Jamie brushed past him without answering.

At twenty, Jamie discovered drinking.

The specifics of that education were provided by Micah—Eli Richardson's foundling, his erstwhile son, a ginger-haired disaster of a human being who approached life with the conviction that anything worth doing was worth doing to excess.

"The secret," Micah announced, swaying slightly as he poured another round, "is to never stop. The moment you stop, that's when the world catches up with you."

"The world's already caught up with me." Jamie accepted the cup. It was his fifth. Or sixth. "It's sitting on my chest asking for the rent."

"Then drink faster."

They were in the alley behind the Ale & Comfort, sitting on overturned crates, passing a bottle of something that had probably been distilled in a bathtub. The night was warm. The stars were blurry. Everything felt very far away and very close at the same time.

"Do you ever think about leaving?" Jamie asked.

"Leaving what?"

"This. Taylor's End. All of it."

Micah considered the question with the gravity of the extremely drunk. "Where would I go?"

"Anywhere. There's a whole world out there."

"There's a whole world in here too." Micah gestured expansively, indicating either the alley or the bottle or possibly his own head.

Jamie laughed. Then he leaned over and vomited into a rain barrel.

Micah patted his back. "That's it. Get it all out. Tomorrow's a new day."

At twenty-one, Rowan was treating Jamie's black eye when he saw her.

"Hold still."

"It stings."

"It's *supposed* to sting. That's how you know it's working." Rowan dabbed the cloth against the swollen flesh. "Who was it this time?"

"Carpenter's boy. The big one."

"What'd he say?"

"Nothing I haven't heard before."

Rowan's hands stilled. He knew what that meant. The same taunts that had followed Jamie his whole life: bastard, orphan, no one, nothing. The words didn't hurt anymore. But the obligation to answer them never faded.

"You won?"

"Eventually."

"Good."

The cottage door was open to let in the morning breeze. Jamie turned his head toward it, wincing at the motion, and went very still.

"Da."

"Hmm?"

"Who's that?"

Rowan followed his gaze. Across the lane, a young woman was drawing water from the well. Dark hair, pale skin, a posture that spoke of hard years and harder lessons. She looked up, saw them watching, and smiled.

It was a small smile. Cautious. The smile of someone who'd learned to be careful with kindness.

But it transformed her face. Made her luminous.

"Lillian Spires," Rowan said. "Jeffrey's daughter. You remember the Spires family."

"She's grown."

"It's been years. People do that."

Jamie watched her hoist the bucket and start back toward her father's house. She moved like she was trying not to be noticed. Like she'd spent her whole life trying not to take up space.

"Is she—"

"Don't." Rowan's voice was sharp. "That girl's got enough trouble without you adding to it."

"I wasn't—"

"You were. I can see it on your face." He pressed the cloth harder against Jamie's eye, drawing a hiss of pain. "Her father's a mean drunk and a meaner sober. She doesn't need any complications."

Jamie said nothing. But his eyes stayed on the lane long after Lillian had disappeared.

The seasons turned. The years piled up like snow. He helped Rowan with the goats, patched the cottage roof when the winter storms tore it open, carried his father home from the tavern on the nights when the old wound ached too badly to ignore and the only medicine was forgetting. He saw Lillian when he could. Spoke to her when he dared. Learned the shape of her silences and the weight of her secrets and the way her eyes changed when she thought no one was watching.

He fell in love. Quietly. Desperately. Without ever quite admitting it to himself.

The castle watched from the hill. Tobias grew older and crueler and sicker. Damien came of age and became something worse. Lionel never quite launched. The kingdom rotted from the inside, and in the village below, a young man with green eyes and a borrowed name waited for something he couldn't name.

In 1601, November had come with pride. The moors were brown and brittle, the last of the root vegetables pulled from hardening ground, the sky the color of slate and promises it wouldn't keep.

They sat inside the cottage. Eating. Turnip stew with the last of the salted pork, steam rising from wooden bowls, the fire popping and hissing against the draft that crept beneath the door. A small honey cake sat between them; lumpy, lopsided, the best Rowan could manage. Twenty-four years old today.

"Da?"

"Hmm?"

"Thank you."

"For what?"

"Everything." Jamie shrugged, like the word was simple. "You know."

Outside, the castle loomed against the stars. Its bells had been silent for decades now. Its walls held secrets that would never come to light. Somewhere in the world, a man who had been a knight was still running. In this cottage, a boy who had been born a prince was finally home.

The fire went out.

Rowan didn't light another one.

He just sat there in the dark, listening to the sound of the wind through the thatch, and let the years wash over him like waves against a shore, the particular weight of a life built on lies that had somehow become love.

SCENE 34

TAVERNKEEPER

The hour had chased away everyone worth knowing and most who weren't.

Taylor's Ale & Comfort wore its emptiness like a drunk wears shame: poorly, and with too much effort to hide it. The candles had guttered to nubs in their sconces, throwing weak orange light across tables still sticky with the evening's commerce. Smoke from the hearth curled against the rafters and hung there, too tired to rise. The floorboards held the memory of a hundred thousand footsteps, warped and groaning in places, silent in others where the wood had simply given up. The place smelled of spilled ale and rendered fat and something older, something that had soaked into the grain over decades of transactions conducted in whispers—debts called in, threats issued, alliances forged and broken while the candles burned down and no one wrote anything down.

Eli Richardson stood behind the bar with a towel slung over

his shoulder and a glass in his hand, polishing it with the mechanical attention of a man whose thoughts were elsewhere.
His cigar smoldered in its case on the bartop, a thin ribbon of
smoke climbing toward the low ceiling. The scars on his face
looked deeper in this light—the white lines that mapped his
history, the ruined socket where his brother's blade had taken
his eye twenty-some years ago. He'd learned to see in the dark
with what remained. Learned to read a room by its sounds
and its silences, by the particular quality of stillness that meant
danger versus the stillness that meant nothing at all.

The figure in the back corner hadn't moved in twenty minutes.

Eli had clocked him the moment he'd slipped through the
door—hooded, hunched, choosing the table farthest from the
fire and closest to the rear exit. The posture of a man who
wanted to be invisible. Or wanted to seem that way. In Eli's
experience, the two were rarely the same thing.

He set down the glass. Picked up another. Resumed polishing.

The figure stayed.

"Oi! Scamper!"

His voice cut through the silence like a blade through
lard—sharp, disinterested, the tone of a man who'd thrown out
a thousand drunks and would throw out a thousand more. He
didn't look up from the glass.

Nothing.

The polishing continued. Three strokes. Four. The figure
remained in his peripheral vision, motionless as furniture.

Eli stopped.

"Mate, I promise you. It's too late to fuck with me."

The words hung in the stale air. Outside, wind scraped
against the shutters; a dry, restless sound, like something trying
to get in. Or get out.

Then the figure spoke.

"A blonde babe... born in blood..."

The voice reached him before the meaning did. Polished.
Aristocratic. Rich with an unnerving elegance that had no

business in a tavern at this hour. A voice that had never begged for anything in its life because it had never needed to.

Eli's hands went still on the glass.

The figure reached up and drew back his hood.

Damien Taylor's face emerged from the shadows like something rising from deep water. Pale skin stretched over sharp bones. Dark hair swept back from a high forehead. And the eyes—Christ, those eyes. Black as wet coal and twice as cold, holding a patience that felt less human than geological. The face of a man who had looked at the world and found it wanting, and had decided, with perfect calm, to make it pay.

Eli's gaze dropped, just for a heartbeat, to the crossbow hanging beneath the bar. He didn't reach for it. Just inventory.

His eyes returned to Damien.

"Jamie. The Red Prince."

The words landed in the silence like bits dropped on a coffin lid. Eli set down the glass.

"Only Jamie I know ran off months ago. Dead, most likely, with the winter we had."

"As is much the contrary, tavernkeeper. The boy lives—despite the winter, despite his father's head rolling in the mud at the hand of your brother."

Eli's eyes betrayed him.

"Jamie's here?"

"How long?"

"You'll have to be clearer, mate."

Damien rose from his chair. The motion was fluid, unhurried. He stepped into the candlelight—fine clothes beneath the common cloak, boots that cost more than most villages earned in a year, the posture of a man who believed the air around him was lucky to be breathed.

"How long have you betrayed the crown?"

Eli's hand found the bar. Steadied against it.

"I owe fuck all to the crown, much less one seeded in the cunni of a loopy whore."

Damien moved.

Eli's hand shot beneath the bar and came up with the crossbow, faster than a man with one eye had any right to move. The bolt was aimed at Damien's chest before the prince had taken a second step.

Damien stopped. Raised his hands in a gesture of surrender that somehow managed to look like condescension.

Their eyes locked. The crossbow didn't waver.

"I wondered when you lot would figure it out."

Eli came around the bar. One step. Two.

"Must be embarrassing. The village has known for years. That and *more*—d'you follow, mate?"

Closer now. Close enough to see the candlelight reflected in Damien's unblinking eyes.

"You come into my tavern, and to what? Scare me?"

Closer still.

"If I hadn't just mopped me floor, I'd do what your whoring usurper daddy should have done the moment you crawled out from that degenerate harlot's filth."

The words hung in the air between them; heavy, final, words that couldn't be taken back and weren't meant to be. Eli stood three feet from the prince of Taylor's End with a loaded crossbow aimed at his chest, and for a long moment, neither man moved.

Then Damien smiled.

"The boy will die tomorrow."

Eli's finger tightened on the trigger. The candles flickered. Outside, the wind picked up, rattling the shutters like the hands of the dead.

"I believe many will."

Damien lowered his hands with the grace of a man who understood that the crossbow wouldn't fire; not tonight, not here, not when the bolt would only make things worse and they both knew it.

He adjusted his cloak. Brushed an invisible mote of dust from his sleeve. Offered a nod.

"Tavernkeeper."

He turned his back on the crossbow and walked toward the door. Each step measured. Each step unhurried. The contempt was worse than any words could have been—the absolute certainty that Eli posed no danger, that nothing in this tavern could touch him, that he was already thinking about tomorrow and all the blood it would bring.

The door opened. The night air rushed in, cold and sharp with the promise of rain. Damien paused on the threshold, silhouetted against the darkness beyond.

He didn't look back.

The door closed behind him with a soft click that sounded, in the silence, like a coffin lid settling into place.

Eli stood alone in his tavern with a crossbow aimed at nothing.

The candles guttered. The smoke from his cigar had gone cold in its case. Outside, he could hear the fading rhythm of hoofbeats—measured, unhurried, receding toward the castle on the hill. Damien Taylor riding home to his schemes and his certainties and his calm, methodical plans for murder.

The boy will die tomorrow.

Eli lowered the crossbow. His hands were steady. They were always steady when it mattered—that was the gift his brother had given him all those years ago, along with the scars. When Arthur's blade had opened his face and taken his eye, something else had been cut away too. The part of him that panicked. The part that froze. The part that wasted time on fear when fear wouldn't help. What remained was harder, colder, and infinitely more practical.

He'd watched Jamie fight in the pit behind the tavern. Had seen the way he moved: economical, instinctive, brutal when he *needed* to be. The kid had something. Not just skill, though he had that. Something else. A gravity. A presence that drew people to him without trying, that made men follow and women notice and everyone else step aside without quite knowing why.

The Red Prince.

Eli set the crossbow on the bar. The wood creaked beneath its weight.

He'd known. Of course he'd known. The whole village had known, or suspected, or chosen to believe—it was hard to tell the difference after twenty-four years of whispers and careful silences. The blonde babe born in blood the night the bells stopped ringing. The child who appeared on Rowan Campbell's doorstep with no explanation that made sense. The boy who grew up looking like no one in Taylor's End, with eyes the color of storm clouds and a jaw that belonged on a crown.

Eli had never said anything. Never asked. What would have been the point? Rowan had raised the boy as his own, and that was enough. That was more than enough. In a world full of men who abandoned their children or beat them or sold them for drink, Rowan Campbell had loved a stranger's son with everything he had.

And now Rowan was dead, his head in the mud, and Jamie was in the castle.

In the castle.

The thought landed like a stone in still water. Ripples spreading outward, touching everything.

What the hell was Jamie doing in the castle? The theatre troupe—Eli had heard rumors, fragments of gossip from patrons who'd come down from the hill. Players from the north, performing for the king's nameday. But Jamie among them? Jamie inside those walls, under the same roof as the men who'd killed his father, the men who'd hunted his bloodline for twenty-four years?

Either the boy had gone mad, or he was playing a game that Eli couldn't see the edges of.

I believe many will.

Damien's words echoed in the empty tavern. That terrible, satisfied smile, like a cat that had already eaten the bird and was simply savoring the memory. He knew something about what was coming, and he'd walked in here tonight to, what? Gloat? Warn? Test the waters before the flood?

No. Eli understood it now. The questions. The probing. How long? Damien had come here to confirm. To fill in his ledger. Identity: confirmed. Complicity: confirmed. The village knew. The village had always known. And now Damien knew that they knew and could plan accordingly.

Eli moved to the window. Pushed aside the shutter and looked out at the darkness.

The castle loomed on the hill above the village, its towers black against the blacker sky. Torches flickered along the battlements like dying stars. Somewhere up there, behind those walls, Jamie was sleeping or scheming or preparing for whatever came with the dawn.

And Damien was riding toward him with murder in his heart and a plan that had been years in the making.

How do you protect someone from inside the beast's mouth?

Eli's mind worked the problem the way it had worked a thousand problems before—turning it over, examining angles, discarding solutions that wouldn't hold. He couldn't ride to the castle tonight. The gates would be closed, the guards would be Damien's men, and even if he made it inside, what then? Grab Jamie by the collar and drag him out? The boy would fight. The boy would demand explanations. And by the time Eli finished explaining, they'd both be dead.

He needed help. He needed people who could move inside the castle without raising alarms, who knew its corridors and its secrets, who had their own reasons for wanting to see Damien's plans crumble.

He needed—

Felix.

The name surfaced from somewhere deep, somewhere he'd buried years ago beneath layers of practical concerns and willful ignorance. The ghost who haunted Rowan's silences. The knight-commander who'd vanished the same night the prince disappeared. The man who'd loved a queen and lost everything.

If Jamie was in the castle, Felix wasn't far behind. Eli would have bet his remaining eye on it.

The question was how to find him. How to reach him. How to get a message through walls and guards and twenty-four years of careful hiding before Damien's trap snapped shut.

Eli turned from the window. His eye fell on the crossbow, still lying on the bar where he'd left it.

Tomorrow.

He had until tomorrow.

He crossed to the bar and looked at his hands—scarred, calloused, the hands of a man who had built something in the shadow of men who wanted him dead—and began to count.

Names.

That was what this came down to now. Names. People who could be trusted. People who would fight. People who had their own reasons for wanting to see Damien's plans crumble and were willing to risk everything to make it happen.

He started with the ones he was sure of. Marcus the farrier. Owes me for his daughter's medicine. Can swing a hammer. Old Thomas from the mill. Lost two sons to the castle's conscription. Hates the Taylors more than he hates his own bones. The Cooper brothers. All four of them. They'd fight a dragon if you bought them enough ale first. Willem the tanner. Quiet, but I've seen him kill a man with his bare hands when the man deserved it. Donovan. Samuel. The O'Reilly clan.

The list grew. Name by name. Face by face. A militia assembling in his mind, ragged and untrained, held together by nothing but shared grievance and the desperate hope that something could be done.

It wouldn't be enough. He knew that. Whatever Damien was planning, whatever slaughter he intended for tomorrow, a handful of villagers with farm tools and old grudges wouldn't stop it. The castle had soldiers. The castle had walls. The castle had Damien, who had been preparing for this moment for years while Eli had been serving drinks and pretending the world made sense.

But it was what he had.

Eli Richardson pulled on his coat, extinguished the last candle, and stepped out into the darkness. Behind him, the tavern held its silence. Above him, the castle loomed against the stars. And somewhere in his mind, the list continued to grow; a roll call of the desperate and the angry and the brave, all of them waiting for someone to tell them that fighting back was possible. That morning would bring something other than blood.

He began to walk. Not toward the castle, not yet, but toward the edges of the village, toward the cottages and farms where the names on his list were sleeping. The night pressed close around him, cold and dark, the stars wheeling overhead, indifferent to the plans of men.

And in the darkness below them, a one-eyed tavernkeeper walked toward war.

SCENE 35

Margaret came without a light.

That alone told him how serious she was. She slipped into the chamber like someone who had already decided the consequences were worth it—barefoot, cloak drawn tight, hair loose over her shoulders. The door closed behind her with a careful click that sounded far too loud in the stillness.

Jamie was sitting on the edge of the bed, boots off, shirt half-unlaced, staring at nothing.

He looked up.

For a moment, neither of them spoke.

Then she crossed the room and kissed him.

It wasn't cautious. It wasn't tentative. It was a kiss that assumed permission because it had already been granted a dozen times in silence, in glances across crowded yards, in fingers brushing during walks through the garden, in everything they hadn't said but had meant. Her hands found his jaw, his neck, the familiar places she had memorized in the dark.

He kissed her back. Too eagerly. As if tomorrow didn't exist.

They moved together without thinking, her cloak sliding to the floor, his hands shaking just enough to give him away. She pressed him back onto the bed, climbed into his lap, the weight of her grounding him, anchoring him to the room, to flesh, to now.

"Take me," she whispered.

He froze.

Not all at once. Not dramatically. But enough that she felt the shift in his breathing, the way his hands stopped moving, the sudden distance that opened between their bodies even though neither had pulled away.

"Jamie."

He rested his forehead against hers. Breathed her in. Then gently, so gently it stopped being sex. He held her wrists.

"*No.*"

She pulled back, confusion flickering into irritation.

"What is wrong with you?"

"I can't," he said. "Not like this."

"Like what?"

"I have to tell you something."

Her mouth curved, half amused, half annoyed. "If this is some vow or apology—"

"I'm not who you think I am."

"You're tired," she said. "You've been strange since the feast. You mustn't let Damien—"

"I'm here for her."

The words landed wrong.

"For *who*?"

"The girl. Lillian. From the dining hall."

"I don't understand."

"I grew up with her," he said quietly. "They took her. I came to get her out."

She sat back on her heels. The space between them widened.

"Is that what this is?" she asked. "Some rescue?"

"It's not that simple."

She laughed once. Sharp. "You men love saying that."

"I loved her," he said. "I mean—I do."

"You do or you did?!" Margaret snapped. "Which is it?"

He didn't answer fast enough.

Her voice rose. "Which is it, Jamie?"

He leaned forward, instinctively, lowering his voice. "*Please*—"

"Don't *shush* me!"

"Margaret—"

"You think me naïve?" she said. "Too green to know love? You think I don't know what it feels like when a man chooses someone else?"

"No," he said immediately. "No. That's not it."

"Then what is it?"

He looked at her like he was memorizing her face. Like he was already losing it.

"The reason I'm telling you this," he said, "is because—"

"Spit it out, for bloody sake!"

"The castle is going to burn tomorrow."

She stared at him.

"What?"

"This castle," he said. "These walls. These people. All of it."

Silence.

Somewhere below them, a door closed. Footsteps echoed, distant, careless. The world continued while the room held its breath.

"You've gone mad," she said.

"I wish I had."

She searched his face for the lie. For bravado. For fear dressed up as destiny.

She found none.

"You're serious."

"Yes."

"And where does that leave me?"

He didn't answer.

She stood. Wrapped her cloak around herself, hands trembling now despite her effort to keep them still.

"You should go," he said.

She laughed again. This time it broke something.

"I came here to be chosen."

He closed his eyes.

"I *have* chosen," he said. "That's the problem."

She crossed to the window, pushed it open a crack. Cold air rushed in. Below, the courtyard lay silvered in moonlight, empty, muted; the stones holding the memory of a thousand footsteps and the promise of blood to come.

She didn't see Damien.

But Damien saw her.

"You're serious," she said again. "About all of it."

"I am."

Margaret let out a short, incredulous laugh. "You're telling me you infiltrated the royal castle—*this* castle—using a theatre troupe?"

Jamie winced. "When you say it like that—"

"When I say it like the truth?"

She shook her head, half amazed, half furious. "Who the *fuck* are you?"

"Someone who ran out of better options."

She paced now, slow, deliberate. Thinking. Not panicking. That mattered.

"So," she said. "You get the girl out. Then what?"

"Then we leave."

"Leave where?"

"Anywhere Damien isn't."

Margaret stopped pacing. "Without me."

"I didn't think—"

"*No*," she snapped. "You didn't allow yourself to."

"I can't take you," he said. "It's too dangerous."

"You think I don't know that? That it's dangerous?"

"Margaret," Jamie said, measured, "if you leave with me, there's no coming back."

She stepped closer, close enough that he had to stop pretending this was theoretical.

"I don't *want* to come back," she all but spat, articulating every syllable with the exaggerated patience one might use for a particularly dim child. "I want *you*, you bloody idiot."

Silence.

The kind that changes the shape of a man.

Jamie stood very still. Something had cracked open in his chest; not pain, not relief, but something rawer. The deeply unpleasant yet twice as intoxicating weight of being chosen by someone who understood exactly what choosing him would cost.

"Margaret—"

"You said the castle burns tomorrow," she said, her voice steady now. "That means there will be chaos. Confusion. Guards running in wrong directions."

"Possibly."

"And then there's the play."

"Yes."

"And during that play," she continued, "half the court will be watching the stage instead of the doors."

He felt it click. The terrible, beautiful logic of it.

"I'll feign illness," she said, her eyes wide and glassy with a terrifying sort of clarity. "Faint if I have to. Women faint all the time. No one questions it."

"It will be noticed."

"I'm already noticed." She let the silence hang. "But not watched."

She stepped closer still.

"You meet me at the stables," she said. "Or the east service gate. Somewhere with horses. Somewhere forgotten."

He searched her face for hesitation.

Found none.

"You don't understand what leaving means," he said softly. "You won't be able to come back."

She smiled. Not lightly. Not sadly. With resolve.

"*Good.*"

Another silence. This one heavier. Final.

"And if we don't make it?" she asked.

He didn't lie.

"Then at least we'll be moving."

She reached for his hand. Held it. Not pleading. Claiming.

"You don't get to decide this alone," she said. "Not anymore."

He squeezed her fingers.

"Alright," he said. "Alright."

Relief crossed her face so quickly it almost hurt to see.

"You should go," he said. "Before someone wonders where you are."

She nodded. Moved toward the door. Stopped.

"Jamie?"

"Yes."

"If we die tomorrow," she said, "I will haunt this place until the stones crack."

He smiled.

"I'd expect nothing less."

She slipped out. The door closed.

Jamie stood alone in the chamber, the plan already alive and dangerous and impossible to unthink. The bed was still warm where she'd been. The room still held the ghost of her perfume, her warmth, her impossible certainty.

He crossed to the window and looked out at the courtyard below.

Empty.

He didn't see Damien.

But Damien saw him.

Damien stood in the shadow of the east tower, pressed against stone that had been cold for centuries, watching the window where the candlelight flickered and the silhouettes moved. He had seen her arrive. Had watched her slip through the door with the careful urgency of a woman who had made a decision. Had waited, patient as geology, while the candle burned and the minutes stretched and the castle slept around him.

He had seen her cross to the window.

Had seen the way she turned back toward Jamie.

Had seen the way she reached for him—not desperately, not possessively, but with something worse.

Love.

Damien's face didn't change. His breathing didn't quicken. He simply stood in the darkness and watched and understood.

She would go with him.

That was the variable he hadn't accounted for; not the girl in the cells, not the theatre troupe, not even Ryder hiding behind his false name and his careful silences. The variable was Margaret. Margaret, who had looked at a doomed man and chosen him anyway. Margaret, who would slip away and ride toward a future that existed only because she believed in it.

Margaret, who loved him.

Damien smiled.

Not with satisfaction. Not with triumph. With anticipation.

Love made men predictable. Love made them reach for things they couldn't protect. Love made them stand in windows lit by candlelight, visible to anyone patient enough to watch, broadcasting their vulnerabilities to the dark.

Jamie would try to flee tomorrow. That was certain now.

He would try to save the girl. That was certain.

And he would try to take Margaret with him.

That was the gift.

Because Damien didn't want to kill Jamie. Not yet. Not cleanly. Killing Jamie would make him a martyr, the lost prince struck down before he could reclaim his birthright, mourned by peasants, immortalized in the same nursery rhymes that had kept his legend alive for twenty-four years.

No.

Damien wanted something else.

He wanted Jamie to watch.

He wanted Jamie to reach for the life he'd been promised—the woman, the escape, the ordinary future that love had made possible—and feel it ripped away. He wanted Jamie to learn what Damien had learned years ago in this same castle, in rooms full of whispers and cruelty and the slow poison of discovering that everything you believed was a lie.

He *wanted* Jamie to become what he had become.

Because if Jamie died a prince, history would forgive him.

But if Jamie lived after losing everything, if he burned and raged and drowned in the same darkness that had swallowed Damien whole, then something else would be proven.

That goodness couldn't survive.

That the Taylor blood was cursed no matter whose veins it ran through.

See? he would tell the ghosts and the gods and whoever else was watching. *He's just like me. He just needed the right pressure.*

The candle in Jamie's window guttered and went dark.

Damien stepped back into shadow.

Tomorrow, the castle would burn.

Tomorrow, many would die.

But first, Jamie would learn what it meant to lose a future.

And Damien would be there to watch.

ACT V

THE BASTARD OF TAYLORS ENDE

ACTUS QUINTUS, SCAENA ULTIMA

Enter PRINCE LEO.

PRINCE LEO. I come to say farewell, thou gentlest beast. My fathers wrath prepareth now a feast Of blades and fire and all that kinges command When pride is wounded and they cannot understande. I planted seedes of truth within his hall, But some soiles are too salt to let them call.

THE DRAGON. I knowe. The harvest kinges doe ever reape Is seldome wheat, but bone, and blood, and weep. Thy father's crowne shall crumble into dust, As all crownes must when built on feare, not trust. The monster he hath hunted all his yeares Was never me—'twas but his own refused teares. And when the throne hath fallen, as it will, The mountaine shall remember who sought skill Instead of slaughter, truth instead of fame. Thou art the prince who askt the monsters name.

PRINCE LEO. What shall become of thee when kinges are gone?

THE DRAGON. I shall endure, as I have ever done. Dragons outlast the crownes that call them foule; The truth outlives the sceptre and the cowle. And somewhere, in some age not yet begot, A boye like thee shall finde this very spot And learne again what thou hast learnt this day: That strength is not in steele, but in the stay, The patient minde, the question fore the blade, The knowing that some monsters are but made.

PRINCE LEO. Farewell, great heart. I shall not thee forget.

THE DRAGON. Nor I thee, prince. The sunne hath risen yet. Goe back unto the world of men and lore; Teach what thou canst; the rest is done before. The harvest comes for kinges who will not bende— But thou art free. And so we are at ende.

Exit LEO. THE DRAGON watches him descend, then withdrawes into ancient mist.

Enter CHORUS, bearing the extinguished taper.

CHORUS. So endeth not in death this tale once steeped in dreade, But in the quiet meeting where no blood was shed. The elder sonne brought steele, as he was taught to doe; The younger brought but questions; and those questions grew To wisedome that no blade could ever cleave or kill, The kinde of strength that kneeleth not, but standeth still. For what is a monster but the shape that feare hath drawne? And what is a king but pride that will not see the dawne? The harvest comes for crownes that cannot bende or heare; The throne shall fall; the dragon sleeps; the truth is cleare: That oft the fiercest monsters in the lore we keepe Are heartes too vast for kinges, and far too kinde for sheepe. Let those who reade this tragedie goe forth and see: That what survives the sword is what was always free.

Exeunt omnes.

FINIS.

SCENE 36

Jamie woke before the bells.

Margaret slept beside him, her face turned toward the wall, one hand resting where he had been. The sheets were tangled without intention, only two people reaching for quiet and finding each other instead. Her breathing was slow and even. He watched the rise and fall as if watching long enough might keep yesterday from ending.

He dressed carefully. Not from tenderness. From habit. He had learned when sound mattered.

The corridors were dim and hollowed, bathed in half-light that belonged to places built to outlast the people inside them. A servant crossed his path without looking up. Somewhere water ran. Somewhere stone shifted as it cooled. The castle was doing what it always did in the morning: pretending nothing had occurred.

Outside, the air was thin and clean and unforgiving. The

light had not yet decided what color it would be. Everything was pale. Sky, stone, breath. The night had not fully released its claim. Birds moved somewhere unseen, their calls distant and unurgent.

She stood near the wall, facing outward.

For a moment he thought she might be waiting for someone else. She looked like she belonged to the morning itself. Plain cloak, hair pulled back without care. A woman shaped by endurance rather than attention.

"Morning always feels like an apology." She spoke without turning. "As if the world is hoping you won't remember what it did yesterday."

"Do you forgive it?"

She watched the light move across the village below. "I'm learning to. Perhaps one of these mornings."

"I'm not very good at it."

"Neither am I."

The village spread beneath them, rooftops smaller than they were, chimneys breathing thin lines of smoke. People beginning again.

"Still," she said, "the village at this hour is certainly beautiful."

"Seems so peaceful."

"Most things do from a distance." She let the words settle. "I used to think mornings like this meant something. That they were proof the world hadn't entirely failed."

"And now?"

"Now I think they're mercy. Brief. Unreliable. But still mercy."

Jamie shifted his weight. "I don't know how to forget."

She glanced at him, just long enough to hear more than he'd said. "Forgiveness isn't forgetting. It's deciding what you'll carry forward."

"And what you leave behind?"

"That's the dangerous part. Most people leave too much."

The light strengthened. A bell rang somewhere far off, then stopped.

"I used to come out here early. Before the day began asking things of me."

"Did it help?"

"It helped me endure." Her voice dropped. "Endurance is often mistaken for survival."

The silence between them held weight.

"You don't lose yourself loudly," she said. "You lose yourself by being reasonable. By agreeing. By telling yourself this is only for now."

"And then?"

"And then now becomes your life."

She drew her cloak closer though the air hadn't changed. When she glanced at him again, something almost like amusement touched her face. "She likes you, you know. The Northborn."

Jamie felt his cheeks flush.

"She's very pretty." She smiled. "Whatever you do, don't run from it." The words came softer now, nearly tender. "And if you ever forgive the world, don't do it by disappearing."

Jamie turned toward her, but she was already stepping away.

"Have a good morning, Jamie."

He opened his mouth. She walked on, her steps making no sound against the stone.

Jamie stayed at the wall, watching the village breathe beneath the pale light. Quiet. Distant. Momentarily untouched.

When the bells began again, steady and indifferent, he turned from the wall.

She was already gone.

SCENE 37

FAULT LINES

The theatre was a cathedral of shadows and sawdust.

Jamie worked the pulley system backstage, hauling canvas and timber into position while stagehands swarmed around him like ants rebuilding after rain. The plan had been clean. Simple. Get Lillian out during the performance while the castle watched Felix play the dragon. The dragon's castle took shape in pieces. Painted flats depicting stone walls. A wooden throne draped in red cloth. Rope rigged to hold the curtains that would part to reveal the monster's lair.

No one spoke much. The work had its own language. Hammer strikes. Rope through iron rings. The scrape of wood across stone. Men moved with practiced efficiency, each knowing their role, each trusting the others to know theirs.

Jamie lifted a beam into place, testing its weight against the bracket.

"Here, let me take that."

A stagehand reached for the beam. Young face, perhaps twenty. Beard still coming in patchy. He wore the same rough tunic as the others, sleeves rolled to the elbow.

Jamie shifted to hand it over.

The man's sleeve rode up.

Chainmail. Just a glimpse. Iron links catching the torchlight before the fabric settled back into place.

Jamie's eyes flicked up.

The man was looking directly at him.

Smiling.

Neither of them spoke.

Jamie's heart kicked hard against his ribs. Once. Twice. His palms went slick around the beam.

Felix.

Snakewater. The lodge. The mercenary in Miranda's room. How clean it had almost been—until Jamie woke. How Felix had already been awake when Jamie came down the stairs, standing in the common room like he'd been waiting. Not surprised. Not alarmed. Just there. Watching.

Miranda hadn't been meant to survive that night. Jamie hadn't been meant to interfere.

Felix didn't punish failure. He rerouted it.

The man's smile didn't waver. Patient. Almost kind. The smile of someone who'd been waiting for this exact moment.

Jamie passed the beam across. The man took it, nodded once, and turned away.

Jamie stood there. His hands empty and damp. Someone called out behind him. A request for rope.

This wasn't a rescue anymore.

Around him, the stagehands continued their work. They moved like stagehands. They spoke like stagehands. They wore the clothes of stagehands.

Jamie looked at their sleeves.

All of them. Long sleeves. In a warm room. Doing physical labor.

Eight. Nine. Maybe ten. Too many for a rescue. Enough for a purge.

He bent down, collected a coil of unused rope as if he had somewhere to take it, and started toward the exit. Not fast. Not slow. The pace of someone going to fetch supplies.

Every step felt observed though no one was looking at him.

The door was three steps away. Then his hand was on the iron ring, cool against his damp palm, and he was pushing it open.

The corridor beyond was dimmer and cooler and empty.

Jamie stepped through.

The door closed behind him with a soft thud that sounded final.

His breath came out all at once. He leaned against the stone wall, feeling its cold solidity against his back.

They were surrounded. The players were gone. Had been gone since Snakewater. Felix had turned a rescue into a slaughter, and Jamie had led them all into it. Every stagehand in that room was a soldier in costume, and in hours, maybe minutes, the performance would begin and the trap would spring and everyone inside that theatre would die.

Margaret would die.

Jamie pushed off the wall. His hands were still shaking but his legs worked. He started down the corridor, faster now, no longer pretending.

He had to find Felix.

He had to find Lillian.

He had to stop this.

Behind him, through the closed door, hammer strikes continued their steady rhythm. Men preparing a stage. Building a slaughter.

SCENE 38

Margaret closed the door to her chamber and turned the lock with hands that wouldn't stop shaking. A small bag sat on the bed, half-packed with the practical things you took when you were planning to disappear and never come back. She'd been preparing to leave, to meet Jamie at the stables halfway through the performance while the castle watched the play and eyes were off the exits.

That was when she saw him.

He stood by the window, half-silhouetted against the night, as though he'd been waiting for hours, as though he'd known precisely when she would return.

"It's such a shame, isn't it?"

Margaret's breath caught. Her spine went rigid against the door.

"What are you doing here?"

He didn't answer immediately, only turned his head enough

that the moonlight caught the edge of his face, his expression calm and empty.

"So many ungrateful souls," Damien said.

Her eyes went to the small table near the bed. A knife sat there, an eating knife with a silver handle and six inches of blade. She'd used it at dinner and deliberately forgotten to send it back down with the tray.

"I wouldn't, darling."

His voice was soft, conversational, the tone she imagined he used in council meetings when suggesting someone be removed from their post.

Margaret's throat was dry. "What do you want?"

"Where were you last night?"

"My chambers."

"Lies."

"Why are you here?"

Damien stepped forward out of the window's light and into the shadows between the furniture. His boots made no sound on the stone.

"I do find it admirable—"

"Answer my question."

"—that even surrounded by the very walls of the opposition, a Beverley woman sees herself as answerable." He took another step. "Much less a Beverley whore. An ornament."

Margaret lunged for the knife. Her fingers closed around the handle as she spun and brought it up between them. The blade trembled. Her grip was wrong, too tight and too high, the stance of someone who'd never held a weapon with intent.

"Guards!" Her voice cracked. "*Guards*!"

No one came. The corridor outside remained silent, either because they hadn't heard or because they'd been told not to hear, and she didn't know which was worse.

Damien smiled. Not the glib kind he wore in public. Something more honest.

"Stay away." Her voice had gone higher now, losing its authority. "I command you."

"Is it the peasant?"

She swung the knife, wild and desperate and without technique, just panic translated into motion. The blade cut through air and missed him entirely. She swung again, and this time the edge caught his raised palm and opened it from thumb to wrist. Blood welled immediately and ran down his forearm in dark lines.

Damien looked at his hand. Then at her.

Then he slapped her.

The impact knocked her head sideways and sent the knife skittering across the floor. Before she could balance, his hand was in her hair, hauling her upright by the scalp.

"How will my dear brother feel when he finds out you've been traipsing around the dark corners of our castle with a common stagehand?"

He threw her into the bookshelf. She hit the floor and he was already on her, hands around her throat.

"Look at me, you cunt."

She couldn't. Her face was pressed sideways against cold stone. She could see the edge of the bed, the knife beneath it, the bag on top half-packed and ready for an escape that would never happen.

His fingers tightened.

The pressure was immediate. Her windpipe collapsed. Air stopped. Her body reacted without permission, hands clawing at his, nails scraping skin, legs kicking uselessly against the stone. Her vision narrowed and darkened at the edges. Red crept in from the periphery. She tried to scream but nothing came out, only a wet and strangled sound that died in her throat. Her lungs burned. Her chest convulsed. Her body tried to inhale and couldn't, tried again and failed, the red spreading inward while her hands began to slow, to lose their grip, to weaken.

Damien squeezed harder. Something in her throat cracked. Cartilage maybe. Or bone. She didn't know. Couldn't think. Couldn't do anything except feel her body shutting down in stages, oxygen deprivation doing its work, methodical and irreversible.

The candles in the chandelier flickered once, then twice. The flames bent sideways as though pushed by wind that wasn't there.

Margaret's vision went black. Not all at once. Gradually. The room fading out like a candle drowning in its own wax.

The last thing she saw was Damien's face.

Still smiling. Still empty.

Still watching.

SCENE 39

The knock came once.

Felix stopped mid-motion, the dagger strap loose in his hand. He'd been expecting it. Dreading it. The conversation that would end everything or begin it, depending on how the boy took the truth.

The knock came again. Harder.

Felix finished cinching the blade to his calf. Tested it. Crossed to the door and pressed his ear against it.

Breathing on the other side. Fast. Controlled. Someone who'd been running and didn't want it heard.

"Who is it?"

"You know who it is. Open."

Felix closed his eyes for half a second. Then he opened the door.

Jamie stepped inside and Felix shut it immediately. Threw the bolt.

"You're late."

Felix walked back over to the bed.

"When's the showing?" Felix asked.

"Less than an hour."

"Good."

Jamie looked at him for a while. Watched him work. Watched him load himself with weapons like a man preparing for war, not a performance.

Finally, Jamie said it.

"You replaced the players."

Felix paused. Then looked at him. Then back down as he continued buckling a knife to his belt.

"I did," he said flatly.

"Snakewater. Miranda. That wasn't random, was it? That was your doing. I'd venture she wasn't supposed to make it."

"Does it matter?"

"To me, yeah."

Felix finished with the knife. Moved to the axe. Weighed it in his hand. Tested the balance. "So what are you gonna do about it? Huh?"

Jamie's jaw tightened. "We came here to rescue my friend."

"You came here to rescue your friend."

Jamie felt his fists clench. "Is it a massacre you want, then?"

Felix slid the axe into his belt loop. Turned back to the sword. Lifted it. "Call it what it is."

"Y'know, I knew you were a cunt, old man, but you've really outdone yourself."

Felix's eyes flicked up. "Watch your step, lad."

"What of the players?" Jamie's voice was rising now. "Where are they?"

"You really want to know?"

"Yes!"

"The swamp." Felix set the sword down. Exhaled. "They didn't suffer."

Jamie's vision blurred at the edges. He'd known. But hearing it confirmed was different. Hearing Felix say it without hesitation, without a speckle of remorse—

"What are you?"

Felix picked up the sword again. Began wrapping the grip with leather cord. "What I've always been, child. A bad man."

"Why?"

"Why what?"

"Why are you doing this?"

"I'm ending it."

"Ending what?"

"All of it."

"What is 'all of it'?" Jamie's voice cracked. His chest was heaving. "What the fuck are you talking about?"

"They butchered the line."

"What line, old man?!"

"Your MOTHER'S!" Felix bellowed.

Silence fell on the room.

Dead silence.

Jamie stood there with his breath caught in his throat. The room felt too small suddenly. Too hot. His ears were ringing. He tried to speak. Nothing came out. He tried again.

"My..."

"You look like her when you're confused. D'you know that?"

Jamie shook his head. Felix set the sword down, slowly, like he was deciding whether to say the next part or let it die with him.

"The crown never belonged to them," he said. "It belongs to you."

"I don't understand."

"Her name was Anya Taylor," Felix explained. "I loved her. She loved me. Then, before we knew it, you showed up." Felix's voice went flat, his eyes elsewhere. "Bloody mess, that was. She died bringing you into this world."

"W-what are you saying?"

"Are you thick?" Felix snapped. "I'm saying I'm your bloody father. Now, are you satisfied?"

A tear propelled from Jamie's left eye and raced down his cheek. "You lie."

Felix's expression didn't change, but something moved behind his eyes, something that looked like pain.

"I never wanted this for you."

Jamie's face twisted. "Well, here we are," he said, his voice taking on a sharper quality. "Did you ever really want to help? Or was I just your stand-in? The last piece to your twisted family vendetta? A pissed-off orphan you could steer toward the Taylors like your very own fucking mastiff?!"

"Would you rather I left you to the savages? Or ditched you in Wolfpine? You wanted vengeance. Well, so did I."

Felix began sharpening a knife, the sound of steel on stone filling the silence; sharp, rhythmic, cold.

"Let me tell you something. Steering you was the best thing that's ever happened in your measly life. A bastard, abandoned, who cocked it all up before he even drew breath, who killed his mother, my Anya, so he could live as a sniveling, cock-up peasant." He didn't look up from the blade. "I gave you purpose. Put a sword in your hand. Made you strong. They brutalized Rowan. Stole your girl. Torched your home." He tested the edge of the knife with his thumb. Blood welled. "And they stole my legacy."

He met Jamie's eyes.

His gaze was black.

"So, either be a man and snap out of your misdirected petulance... or do what boys do and fuck off."

Jamie's hand went to his knife.

His fingers closed around the handle. His vision tunneled. Felix was three steps away. Back turned. Vulnerable.

He moved.

Two strides. His shoulder drove into Felix's back. They hit stone. Jamie's knee found spine.

Knife found throat.

Felix didn't move. Eyes on the ceiling. Breathing steady.

Jamie's hand trembled. The blade pressed. Blood leaked. His breath came fast. Tears fell.

"Do it."

Jamie's hand shook.

"It's what you want."

The blade trembled. More blood.

"I taught you where to cut. So do it."

"I can't."

"Why not?"

"Because you're all I have left."

Jamie's hand loosened.

The knife clattered.

Jamie rolled off. Sat against the wall. Face in hands.

Felix pushed himself up. Touched his throat. Fingers came away red.

He crossed to the bed. Found a cloth. Wiped his neck. Jamie's breathing steadied. Hands fell. Eyes dry. Felix picked up the sword. Slid it into the sheath on his back. Continued arming himself as though nothing had happened.

The silence stretched.

Finally, Jamie spoke. His voice was hoarse. "What about Lillian?"

Felix didn't turn around. "Dungeon. Locked chamber near the stairwell. Two guards."

"And Margaret?"

"I suggest you get her out as soon as you can. I can't guarantee the well-being of a Beverley."

"What about you?"

"I told you what I'm doing."

Jamie's throat tightened. "You're not walking out of here, are you?"

"No."

His inflection couldn't have been more final.

Jamie stood. His legs were unsteady but they held. He crossed to the door. His hand met the handle.

"Jamie."

He stopped. Didn't turn around.

Felix's voice was different now. Quieter. Raw. "You were worth it. All of it. Even if I wasn't."

Jamie's hand tightened on the door handle. His throat closed.

He didn't respond. Couldn't.

He just opened the door and walked out.

The corridor was cold and empty.

Behind him, the door closed.

Felix stood alone in the quiet. Touched his throat. Blood drying.

Mercy.

The boy had chosen mercy.

Just like his mother would have.

By God's wounds, they would've loved each other.

Felix picked up his helmet—worn, dented, scratched to oblivion—and looked into it, his reflection distorted in the black metal.

"I'm coming," he said quietly to the empty air.

Then he put on the helmet and became the Black Rider one last time.

SCENE 40

The theatre was full, every seat occupied, nobles in silk and merchants in wool pressed together in the heat of too many bodies, the air thick with perfume and sweat and that particular anticipation which precedes spectacle. Guards stood stationed at the exits, and high above, the rafters disappeared into shadow.

Barnaby stood center stage with his arms spread wide, swaying slightly in a manner that suggested drink or terror or some uncertain marriage of both, and when he spoke his voice carried to those distant rafters with the practiced projection of a man who had spent his life making himself heard. "Ladies and gentlemen," he called. "Thank you. Thank you for your presence this evening. We are honored, truly honored, to perform for His Majesty King Lionel Taylor and the noble houses of England."

The applause that followed was polite and scattered, the sound of duty rather than enthusiasm.

Barnaby bowed too deep, nearly lost his balance, and recovered with the desperate grace of the chronically inebriated before gesturing grandly toward the wings. "And now, without further delay, we present to you: The Dragon and the Prince!"

He wobbled offstage as the curtains began to part.

In the front row, Lionel leaned toward Richardson, his voice low and casual. "Where is my wife?"

Richardson kept his eyes on the stage, his hand resting on the pommel of his sword. "Ill, Your Grace."

"Ah. Odd."

Margaret looked smaller in death than she had in life, her warmth already fading, her body given over to meat and bone. She lay crumpled on the marble like discarded clothing, her hair covering half her face and one arm bent at an odd angle beneath her, her mouth slightly open.

Across the room, Damien stood before the mirror wrapping his hand in clean linen. The cut across his palm had stopped bleeding, shallow and precise, the kind that would heal in days. He hummed while he worked, an old tune, simple and repetitive, the kind washerwomen sang while beating clothes against river stones.

Hurdy gurdy, turn and spin, Round and round, the wheel within...

His eyes went to the bag on the bed across the room, half-packed, clothes and bits visible within, evidence of a plan that had ended long before it began. He regarded it for a moment without expression, then returned his attention to the linen.

He tied off the bandage slowly and with care, wrapping the final length of cloth around his palm and securing it with a neat tuck. He tested his grip and flexed his fingers, watching the tendons move beneath the clean white fabric until he was satisfied.

The chamber was quiet save for that tuneless melody and the faint settling of the fire in the grate. Candlelight played across the walls in gentle undulation, casting long shadows that shifted with each flicker of the flame.

He stood a moment longer before the mirror, his reflection watching him with the same flat calm, and then he turned and crossed to the door. He left the chamber and locked it behind him and pocketed the key. The corridor stretched empty in both directions, torches burning at intervals, their light dancing on the stone.

Somewhere below, music had begun, organ pipes deep and resonant, playing the same tune he had been humming.

The curtains parted and velvet slid smooth on iron rings, revealing the stage in slow unveiling as the audience leaned forward in their seats. The rustle of fabric and the creak of wooden benches filled the theatre, a collective breath drawn and held in anticipation. Applause rippled through the crowd as actors took their places and the dragon's castle rose from darkness, its painted towers catching the light of a hundred candles.

Somewhere beyond the theatre walls, Jamie sprinted through corridors with breath ragged and boots striking stone. The sound of his footfalls echoed off the vaulted ceilings and chased him around each corner, his shadow leaping wild against the torchlit walls. He turned sharply and nearly stumbled, caught himself, and ran on without slowing, the distant swell of organ music reaching him like a summons he couldn't yet answer.

In the tiring room behind the stage, Felix stood before a cracked mirror with black paint streaked beneath his eyes. He studied his reflection with the detachment of a man regarding a stranger, noting the hollows in his cheeks and the stillness in his gaze. The helmet rested heavy in his hands, and he lifted it slowly, turning it so the candlelight caught the curve of its surface before raising it toward his head.

Deep in the bowels of the castle, Lillian shivered in her cell with chains rattling as she pulled her knees to her chest. The cold of the stone floor seeped through her thin clothing and settled into her bones, and the darkness pressed close around her. She closed her eyes against it, listening to the faint vibration of music filtering down through layers of rock and mortar, and waited for whatever would come next.

Above her, the torches burned and the music swelled, and everything converged at once toward the moment when masks would fall and steel would speak and blood would answer for blood.

SCENE 41

Jamie saw the guards before they saw him.

Two of them, walking their patrol at an unhurried pace, coming straight toward him down the corridor with torches in hand and swords at their hips. Thirty feet separated them. Then twenty. The distance closed with each echoing footfall, and Jamie found himself caught in the open with no alcove to slip into, no doorway to duck through, nothing but bare stone walls and the guttering light of wall-mounted torches that left nowhere to hide.

To his left, a door. Heavy oak banded with iron, set deep into the wall as though the masons who built it had intended it to hold back something substantial. He remembered Damien gesturing toward it during the tour of the castle's lower passages, remembered the casual warning to avoid it, remembered nothing of what lay beyond. The guards were fifteen feet away now, close enough that he could hear the creak of their leather armor and the low murmur of their conversation.

Jamie grabbed the handle and pulled.

The door opened with a groan of rusted hinges that echoed down the corridor behind him, and he slipped through the gap and let it fall shut at his back before the sound could reach the guards or draw their attention. Darkness swallowed him instantly, complete and absolute, true, absolute, total darkness that pressed against the eyes and made them ache with the effort of seeing. He stood still and let his breathing slow, felt for the wall, found cold stone beneath his palm slick with condensation. Somewhere ahead of him, a staircase descended into nothing.

He waited until his eyes adjusted, until the faintest suggestion of light from somewhere far below revealed the shape of the passage before him. The stairs were steep and narrow, carved directly into the rock rather than built from fitted blocks, and the torches meant to light them had been spaced so far apart that each one served only to deepen the shadows between. Jamie began his descent with one hand trailing along the wall and his footsteps careful on the worn steps.

The air changed as he went deeper. It grew colder and damper with each flight, and the smell of the castle above gave way to something older. Earth and standing water and the mineral breath of deep rock. The walls lost their dressed surfaces and became rough and uneven, natural formations rather than architectural choices, and Jamie understood with growing unease that he was descending into something that predated the castle itself. A cavern system, perhaps, or a fissure in the bedrock that the original builders had incorporated into the foundations rather than filling. The stairs didn't end so much as dissolve, the final steps giving way to an uneven floor of packed earth and scattered stone.

A corridor opened before him, if it could be called a corridor. The ceiling hung low and irregular overhead, and water dripped somewhere in the darkness with a slow and patient rhythm that suggested it had been dripping for centuries. Jamie pulled a torch from the last iron bracket on the wall and held it before him, and the flame pushed back the darkness perhaps ten feet before exhausting itself against the black.

He should turn back. He knew this with the certainty of instinct, the same wordless knowledge that told a man when he was being watched or when the ground beneath his feet was unsound. But Lillian was somewhere in the depths of this castle, locked in a cell, and every passage he had not yet searched was a passage that might lead to her. He moved forward into the dark.

The silence was immense. His own breathing sounded loud and foreign, and his footsteps seemed to travel outward into distances he couldn't measure. The corridor widened as he went, the walls pulling away from him on either side until the torchlight could no longer find them, and the ceiling rose until it too disappeared into darkness overhead. Jamie slowed and then stopped, overcome by the sudden and vertiginous sense that he had stepped out of a passage and into a void.

A sound reached him. Low and rhythmic, like breathing, but vast in a way that made his own lungs feel small and insufficient. The kind of breathing that displaced air, that created currents in the darkness, that stirred the dust on the cavern floor with each exhalation. Jamie's free hand went to the knife at his belt and found the handle, though he didn't draw it. He understood instinctively that a knife would do nothing against whatever made a sound like that.

He lifted the torch higher and the flame caught something ahead.

Scales. Dark green and edged with black, each one larger than his spread hand, layered in overlapping rows that curved away from him into shadow. They rose and fell with that massive breathing, a wall of armored flesh that stretched beyond the reach of his torchlight in every direction. Jamie's mind tried to process what he was seeing and failed, tried again and produced only fragments. A flank, perhaps. A section of coiled body. The suggestion of mass so enormous that his torch illuminated only a fraction of its surface.

He turned slowly, following the curve of scales with the

torchlight, and found the tail.

It lay across the floor like a fallen pillar, thicker through than a carriage was tall, its weight pressing a shallow furrow into the packed earth beneath it. The scales along its length were scarred and worn, some of them cracked or missing entirely, the accumulated damage of an existence longer than Jamie could comprehend. The tail disappeared into the darkness in both directions, and Jamie understood that he was standing in the coiled center of something that could fill this cavern from wall to wall.

The breathing continued. Steady and deep and undisturbed. The sound of something ancient, something that had been sleeping in this darkness since before the castle above was built, since before the kingdom itself perhaps, dreaming whatever dreams such creatures dreamed.

Jamie's legs wanted to run. Every instinct he possessed screamed at him to turn and climb those stairs and seal that door behind him and never speak of what he had seen. But he couldn't move, couldn't look away, couldn't do anything but stand in the presence of this impossible thing and feel the inadequacy of his own existence.

He lifted the torch higher still, and the flame found the head.

It lay perhaps twenty feet from where he stood, resting on the cavern floor with the easy weight of a thing that feared nothing in the world. The skull alone was larger than a wagon, the snout long and heavy and armored with scales that looked thick enough to turn a blade. The nostrils were dark slits that flared slightly with each breath, drawing in air and releasing it in warm currents that Jamie could feel against his face even at this distance.

The eye was closed. A single lid, scaled like the rest of the body, covering an orbit the size of a wagon wheel. Jamie stared at it and felt his heartbeat in his throat and his temples and his wrists, felt the sweat break out along his spine despite the cold of the cavern, felt the torch tremble in his grip.

Then the eye opened.

The lid pulled back and revealed an iris of deep gold surrounding a pupil that contracted instantly in the torchlight, narrowing to a vertical slit as it focused. The eye found Jamie and fixed upon him with an intelligence that was neither human nor animal but something else entirely, something older than either, something that had been watching the world since before men had words for what they feared.

Jamie's breath stopped in his chest.

The beast moved, faster than something so large should have been able to move, the great head lifting from the floor and swinging toward him in a single fluid motion that displaced the air of the cavern and sent the torch flame guttering sideways in Jamie's hand. The mouth opened, revealing teeth longer than swords set in rows that disappeared into the darkness of the throat, and it roared, though the sound was not a sound. It was a physical force, a wall of noise that struck Jamie's chest and drove the breath from his lungs and filled his skull with a pressure that blotted out thought. The torch flew from his hand and clattered across the cavern floor, its flame somehow holding, throwing wild shadows across the cavern walls as the roar continued and continued and seemed as though it would never end. Jamie's knees buckled. He caught himself against the cavern floor, palms scraping against rock, ears ringing, vision swimming, every part of him convinced that he was about to die.

The roar stopped.

Silence rushed in to fill the void it left, a silence so profound that Jamie could hear his own blood pounding in his ears. He looked up, gasping, and found the dragon's head directly before him, so close that he could see the texture of individual scales, could count the scratches and scars that marked its snout, could feel the heat radiating from its body like a banked furnace. The eye watched him, that golden eye with its slitted pupil, and Jamie saw his own reflection in its surface, tiny and pale and trembling.

The nostrils flared.

Once. Twice. Drawing in great drafts of air, scenting him the way a hound might scent a trail. The dragon's head tilted slightly, that massive skull shifting with a curiosity that seemed almost uncertain, almost confused. The tension in its body changed. The coiled readiness that had preceded the roar softened into something else, something Jamie couldn't name.

The great head pulled back. The breathing slowed, deepened, settled into the rhythm Jamie had first heard when he entered the cavern. The eye watched him a moment longer with an expression he couldn't read, and then the lid descended and closed, and the dragon lowered its head and was still.

Jamie didn't move. Couldn't move. He remained where he had fallen, palms pressed against the cold rock, heart hammering against his ribs, staring at the impossible creature before him as it settled back into sleep. He didn't understand what had happened. Didn't understand why he was still alive, why the beast had roared and then relented, why it had scented him and then turned away. There was no logic to it, no explanation that his mind could grasp. There was only the fact of his survival, inexplicable and absolute.

He rose slowly, his legs unsteady beneath him. He crossed to where the torch lay on the cavern floor and bent to retrieve it, his eyes never leaving the dragon's sleeping form. The flame had steadied, casting its small circle of light against the darkness, illuminating a fragment of scale and shadow and nothing more.

He backed away. Step by careful step, keeping the torch between himself and the beast, not daring to turn his back until the corridor swallowed him and the dragon disappeared into the dark. Only then did he allow himself to breathe. Only then did he turn and run, taking the stairs two at a time, climbing toward the light and the world above and the door that should never have been opened.

SCENE 42

ANYA

She returned when she was ten.

Not because she meant to, not exactly. The door was there and she was there and the memory of what lay beneath had not faded the way she hoped it would. She told herself she only wanted to see if the stairs were real, if the darkness was as deep as she remembered, if the breathing had been something she imagined in her fear.

She descended with a torch too heavy for her arms and stood at the edge of the vast space and listened. The breathing was there. Slow and patient and unchanged, as though the months between her visits had been nothing, as though time moved differently in the dark. She did not sing. Did not speak. She stood until her torch burned low and then she climbed the stairs and closed the door behind her.

It was enough to know that it was real.

At twelve she brought a candle instead of a torch, smaller and easier to carry, and she sat on the bottom step with her back against the cold stone wall. The breathing filled the cavern the way water fills a vessel, present in every corner, pressing gently against the boundaries of the space. She stayed longer this time. Let the silence settle around her. Let herself grow accustomed to the weight of the air and the rhythm that moved through it.

She didn't go closer. Didn't need to. The presence was enough, vast and indifferent and strangely calming in its indifference. Whatever lived in that darkness didn't care that she was there. Didn't mind. Didn't want anything from her at all.

She found comfort in that. In being small and unimportant. In sitting at the edge of something ancient that asked nothing of her and offered nothing in return.

By fourteen she had learned how to move in the dark without disturbing it. She would descend the stairs and cross the uneven floor and find a place to sit, always the same place, a flat stone near the far wall where she could rest her back and fold her hands in her lap and simply be. The breathing continued around her, unchanged by her presence, and she would stay for an hour or more, watching the darkness and thinking about nothing.

Sometimes she spoke. Not to the breathing, not to whatever made it, but near it, the way one might speak near a fire or a window or any other thing that couldn't hear. She talked about her lessons and her tutors and the particular cruelty of certain girls at court. She talked about her mother's expectations and her father's distance and the way the castle felt like a cage she had been born inside. She talked because the silence was large enough to hold her voice without judgment, and because the words sounded different in the dark, smaller and truer and less important than they seemed in the light above.

The breathing never changed. Never quickened or slowed in response. It simply continued, vast and patient, and Anya found that she preferred it that way. She didn't want to be heard. She only wanted a place where she could speak without consequence, where her voice could fall into the dark and disappear.

She was nineteen the last time she descended those stairs.

It was autumn and the leaves were turning and she had spent the morning walking the castle grounds with a man she should not have been walking with, a man whose name she couldn't say aloud without her chest tightening, a man who looked at her in ways that made her feel seen and terrified in equal measure. She had smiled at him and he had smiled at her and she had understood in that moment that something was beginning that she didn't know how to stop.

She sat in her usual place with her hands folded in her lap and her back against the cold stone. The breathing moved through the cavern the way it always had, slow and steady and indifferent to her presence. She sat for a long time without speaking, longer than she ever had before, letting the silence press against her skin and fill her lungs and quiet the noise inside her head.

When she finally spoke, her voice was barely a whisper.

"I don't know what I'm doing," she said. The words fell into the dark and vanished. "I don't know what I'm supposed to do. Everyone expects me to be something and I don't know what it is and I'm so tired of pretending I understand."

The breathing continued. Unchanged. Unhurried.

"I love someone," she said. "I think I love someone. I'm not supposed to. I know I'm not supposed to. But I don't know how to stop and I don't know if I want to and I'm afraid of what happens if I don't."

She pressed her palms flat against her thighs and stared into the darkness where the breathing lived.

"Something is ending," she said. "I can feel it. Something is ending and something else is beginning and I don't know what any of it means."

The silence held her voice and offered nothing back. The breathing moved through the cavern, patient and vast, and Anya sat with her hands folded and her heart aching and the knowledge settling into her bones that she would not come here again.

She didn't know why she was certain. Didn't know what had changed. But she understood, the way she had always understood forbidden things, that this was the last time she would descend these stairs, the last time she would sit in this darkness, the last time she would speak her secrets into the silence and let them disappear.

She rose. Crossed the uneven floor. Climbed the worn stone steps without looking back.

The door closed behind her with a sound like a held breath released.

She never returned.

SCENE 43

DETONATION

Sir Rodham stood with his back to the door, half-naked and glistening in the candlelight, his right hand wrapped around the braided handle of a cowhide whip. Before him stood two girls, neither of them older than fifteen, their shoulders hunched and their faces turned away. One of them trembled visibly. The other had gone still in the manner of small animals who have learned that stillness is sometimes the only defense available to them.

Rodham paced behind them with the unhurried confidence of a man who had done this many times before and expected to do it many times again. He studied the first girl the way a buyer studies livestock, his gaze moving across her back with proprietary satisfaction.

"Hmm."

A shadow passed across the far wall, quick and fleeting, easy to dismiss as a trick of the guttering candles.

Rodham reached forward and pulled the first girl's dress down from her shoulders, exposing the pale skin of her back. He ran his hand across it, testing the texture, and brought the whip up close to her ear so she could hear the creak of the leather in his grip.

"Do you know why I like peasant girls?" he asked. "Ones that crawl in the shit?"

He drew his arm back and struck her across the shoulders. The sound was sharp and wet, and the girl cried out before she could stop herself.

"You're used to a little beating."

The second girl had been staring at something across the room, her eyes fixed on a mirror mounted on the far wall, and now her body went rigid. A shudder passed through her, visible even from behind, and Rodham noticed.

"What is it, girl?"

He turned to follow her gaze, turned to look into the mirror, and in the glass he saw a figure hurtling toward him at full speed.

Jamie hit him low and hard, driving his shoulder into Rodham's midsection with enough force to carry them both three yards across the room before they crashed to the floor. The impact drove the air from Rodham's lungs in a wet grunt, and before he could recover Jamie was on top of him, one knee pinning his chest, a dagger drawn and pressed against the exposed flesh of his throat.

"Lillian Spires." Jamie's voice was tight and controlled, the voice of a man holding something back. "Where can I find her?"

"Get stuffed, you little rat."

Jamie brought the pommel of the dagger down hard into the hollow of Rodham's collarbone. The bone didn't break, but the pain was immediate and clarifying, and Rodham's face went white. Jamie looked up at the two girls, who stood frozen where he had found them, their eyes wide and their bodies trembling.

"Run."

They ran. The sound of their bare feet on the stone floor faded quickly, and Jamie returned his attention to the man beneath him.

"Brown hair. Blue eyes. She's new." He pressed the blade more firmly against Rodham's throat. "One of your 'peasant girls.'"

"*Please...*" The word came out slurred, dazed.

"*Where is she, you cunt*?!"

"They moved her." Rodham's eyes were darting now, looking for something, calculating something. "They moved her."

"Moved her?"

"Oi. To the prison. She wouldn't cooperate."

"Cooperate, aye?"

Jamie hit him in the face with his closed fist. The cartilage of Rodham's nose gave way with a sound like a green stick snapping, and blood poured down across his lips and chin in a dark sheet.

"I should cut your fucking balls off." Jamie wiped his knuckles on his sleeve without looking at them. "In the prison, you say?"

"Yes." Rodham was holding his face now, his voice thick and wet with blood. "*Fuck*. Yes!"

"Where is it?"

"Down below. Underneath here."

"Where's the key?"

"The pants." Rodham gestured weakly toward the bar on the far side of the room. "By the bar."

"Good." Jamie shifted his weight slightly, easing the pressure on Rodham's chest. "Now I'm going to stand up. Can you just promise—"

Rodham lunged. His hand shot out toward a bottle on the floor beside them, his fingers closing around the neck, and Jamie reacted without thought. The dagger came down and buried itself in the soft tissue of Rodham's throat, just below the jaw, punching through the esophagus and into the meat beyond. Blood welled up around the blade, dark and arterial, and Rodham made a sound that was not quite a scream and not quite a gurgle but something between the two.

Jamie held the handle. His knuckles went white around it. He held it and watched as Rodham's legs kicked against the stone floor, as his hands clawed weakly at the air, as the life drained out of him in hitching spasms that seemed to go on far longer than they should have. The kicking slowed. The clawing stopped. The gurgling faded to silence.

Jamie sat there for a moment, his hand still wrapped around the dagger, his breath coming hard and shallow. The room was quiet now except for the hiss of the candles and the distant sound of music from somewhere above. He looked at his hand, at the blood that had run down across his wrist and soaked into his sleeve.

"Fucking hell."

He pulled the dagger free. Wiped it on Rodham's shirt. Found the pants by the bar and retrieved the keys from the pocket, his fingers clumsy and trembling as he worked. He was almost to the door when he saw the sword leaning against the wall, a heavy blade with a worn leather grip, and he took it without thinking, without deciding, simply because it was there and because he understood now that he would need it.

The prison was warmer than he expected, a long corridor lined with cells on either side, at least thirty of them, lit by torches that cast unsteady shadows across the grimy stone walls. The air smelled of human waste and old straw and the particular despair of people who have been left to rot. Jamie moved past the first cells without stopping, his eyes scanning the darkness behind each set of bars until he found her.

She was huddled in the corner of her cell, her dress torn and filthy, her hair hanging damp and matted across her face. There was blood on her, dried brown against her skin, and she didn't look up when he approached.

Jamie knelt before the bars and wrapped his fingers around the iron.

"*Lily*." His voice cracked on the word. "Sweetheart."

She lifted her head. Her eyes were glassy and unfocused, the eyes of someone who had retreated somewhere far away, and for a moment she didn't seem to recognize him.

"It's me. Jamie."

"Jamie...?"

He fumbled with the keys, trying one after another until he found the one that fit, and the lock opened with a heavy clunk. He pulled the door open and crossed to her and knelt beside her and put his arms around her, feeling how thin she had become, how fragile, how close to breaking.

"Are you all right?"

"Thirsty."

"Of course." He helped her to her feet, guiding her arm around his shoulder, taking her weight against his side. "Put your arm around my shoulder."

In the theatre, the play continued.

Clemence stepped forward, his young face tilted upward toward the towering figure before him. "Farewell, great heart," he said. "I shall not thee forget."

Felix stood in the dragon costume, his face hidden behind the painted mask, his body wrapped in scales of leather and lacquered wood. He delivered his line with the projection of a man who had performed a thousand times before.

"Nor I thee, prince. The sunne hath risen yet. Goe back unto the world of men and lore; Teach what thou canst; the rest is done before." He paused, and when he spoke again the words seemed to hang in the air above the audience like smoke. "The harvest comes for kinges who will not bende. But thou art free. And so we are at ende."

Felix turned to leave the stage.

"Oi!" Lionel blurted.

Felix stopped. The audience shifted in their seats, uncertain whether this was part of the performance.

"The funny man, in the dragon hat."

Lionel's voice was casual, almost bored, the voice of a man accustomed to interrupting whatever he pleased. He sat in the front row with one hand draped over the armrest, his posture loose and entitled. Richardson stood behind him, hand on sword, eyes scanning the stage.

In the wings, Miranda felt her stomach drop. She could see Felix from where she stood. The stillness that had come over him.

Her eyes shot to the entrance of the theatre.

"I do apologize, for you are quite the talent," Lionel said, ever glib. "However, I *beg* of you. Show yourself, just this once."

The theatre held its breath. No one moved. The candles guttered in their sconces and the shadows swayed and Felix stood at the center of the stage with his back to the King, the painted dragon mask hiding whatever moved across his face.

Felix turned. Through the eyeholes of the mask, he found Lionel's gaze and held it.

The silence stretched. In the galleries, a woman coughed. Someone shifted in a wooden seat, the creak of it obscenely loud. Miranda pressed her hand against her mouth and watched and understood that the world was about to break.

Felix raised his hands to the base of the mask. He gripped the painted leather.

And he pulled it off.

Lionel's face changed. The recognition came slowly at first, then all at once, the blood draining from his cheeks as he understood who stood before him. His mouth opened. No sound came out.

In the booth above the stage, Damien smiled.

Felix's hand dropped to his calf. The knife was in the air before anyone could move, a thin silver line that crossed the twenty-foot distance between stage and royal seat in less than a heartbeat. It struck Lionel in the throat dead-center.

For a moment, nothing happened. Lionel sat in his chair with the handle protruding from his neck, his expression one of pure confusion, as though he couldn't quite believe what had occurred.

Then the blood came. It erupted from his mouth and nose in a dark flood, pouring down his chin and soaking into the velvet of his doublet. He began to make sounds that were not words but wet, choking gasps, his hands clawing at the knife, his body convulsing in the chair. He slid sideways. His legs kicked. Finally, he gave way, slumping into the leather like a sack of grain tossed into a corner, his weight slowly, lifelessly settling into the seat.

The screaming began.

It started in the galleries and spread outward like fire through dry grass, a rising wave of sound that filled the theatre and drowned out everything else. People surged from their seats. They pushed toward the exits and found them blocked, pushed back by the crush of bodies, trampled by the weight of those behind them. A woman fell near the doors and didn't rise. A child screamed for a mother who couldn't reach her. The theatre became a single thrashing organism of panic and terror and incomprehension.

Felix was already moving. He drove his sword through the chest of the nearest guard and stripped the bow from his hands in the same motion. He dropped to one knee, nocked an arrow, drew, and released. The shot flew toward Damien's booth. Damien ducked. The arrow took Falstaff instead, punching through the corner of his chest and pinning him to the wall behind.

Felix cast the bow aside and drew his sword.

His men poured from the wings, from behind the painted flats and beneath the stage, armed and armored and moving with the coordination of soldiers who had rehearsed this moment. They met the first wave of guards in the center of the theatre, and the sounds that followed were not the sounds of staged combat. Steel on steel. Steel on flesh. The grunt of effort and the cry of surprise and the wet noise of bodies opening.

Mercenaries in black armor crashed through the main doors and the fighting spread, filling the aisles and the galleries and the space before the stage. Felix cut through them without hesitation or ceremony. A guard raised his sword and Felix opened his throat. Another lunged with a spear and Felix stepped aside and drove his blade through the man's ribs.

In his booth, Damien watched the theatre become an abattoir. His face betrayed nothing. He observed the bodies falling and the blood spreading and the systematic destruction of everything Lionel had pretended to preside over, and his expression remained composed as though he were watching something happen very far away to people he had never met.

He glanced at Falstaff. The man was still alive, pinned to the wall by the arrow, his breath coming in shallow hitches, blood running from the corners of his mouth. His eyes found Damien's. They held a question, or perhaps an accusation, or perhaps nothing at all.

Didn't matter. Damien turned away. He moved to the back of the booth and found the door and slipped through it into the corridor beyond. The sounds of the massacre faded behind him, muffled by stone and distance, and he walked without hurrying toward whatever came next.

Miranda found a sword in the hand of a dead man and used it, fighting the way a cornered animal fights, without technique or grace, swinging at anything that came near her with the desperate strength of someone who understood that stopping meant dying. She killed a man, though she didn't know if he was a guard or a mercenary or simply someone who had been in her way.

"Felix!"

Her voice cut through the chaos, and he turned.

A mercenary in black stood fifteen yards behind her with his bow raised and arrow drawn, and Felix saw him, saw Miranda, saw the angle of the shot and understood what was about to happen in the same instant that it happened. The arrow passed through her heart cleanly, and she dropped straight down as though someone had cut the strings that held her upright, dead before her body struck the floor with no final words and no last breath drawn, the space where she had been standing suddenly empty.

Felix and the mercenary locked eyes across the carnage, and something shifted in the man's face behind the helmet, behind the black iron, as he understood what he had done and who was now looking at him. His hands began to move, reaching for another arrow, fumbling at his quiver.

Felix sheathed his sword and began to walk.

The distance between them was fifteen yards, perhaps less, and the mercenary's fingers found an arrow and nocked it and drew, his hands shaking as the bow came up and he loosed.

Felix caught the shaft out of the air without breaking stride, snapped it between his fingers, and let the pieces fall.

The mercenary stumbled backward with his hand going to his quiver again, finding it empty, going to the short sword at his hip. He had time to draw it but not to raise it.

Felix closed the distance in three steps, his left hand seizing the mercenary's wrist and wrenching it sideways with a sound of the joint separating that was audible even above the noise of battle, the sword clattering to the floor as his right hand found the man's throat and squeezed, lifting him off his feet. For a moment they stood like that, Felix's face inches from the mercenary's, close enough to see the whites of his eyes and the terror in them.

Then Felix drove him down into the stone floor headfirst, and the sound that followed was unthinkable.

They moved through the castle like hunted animals, Lillian's arm around Jamie's neck and her weight dragging at his shoulder with every step. The corridors were wrong now, transformed by violence into something unrecognizable, blood smeared across stone and bodies slumped in doorways and the sound of fighting bleeding through the walls from every direction. Steel and screaming and the heavy rhythm of boots on stone. Jamie didn't stop. Didn't look. He kept his sword up and his eyes forward and pulled Lillian along with him through the labyrinth of passages that led toward the outer ward.

They burst through an archway into cold night air, and the stables were there, fifty yards across the courtyard, torchlight spilling from the open doors and horses screaming in their stalls. Grooms and guards fled in every direction, some mounted, some on foot, all of them running from something Jamie couldn't see. The gates beyond stood open. Freedom was right there.

Jamie scanned the courtyard. The fleeing figures. The horses. The faces lit by torchlight and shadow.

He scanned again.

"Jamie." Lillian's voice was raw. "Jamie, we have to go."

Margaret wasn't there. She wasn't among the runners or the riders or the guards scrambling for the gates. She wasn't anywhere.

"*Jamie.*"

She wouldn't have left without him. She couldn't have left without him. Which meant she was still inside, somewhere in the burning wreck of the castle behind them, alone.

He stopped. Lillian felt it and looked at him and understood.

"Come with me," he said.

"Why?"

"I need to see about someone."

He turned back toward the castle. Lillian followed, and the open gates fell away behind them, and the darkness of the corridors swallowed them again.

Eli Richardson sat on the steps of the tavern with his crossbow across his knees and watched the road. Around him, his men waited in silence, the last light of dusk bleeding out across the sky in bands of copper and ash. They carried what they had brought from home: axes and cleavers and clubs wrapped in leather, a few swords that had seen better centuries, one rusted halberd that Terrence had pulled from his grandfather's barn. The mud sucked at their boots where they stood, and the sounds from the castle carried farther than they should have, steel and screaming drifting down through the fading light.

The second wave appeared on the hill to the east, perhaps four hundred yards out. Black armor. Mounted. But something was wrong with them. They came over the ridge in a ragged line, horses jostling into each other, riders sawing at reins and shouting commands that overlapped and collided in the air. One man's mount balked and spun, nearly throwing him. Another drove his horse into the flank of the rider beside him. They dismounted in a chaos of clattering steel and tangled stirrups, one man going down to his knees in the mud before someone hauled him upright by his pauldron.

Then they moved.

They ran uphill toward the castle with their armor banging against their bodies and their breath coming hard and visible in the cooling air, formation dissolving within the first twenty yards. Someone cursed at someone else to move. A soldier stumbled on the uneven ground and crashed into the man ahead of him, and both of them staggered before finding their feet. Their weapons rattled. Their boots churned the mud. They moved like men who believed they were already too late.

Eli watched their scramble with a detached, somewhat amazed disposition. His men watched him, suspended in silence, ready to move at the barest indication, standing half-sunk in mud-caked boots with their fathers' tools in their hands and nothing between their skin and the dusk but wool and leather.

"*Well*," Eli finally spoke, rising from the steps and shifting the crossbow onto his shoulder, leaving his sword where it hung at his hip. "That's us, boys."

He stepped off the porch and started walking toward the castle, his own boots sinking into the muddy road with each step. Behind him, his men followed without comment, and the village fell away into darkness at their backs.

SCENE 44

The theatre had gone quiet. Felix stood among the dead with his sword hanging at his side, blood running from his knuckles and soaking into his sleeve, and listened. Beyond the walls, coming from the direction of the main gates, he could hear the second wave arriving: boots on stone, shouted commands, horses screaming.

He looked up toward the upper galleries.

Six of his men remained standing. They watched him with the flat eyes of soldiers who had stopped expecting to survive.

"Hold the gates," Felix said. "Buy time."

He didn't wait for acknowledgment. He crossed the blood-slicked floor of the theatre and passed through the archway that led into the castle's interior, and the sounds of his men preparing to die faded behind him.

The first stairwell was narrow and torchlit, spiraling upward through stone that sweated condensation in the heat. Felix took the steps two at a time, his breathing steady, his sword angled forward. A mercenary waiting at a blind corner wore black leather and carried a short blade in each hand, and he came at Felix the moment he appeared around the curve. Felix caught the first strike on his crossguard and drove his shoulder into the man's chest, pinning him against the wall, and opened his throat with a short lateral cut before the second blade could find its mark.

He shoved the body down the stairwell and continued climbing.

Two more waited at the top of the stairwell, positioned on either side of the archway with their weapons drawn and their stances wide. They moved together, coordinated, one driving high while the other swept low, and Felix retreated down three steps to draw them forward onto uneven footing. The high man overextended. Felix took his hand off at the wrist and buried his blade in the man's chest before the severed appendage hit the stone. The low man's sweep caught Felix across the thigh, a shallow cut that parted fabric and skin and sent a bright ribbon of blood running down toward his boot. Felix pivoted on his wounded leg and brought his sword down through the man's collarbone, driving it deep into the chest cavity, and had to brace his foot against the body to wrench the blade free.

The corridor beyond stretched for thirty yards before branching. Torches guttered in their sconces. Somewhere ahead, a door slammed.

Felix moved forward, favoring his injured leg, his breathing no longer steady. Blood filled his boot with each step, warm and slick, and the fabric of his trousers clung to the wound. He could feel his heart beating in the gash, a dull pulse that matched his footfalls.

Three mercenaries emerged from a side passage and spread across the corridor to block his path. They carried longswords and wore hauberks of blackened mail, and they watched him approach with the patience of men sent to bleed him. Felix closed the distance at a dead run and hit the center man before the formation could collapse on him, driving his blade through the gap between helmet and gorget. The body sagged but didn't fall, the weight of it hanging from his sword, and Felix wrenched at the grip but the blade held fast, caught on bone or mail or something that wouldn't give.

The man on his left was already swinging. Felix hauled the dying mercenary between them and felt the blow meant for him shudder through the body instead. His hand found a hatchet on the dead man's belt, ripped it free, and swung across his own chest without thought or aim, and the blade caught the left mercenary in the neck where it met the shoulder and sank deep into meat and gristle. The man made a sound like air escaping a bellows and went down. Felix left the hatchet where it was.

The third came around the body of his companion with his sword already descending. Felix stepped inside the arc, too close for the blade to land, and brought the heel of his hand down hard across the man's wrist. The sword clattered to the stone. The mercenary grabbed for him with his free hand, fingers scrabbling at Felix's collar, and Felix seized the knife from the sheath strapped to the man's thigh. He drove it upward into the gap above the breastplate, into the soft hollow of the clavicle, and the mercenary made a sound like something tearing. Felix stabbed him again. And again. The man's legs gave out and Felix followed him down, still driving the blade into that same narrow opening until the body stopped moving and the only sound was his own breathing, ragged and wet in the empty corridor.

He retrieved his sword. The wound in his thigh was bleeding freely now, worse than he thought. His breath came in short, sharp pulls, and his hands had begun to shake with a fine tremor he couldn't control. The corridor ahead forked left and right, and Felix paused to listen, pressing one hand against the wound to slow the bleeding, and heard footsteps retreating up the leftward passage.

He followed.

The stairs here were broader, built for ceremony rather than defense, and the torchlight gave way to candlelight as he climbed into the residential quarters of the castle. Tapestries lined the walls, hunting scenes and battle standards, and the floor beneath his boots changed from bare stone to polished wood. Felix left bloody footprints behind him with every step, a trail that anyone could follow, and he didn't care.

Two more mercenaries waited at the top of the stairs, and they came at him the moment he appeared. Felix parried the first strike and let the momentum carry him into a spin, bringing his blade around in a wide arc that caught the second man across the throat, ear to ear. The man spun back gurgling, hands clutching at the wound, and collapsed. The first man pressed forward, driving Felix back against the wall, and their blades locked at the crossguards, faces inches apart, breath mingling in the narrow space. Felix could feel his strength failing, could feel the edges of his vision darkening, and he drove his forehead into the man's nose and felt the cartilage give way. The man stumbled. Felix ran him through.

The corridor ahead was empty.

He stood for a moment with his hand braced against the wall, his chest heaving, his body screaming at him to stop. Blood ran from his thigh and from a gash across his cheek he didn't remember receiving. His sword felt impossibly heavy in his grip. His legs trembled beneath him.

He pushed off from the wall and kept moving.

The last three found him in the gallery outside the royal chambers, a long corridor lined with portraits of dead kings and lit by candelabras that cast dancing shadows across the ceiling. They spread out as he approached, circling like wolves. One of them smiled.

Felix attacked the smiling one first, driving forward with everything he had left, his blade a blur of steel that the man barely caught on his crossguard. The impact drove the mercenary backward into one of his companions, and Felix followed, pressing, refusing to let the distance open, his strikes growing wilder as his control slipped. A blade caught him across the back, shallow but agonizing, and he spun and severed the man at the midsection. The smiling one recovered and thrust for his heart, and Felix twisted away too slowly, the point scraping across his ribs and leaving a furrow of exposed bone. He caught the man's arm on the backswing and broke it. The sword clattered to the floor. Felix picked it up and swung diagonally as the man knelt clutching his ruined arm, and took his head off clean.

The last mercenary dropped his sword and ran.

Felix let him go. He didn't have the strength to chase.

He stood in the gallery with his sword point resting on the floor, his weight sagging forward over the pommel, his breath coming in wet, ragged gasps. Blood pooled beneath him, spreading slowly across the polished wood. The portraits watched him from their frames, silent and indifferent.

The door to the royal chambers stood at the end of the gallery.

Felix straightened. The movement cost him something he wouldn't get back. He lifted his sword and walked forward, leaving a trail of red behind him, and the silence of the gallery swallowed the sound of his footsteps.

Outside the castle walls, in the fading copper light of dusk, the front gates collapsed into violence.

Felix's men met Damien's second wave in the narrow passage between the outer walls, blades crashing together in a space too confined for formation or strategy. Men pressed against men, killing at arm's length, grunting and screaming and dying in a tangle of limbs and steel. The mercenaries had numbers and armor. Felix's men had nowhere to retreat and no reason to try.

Eli and his villagers arrived at the flank of the fighting, spilling up from the muddy road with their axes and clubs and rusted swords, and hit the mercenary line before anyone understood what was happening. A blacksmith drove his hammer into the back of a helmeted head and sent the man sprawling. A farmer with a pig-sticking knife opened a mercenary's thigh and watched him fall. The line buckled, re-formed, buckled again. It was chaos.

The fighting spread across the gatehouse and into the outer courtyard, small knots of men hacking at each other in the dying light, no commanders, no signals, no plan. A villager went down with a sword through his chest. A mercenary stumbled on the cobblestones and three men fell on him before he could rise, ripping him apart. The noise was enormous, steel and screaming and the wet sounds of bodies opening, and above it all the castle loomed dark and silent, keeping whatever was happening inside to itself.

Eli fired his crossbow into the chest of a mercenary at fifteen yards and dropped the weapon where he stood. He drew his sword, the one he had not touched in the tavern, and walked into the fight with a bellowing cry.

SCENE 45

LEAVE THE BOY BE

Margaret's chamber was quiet in a way that felt wrong, the silence too complete, too untouched by the violence that had consumed the rest of the castle. The candles still burned in their sconces. The furniture stood upright and undisturbed. The tapestries hung straight on the walls. It was as though the room existed outside of time, preserved in amber while the world beyond its doors tore itself apart.

Jamie pushed through the entrance with Lillian behind him, his sword raised, his breath still ragged from the climb, and found Margaret on the floor.

She lay crumpled near the window with her hair fallen across her face and one arm bent beneath her at an angle that looked uncomfortable. Her eyes were open. They caught the candlelight and held it without reflection, fixed on a point somewhere beyond the ceiling, beyond the castle, beyond anything Jamie could follow.

He crossed to her and dropped to his knees.
"*Margaret.*"

The door to the king's chamber stood open.

Felix paused at the threshold, his sword heavy in his grip, his breathing wet and labored. Blood ran from his side and his thigh and his back and a dozen other wounds he had stopped counting, pooling in his boot, dripping onto the stone, leaving a trail behind him that anyone could follow. The corridor was silent. The bodies of the men he had killed lay where they had fallen, and the candles burned on in their sconces as though nothing had changed.

He stepped through the doorway.

The chamber was empty. A fire crackled in the hearth. Candles flickered on the mantle and the writing desk and the table beside the bed. The room smelled of wood smoke and something else beneath it, something metallic and wrong, and Felix's eyes moved across the space, searching for movement, searching for threat, searching for the man he had climbed through hell to find.

The blade entered his back just below the ribs on his right side, accompanied by a muted mechanical *click* Felix barely registered before the pain arrived.

He felt it punch through muscle and organ, felt the edge scrape against something vital. The pain arrived a moment later, enormous and clarifying, and then the blade twisted and tore upward and the pain became something beyond pain, something that whited out his vision and buckled his legs and dropped him to the floor before he understood he was falling.

He landed on his side. His sword clattered away across the stone. He tried to rise and his body refused, tried to reach for the weapon and his arm wouldn't obey, tried to breathe and found only a wet gurgling sound where breath should have been.

Footsteps circled into his field of vision. Polished boots. Dark trousers. The hem of a velvet doublet unstained by blood or battle.

Damien crouched before him.

"Impressive work, Sir Felix."

The name landed like a blow. Felix's eyes found Damien's face and held there, and he saw the knowledge in that gaze, the recognition, the absolute certainty of a man who had been working toward this moment from the very beginning.

"I must confess, I rather enjoyed watching you fling your blade into my sniveling brother's throat. Twenty-four years of exile, and you haven't lost a step." He smiled, thin and bloodless. "The mercenaries were from Ashford, you know. Rather expensive, as these things go. I had hoped they might slow you down, but I confess I am not disappointed that they failed." The smile widened slightly. "Oh, I did enjoy watching you work, Black Rider."

Felix tried to speak. His mouth opened. Blood welled between his lips and spilled down his chin, and the only sound that emerged was a thick, wet rasp that might have been a word or might have been nothing at all.

"You and your bastard caused quite a disruption this evening." Damien rose and moved to the window, gazing out at the evening beyond as though the dying man on his floor were merely an inconvenience to be tidied later. "The theatre will need to be rebuilt. The noble houses will demand explanations. The succession will require delicate framing." He turned back, his hands clasped behind his back. "But these are small matters, in the end. Administrative concerns."

He crossed back to where Felix lay and crouched again.

"I want you to know that I intend to make the boy suffer. The girl, perhaps less so. When I find her—and I *will* find her—it may even be quick. A blade across the throat. A snap of the neck. A moment of confusion, and then nothing."

He leaned in.

"But the boy? *Your* boy?" He exhaled. "Him I will take my time with. Days, if I can manage it. Everyone who's met him seems to believe there's something so special inside. I intend to open him up and find it."

Felix's hand twitched toward his sword. The weapon lay

three feet away, impossibly distant, and his fingers scraped uselessly against the stone as his body refused to close the gap.

Damien watched the attempt. Didn't even bother to thwart it.

"I am a cruel man, Sir Felix. I was cruel before my father died, I was cruel when I felt him breathe his last breath beneath my weight, and I have been cruel ever since. I was cruel as Prince, and I will be cruel as King. It is not a flaw I fight against, nor a demon I wrestle in the dark or a sickness I hope to cure. It is simply what I am. And what I am is effective."

He brought his face close to Felix's, close enough that Felix could smell the wine on his breath and the perfume on his collar.

"It is a curious thing, is it not? The way love unmakes men. You loved Anya. You loved her so completely that you threw away your name, your honor, your place in the world, all for the privilege of abandoning your son and slaving for bounties in some provincial blackwater. And now the boy loves Margaret, loves her with the same blind devotion, the same willingness to sacrifice everything for a woman who was never his to have."

He reached out and brushed a strand of blood-matted hair from Felix's forehead.

"It is the same weakness, passed from father to son. The same vulnerability. The same door through which a patient man might enter and take everything." His hand withdrew. "Oh, and I have been patient, Sir Felix. I have been so very patient. And now the door stands open."

Felix's lips moved. A sound emerged, barely audible, shaped like a name that might have been Jamie or might have been something else entirely.

"Oh, yes. The Northborn." Damien stood and adjusted his cuffs. "She was quite lovely, in her way. Quite determined. She *actually* believed she might escape. She fought at the end, as they do. But it was over quickly enough."

The words reached Felix through a growing darkness, through a cold that spread from his center outward, through the wet labor of lungs that were filling with blood. He understood them. He understood everything. And there was nothing he could do, nothing he could say, nothing left in his failing body that could change what had already been decided.

He tried one more time to reach for his sword. His arm moved perhaps an inch before the strength left it entirely, and his hand fell still against the stone, fingers half-curled, reaching for something they would never grasp.

Damien looked down at him for a long moment, his expression unreadable, and then he turned and walked toward the door.

"Goodbye, Sir Felix. It has been an honor."

The footsteps receded. The door closed. The fire crackled in the hearth, and the candles burned on their wicks, and the room grew quiet around the man bleeding out on its floor.

Felix's vision narrowed. The edges went gray, then black, then nothing at all. His breathing slowed, hitched, slowed again. His thoughts scattered and reformed and scattered once more, chasing something he could no longer name, reaching for someone he could no longer see.

His last breath left him in a long, rough sigh, and the Black Rider was still.

Margaret's body was still warm beneath Jamie's hands when he took her by the shoulders, warm enough that for one terrible moment he allowed himself to believe he had arrived in time, that she was merely unconscious, merely injured, merely waiting for someone to wake her. He shook her, gently at first, the way one might rouse a sleeping child.

"Margaret."

Her head lolled sideways. Her mouth fell open slightly. Her eyes didn't move.

He shook her again, harder this time, his fingers digging into the fabric of her dress, and her body responded with the loose, unresisting weight of something no longer occupied. There was no tension in her limbs, no resistance in her neck, no flicker of awareness behind those open eyes. She moved when he moved her and stopped when he stopped and that was all.

"Oh, Margaret."

His voice cracked on her name and he heard the sound of it as though from a great distance, the raw desperate noise of a boy who had arrived too late and knew it and couldn't make himself stop trying anyway. He pulled her toward him, cradling her head against his chest, and rocked back and forth with his face pressed into her hair, breathing in the fading scent of her, feeling the warmth that wouldn't last much longer seeping out of her body and into his hands.

"Please wake up." The words came out broken and wet. "Please, please wake up."

She didn't. She would never. He knew this with a certainty that sat in his chest like a lodged blade, excruciating and immovable, but he rocked her anyway because stopping meant accepting and he wasn't ready to accept, or if he would ever be.

Lillian stood frozen in the doorway with her hand pressed to her mouth and tears running silently down her cheeks, watching Jamie hold a dead woman and beg her to come back, and the room remained quiet around them, quiet and still and utterly indifferent to the grief unfolding within its walls.

"Well, would you look at that?"

Jamie's body went rigid. The voice came from the doorway to the bedroom, calm and unhurried, carrying the particular cadence of a man who had been waiting and was pleased that the waiting had finally ended. He turned his head, still holding Margaret, and saw Richardson emerging from the shadows with his sword hanging loose at his side.

The knight looked untouched. His armor was clean. His boots showed no mud, no blood. He might have been preparing for a formal dinner rather than standing in a room with a dead woman and a grieving boy.

"The blacksmith's bastard," he marveled. "I knew I recognized you."

Lillian's breath caught. Richardson's gaze shifted to her.

"And the Spires girl. How thoughtful."

Jamie lowered Margaret's body to the floor. He rose and put

himself between Lillian and the knight.

"Get behind me."

She moved without speaking.

"Come to rescue her, have you?" He walked forward, sword low, stride unhurried. "Honorable."

"Don't."

"Or what?"

Jamie lunged.

The blow was fierce and committed, driven by rage and grief, and Richardson caught it on his blade without apparent effort. Before Jamie could recover, Richardson had deflected the strike and reset his stance as though swatting away an insect.

Jamie came at him again, driving forward with a combination Felix had taught him, and Richardson slipped the first strike and parried the second and opened a gash across Jamie's forearm with a casual flick.

"Who taught you to fight? Some hedge knight?"

"A better man than you."

Richardson feinted high and cut low. Jamie barely caught it. They traded blows across the chamber, Jamie pressing forward, Richardson retreating just enough to stay comfortable.

Then Richardson stopped retreating.

He caught Jamie's blade and turned it aside, then drove his shoulder into Jamie's chest. Jamie flew backward into a portrait on the wall. The frame cracked. Glass shattered. He staggered forward, dazed, and Richardson swung for his head.

Jamie ducked. Cut low. Felt his sword bite into Richardson's thigh.

Richardson's face changed. The amusement drained away. He charged.

He hit Jamie like a wall of iron and drove him to the floor. Their swords clattered away as Richardson's hands found Jamie's throat. The fingers tightened with a pressure that crushed Jamie's windpipe and turned the world gray at the edges.

Jamie clawed at the hands. Bucked. Thrashed. Accomplished nothing.

"You should have stayed in the woods," Richardson said. "That was the life you were made for."

"Oi."

Richardson's hands stilled. His head turned.

Eli stood at the far end of the corridor, sword drawn. He was covered in blood and mud, but his stance was solid and his eyes were clear.

"Leave the boy be."

The brothers regarded each other. Years of history compressed into a single look.

"Eli." Richardson's grip loosened. "I wondered when you'd arrive."

"*Let him go!*" Eli boomed.

Richardson released Jamie and rose, retrieving his sword. Jamie rolled onto his side, gasping, sucking air into his bruised throat.

"Take your girl and go, Jamie," Eli said, his attention fixed on his brother.

Jamie pushed himself up. His throat burned. He looked back at Margaret's body, at the stillness of her face, and understood he was abandoning her.

"Thank you," he said.

Eli didn't respond.

Jamie took Lillian's hand and walked past him, and the corridor swallowed them both.

The brothers were alone.

"You look tired," Richardson said.

"I am tired." Eli began to circle. "Tired of you. Tired of hearing what you've become."

"I serve the crown."

"You're a murderer."

Richardson attacked.

The first strike came fast and hard, aimed at Eli's head. Eli caught it with a force that drove him backward. Richardson pressed forward, hammering at his guard with heavy overhand blows.

Eli gave ground. Parried. Deflected. His arms ached. His

shoulders burned. The wound from the fighting below had reopened.

Richardson overextended. Eli stepped inside and drove his pommel into his brother's jaw, followed by a cut across Richardson's bicep.

"There he is!" Richardson spat blood. "The brother I remember. Come on!"

Richardson came at him again, faster. Their blades locked. Faces inches apart.

"You're the same as me, Eli. It's in your eyes."

"We're nothing alike."

"We're Father's boys." Richardson shoved him backward. "Made for violence. Made for blood. Only difference is I embraced it while you ran away to pour drinks for peasants and pretend you were something better than what you are."

Eli caught a strike and redirected it into the wall. Sparks flew. His arms were failing.

Richardson feinted low and cut high. Eli's parry came too late. The blade sliced his forearm. His grip faltered.

Richardson drove forward with a thrust aimed at Eli's chest.

Eli twisted. The blade meant for his heart took him in the side instead. The pain was enormous. His knees buckled.

He went down.

Richardson pulled his sword free with a wet sound and stepped back to examine his work. Blood poured from the wound in Eli's side, pooling on the stone beneath him, spreading in a dark tide that caught the candlelight and shimmered.

"Look at that." Richardson was breathing hard, but his voice carried the satisfaction of a man who had achieved something he had been working toward for a long time. "The great Eli Richardson, brought low at last. Father would be proud."

Eli pressed his hand against the wound. He knew this was it. He could feel it in the wrongness of his breath, in the way his vision pulsed at the edges, in the cold that was already spreading through his limbs.

"You always thought you were better than me," Richardson said, and for a moment he sounded like a boy. "Smarter. Better liked. Always looking down from your moral heights, judging everything I did, pretending you had the right to condemn me for being what our father made us."

"I never thought I was better than you," Eli said, breath almost up. "I just knew where you really belonged."

"Where's that?"

"Hell."

Eli surged up from the floor and drove his sword into Richardson's stomach before he could react. The blade punched through leather and muscle and viscera and emerged from Richardson's back in a spray of dark blood, and Eli kept pushing, driving forward, using the last of his strength to bury the steel to the hilt.

Richardson's eyes went wide. His mouth opened. His hands came up to grip the blade emerging from his gut, and blood welled between his fingers and spilled down the front of his armor. Eli's face was inches from his brother's, close enough to see the terror dawning in his eyes,

He twisted the blade.

Richardson screamed, a sound without dignity or control, the scream of an animal dying badly. His legs gave out and he collapsed forward against Eli, and they sank to the floor together.

Eli released the sword. He didn't have the strength to withdraw it. He lay on his back with his brother's weight pressing down on him and his own blood spreading beneath them both, and he stared at the ceiling and listened to Richardson's breathing grow ragged and shallow.

"Eli." The voice was barely a whisper now, wet and broken. "Eli, I—"

"Don't."

"Eli, it burns—"

"I said don't."

Richardson's breathing hitched. His body convulsed once, twice, and then went still.

Eli lay beneath him and watched the candlelight flicker on the ceiling and felt the cold spreading through his chest. His thoughts grew distant and strange. He thought about the tavern, about the smell of wood smoke and spilled ale, about the sound of laughter on a busy night. He thought about the boy he had just sent away with a stolen girl and a stolen sword and a lifetime of grief ahead of him. He thought about whether any of it had mattered, whether anything ever mattered, whether the choices men made in their brief lives amounted to anything more than noise against the silence that swallowed everything in the end.

He didn't find an answer.

The candles burned. The blood spread. The room grew quiet.

SCENE 46

THE COTTAGE

Felix walked.

The stone had gone soft beneath his boots. The air had changed. He did not know how long he had been walking, or where he was going. There was a path, faint and worn, and his boots followed it without thought.

The trees thinned and opened onto a rise. Below it, a cottage sat in a shallow valley; whitewashed walls, thatched roof, smoke rising from the chimney. Light came through the windows. Chickens moved in the yard. In the yard, a chestnut mare stood with her head lowered toward a girl brushing her flank, the rhythm of her arm slow and familiar.

Miranda looked up as he approached. She met his eyes, smiled politely, and turned back to the horse, as if he had simply arrived a moment later than expected.

Felix walked on.

Beneath the oak at the edge of the yard, Margaret sat in

a wooden chair with a book open in her lap. Light moved through the leaves and crossed her face, then passed on. She did not look up. Her breathing was even. The page did not tremble.

Felix climbed the three steps to the porch.

Anya came out before he reached the top.

There was grey in her hair now, pulled back simply, and fine lines at the corners of her eyes. Her dress was plain linen. Her hands were bare. She watched him take the last step. Her expression did not change. She had been waiting.

She crossed to him and put her arms around his neck and drew his head down against her shoulder. He smelled rose water and woodsmoke and skin. His breath left him all at once.

His hands found her back and stayed there.

She held him. Time passed. Her fingers moved through his hair the way they had when he was young and frightened and hers.

When she let go, she kept one hand on his chest, as if to steady him, or herself.

"Will Jamie be joining us?"

Felix looked out at the field behind him. The grass bent and rose again in the wind.

He looked at her feet. Swallowed.

"I don't think so."

She smiled. Another answer had already reached her.

"I know," she said.

She stepped past him to the edge of the porch.

"Girls," she called. "Supper's ready."

Miranda gave the mare one last pat and started toward the cottage. Margaret closed her book and rose from the chair beneath the oak. They moved toward the cottage.

Anya squeezed his hand.

"Come inside."

Felix walked through the door.

SCENE 47

JAMES ALDRIC TAYLOR

The throne room stood in ruins at the heart of the dying castle. The great doors hung crooked on their hinges, and the windows along the eastern wall had shattered inward, scattering glass across the flagstones like frozen rain. Smoke drifted through the space in lazy coils, carrying with it the smell of burning timber and spilled blood and the particular acrid tang of a world unmade. The banners with the Taylor crest still hung from the rafters, torn and streaked with soot, the twin dragons barely visible beneath the residue of violence. Beyond the main doors lay the courtyard and the stables and the road that led away from this place forever, and the last light of dusk bled through the ruined windows in bands of copper and ash.

Jamie and Lillian crossed the threshold at a run, her hand tight in his, their footsteps echoing in the vaulted space. They were almost there. Almost free.

"Jamie Campbell."

The voice came from behind them, calm and unhurried, and Jamie's blood went cold. He stopped. Lillian stopped with him. They turned together and watched Damien emerge from the shadows of the gallery above, descending the grand staircase with the measured tread of a man attending a function he'd organized himself.

He was untouched. His doublet showed no stain, his hair no disarray, his boots no mud or blood. He might have been arriving at a coronation rather than walking through the wreckage of the kingdom.

"Or should I say, James Aldric Taylor. Son of Queen Anya and Watch Commander Sir Felix Ryder, true heir to the throne of England, The Red Prince." He smiled, wide and bloodless. "I must confess, I've wondered what this moment would feel like. Whether you would be taller, perhaps. More imposing. But then, myths so rarely survive their meeting with reality, do they?"

Jamie's hand tightened on his sword, Lillian pressed close against his side.

"I've known of you long since before you arrived at this castle," Damien said, walking toward them. "Since before your dear Margaret was offered to my brother. Since before this whole particularly absurd but admittedly compelling charade. Since before everything. You were never hidden, Jamie. You were merely a stone I hadn't yet turned over to crush."

"Stay back."

"I strangled her myself," Damien said, gleaming. "Margaret. Quicker than she deserved, if you ask me."

Jamie's sword trembled in his grip.

"And now here we are." Damien stopped fifteen feet away. "The last of a dead line, standing in a burning castle, holding a sword he hardly knows how to use." He tilted his head. "I'm going to kill you now, Jamie. That is how this ends."

"Oi."

Damien's expression shifted, and he turned.

Peter Beverley stood at the far end of the throne room, framed by a doorway Jamie hadn't noticed, his armor battered and bloodstained, his sword drawn. Behind him, emerging from the shadows like ghosts taking form, came others: the Strays of Harthfell in their mismatched armor, carrying weapons that had seen generations of use. The village militia followed, spreading along the walls with their axes and clubs, until the throne room was lined with men who had come to witness something end.

Damien was surrounded.

He turned in a slow circle, taking in the scope of what had arrived. "It seems we have company. The Strays of Harthfell and Peter Beverley himself." His composure held, but something had become undone behind his eyes. "I'd imagined you were dead."

"Your imagination betrays you."

"And what is this? Retribution? Whatever you hoped to accomplish—"

Peter thrust forward, fists readied at his sides. He didn't wait for Damien to finish.

Damien's right arm came up with a snap of metal and spring, the long thin spike of steel shooting toward Peter's throat. Peter caught it on his gauntlet, the impact ringing through the room, and before Damien could retract the weapon, Peter's fist drove into his stomach with the force of a battering ram.

Damien doubled over. Peter's boot came down on his extended arm, pinning it to the floor, and his full weight followed. Metal warped. Wood splintered. Bone gave way with a sound that echoed through the throne room.

Damien screamed.

Peter hauled him upright by the collar and hit him. Not with weapons, not with technique, but with his hands, blow after blow landing with the sustained, repetitive rhythm of necessary labor. Damien's nose broke. His lip split. His left eye swelled shut. After some time, he sagged in Peter's grip, blood streaming down his face and bubbling from his lips, and Peter let him fall like a doll.

Two of the Strays moved forward and pinned him to the flagstones.

All was silent.

Peter turned to Jamie, breathing hard, his knuckles split and bleeding.

"And what of my sister?"

Jamie tilted his head toward Damien, a small motion which Peter absorbed solemnly.

"The matter is settled, then."

Jamie nodded.

"So, you're it," Peter said. "The Red Prince. First and only offspring of Anya Taylor. True heir to the throne, as things have it. The reason for all this mess, I presume."

Jamie didn't answer.

Peter stepped back and lowered himself to one knee, his sword laid across his thigh, his head bowed. Behind him, the Strays followed suit, and then the militia, dozens of men kneeling in the ruins of the throne room before a boy who had never asked for any of this.

"The cycle is yours to break, my lord."

Jamie released Lillian's hand and stepped forward.

The room held its breath.

"I don't want it."

The words fell into the silence and lay there.

"I don't want the crown, and I don't want the throne." Jamie looked at Peter, at the kneeling men, at the ruins of everything that had been built on lies and blood. "I just want to leave." He looked at Lillian. "*We* just want to leave."

After a while, the surprise faded from Peter's expression, and— following a glance at Lillian behind him—was replaced by something like empathy.

"Understood."

Peter rose.

"Then take your leave. We'll attend to this cunt." He spat beside Damien, then turned to his army. "Clear a path for the Prince."

Slowly, The Strays and the militia parted, forming a corridor through the throne room, and Jamie and Lillian walked through them without speaking. The men watched them pass, inclining their heads as they went, and though no one knelt again, there was something in the way they held themselves that felt like reverence. Like hope. Like the beginning of something new.

They emerged into the night.

A horse stood waiting in the courtyard, saddled and ready. One of the Strays helped Lillian up, and Jamie mounted behind her. The animal shifted beneath them, eager to run.

He didn't look back.

They rode out through the village at speed, the hoofbeats echoing off the silent buildings, the wind cold against their faces. The road opened before them, dark and empty and free.

In the throne room, Peter Beverley raised his sword.

Damien lay on the flagstones, broken and bleeding, his ruined arm bent beneath him. The Strays held him in place, though there was no need.

"Any last words?"

Damien laughed, wet and bubbling. "The wheel keeps turning, Beverley. It always—"

The castle shuddered.

The sound came from somewhere deep below, a rumble that built and built until the flagstones cracked beneath their feet and the walls groaned and dust rained from the ceiling. Peter stepped back. His men looked at each other with widening eyes.

One of the Strays whispered it first, his voice cracking with terror.

"Varska."

The last thing they saw was a spark.

The floor of the throne room exploded upward.

Rather, it ceased to exist. Stone and mortar and the weight of centuries became shrapnel moving at speeds no human body could survive, and Varska came through the breach like a battering ram made of scale and bone and two hundred years of captivity, her mass displacing everything in her path, her velocity turning the air itself into a weapon. Damien Taylor was vapor before the sound reached him. Peter Beverley was gone in the same instant, his sword still raised. The Strays and the militia died without knowing they had died, their bodies unmade by debris and pressure and the simple physics of something enormous moving through a space built for men.

Varska tore through the ceiling as easily as she had torn through the floor, through the rafters and the roof beams and the ancient stonework of the keep, and she was gone into the night sky before the collapse began, trailing fire and ruin, leaving behind her a castle that was already falling, already burying its dead, already becoming rubble.

Outside Taylor's End, riding hard down the open road, Jamie and Lillian heard the sound and turned in the saddle.

Varska climbed into the darkness with wings that blotted out the stars and the moon together. She circled once above the burning wreckage, her silhouette vast against the flames, and then she turned toward the road where two riders fled on a single horse.

Jamie kicked the horse harder. Lillian's arms tightened around his waist.

Varska's shadow passed over them, cold and enormous, and Jamie braced for fire, braced for death, braced for the ending he'd always known was coming.

It didn't come.

The dragon soared overhead and kept flying, following the road they traveled, following the direction they fled. Her wings beat steady and slow, carrying her forward into the darkness ahead of them, and she didn't look back.

Jamie slowed the horse to a canter, then to a walk. He stared at the shape moving against the stars, at the impossible creature that had chosen not to kill them, and he understood without knowing how he understood that something had changed. Something old had ended. Something new had begun.

Lillian pressed her face against his back. Her breathing steadied.

"Where do we go?" she asked.

The road stretched before them, empty and dark and full of possibility. Behind them, Taylor's End burned against the horizon, a funeral pyre for everyone who had tried to control what couldn't be controlled. Ahead of them, the dragon flew on, a shadow against the stars, leading them toward whatever came next.

"Forward," he said.

"London?"

"London."

He kicked the horse back into a gallop, and they rode into the night, chasing the dragon, chasing the dawn, chasing the future that no one had written yet.

The world had changed.

And for the first time in his life, Jamie Taylor was no longer in it alone.

This story has been with me since I was nineteen. It began as a screenplay while I was working at a hometown movie theater in the Bay Area, back when I thought it would live on a screen long before it ever reached the page. When the world shut down in 2020, it was left unfinished, but its essence, what I knew it could be, never left me. There was never any doubt I would return to it.

Bastard stayed with me through jobs, a pandemic, the sudden passing of my father in 2023, breakups and relationships, friends lost and friends made, and *somehow* held its ground long enough to become the mic-drop title of a 2025 I never could have seen coming.

Before I even started *Made in America* in June, I knew this would be the book that followed. It is, without question, one of my favorite stories I've had the privilege to develop. These characters have lived with me for years, and I feel them as deeply now as I did at the beginning—perhaps more, having spent just under five hundred pages with them, and more than that, finally giving them the ending they deserved.

If there is anyone to thank, it is my mother, who has never left my side; my aunt, who is always ready, without hesitation, to shoulder the weight of the world for the people she loves; Mulan, for making me less alone on nights when characters give way to the noise of reality; my late father, for being as strong as he could for as long as he could; and God, for refusing to let me abandon this craft.

Cheers,
Jack

Jack Chase is an American novelist, screenwriter, and graphic designer, and the founder of Abbycat Group & Publishing Brands, a boutique press devoted to cinematic fiction and high-end book design. He writes, designs, and publishes each of his works under the multi-imprint AGP umbrella, building a unified body of literature that blurs the line between novel and film. After the seismic release of *Made in America: or The Tragedy of Billy Castle and Unexpected Absolution of Dean Willis*, Chase has returned two months later with *The Bastard of Taylor's End*, a dark, operatic tale of inheritance, theater, and rebellion set in an alternate 1602 England.

Led by Abbycat Group (*Beat Cop: A Love Letter to the City of Fog, Ghosts, and Lost Men*, *Made in America: or The Tragedy of Billy Castle and Unexpected Absolution of Dean Willis*, *The Bastard of Taylor's End*), his imprints, including Abbycat Liminal (*Immundus: A Western Navajo Folktale, Remastered and Expanded Edition*), Abbycat Black (*Overtime: The Ballad of Marcus Graves*, *Violent Crimes: The Butcher of Westchester*), and FRAMEWORKS, the visual design division responsible for everything from layout and covers to promotional art, have further defined his reputation for precision and uncompromising creative vision.

His next major novel and eighth publication, *The Schultz Brothers*, arrives as a decade-in-the-making crime saga of brotherhood, consequence, and the ghosts that refuse to stay buried. It will serve as the first installment in a 4-part franchise and be published under the Abbycat Group imprint as well.

He lives in Southern California with his cat, Mulan.

*IMMUNDUS: A Western Navajo
Folktale*

*Beat Cop: A Love Letter to the City of
Fog, Ghosts, and Lost Men*

*Overtime: The Ballad of Marcus
Graves*

*Violent Crimes: The Butcher of
Westchester*

*Immundus: A Western Navajo
Folktale, Remastered and Expanded
Edition (II)*

*Made in America: or The Tragedy of
Billy Castle and Unexpected
Absolution of Dean Willis*

IN 2026

The Schultz Brothers

She's Still Here

Bears in Winter

Citizen Unknown

Twenty-Five Thousand

Overtime 2: Buenos Aires

Day of the Scorpion

Violent Crimes: Los Angeles

Cyber City

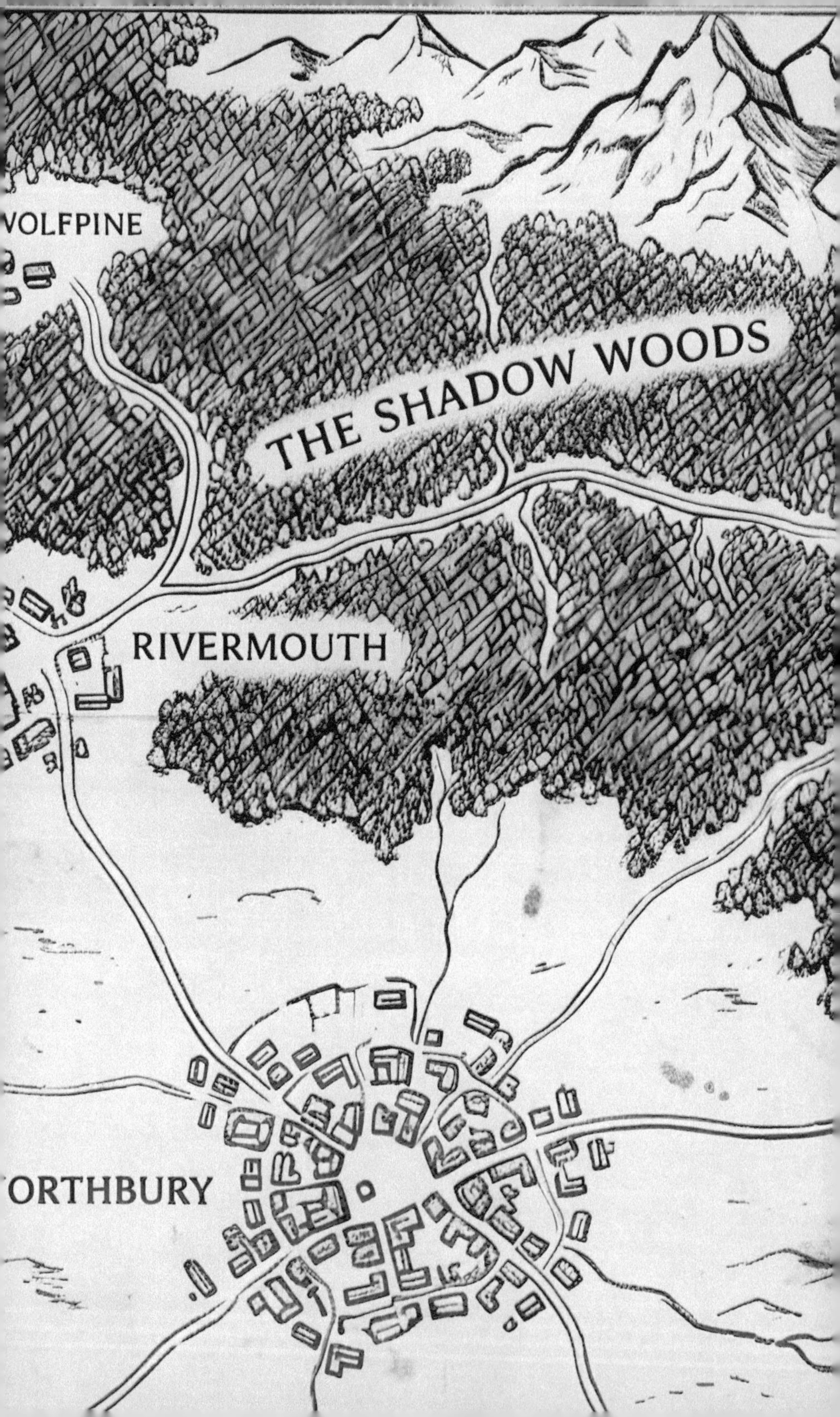

VOLFPINE
THE SHADOW WOODS
RIVERMOUTH
ORTHBURY

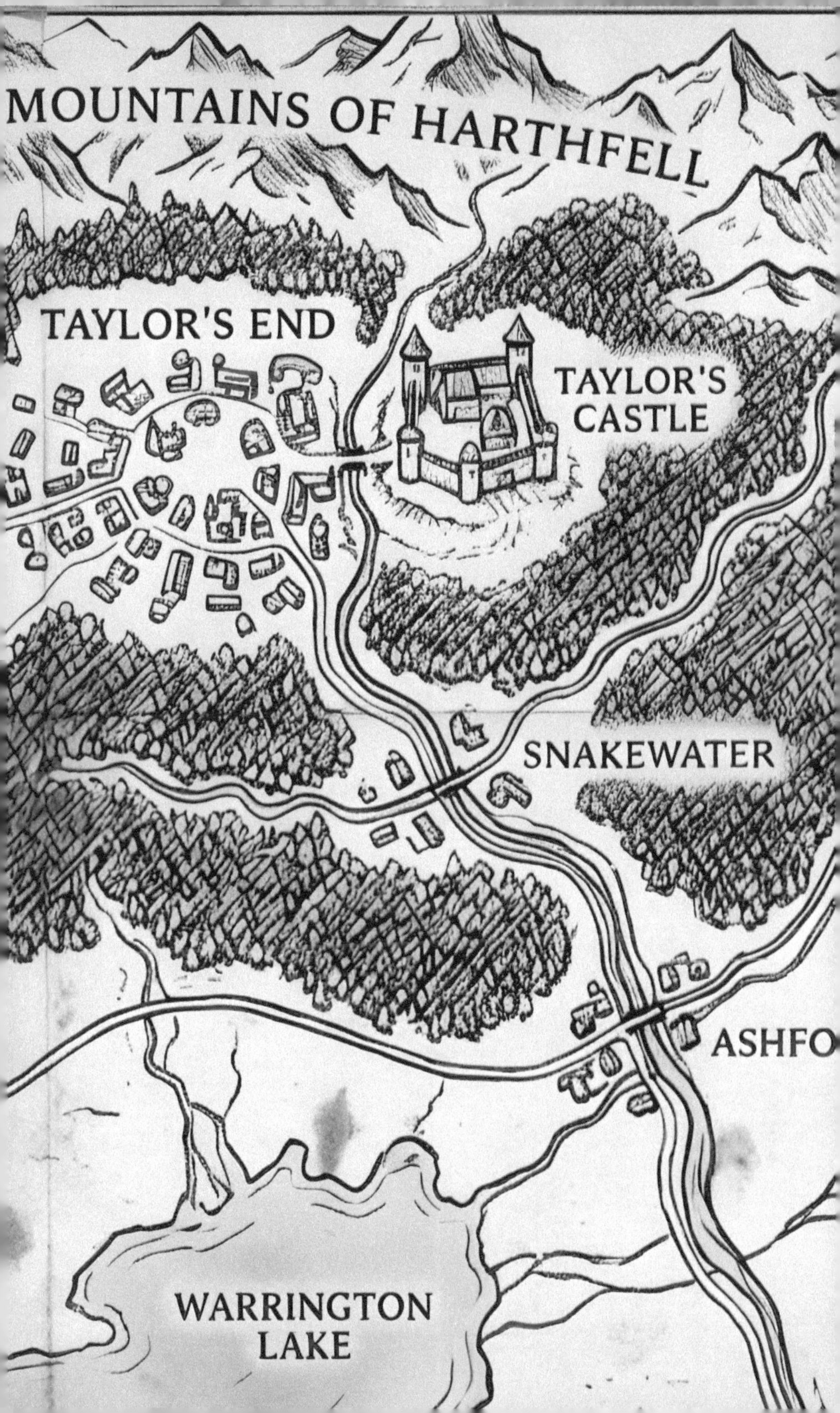

MOUNTAINS OF HARTHFELL
TAYLOR'S END
TAYLOR'S CASTLE
SNAKEWATER
ASHFO
WARRINGTON LAKE